THE GIRL IN THE WOODS

LYNDA RENHAM

BLOODHOUND
— B O O K S —

First published in 2024 by Bloodhound Books.

www.bloodhoundbooks.com

Print ISBN: 978-1-917214-26-1

In Memory Of
Simon Gowen, Adele Blair and Penelope Smith.
Three of my greatest supporters,
whom I miss terribly.

CHAPTER ONE

SEVEN YEARS EARLIER

L aurie stumbled from the heaving pub. Wobbling on her stiletto heels, she grasped the door while her stomach lurched and gurgled as nausea overwhelmed her. She needed fresh air.

'Come on, Laurie,' someone called. 'One for the road?'

'I feel sick,' she said, clutching her stomach. The cold night air breathed into her face, its iciness sending her reeling. She leaned her hot body against the pub's cool walls and took several deep breaths. Her low-cut top and short skirt did nothing to ease the fire burning within her. It was that last shot that had finished her off.

No one noticed her slouching against the wall out of everyone's way in the pub's side alley. Why would they? Who didn't get wasted on a Friday night? People swayed and zigzagged out of the pub, laughing and bumping into her. That's when she saw him, but somehow he seemed different. The charm he'd shown in the pub had gone, as had the friendly sparkle in his eyes. Without her noticing, he must have followed.

He was now so close that she could feel his breath on her

face. He grabbed her breast, and whispered into her ear. 'Take off your knickers.'

A stab of fear shot through Laurie, and her heart raced. The man wasn't behaving as he had earlier. He'd been different to the others. Considerate and thoughtful.

'I'm Laurie–' she began.

'Don't need your name,' he said, breathing heavily. He swept her hair over her ear and kissed her neck roughly while pushing her back against the wall. Laurie's insides turned cold. This wasn't right. This wasn't the funny man who'd told her jokes over the music; he wasn't the gentle man who'd held her hand in the pub a few moments earlier when she'd said she felt ill. Her body froze as he began to pull at her underwear.

'No, don't.' Laurie pushed at his chest. Her heart was pounding so hard and fast she thought it would explode. He moved his head back to meet her eyes; his were so full of disgust that Laurie couldn't bear to look into them.

Everything Laurie despised about herself was mirrored back in those eyes, and the truth was unbearably painful.

'No?' he mocked. 'You've been gagging for it all night. So don't start that fucking prick teasing with me. You're just a bit of rough from the gutter, girl. If you think Prince Charming is waiting for you, forget it. Welcome to your life, one-night stands, lonely regrets. It's what slags like you were made for.'

Tears blurred her eyes. Why was he being so hurtful? It was true, of course. A bit of rough from the gutter, that's exactly what she was, an uneducated, useless failure at everything. *I will always be a target for people like him*, she thought sadly. Then, his words hit her like a red rag to a bull. He might believe it, but he had no right to say it. No right to abuse her like that.

'Get off me, you piece of shit,' she snarled before lifting her knee hard into his groin. Maybe she was a bit of rough from the gutter, but that didn't mean she couldn't take care of herself.

He doubled over, grimaced and growled, 'Bitch.'

Laurie tugged down her skirt and turned to run, only to collide with someone else. Strong arms held her firmly, and the familiar aftershave made her feel safe.

'Hey, Laurie, are you okay?' said a steady, deep voice. Laurie saw his eyes turn to the angry young man at her side. 'What's going on?'

'She's a fucking tease, that's what's going on,' said the young man angrily. 'Not that it's any business of yours.'

'She's fifteen,' the man shot back.

The young man laughed. 'Fifteen my arse. You can have the little slut,' he spat before limping into the night, clutching his crotch.

Laurie looked into her rescuer's eyes and thought that no feature makes a man handsome, but his eyes came close. From them came an intensity, an honesty, a gentleness Laurie had never known. Suddenly, she became conscious of the shortness of her skirt and the low cut of her top and wished the lights outside the pub weren't so bright.

'It's a friend's hen night,' she lied. 'Everyone has had too much to drink.' She didn't want him to know this was her regular haunt.

He smiled. He had a friendly smile. *I bet he never gets drunk or loses control*, thought Laurie. *He's clever, educated, and undoubtedly on his way home to his lovely detached house and equally pretty and intellectual wife.*

'Don't you have a coat?' he asked.

Laurie shook her head.

He pulled off his jacket and wrapped it around her. 'Would you like me to walk you home?' he asked. 'In case that guy is still hanging around?'

God no. The last thing she wanted him to see was the hell

hole she called home. His scent was all over the jacket, and she inhaled deeply. 'I'll be fine,' she said.

'If you're sure,' he said, and she realised he was gazing at her breasts.

'Honestly.' She nodded, pulling the jacket tighter around her body.

'I'll see you Monday at six,' he said. 'You can bring the jacket then.'

'Yes,' she said, tugging at her skirt again. Then, as soon as he turned the corner, she threw up violently into the gutter.

CHAPTER TWO

PRESENT DAY: SATURDAY MORNING

With each stride, Ana's mind became clearer and more resolute. She'd made it, and there was no going back. Then, as the sunlight caressed her skin, she took a deep breath of the warm air and steeled herself to think only of her future. With each stride after that, she felt more in command. Ana's clear brown eyes scanned the concrete tower block and landed on the fourth-floor window. She smiled. It was ideal. Across the street stood an identical building. Its grey concrete galloped up to the clouds. Yes, it was more than ideal; it was perfect.

'They make 'em too high if you ask me,' said the estate agent approaching her. 'Ana Rawlins?' he asked.

She nodded. 'Great views, though.'

'If you've got a head for heights.' He pulled a key from his pocket and opened the main doors to the smart foyer. There was a click, and the place was flooded with light. It smelt of polish and someone's floral perfume. The black and white tiled floor was spotless.

'Cleaners come twice a week. All part of the maintenance,' he explained. 'All included in the rent. The security light stays on for two minutes. Long enough to reach the lift, but there's another button by the lift doors.' He turned to her. 'Sure you don't want to see the flat on the first floor. Unfurnished and slightly cheaper.'

Ana shook her head. 'I like a good view,' she said, and the fourth floor would give her precisely the view she wanted.

The estate agent noticed she barely looked around the flat or took in the tasteful décor and furnishings. Instead, she went to the window and looked at the block across the street. The fourth-floor window of the opposite flat had pretty curtains with tiebacks, embellishing the window like a picture frame.

'Like a goldfish bowl. You need to remember that,' he said, standing beside her. 'You can see right in here from over there.' He leaned in like he was about to share a secret with her. 'There was this story in the paper about this guy who was stalking some girl from a flat window. Took photos of her undressing using one of those long lenses.'

'I didn't read it,' she said absently. *I wonder if she's home,* Ana thought. *Probably not.*

'All the same, best to get nets,' he advised.

'I'll take it,' she said, turning from the window.

He raised his eyebrows. 'But you haven't seen the other rooms.'

'It's exactly what I want. I've been waiting for a flat like this.' She'd waited long enough, and now the time had come.

CHAPTER THREE

SATURDAY EVENING

The lad making his way home from the Chelsea match was Sajid Singh. Chelsea had won 3–1 against Spurs, and Sajid was elated and slightly drunk. Next was the quarter-final, and Sajid felt sure they would win. Warmth radiated throughout his body, partly from excitement and partly from the alcohol he'd consumed. A few of the supporters he'd sat with had invited him to celebrate with them at a place in Soho whose name he couldn't remember. He remembered being happy, though; his eyes still shone with the pleasure only winning could bring.

He climbed aboard the coach at Marble Arch, heading for Oxford. If the traffic was okay, it would take an hour and a half, maybe less. There were only a few empty seats. He debated sitting with the lads wearing Chelsea shirts, thinking it would be fun to share the excitement of winning, but their expressions made him uneasy. Their shaven heads and tattoos told him he wouldn't be welcome into their clique. Instead, he sat next to an old man who stank of sweat and nicotine. He could hear the lads behind him sniggering and swearing.

'You shouldn't be doing that,' someone said.

'Is that right?' One of the lads laughed.

Sajid turned to see that one was spraying black paint on the CCTV cameras. He quickly turned back and glanced down at his phone.

As time went on, the lads got rowdier. Sajid could smell the beer they were drinking. The more they drank, the more boisterous they became. He pulled his earphones from his pocket, accidentally hitting the old man with his elbow.

'Hey, watch it,' said the man harshly.

'Sorry, the seats are so close,' apologised Sajid.

'Yeah, well, just be more careful next time.'

'Of course, I'm–' began Sajid, but he stopped when a hand slapped him on the shoulder.

'Is this Paki upsetting you, mate?' The voice was coarse and common. Sajid knew without looking that it was one of the lads he'd chosen not to sit beside. The lad leaned over him, his alcohol-fumed breath wafting into Sajid's face.

The word *Paki* drove through Sajid's heart like a knife. Only one kind of person used words like that, and Sajid knew from experience that they weren't the best kind.

'He's all right,' said the old man nervously.

Sajid wanted to say that he wasn't from Pakistan, that he'd been born in Oxford, and that his parents were from India, but his throat had tightened up, and he could barely speak.

'Well, I think he should apologise. I'm Needles, by the way. Cool name, yeah? It's on account of the tattoos, see?' He proudly held up a tattooed arm.

Sajid wanted to run and hide somewhere. Images of what could happen flashed through his mind. A friend of his had been stabbed just the other month because he was Muslim, so Sajid's heart was nearly exploding with fear.

'Now fucking apologise, Paki,' Needles snapped.

Sajid looked up into the man's hard brown eyes. They were

dark and chilling. Every muscle in his face was tight. He expressed intense anger and contempt.

The coach had turned quiet. No one wanted the tattooed skinhead to pick on them. Sajid wished the man named Needles would take his hand off his shoulder. He didn't want him to feel the trembling of his body.

'I did apologise,' he said softly.

'Whaddya say, Paki? Speak up, or has the cat got your tongue?' mocked Needles.

The other lads laughed, and Sajid felt a chill of fear run through him. 'I did apologise,' he repeated.

'Is that right, Granddad?' asked Needles.

The man bristled at the word *granddad*. 'Yes, he did.'

Sajid was relieved when the coach driver barked, 'What's going on back there? Please go back to your seats.'

'What right yer got to tell us what to do? What do yer think you're playing at letting a Paki onto this coach?' said Needles, vitriol pouring from his mouth like venom.

Sajid could smell the odour of his own sweat and felt ashamed of his fear.

'Yeah,' shouted another. 'The coach stinks of fucking curry now.'

Sajid could see the driver didn't know what to do either. Sajid just prayed he would call for help. They were on the M25, and Sajid knew they couldn't just stop. His legs trembled so much that he knocked them against the older man's knee.

'I bet he doesn't even have a fucking ticket,' said Needles, grabbing Sajid by the arm. 'Show it to us then?'

With fumbling hands, Sajid felt in his pocket for the coach ticket.

At that moment, Sajid saw one of the lads pull a hammer from his rucksack, and for one awful second, he thought he was going to use it on him, but Sajid saw his aim was for the radio that the coach driver had in his hand. Someone screamed and Sajid watched in horror as the hammer smashed into the radio. Sharp pieces of metal, like small razor blades, flew everywhere. The coach swerved dangerously across the lanes for a few desperate seconds as the driver tried to get the steering wheel back under his control.

'Why don't you just keep your eyes on the road, mister,' shouted the lad waving the hammer. His tone was threatening, and Sajid's hands had turned clammy.

'All right, all right,' the driver said shakily. Sajid saw blood dripping down his face.

'And why don't you drop that hammer and sit back down, you piece of trash,' said a voice behind them.

The lad spun around, and his face turned ashen. Several times his mouth opened, but nothing came out of it. Standing with a machete at Needles' throat was a figure dressed in combat trousers and a khaki jacket. A balaclava hid his face, and he wore black gloves. Sajid stared at him in shock and confusion.

'Where the hell did he come from?' yelled one of the lads.

Sajid was wondering the same thing.

'Christ,' cried one of the other lads, reaching into his pocket.

'Watch it,' someone yelled.

The figure turned, wrenching Needles around with him. 'Unless you want your mate's throat slit from one side to the other, I wouldn't reach for that flick knife, if I were you. Trust me, I'll slaughter this little scumbag if you do.'

'Needles?' asked the lad. 'What do I do?'

'Do as he fucking says,' screamed Needles. For the first time that evening, Sajid saw fear in Needles' eyes.

All his arrogance had left him, and Sajid felt sorry for him in a strange way.

'I am The Vigilante,' said the masked figure. 'Nice to meet

you, you pieces of shit. Now, I think it's time you and your mates move on, don't you? I suggest you get off at the next stop, which is quite soon, isn't that right, driver?'

The driver simply nodded. He pulled in at the next stop with such a jerk that all the passengers were thrown forward.

'Just in case you think I'm a bit of a joker,' said The Vigilante calmly, and then, before Needles could blink, The Vigilante gently slid the machete across his neck. A trickle of blood ran down Needles' throat. The crimson liquid continued its journey down his shoulder and onto his arm. He screamed like a girl and clutched at the wound. In seconds all the lads had hurried off the coach, and the driver was bombing it down the A40 like a rocket was up his coach's backside.

Sajid sat stiff as a poker, waiting for The Vigilante to turn on him, but instead, he asked, 'Are you okay, mate?'

Sajid nodded dumbly, staring in fear at the machete.

The man slid it into his backpack and handed Sajid a card. Then he walked up the coach to the driver. 'Stop here,' he said.

As directed, the driver pulled into the layby, and the masked man handed him a card, too, before jumping off the coach.

The driver didn't wait to see where The Vigilante went but pushed his foot hard on the accelerator.

'Who the hell was that?' someone asked.

'I didn't see him get on,' said another.

'Well, it sure wasn't bloody Superman,' said the driver.

Sajid wiped the perspiration from his forehead and thought he wasn't far off being Superman as far as he was concerned. He looked down at the card in his hand. Big, bold letters read, 'When the law fails to serve us, we must serve as the law', and then handwritten were the words 'The Vigilante'.

'Who the fuck was that?' said Skinner eyeing up the cut on Needles' neck.

'Where did he come from?' asked Digger.

'I don't know,' said Needles. 'I'm sure as hell going to find out, and when I do, we'll show that Paki lover who's in charge. Is it bad?' he asked, gently feeling his neck.

'Nah,' said Skinner. 'He wasn't aiming to cause damage.'

'Some kind of vigilante,' said Twitch.

Needles let out a small laugh. 'We'll be ready for him next time, right?'

They all nodded. They knew better than to disagree.

'What are we going to do now?' asked Skinner.

'Get the next coach, you wanker. Only we don't sit together. We don't want them making connections, just in case that dickhead driver phoned and reported it. Viper promise, lads.' Needle held his right hand up.

The others followed suit. 'Stand together, fight together, die together,' they all said solemnly.

'The enemy will never win,' said Needles.

'Never,' they chorused.

Further down the road, The Vigilante removed the khaki jacket and balaclava before shoving them into his rucksack. He covered his head with a beanie, walked to the next coach stop, boarded the second coach with several others, and sat at the front with his head deep in a book.

None of the lads was aware of him.

CHAPTER FOUR

SEVEN YEARS EARLIER

Laurie debated whether to cut through the alley. It would save her the fifteen minutes it took to go through town. Her guts cramped so much that she didn't think she could face the Friday night ruckus. If only she'd accepted his offer of a walk home. No, that had been unthinkable.

For the third time, she glanced behind her and decided it was safe enough to cut through as usual. A cat rooting through a black rubbish bag stopped to glare at her for a second and continued scavenging when it realised she wasn't a threat.

Laurie continued, the pulsating pain in her head making her dizzy. There was a jingle of keys as someone locked or unlocked a door, and she desperately wished it were her and that she was home and safe. It was freezing now, and she slid her arms into the sleeves of the jacket. His warmth and smell were all over her, as if he were holding her tightly against him.

The pungent aroma of dope reached her nostrils, adding to her nausea. Several homeless men sitting on tatty blankets shouted out to her. 'Hey, love, spare us a bit of change?'

She ignored them and held her breath until she'd passed. Finally, she came to the end of the alley, and a cloud of relief enveloped her when she saw the group of houses and flats huddled together on the estate. The familiar sound of her neighbour's dog barking reached her ears, followed by the loud blaring of a television.

Laurie inserted her key into the lock of the small terraced house and entered the hallway cluttered with boots and shoes.

'Is that you, Laurie? What time do you call this?'

Laurie entered the living room, where the television was deafening. 'It's nearly one,' she said, yawning. 'You know you can hear the telly outside. How are Anika and Dil supposed to sleep?'

Without waiting for Arthur to reply, she headed to the kitchen. The sink was full of dirty dishes, and the table was littered with the remains of a Chinese takeaway. Laurie wrinkled her nose and then opened a cupboard door that hung on one hinge, took a tea-stained cup and filled it with water from the leaky tap.

'I'm going up,' said Arthur from behind her. He had been her mother's partner for close to three years now. Laurie liked him. Not enough to call him dad, but enough to hope he stayed for her mother's sake.

'Anika will be pleased.'

'How much you had to drink? You're only fifteen years old, for Christ's sake.'

'So? You're not my dad, so sod off.'

'You telling this social worker bloke how you get tanked up most nights?' he asked.

'It's none of your business what I tell him,' she said tiredly. 'Where's Mum?'

'Gone to bed.'

'Is she okay?'

'You know.'

Laurie knew, all right. Brenda had drunk too much, and the

pain had come, sending her to bed. 'She ought to see a doctor,' said Laurie.

'You try telling her that.'

'Couldn't one of you have cleaned up?' Laurie said, looking at the table in disgust.

'Since when did you care about the place being clean? Ain't you got enough problems?'

Laurie gave a sad laugh. 'Yeah, well, they say it's your parents that fuck you up, don't they?' Nausea welled up in her again, and she pushed past him, making it to the loo just in time.

'I hope you're gonna clean that up,' he called from behind the door.

Laurie splashed cold water on her face, and then, much to her surprise, she began to cry.

CHAPTER FIVE

PRESENT DAY: EARLY HOURS

The quiet village of Stonesend and its neighbouring hamlet, Longbridge, were mostly in darkness, aside from the warm glow of the moon that enshrouded them, but Needles was too hyped up to sleep.

Chelsea's win had excited him, and then that fucking vigilante had gone and ruined everything. Standing up for a Paki, of all people. It made his blood boil. It was no good. He needed to get it out of his system and knew exactly how. Needles' joyriding had been driving the locals mad for some months. Needles couldn't care less about them. He was angry and needed to get it out of his system.

The Vigilante was exhausted. The adrenalin was pumping through his veins, and his head was still buzzing from earlier.

He would have been thrilled to know that Sajid had thought him Superman. He'd felt far from Superman when he'd climbed from the coach. The sweat bead on his forehead had been a stark reminder of his vulnerability. His trembling hands had eventually stilled, and the frantic rhythm of his heart eased. But he had acted decisively and without hesitation.

The law, often sluggish and bureaucratic, had failed to act swiftly. So, he'd stepped in, fuelled by duty and a sense of injustice.

Looking back, he acknowledged the thrill that had surged through him – the adrenalin, the purpose. Now he had begun, he knew he couldn't stop. Tonight, he would sleep well, knowing he'd put an injustice to rights.

Down the road in Longbridge, Leigh wasn't surprised when the sound of the trail bike broke Will's guttural snores. She saw his eyes snap open. 'It's one o'clock,' she said wearily.

It was too hot to close the window, and Leigh did not feel that having it open made much difference. The air was still and stifling.

'I swear I'll kill the bugger,' yelled Will, jumping from the bed.

The trail bike roared, heading their way again, and Leigh turned on the bedside lamp. 'Be careful, Will. You know what they're like,' she said nervously. Her hair had rearranged itself during the past few hours and now stood on end like a soldier standing to attention, waiting for Will's next command.

He hurriedly pulled his trousers over his pyjama bottoms and a jumper over his top. 'Enough is enough. Racing through here in the evening is one thing, but I'll be buggered if I'll listen to the little sod at night too.'

The bike thundered past, and Leigh covered her ears before hurrying to the window.

'Hale's out there,' she said, seeing her next-door neighbour's large frame lit up by their security light. Leigh felt her confidence rise at his presence. If Will had to go outside, he wouldn't be alone.

The rider had roared past the houses on his circuit and apparently hadn't even noticed Hale standing in the street.

'Right,' said Will, pulling on his trainers and grabbing the torch from the bedside cabinet.

Leigh hurried down the stairs behind him. When they opened the front door, they saw several neighbours standing in the street.

'What the hell is he playing at?' asked Hale. His torch blinded Leigh briefly, but then he lowered it, and she was shocked that he was in his pyjamas. She'd only ever seen him in a suit on his way to and from work, so seeing him in his striped nightwear felt like an invasion of privacy.

'I've had enough of this,' he complained. 'No licence plate and no silencer, and he's most likely not insured, and what's the bloody police doing?'

'Sod all,' replied Will. 'I've reported the little bugger three times.'

Leigh stood at the front door, listening to their conversation and praying they wouldn't do anything silly. Everyone knew what some of those lads who lived at Ludbrook Grove estate were capable of. The last thing she wanted was their car floured, the house egged, or something worse.

'Wait here,' said Hale. 'I've got an idea.'

The rumbling of the trail bike was getting nearer. Leigh edged back into her hallway. Hale returned with a long ladder, and Leigh stared in surprise. The bike was getting closer, and Leigh's heart was thumping like crazy. What were they going to do? Surely, they weren't planning on knocking him off the bike. What if he got injured? There'd be hell to pay.

'I think we should call the police,' she said. 'It's safer that way.'

Will turned on her. 'If you've got nothing more useful to offer, keep quiet.'

Leigh stepped back and watched Will help Hale position the ladder across the road. The roar of the trail bike was growing nearer, and the noise seemed to vibrate in Leigh's head.

'You block him with the ladder,' said Will. 'Then when he turns back, I'll follow him in my car and see where he goes.'

'No, Will,' cried Leigh. 'Don't go to Ludbrook Grove estate.'

'I'm not stupid. Stop nagging me.'

Then, the helmet-less rider was close to them. The brightness of the torches must have temporarily blinded him because, for a split second, he swerved, and Leigh gasped. What if he fell and injured his head? As he drew closer and saw the ladder, Leigh thought she saw his eyes turn wild and fierce. The screech of brakes made Leigh's teeth tingle. She was reminded of that scene in the film *The Great Escape* when Steve McQueen tries to jump the wire fence, but of course, this wasn't Steve McQueen but some ruffian from Ludbrook Grove.

Hale aimed his phone at him and took a photo. Leigh thought, *He won't forget your face in a hurry.* She stepped further back into her hallway.

After several attempts to get past them, the rider turned and roared off, deliberately scraping Hale's car as he did.

Will in his own car accelerated and followed the bike.

'I got a photo.' Hale grinned, holding his phone up so Leigh could see. 'Let's wait for Will, and then we'll get the police here.'

Leigh could barely breathe. She'd heard all sorts about the families that lived at Ludbrook Grove. What if Will got beaten up? It seemed a lifetime before she saw Will's car turn the corner.

'I lost the bugger,' he said. 'He shot down an alleyway near Ludbrook Grove. I couldn't get the car down there, but he's from the estate. I'm phoning DS Beth Harper,' he snarled, marching into the house.

'You can't phone her now, Will,' protested Leigh, hurrying after him. 'It's one in the morning. Shouldn't you phone the police station?'

'What and be fobbed off again? I don't see why she shouldn't be awake too,' argued Hale. 'These yobs are harassing and tormenting us daily because they can get away with it. They've damaged my car as well.'

'Stonesend station covers all the surrounding villages, not just sodding Stonesend,' agreed Will. 'I think we should phone Beth Harper, not some night sergeant.'

'He saw your faces,' Leigh said, the tremble evident in her voice.

'Who gives a shit?' said Hale arrogantly.

You don't know what they're like at Ludbrook Grove, thought Leigh. *You've only lived here a few months.*

'What's the point in the police if they do bugger all?' said Will. 'If you ask me, it's time for the public to take the law into their own hands.'

'I couldn't agree more,' said Hale.

'You don't have her number, Will,' Leigh argued.

'She's on the village WhatsApp group.' Will grinned.

Leigh didn't see the point in arguing as Will was already tapping Beth's phone number into his mobile.

CHAPTER SIX

LAURIE

———————

S ome might have said Laurie McDuff's life was doomed from the moment she was born.

She was raised on a council estate by an alcoholic mother and so many daddies that she eventually lost count. Life was never going to be easy. Some of the dads stayed longer than others. The nice ones gave her sweets or toys, usually to get her out of the way. Even at seven, Laurie knew why they wanted her out of the way, but it didn't bother her as long as she got the toys.

Brenda McDuff hadn't been a bad mother; it was just that everything had been against her from the moment she had met Charlie McDuff.

'I was dealt a bad hand of cards,' she would tell anyone who would listen.

The truth, however, was that Brenda had known Charlie McDuff was trouble. He'd been in the nick twice for burglary. It had been the air of danger and excitement enshrouding him that had made him more attractive to Brenda.

Sometimes, she would wonder what life might have been like if she hadn't married Charlie McDuff. But thinking about what could have been doesn't pay the rent. Charlie had been the best-looking bloke on the estate. All the girls fancied him, but Charlie wanted Brenda with her natural curly locks and big bright blue eyes. Brenda had been flattered that it was her he'd chosen. She'd been seventeen when they started going out together. Charlie had been twenty, worldly, and knew, it seemed to Brenda, just about everyone and everything.

Within a year, Brenda was pregnant. It had never occurred to her to go on the pill. She'd just assumed Charlie would take care of that side of things.

Once they were married, Brenda quickly learned that her ideal boyfriend wasn't such an ideal husband. He resented her for the pregnancy and claimed she had trapped him into marriage. Because of Brenda's pregnancy, they got a small council house on the Moorgate Estate. Charlie had grand ideas, and the Moorgate Estate wasn't one of them. He was disappointed and became even more resentful.

They couldn't afford furniture, so Charlie brought home tatty sofas that someone had thrown in a skip. The curtains left by the previous tenants were threadbare and smelt of stale cigarette smoke, but Brenda consoled herself that at least they had curtains, unlike some of the other tenants.

On the second day in their new home, their neighbour, Anika, came by with some homemade samosas. Brenda immediately felt a kinship with this pretty Indian woman, who wore the most colourful sari.

But that night Charlie refused to eat the samosas. 'You've got to be joking,' he scoffed. 'God knows what their house is like or if her hands were clean when she made them.'

'Charlie,' exclaimed Brenda, shocked.

'I don't want Indians in our house, got it? Or touching our baby.'

So Brenda would go to Anika's house, which always smelt of

the most fragrant spices. Together, they made new curtains for Brenda's living room out of cheap material they'd bought at the market. Anika helped hang them when Charlie was out.

Charlie spent more and more time away from home, and it wasn't long before Brenda discovered that her husband had a split personality and that the man she had married was actually a drug-addicted abuser.

CHAPTER SEVEN

PRESENT DAY

The high trill of Beth's mobile shattered the night's silence and pierced through her brain like sharp needles. Her hand fumbled around the bedside cabinet, hitting a glass of water and sending it smashing to the floor. *Shit.*

An incessant throb drummed across her right temple in time with the relentless ringing. The time on her phone read 1.15am. *What the hell?* That familiar churning in her stomach returned, and she felt nauseous.

'DS Harper,' she mumbled into the phone, her voice croaky. God, she'd needed that water.

'It's Will Moulson here,' said the voice at the other end.

'Who?' asked Beth, trying to get her fuddled brain into gear. Who was Will Moulson, and why was he calling her at one in the morning? 'I think you have the wrong number,' she said, about to hang up.

'Will Moulson from Longbridge, you know, the next village.'

Beth sensed the sarcasm and leaned over to switch on the lamp. As she sat up, her arm brushed the empty wine bottle. 'It's one in the morning,' she said sleepily. 'Is this a police matter?'

'Oh, I'm well aware of the time,' he said sardonically. 'As is half the bloody village. We've had that trail bike here again and–'

'Have you phoned the station, Mr Moulson?' Beth broke in.

There was a scoff from the other end of the line. 'Like all the other times? Where no one does anything. We're not prepared to put up with this intimidation any longer. We've got photos. Either you do something, or we'll take it into our own hands. I'm number 23 Oakfields Road.'

Beth sighed. 'I would advise you not to do anything stupid, Mr Moulson.'

'Perhaps *you'd* better do something then. I'm sorry this isn't an exciting murder case for you.'

Beth sat forward, her shoulders tensed. 'What did you say?'

Mr Moulson had already hung up. Beth exhaled heavily, climbed from the bed, gingerly stepped over the broken glass, and walked to the kitchen. Then, after filling a glass with water and swallowing two painkillers, she phoned the station.

DC Matt Wilkins had barely answered before she said, 'Matt, get over to Longbridge. Someone called Will Moulson just phoned me. That trail bike brat is at it again. They've got photos of the kid. Go over to Moulson before he does something stupid. He's all worked up. 23 Oakfields Road. I'll meet you there. See if you can catch the lad on the bike.'

'What, now?' asked Matt surprised. 'It's half past one.'

'No kidding, Sherlock. Have you got something better to do?'

'No, ma'am,' sighed Matt. 'I'm on my way.'

Beth flopped into a kitchen chair and laid her throbbing head on the table. Were they ever going to let her forget the murder last year? It had been frightening for everyone, including her, but now everyone seemed to think that unless it was some gory murder they were reporting, then she wasn't interested.

Her thoughts wandered to Tom Miller and the events of a year ago, the horrific attacks and how they had changed everyone. Tom had been traumatised, and when he'd left as the station's DI three months ago, Beth felt like her heart had been broken again.

'It's too soon,' he'd told her. 'Please forgive me.'

She sighed heavily and decided to have an early night later. Then, with a jolt, she remembered her sister's birthday dinner that evening, which, in turn, reminded her that today would have been her wedding anniversary.

Beth cursed the trail bike kid and quickly dressed. Outside, the air was cool and fresh. The street was eerily quiet, with just the odd cry of an owl breaking the peaceful silence. She never ceased to appreciate the beauty of Stonesend village. Wands of rising branches became dancing silhouettes in the moonlight. The stone cottage windows were wide open to relieve the day's heat.

Beth drove slowly by the churchyard and forced her eyes away from the small empty cottage beside it where Tom had lived, keeping her gaze firmly on the road. It took five minutes for her to reach the village of Longbridge.

Here, the houses were different from those in Stonesend. They huddled together, sharing walls and forming a row of rooftop peaks. The front gardens were decorated with scooters, bikes, and Wellington boots. Beth parked behind Matt's panda police car and pushed open the gate of number 23, where the front garden displayed a neatly trimmed lawn and terracotta pots holding petunias.

Matt met her at the front door. 'They're pretty worked up,' he said. 'Can't say I blame them.'

Beth flexed her neck and wished the painkillers would kick in. 'Any sign of the kid?'

'No, nothing.'

Several people were standing in the Moulson's living room.

'Mr Moulson?' she asked, looking around. A man stepped in front of her. Beth guessed him to be in his early fifties. His face was pock-marked like he'd had terrible acne when he was younger.

'That's me,' he said, his voice cold and hard, his face twisted in anger.

Beth met his angry eyes. 'I'm DS Harper. You called me.'

A younger, good-looking man stepped forward. 'I'm Hale–'

'I'll speak to Mr Moulson first if you don't mind,' said Beth firmly.

Hale glared at her before stepping back.

'This is him,' said Will, shoving his phone with the photo into her face. The image was grainy, and the features were unclear.

'What was the ladder for?' asked Beth

'We were trying to stop him,' said Hale. 'He woke up my baby. It takes long enough to get her to sleep as it is.'

'You do realise that if you'd knocked that lad off his bike and caused him an injury, serious or otherwise, you'd be looking at a charge of grievous bodily harm?'

Moulson gave a sarcastic laugh. 'Are you serious? That kid is tormenting everyone. Unbelievable.'

'I'm just putting you in the picture for the future, Mr Moulson.'

'He races through here all the time. He doesn't wear headgear, and the bike has no number plates or silencers. Surely you can take the bike off him,' said Hale.

'I understand your frustration–' she began.

'Do you?' Moulson broke in sharply. 'Was he racing through Stonesend? Did he wake you up?'

'The only person who woke me up, Mr Moulson, was you.'

'No one from Stonesend reported it,' said Matt.

Will's hands were tightly clenched, and his shoulders rigid. Beth felt his anger seemed out of control, and for a second, it crossed her mind that he might hit her, and she stepped back slightly.

'Can't you confiscate the bike?' asked Hale.

'It's not as easy as that, I'm afraid,' said Beth, becoming aware of the slim, auburn-haired woman standing to her right, attempting to fade into the wallpaper.

'Well, it bloody ought to be,' said Hale.

Beth ignored him. 'Do you know the lad, Mr Moulson?'

'If I did, he wouldn't still be doing it. We think he's from that dump at the end of the village, Ludbrook Grove.'

Beth saw the woman flinch at the name.

'Did he threaten you?' Beth asked, turning to her.

Leigh shook her head. 'Oh no, but they're a bit of a rough crowd by all accounts.'

'We're aware of them,' said Matt.

'So, why don't you do something?'

'I assure you we're doing our best. Unfortunately, this isn't a very clear photograph. Until we know who the bike belongs to, there isn't much we can do. Catching them in the act isn't easy.'

Beth handed Will a card with the station's number on it. 'Contact the station if you have any more trouble with them.'

'You're going to do something, aren't you? Because if not, we'll take things into our own hands,' said Will determinedly. 'If the law doesn't do something, we'll have to. Too many yobs are getting away with things.'

'Well, I didn't ask you, Mr Moulson. The police handle matters of the law, not the public. So I wouldn't advise that. Leave these matters to those trained to deal with them. If there is any more trouble, phone us right away.'

'You mean like when those joy riders race through the

village every year when they have the car rally? I don't see you doing much about that.'

Beth sighed. 'I know it's a problem, and we do try to catch them–'

'Huh, try is the operative word,' said Will scathingly.

'What will you do in the meantime?' asked Hale. 'About this biker?'

Beth forwarded the photo to her phone. 'We'll get some work done on this photograph and see if we can get a clearer picture of this rider. Meanwhile, we'll visit Ludbrook Grove and see if anyone there has a trail bike.' She nodded to Matt, and they headed for the front door.

'If the police can't catch a kid on a bike, it comes to something,' said Will sarcastically.

'Leave it with us,' she said calmly, walking from the house.

'Wanker,' muttered Matt.

'Probably pissed off. Let's visit Ludbrook Grove.'

Matt gave her a sideways glance and said carefully, 'You look a bit rough.'

'I don't do my Jennifer Aniston look at one in the morning, and you don't exactly look like Brad Pitt, yourself.'

'Point taken.' He smiled, climbing into the panda.

'See you there,' he said

CHAPTER EIGHT

PRESENT DAY: EARLY HOURS OF SUNDAY MORNING

Needles gently eased the trail bike onto the concrete floor of the darkened garage. He didn't want to turn on the light and draw attention to himself. Fortunately, he didn't need any extra light. The street lamp was enough, and Needles knew the dilapidated building like the back of his hand. The smell of oil and grease calmed him slightly, but not enough to extinguish the roaring anger burning within him.

He'd needed that burn-up. What was the world coming to? A Paki wearing a Chelsea top and some vigilante standing up for him. *It's a fucking disgrace; that's what it is. Whose bloody country is this, anyway?*

Now he had some burnt-out old farts trying to be clever with their ladder. They'd be sorry soon enough. He gently ran a finger along his neck and grimaced. It stung like hell. 'Shit,' he groaned.

Carefully locking the garage door behind him, he looked around to ensure no one had seen him. After all, you never knew what nosy parker might question why he was using Jim Carter's garage.

Jim would be fast asleep by now. *Poor sod*, thought Needles,

losing your mind and with no one to care for you. Life is a bugger.
Still, dementia had its bonuses. It meant Needles could use Joe's
garage as much as he liked. The poor old sod had forgotten he
even had a garage, and no one would ever suspect an old bloke
with dementia would be housing a trail bike in his garage.

He would pop in tomorrow and check that Meals on
Wheels had delivered Jim's food.

His parents' house was quiet when he went in, and he crept
up the stairs, avoiding the creaky one at the top. One of these
days, his useless father would fix that. Still, Needles wouldn't
have to worry about that much longer. Richie had said he could
rent the rooms above the garage. All he needed was the deposit.
Needles only had to save another hundred, and he could move
out of this dump.

'I heard you on that bike.'

He turned with a start to see his sister, a loose jumper
covering her nightgown.

'That weren't me.'

'Liar,' she hissed, following him into his room. 'You'll get
caught, and they'll take the bike off yer.'

'They'll never find the bike,' he said confidently.

It was when he clicked on the light that she saw his neck.
'Jesus, what the hell happened to you?' she asked, reaching up to
feel the cut.

Needles pulled away. 'Nothing, he said dismissively.

'*Nothing* doesn't leave a mark on your neck – unless that
was his name. When did that happen?'

Needles sighed. Laine could be like a dog with a bone
sometimes. He studied the cut in the mirror. It looked worse
than it felt. He stroked it gently. He'd wear it as a badge of
honour. After all, he hadn't been the coward hiding his face
behind a mask.

'Some wanker who took it upon himself to defend some

Paki on the coach tonight. He slashed me with a machete. If he hadn't been wearing a balaclava, I'd 'ave 'ad 'im by now.'

Laine's eyes widened. 'A machete? Are you shitting me?'

'Ask the others.'

'Did you go to the hospital?'

'Don't be soft.'

'You lot are going to get into serious trouble one day.'

Needles laughed. 'Says the sister who's been referred to social for bunking school and abusing the staff.'

Laine sighed.

Needles knew she'd planned to bunk school the day of the counselling and go shopping with her best friend, Jassy.

'You should go,' he said. 'Else, you'll be in worse trouble.'

'They can't make me. Playing truant and nicking a few things isn't the same as racial harassment. Mum would go mad if she knew what you got up to. Anyway, school is boring. All the teachers are a pain.'

'You're not supposed to tell the teachers that.' He laughed.

'It's not as bad as what you get up to.'

'I don't get up to anything. Anyway, Mum can't do nothing. I'm nineteen.'

'You're going to get into trouble one day. You need to be careful.'

He laughed bitterly. 'There're a few people who need to be careful, but I ain't one of 'em.'

Laine looked at him sorrowfully from under her long fringe. 'It's not fair,' she said sullenly. 'I have to have an assessment about my behaviour while you get away with murder. Seriously, you're making enemies,' she added worriedly.

'I ain't scared of no one,' Needles boasted. 'Who are you to tell me what to do? You're just a kid.'

'I'll be sixteen soon. I'm not a kid.'

'You're not sixteen for another six months.'

Laine shook her head in exasperation before turning and leaving his room.

Needles studied the cut more closely. Yes, it was a badge of honour, not the mark of a coward, and that fucking joker would soon learn that Needles didn't much like a joke.

CHAPTER NINE

Ludbrook Grove estate was one of those places people avoided unless they had the bad luck of living there. Even though Beth knew of its reputation, the state of the place always surprised her. Why they stuck social housing estates close to small middle-class villages was a mystery to her. It just emphasised the class distinction and caused trouble all around, especially for the police, who were forever being called out about house egging or car flouring.

'Never been here at night?' Matt smiled, taking in Beth's expression at the girls hanging out on the corner of the street in their short skirts and laddered tights, touting for punters.

'Can't say a night visit to Ludbrook Grove was on my bucket list.' She grinned.

'It's on my patch, so I've had the pleasure. Can't see it in all its best points in the dark.' Matt smiled, climbing from the car.

'When you say you've had the pleasure. I'm presuming you don't mean literally,' she said, nodding at the girls.

'Do I look that desperate?' he asked, affronted.

'I bet they egg you on, though, a good-looking lad like you.'

'I feel sorry for them. It's a rough start in life, and no one bothers to help them or highlight the problem. They have their banter with me. I don't mind. Let me show you Ludbrook Grove in all its glory.'

'I can see enough,' said Beth, taking in the piles of rubbish.

'You're not nicking us tonight, are you, sweetie?' called one of the girls.

'More important things to do,' replied Matt.

'Aw, more important than us?' The girl pouted.

'I'm afraid so.'

'Let's stroll around and see if we can spot a trail bike,' Beth said, tripping over something on the ground and wobbling slightly. Matt's hand steadied her. She realised that any other time, he wouldn't have needed to do that. *I've got to stop drinking,* she thought. Could Matt smell the alcohol on her breath?

'What the hell was that?' she said, shining her torch onto the ground. She'd tripped over an empty beer can. Beside it were cigarette butts and used hypodermic needles.

'Not again,' exclaimed Matt.

Beth sighed. 'We need to contact social services.'

Matt shrugged. 'I've already done it. You know how it is. Cutbacks everywhere.'

'I don't give a shit about cutbacks. Get onto them first thing.'

'Right,' he said, looking at her oddly.

Beth let her shoulders sag and felt the tension ease slightly. 'Sorry,' she said quietly. 'Not a good day.'

'I know,' he replied softly. Matt shone his torch on a garage that read 'Benson's Repairs.'

'No sign of a trail bike here,' he said. 'It could be inside, of course.'

A cat scurried from behind a bin, making Beth jump.

'Be grateful it wasn't a rat.' Matt smiled.

Beth shuddered. 'You're really cheering me up tonight, aren't you?'

From across the street, loud music blared out from an open window. Beth crossed the road and entered the garden, carefully stepping around a broken satellite dish. The doorbell didn't seem to work, or she didn't hear it over the sound of Harry Styles.

Matt looked at her and then hammered on the door. Through the door's glass panels, they saw the light go on in the hallway, and then the door was opened just enough for Beth to glimpse through the crack into a cluttered hallway.

'Who is it?' a woman asked.

'Police,' said Beth, pushing her ID through the gap.

'What's the problem?'

'The music, Mrs...' began Matt.

'Skinner,' said the woman. 'I 'ave told him. Just ignores me. Freddie!' the woman yelled, and Beth thought her thumping head would burst.

The door opened wider, and a diminutive figure in a flannelette nightgown appeared. 'I keep telling him to turn it down,' she said. 'He never does what I tell him.'

'Can you call him, please?' asked Matt, who struggled not to inhale the atrocious smell of stale sweat, food grease and urine.

'No, it's fine,' broke in Beth, who didn't think her head would survive another yell. The music continued, pulsating through her brain like an African war dance. 'Can we come in?'

Matt took a deep breath as the door opened wider. Beth reeled back at the stench before dodging past several cat litter trays that looked like they hadn't been cleaned in months and made her way upstairs. The stench of cat piss mixed with stale tobacco and fried food almost made Matt gag.

'Don't you dare,' Beth warned him.

'I'm not,' he said determinedly.

Beth banged on the door, where the music was deafening. 'Freddie, it's Detective Sergeant Harper. Open the door, please.'

The music continued.

'Bugger this,' she said and turned the door handle. The door was locked.

'Freddie,' she shouted, 'open the door, now!'

The music stopped, and after some minutes, the door opened. In the sudden silence that followed, Beth heard the faint sound of a dog whining somewhere in the house. Freddie stared at her, and Beth saw something she could only define as evil in his eyes. His close-cropped hair revealed a skin rash on his scalp.

'So, what's up?' he said, chewing noisily on some gum.

'I'm DS Harper, and this is DC Wilkins. The music,' she said. 'Let's keep it off until a more sociable time, shall we?'

'Whatever you say,' he said cockily. 'It's only my house, ain't it?'

'You have neighbours that don't appreciate your taste in music.'

'Someone complained?'

'I'm complaining,' said Beth, fighting back the impulse to whack the little sod around the head. The dog's continual whining was annoying her.

'Do you own a trail bike?' asked Matt.

Freddie Skinner grinned. 'Where would I keep a trail bike? Have you seen the crap my mum keeps in this dump?'

'Polite, aren't you?' commented Matt.

'It's my strong point.' Skinner smirked.

'Maybe you've got a garage you keep it in?' suggested Matt.

'I ain't got no trail bike, all right?'

'Did you hear a trail bike tonight?'

'In case you hadn't noticed, I had me music on.'

'Do you know anyone who owns one?' asked Beth.

Skinner shrugged. 'Am I my brother's keeper?'

Beth stared into the dark depths of his eyes. 'Don't make me come back because I might not be so pleasant next time,' she said quietly, but the threat in her voice was deadly.

Skinner, feeling more confident now, pretended to shudder. 'Oh, I'm so scared,' he said mockingly.

Maybe it was the hangover, the anniversary, or just the headache, but before Matt could react, she had Skinner pushed up against the wall of his room with his arm twisted behind his back.

'Beth–' began Matt, shocked.

'DS Harper,' she corrected before returning her attention to Skinner. 'Now, listen carefully, you little turd. I've got a bloody awful headache, and you're not helping it. You start showing some respect to your mum and the police, or next time I'll break your arm, and if I hear any more complaints about your music, I'll confiscate all the equipment you own, and that's not a threat. It's a promise.'

She released him, and Skinner fell, shaking, onto his bed.

'This is fucking harassment; that's what this is,' he snarled. 'I could do you for assault.'

'Yeah, make my day,' said Beth.

Matt followed Beth downstairs to where Mrs Skinner stood wringing her hands nervously. 'I tried to tell him,' she said.

'We'll be in touch with the RSPCA,' said Beth. 'These animals are being mistreated, and if either of you should suddenly remember who owns a trail bike, call the station.'

'Bloody hell!' exclaimed Matt as the door closed behind them. 'That was a bit OTT, wasn't it?'

'No discipline anymore,' she said, yanking open the car door.

'Ah,' said Matt, like that explained everything.

CHAPTER TEN

LAURIE

At seven months pregnant, Brenda began to worry about their finances. Charlie was hardly home, claiming to be working overtime, but there seemed to be less and less money coming in, and Brenda was concerned for their baby.

The cranky radiators barely gave out any heat, so Brenda had borrowed an electric heater from her mum, which Charlie would turn off as soon as he came home. 'We're not fucking made of money,' he'd shout.

The money Brenda earned working as a cleaner at the Co-op hardly brought in a fortune, and she knew that would have to stop once the baby came. The night Brenda confronted her husband about money was the worst night she could have chosen. Charlie, having just lost on the horses and fuelled by cocaine and booze, had given Brenda the beating of her life. He'd hit her before. A slap here and a slap there, but Brenda had put it down to Charlie being stressed about money. This time, it was different. This time, it wasn't just a slap.

'Don't you dare ask me about my business or my whereabouts,' he'd yelled while his fists rained down on her pregnant body. Brenda had shielded her unborn baby as best she could, taking the beatings to her face, arms and back while begging him to stop.

'The baby,' she'd pleaded. 'Please, our baby.'

There was blood. Brenda felt it flow down her face and tasted the metallic liquid as it ran into her mouth.

'That fucking baby,' he'd screamed. 'It's all you fucking talk about.'

Charlie had stormed from the house, leaving his bleeding pregnant wife lying on their living room floor. Brenda had crawled to the phone and called Anika.

The sound of her pregnant friend begging for help had made Anika sick to her stomach. 'Dil, phone for an ambulance,' she'd called to her husband. 'Charlie's gone too far. I'm going round.'

'No,' he shouted. 'Not on your own. Not while that bastard is still there.'

'He's gone,' said Anika, hurrying from the house.

Brenda was barely conscious when Anika arrived. Blood flowed from her ears, and her eyes were so puffy that Anika barely recognised her.

'Oh my God, what has he done to you?'

Brenda opened her swollen lips to speak but realised she was unable to.

'You're going to be fine,' Anika said gently, stroking Brenda's forehead. 'So is the baby.'

Dil stood in the doorway, fuming. He wanted to beat the shit out of Charlie, but the coward had legged it.

Anika held back her tears until they reached the hospital, and Brenda was ushered into a treatment room. Only then did Anika cry.

In the early hours of the following day, Laurie came prematurely into the world, carrying emotional baggage before she'd even opened her eyes. Charlie never visited them in the hospital. Dil drove Brenda home a few days later with a new baby, a black eye and a broken wrist. Holding her baby in her good arm, Brenda arrived at the house to find her husband and all his belongings gone.

Things were never the same after that for Brenda. Life was a constant struggle, and her financial dependence came from the state and anyone who would help. Loneliness drove her to drink. Life looked rosier after a few vodkas. It was easier to cope when the blood running through her veins was pumped with alcohol. Then there were the men. They were happy to help out in return for a fun night. It helped pay for the vodka and heat for the house and allowed her to put food on the table.

Laurie had no idea who her biological father was, and as she grew older, she decided she didn't want to know.

It was curiosity that drove her to the vodka bottle one night. The last dregs of that bottle had been her first taste of alcohol. Laurie had always been curious about the bottle that her mother seemed to love more than her. At first, the liquid had burned her throat, making her cough, but then it made her feel good and more confident.

Now, at fifteen, she had a mature face, and once made up, she could easily pass for eighteen. It hadn't been difficult for her to get what she needed from the off-licence. Soon, like her mother before her, vodka would become Laurie's drink of choice and, with it, her downfall.

CHAPTER ELEVEN

PRESENT DAY: SUNDAY MORNING

S tonesend police station was a small building beside the village library and opposite the bakers. Neil Watson, head computer analyst, was thinking about doughnuts, but Beth's eyes were trained on him as he finished working on the photo, so he knew doughnuts would have to wait.

'That's the best I can do,' he said.

Beth looked closely at Neil's computer screen. The photograph that Hale had given her was still blurry. She'd hoped for a better outcome.

'Features are impossible to see. There are some marks on the arms,' said Neil, pointing. 'I'd wager ten to one that they're tattoos, but deciphering them is impossible. They could be scars. Like I say, hard to tell.'

'Someone here to see you, ma'am,' said DC Carpenter, popping his head around the door.

'Right,' she said, standing up. 'Can we try and get a closer view of those tattoos?'

'I'm a computer expert, not bloody Jesus,' replied Neil.

'I'm not asking you to walk on water,' she sighed. 'Just try to get a close-up. Otherwise, one of us will have to catch the bugger red-handed at one in the morning. All volunteers write their names on the board.'

Beth picked up her phone from the desk, checked for any messages, then scrolled into her contacts and stared at Tom Miller's details for the hundredth time. She deliberated again whether to message. Insiders had told her he'd returned to work at Notting Hill station. Had she imagined the chemistry between them? It had felt so real at the time. Or had it been the closeness they'd shared because of the murder and suspicion surrounding the village at the time? Impulsively, she typed a message and then hit the send button. It simply read:

> Can you believe it's been a year since we
> worked on that case together? How are you?

Then, pocketing her phone, she walked to the outer office where, according to the desk sergeant, someone was waiting to see her.

The woman looked up as Beth entered. Beth felt uncomfortable meeting her gaze. She knew she didn't look her best. There were dark circles under her eyes where she'd not slept enough, and there never seemed to be enough time to put on make-up.

'Can I help you?' asked Beth.

'I'm Constable Rawlins. I was told to report to you today.'

Beth fought back a sigh. Shit, how could she have forgotten? *Blimey, constables are getting younger*, she thought, *or maybe I'm just getting older.*

'Have I got the day wrong?' asked Ana innocently.

'Of course not. Sorry, it's been a long night. Come in and meet the team. Are you old enough for this job? You look about sixteen,' said Beth as they walked.

'I'm well over sixteen, I assure you.' Ana laughed, confidently following Beth through reception and into the busy department. Beth clocked the admiring glances the men gave Ana, but the new DC seemed unaware of it, as if it was something she had experienced often.

'Everyone, this is DC Ana Rawlins. Ana's joining the team. Make her welcome. No filthy jokes, and watch your language until she gets used to it here,' announced Beth. 'Ana, this is DC Luke Carpenter, and that's DC Matt Wilkins. We're a small department, as you can see. You'll meet the DI later.'

'Hi, I'm pleased to be part of the team,' Ana said, her accent taking them all by surprise. 'And I think it's my language we'll have to watch.'

'You from up north then?' said Neil.

'Meet "state the bloody obvious" Neil Watson. He's one of our computer analysts and not bloody Jesus, as he keeps reminding me.' Beth laughed.

'Aw, not Jesus, then. That's a disappointment,' said Ana, smiling. 'I could have taken to someone who turned water into wine.'

'*Head* computer analyst,' Neil corrected. 'And as close to God as they come.'

Matt nudged Luke in the ribs. 'Bet you get her, you lucky bastard.'

'DC Matthew Wilkins, you'll be working with DC Rawlins. Fill her in on this trail bike rider. Show her around and take her with you to Ludbrook Grove. See what you can find out about that trail bike.'

'Who's the lucky bastard then?' Luke smiled.

Matt grinned and wished he could show her around somewhere better than Ludbrook Grove. 'We'll also do a tour of Stonesend,' he said. 'Get to know the locals.'

Beth noticed the team staring at Ana and rolled her eyes. 'Has nobody got any work to do around here?'

In her office she checked her phone and felt disappointed

that her message hadn't been read. Then, she stared at it for a few seconds and, without a moment's hesitation, deleted it. For some strange reason, when the phone on her desk rang, she thought it was him and answered breathlessly.

'Hello?'

'Beth, my office, please,' said Chief Superintendent Lewis.

Beth stifled a sigh. 'Yes, sir.' Had Matt put her in it? Surely not. Beth felt sure she had his loyalty.

Lewis looked up and smiled when Beth entered, and some of her anxiety eased. 'Sit down, Beth,' he said.

Beth sat down reluctantly. 'Will this take long, chief? Only...'

Lewis pushed the papers he'd been reading to one side, leaned his elbows onto the desk, and clasping his hands, looked at Beth and said bluntly, 'DI Stephens isn't coming in today or any other day in the future, come to that.'

'What?' Beth said, surprised. 'What's happened? Is he all right?'

DI Stephens had replaced DI Miller just over three months ago, shortly after the Blanche Lethbridge case. He was an okay boss, if not a touch chauvinistic. There'd been no hint that he'd been thinking of leaving.

'We've received a complaint of sexual misconduct,' the chief super said.

Beth groaned. She remembered Craig Stephens dribbling like a baby whenever Leah, the communications officer, entered the building. *He's as horny as a tomcat*, Beth once remembered thinking. 'Who complained?' she asked.

'That's confidential, Beth. You don't seem surprised.'

'I was aware that he thought himself a ladies' man, but I never saw any sexual misconduct, and he certainly never said anything out of line to me... But he was a bit, well, you know.'

'This sexual misconduct was quite blatant, and he's been

suspended until the complaint is fully investigated. I will make the team aware. However, he has insisted that whatever the outcome of the investigation, he doesn't want to return to this division.'

'Yes, sir, thanks for letting me know,' said Beth, standing up.

'Beth, sit down. There's something else.'

Beth swallowed. She somehow felt this wasn't going to be good.

'Beth, any other time, you know I would have recommended you for the job. I believe you have what it takes to be a good DI, but I've noticed that your personal problems are affecting your work. Your behaviour was unprofessional when you visited Ludbrook Grove. A young lad's mother complained. Luckily for you, she isn't taking it any further.'

Beth was about to protest, but he held his hand up to stop her. 'You've been late several times. You arrived at court smelling of alcohol last week, and I know you've left early on several occasions when you should have been here.'

Beth's throat turned dry. The chief was waiting for her response, so she attempted to laugh it off. 'It was a lunchtime drink with a friend. I'd only had one glass of wine. The case was running late.'

'It's not the first time, Beth, and I understand some personal issues are still ongoing.'

'I don't have personal issues,' she said sharply. 'Can I ask who reported me, sir?'

'You know I can't reveal things like that. You and I know how important it is to be on top of the job. It only takes one mistake for a career to be over. DI Stephens is a clear example of that. I don't want another. I know it's been a challenging year for you, but we have people you can talk to.'

Shit, she couldn't afford to lose her job on top of everything else. 'I'm fine, sir. I'm on top of the job.'

'Let's make sure things stay that way, shall we?'

'Yes, sir,' she said, standing up. 'Can I ask who the new DI will be?'

He hesitated, looked her in the eye and said, 'DI Tom Miller.'

Hearing his name brought back an avalanche of memories that made her head spin. 'Tom Miller?' she repeated, leaning on the back of the chair.

'I requested him, and he agreed as long as you're happy with the decision. He's been through trauma while on the job, and he understands the personal issues you may be going through.'

Beth's eyes hardened with anger. 'So you've gone behind my back, just like the first time you took him on. You didn't mind having an alcoholic DI then, did you?' She was raising her voice, but she didn't care.

'Beth,' Lewis said, leaning across the desk. 'Are you telling me you're an alcoholic?'

'Of course not,' she denied hotly, feeling her face grow red. 'You had no right to talk to him about my private life.'

'I'll overlook your disrespectful manner, DS Harper, as I can see you are upset, but may I remind you that as head of this department, I have every right,' Lewis said sharply. 'As chief superintendent, running a tight ship is my job. I can't have officers on my team who will likely make mistakes.'

'Yes, sir,' she said.

Lewis nodded. 'That's good. If you have any problems in the future, come straight to me. We can offer help, Beth. Don't struggle alone.'

Beth stood outside his office for a few minutes, her mind whirring. How many of her colleagues knew about the drinking? Had someone reported her leaving early?

'Shit,' she muttered.

Beth tried to picture Tom Miller and wondered if he had

changed much. Then she realised she hadn't asked when he was starting. The anticipation of seeing him again made her body tingle.

The attacks in Stonesend a year ago had changed them all. How could it not have? They had learnt the harsh reality that nowhere you lived was safe, that leaving doors unlocked was foolhardy, and that no one did that anymore. Seeing Tom Miller again was going to feel strange for everyone.

CHAPTER TWELVE

'What's she like to work for?' Ana asked as they strolled through the village. The smell of yeasty bread wafted over them as they passed the bakers.

'Best doughnuts in the world,' Matt said, waving at a young girl behind the counter. 'I can vouch for their custard ones.' Matt's mouth watered at the thought.

'So, what's she like?' repeated Ana.

'Not a doughnut girl then?' said Matt.

'Custard tarts,' she said with a smile. 'So what's she like to work for?'

'Beth?' Matt grinned. 'I mean DS Harper. Yeah, she's okay. She's a good boss.'

'All right, Matt.' Nat from the butchers waved.

'I'm good, mate. Save me a nice lamb chop, will you?'

'Sure thing,' said Nat, staring openly at Ana.

'This is DC Rawlins. She started with us this morning.'

'Right,' said Nat. 'Welcome, not one of those vegetarians, are you?'

Ana laughed. 'No, give me a good steak any day.'

'That's my speciality.' Nat grinned.

'Good butchers,' said Matt. 'You won't get a better steak.'

Ana smiled. 'Is food all you talk about?'

'No,' he laughed, 'just most of the time.'

Ana glanced at the yarn store on the corner. 'Such a cute place.'

As they continued walking through the village, Matt stopped several times to talk to people or wave to others.

'Is there anyone in this village you don't know?' asked Ana.

Matt laughed. 'Yeah, loads.' He glanced sideways at her. She was pretty enough to be a model, and he couldn't help wondering why she had chosen to be a copper. 'So how come you got sent here?' he asked.

'I requested a transfer,' she said, stopping to stroke a dog.

'From up north?'

'You ask a lot of questions.' She smiled.

Matt liked her. He hadn't had a girlfriend since Jo. He hadn't wanted all that aggravation again, but Ana might be worth it. 'I'm a nosy sod.'

'From Kirby, actually,' said Anna. 'I wanted to experience police work outside of Kirby. I felt like I spent most of me time breaking up fights at the footie, you know?'

'I don't think you'll find it much more exciting here.'

'We'll see,' she said ominously.

Matt was about to ask her what she meant when she spotted a man struggling to get a wheelchair over the high kerb and hurried towards him.

'Let me help you,' she said.

'They've closed the bottom of the road,' said the man. 'The kerb is much lower there. Honestly, I can manage.'

'She's new,' joked Matt. 'Let her make a good impression.'

Ana pushed the wheelchair up the kerb, deliberately rolling it over Matt's foot.

'Touché.' Matt laughed.

'This is Tim Smith,' said Matt. 'Tim is part of our neighbourhood watch scheme.'

Ana smiled, but her eyes were on the woman in the wheelchair.

'Ah,' said Matt, remembering. 'Did you hear that trail bike in the early hours, Tim?'

Tim straightened his rucksack, which had slipped when struggling with the wheelchair and shook his head. 'Not this time. I wear earplugs these days. I've heard it before. Little buggers. Do you know who they are?'

'We're looking into it today. Have you ever seen any of them close up?'

'You must be joking. The way they race through here, you never get to see their faces. They're going to kill someone one of these days.'

Meanwhile, Matt noticed Ana was attempting to chat with the woman in the wheelchair.

'It's not one of her best days, I'm afraid,' Tim said apologetically. 'Some days, she's more with it than others.'

Ana looked up. Tim was frowning, so she quickly backed away and let him take the wheelchair.

When he was out of earshot, Ana said, 'What's up with the old woman?'

A pained expression crossed Matt's face. 'She's not that old as it happens. I don't think she's even sixty.'

Ana looked upset. 'You're kidding. What happened to her?'

Matt's throat thickened with emotion. He'd known Tim since their school days, and his memories of tea at Tim's house had been good ones. Vanessa had made these enormous scones. They'd lather them in jam and clotted cream and eat them until the jam ran down their chins.

'Hit and run,' he said, struggling to disguise his emotion.

'Three months ago, April 14th, Vanessa, Tim's mum, was on her way home from bingo. The driver came out of nowhere. Vanessa's friend said the impact threw her in the air. The bastard drove off. We never caught him. The accident left her with a severely injured spine and mild brain damage. Some days, she's really with it, like Tim said, and at others, not so much. Tim's been her carer ever since. He refuses to allow her to go into a home. It will be a slow recovery, but he worries a rehabilitation home will depress her.'

Ana gasped. 'Oh my God, that's awful.'

Matt took a deep breath. 'That's life. He's a good bloke, Tim. We've been friends since our school days. His aunt sits with her when Tim gets some work. He's a gardener. So, if you ever need one–'

'I live in a flat,' Ana broke in.

Matt wanted to ask her where but decided against it.

Ana frowned. 'What about CCTV cameras?'

'What CCTV cameras?' Matt asked, puzzled.

'Where Vanessa was knocked down.'

'It was a residential road. They were walking to the bus stop. There were no CCTV cameras.'

Ana sighed. 'There must have been something.'

'I wasn't on the case.'

'Can I look into it?'

Matt looked surprised. 'You'd have to speak to the guv.'

'DS Harper?'

Matt shook his head. 'DI Stephens. You'll meet him. I doubt you'll find anything new, though.'

Ana smiled. 'No harm in looking.'

'Let's get to Ludbrook Grove. I should warn you the clientele there are very different.'

Ana didn't turn a hair when they arrived at Ludbrook Grove. 'No one here is going to dob in your trail bike rider,' she said.

Matt raised his eyebrows in interest. 'Why do you say that?'

'People on estates tend to stick together out of loyalty; or because they are too afraid to do anything else.'

'Let's have a wander,' he said. 'Mind the used needles.' He had hoped to shock her, but Ana seemed to take everything in her stride.

'I'm surprised you've got heroin addicts here in Oxford. Do the council know about the needles?' she asked.

'I got on to them today. I'm always on at them.'

A group of lads were kicking a football around in the park. They looked over at Ana and Matt. 'Here are the pigs in their candy car.' One laughed.

Matt said to Ana out of the corner of his mouth, 'That's Freddie Skinner, with the shaven head. We visited him last night.'

Ana stepped confidently towards the lads. 'Are you as good with that ball as you are with your mouth?' she asked, a slight smirk on her face.

'Better,' said Skinner, his eyes boring into hers.

'Good on a trail bike, too, are you?'

Skinner gave her a lopsided grin, turned and spat onto the ground, just missing her foot.

Ana looked impressed. 'Good shot,' she said. 'I couldn't have done better myself.'

'Yeah, I'm good at everything,' he boasted.

'What about on a trail bike?'

'I already told him,' he said, nodding towards Matt. 'I ain't got no trail bike.'

Matt was trying not to look at the scabs on Skinner's shaved head.

'We're at college, mate, summer holidays.'

'Good at college too, are you?' asked Ana.

He grinned. 'Yeah, as it 'appens, I am.'

'But not good on a trail bike?' said Ana, turning her back and walking away.

'I told you I ain't got no trail bike.'

'I'm disappointed because that means you're not good at everything – because I hear that bloke is ace on that bike,' she threw over her shoulder.

'He ain't that good,' said Skinner without thinking.

Ana turned and smiled. 'So you do know him?'

Matt looked at her admiringly.

'I didn't say I knew him. I just seen 'im,' said Skinner.

'Well enough to know how good he is on it,' said Matt.

Ana turned to the other lads. 'Who's the boss of this gang then?'

'We ain't in no gang,' said Skinner.

'Yeah, right, and I ain't a copper. He wouldn't protect you. You know that?' she said, staring straight into Skinner's eyes.

'We don't know nothing,' said Skinner.

'We'll be back,' said Ana, walking away. 'I'd see a doctor about that eczema if I were you,' she added.

When they were out of earshot, Matt said, 'You made an impression.'

'That was my intention,' said Ana with a wink.

They walked past run-down houses with shabby net curtains and shopping trolleys in the front gardens.

'I never get why people nick trolleys,' said Ana.

'Good for stacking the stolen goods in,' said Matt, in a matter-of-fact tone.

They strolled past several garages scrawled with graffiti until they reached a small block of flats.

'Local brothel,' said Matt. 'We get called out a few times here. You know, neighbours complaining about shouting and whatnot.'

Ana raised her eyebrows in surprise. 'Is this part of your patch, then? I always thought Oxford was a posh place.'

Matt laughed. 'Not all of it.'

'Got a new mate?' shouted a female voice.

Ana turned to see a young, pretty girl carrying a rubbish bag to the bins. 'Yeah, I'm new,' she called back. 'DC Ana Rawlins.'

'Is that right,' said the girl, dumping the bag into a recycling bin. 'Bit early to catch us, ain't yer?'

Ana smiled, walking toward her. 'Just exploring.'

'Well, you've seen us now, so you can bugger off.'

The insult was like water off a duck's back to Ana. *She can't be more than eighteen if she's that*, thought Ana, walking closer. Ana could now see the streaked mascara around the girl's deep-set eyes and smell the faint odour of stale alcohol on her breath. 'You don't know the prick who owns that trail bike, do you?' she asked.

The girl's eyes widened and she turned to Matt. 'Is she for real?'

Matt was too surprised to answer.

'Nah, I don't, but you're right. He's a pain in the arse, prick,' she said to Ana. 'Drives us fucking bonkers.'

Ana smiled. 'If you do hear anything, can you let us know?' She handed the girl her card.

'Yeah, sure. Ta.'

'Thanks...' Ana deliberately hesitated.

'Frankie,' said the girl.

'Great, well, you take care, Frankie.'

Matt followed her as she returned to where the panda was parked. 'Making new friends?' he asked.

Her steely eyes met his. 'It's the bastard pimps that use those girls you ought to be watching,' she said and got into the car without another word.

CHAPTER THIRTEEN

SEVEN YEARS EARLIER

A nika hurried along the street. Her hands carrying the shopping bags were numb from the cold. Above her, the grey clouds were threatening snow.

'Nippy, ain't it?' said Martha, her neighbour.

'Going to get colder,' said Anika. 'They say snow is coming.'

'Cheer us up, why don't yer.'

Anika laughed and crossed the estate to her house, the shopping bags knocking against her legs as she walked. It would be good to be home and in the warm. *I'll unpack,* she thought, *and then I'll go and check on Brenda and make sure she's got some heating on.*

When Brenda opened the door, Anika had to fight back a gasp. Brenda had lost even more weight. 'Cold out today,' she said, stepping into the hallway that needed a good vacuum. 'Arthur at work?'

Brenda nodded. 'I'm making dinner.'

Anika touched the radiator as she followed Brenda to the kitchen. It was stone cold. 'Put the heating on, love,' said Anika. 'It's bloody freezing.'

Brenda smiled. The word bloody coming from Anika's lips

in her Indian accent always sounded strange. 'The electric heater is on in the living room.'

It seemed to take Brenda forever to walk to the kitchen. The state of the kitchen stopped Anika in her tracks. The rust-stained sink was full of dirty dishes. Anika glanced at the cluttered kitchen counters and began collecting half mugs of tea and empty beer bottles. 'You sit down,' said Anika. 'I'll put these in the recycle bin and then put the kettle on.'

I'll also give the place a good vacuum before I leave, thought Anika. A casserole dish sat on the kitchen table, surrounded by onions, carrots and stewing beef.

Anika clicked the kettle on and opened the cupboard to get mugs.

'Behind the boxes of teabags is a bottle of painkillers. Can you get them for me, love?' Brenda asked.

Anika turned. 'Brenda?' she said worriedly, seeing that her friend was breathing heavily.

'Give me two of those, darling,' said Brenda.

Anika shook out two capsules from the bottle and gave them to Brenda. She made the tea in silence and then sat opposite Brenda, who hurriedly swallowed the capsules with the hot tea before relaxing back in her chair.

'Let me finish the casserole,' said Anika, jumping up again and busying herself with chopping carrots and onions. 'Or better still, I've made a large batch of lamb biryani, Arthur's favourite. I'll drop some in. You have your tea, and I'll wash up those bits.' She nodded to the sink.

'Anika, sit down. I need to tell you something.'

The tone of Brenda's voice turned Anika's body cold. *I don't want to hear it*, she thought. *I can't listen to what you're going to say.* But she dropped back into a chair, realising she still had the knife in her hand. Gently, she laid it on the table.

'I'm very unwell, Anika,' Brenda said softly.

'Let me call the doctor.' Anika went to get up from the chair, but Brenda's hand stopped her.

'There's no point.'

Anika swallowed the lump that had formed in her throat. 'Of course there is.'

'I've told no one, Anika. I don't know how to tell Arthur. He's not very strong, and Laurie mustn't know. You know how badly she's doing at school, and I know she's drinking. I've made such a mess of things, Anika. I was dealt a bad hand of cards. That's what it was.'

'Don't be silly. You've not made a mess of anything.'

From Brenda's face, Anika could see the pain had eased. Brenda slipped her hand from Anika's and sipped at her tea.

'Have you seen a doctor? Do they know what's wrong?'

'I've seen them all, pet, all the quacks. I've had the scans. It's my liver. The drinking, you see. I've got advanced liver cancer. They're not sure how long I've got.'

Anika let out a small gasp before she could stop herself.

'Now, don't start feeling sorry for me. If you're going to do that, you can fuck off now,' snapped Brenda.

'Brenda...' Anika faltered.

'No fucking crying, either. I'm depending on you.'

Anika took a deep breath. 'I'm not crying.' Inside, though, her heart was breaking. Brenda had been her best friend from the day they first moved to the estate, and if anyone had ever made one racist comment, Brenda had shot them down in flames before they had time to open their mouth again.

'I want you to take care of my girl. Arthur will bugger off, and I can't blame him. I've been lucky he's stayed this long. He's a good sod. Got a good heart, but she's not his. You've been a good friend, and I know you won't let me down.'

'You should go to the hospital,' Anika said. 'They can take better care of you.'

'I'm staying here. I don't want strangers looking after me. Make sure Laurie finishes school and gets a decent job.'

'You'll be here to see to that. Now I've had enough of talking this rubbish. I'm going to call an ambulance.'

'You do that, girl, and we're not friends.'

'You're an awkward cow. I'm going to clean up and then get that curry for you. Dil and I will never eat it all; the kids always want pizza. Pizza, pizza. I ask you.'

Brenda smiled.

Anika got up from the kitchen table and began hoovering the living room with tears rolling down her cheeks.

CHAPTER FOURTEEN

Beth scanned the packed pub, hoping to quickly find her sister, Sandy, and her husband, Ray. The last thing she wanted to do was attract some half-loaded guy determined to buy her a drink. Maybe they should have gone to The Bell. At least she would have known everyone, but that would have held too many memories. Waitresses hurried past her with trays of food. The smell of grilled hamburgers made her stomach rumble.

A hand on her shoulder startled her. What was happening to her? She'd become a bag of nerves.

'Beth, sorry, are you okay?'

She turned to her sister, Sandy. *She's immaculate as always,* thought Beth, looking down at her own black slip dress that she always wore for these occasions. *I ought to buy a new dress and get my roots done.*

'You're early,' Sandy said, kissing her and leaving the air fragranced with Chanel Chance. Beth couldn't remember the last time she wore perfume. Ben had bought her a bottle of Jo Malone's Grapefruit the last Christmas they'd spent together. The thought of wearing it made her feel sick.

'No, you're late,' said Beth.

'Sorry, my last client was late.'

'Honestly, Sandy, your clients take advantage of you.'

'I'm a caring counsellor,' said Sandy.

'Where's Ray?'

'He's running behind. You know how it is. He'll be here soon.'

The waiter took them to their table, where they ordered a bottle of Chardonnay while they waited for Ray.

'Happy birthday, sis and here's to many more.'

They clinked glasses and drank. Sandy looked at Beth over the rim of her glass. 'Beth, I know it's been a tough year, but we're all worried about you,' she said gently.

Beth lowered her eyes and fiddled with the salt pot. 'You don't have to worry about me. I'm fine.'

Sandy watched as Beth topped up her glass. 'You're drinking too much.'

Beth's head snapped up. 'Is everyone counting my alcohol intake now?'

Sandy sighed. 'Of course not. It's just that—'

'I'm off duty,' said Beth. 'So, you don't need to report to Lewis.'

'What do you mean?'

'Well, someone told him I'd been drinking too much.'

There was a sharp intake of breath from Sandy. 'It wasn't me, Beth. I wouldn't stoop that low.'

At that moment, the waitress stepped forward with menus. As soon as she'd left, Sandy leaned forward across the table. 'I know it can't have been easy with Ben leaving you for another man.'

'That's got nothing to do with it,' Beth retorted.

'I know about the baby,' Sandy said softly.

Beth took a long swig of her wine and swallowed it down with her unshed tears. She wouldn't fucking cry.

'Beth, you've got to let it go.'

'Let it go?' Beth thundered. 'They've got a fucking surrogate mother. Don't you think Ben's humiliated me enough, and you say, let it go? How fucking dare you. Don't you think I wanted kids? It's all right for you with your daughter. Can you imagine what it will feel like seeing him and Mark with their child?'

'Beth, keep it down,' said Sandy, aware of the looks the other diners were giving them.

Beth felt a tightness in her neck. 'Whose side are you on, Sandy?' she asked, trying to control her anger.

'Beth, it's not a matter of sides.'

At that moment, Ray bounced happily towards them, a prettily wrapped present in his hand. 'Sorry I'm late,' he said, kissing Sandy and hugging Beth.

'You look knackered,' he said.

Beth sighed. 'Don't start. I was woken at one this morning by the villagers at Longbridge over that bloody trail bike.'

'I saw Leigh Moulson today. She's terrified about the whole thing. They can be nasty buggers on the Ludbrook Grove estate,' said Sandy, relieved to change the subject.

'Her husband, Will, phoned me at two this morning. He is not the most pleasant man I've ever met.'

'He's a bit of a rough diamond,' said Sandy. 'This lad is from Ludbrook Grove, isn't he? Don't you know the social worker who deals with some of them?' she asked Ray.

Ray called over a waiter. 'It's humid as hell out there. I'm parched. Did any of you alcoholics think of ordering a jug of water?'

It was a throwaway comment, but Beth blushed as she felt Sandy's eyes on her.

'Not yet,' said Beth.

'You're ignoring my question, Ray,' persisted Sandy.

'You know I can't discuss things like that,' he said, as he studied the menu.

Then Beth's phone rang, and for one awful moment, they were all thrown back to that evening a year ago when Tom Miller had phoned her to say a woman had been attacked in the village. They'd been celebrating Sandy's birthday just as they were doing now.

'Blimey, we're not even on to pudding yet,' said Ray. 'This is a bit déjà vu.'

No one spoke, and Ray realised his mistake immediately.

'Thoughtless as ever,' muttered Sandy.

'It's okay,' said Beth.

Ray poured wine into his glass. 'Sorry,' he said.

Beth glanced at the screen; the caller *was* Tom Miller. Ray was right, déjà vu or what?

'I need to take this,' said Beth.

No one commented as she got up from the table and made her way to the exit. The muggy air was a shock after the restaurant's air conditioning.

'Hello,' she said.

'Beth?'

The sound of his voice took her right back to a year ago when they'd first met. It had been even hotter then. Beth remembered she'd had a hangover. There had been a leaving party the night before, and to top it all off, some idiot had parked in her spot in the station's car park.

'Okay, which one of you wankers parked in my space?' she'd demanded, and then she'd seen him.

'I think the wanker might be me,' he'd said.

She'd always known he was handsome, but his looks had left her breathless.

'Hi,' she said.

'I got your text.'

Shit, she was sure she had deleted it. 'Oh, I thought I'd deleted it.'

'Clearly too late,' she heard the smile in his voice and pictured him in her mind.

'The chief told me,' she said. There was silence for a few seconds.

'He said you're having a hard time.'

'I'm not,' she said defensively. 'He had no right to tell you that.'

'You were there for me, Beth.'

Don't cry, she thought, *don't you dare fucking cry*. 'Anyway, he's the chief,' she said.

Before he could speak, she said quickly, 'I have to dash. I'm out with my sister. It's her birthday.'

'I know. Wish Sandy a happy birthday from me. I'll see you soon.'

'Yeah,' she said flippantly, not wanting him to hear the emotion in her voice and hung up.

Shit, she didn't ask when he was coming. She managed to keep the tears under control until she reached the ladies' loo, and then she let them flow freely.

'Sod it,' she muttered and wondered again, when did this become her life? There was a time when she was an ecstatically happy married woman whose thoughts were on a future family until the day her husband told her he loved someone else and that someone else was a man. Now, he would have the family she'd always dreamed of, but not with her. Some fucking anniversary this was.

CHAPTER FIFTEEN

PRESENT DAY: MONDAY EVENING

If Needles believed no one had followed him to Jim's garage, he'd been very much mistaken. Several people on the Ludbrook Grove estate were sick of Needles and his trail bike but were too frightened to report him. The Vigilante wasn't afraid, and late Monday night, he took things into his own hands.

It took just a few minutes to break the lock on Joe Carter's garage door. The Vigilante studied the bike admiringly. It was a beautiful piece of workmanship. He was not into bikes much, but he knew a good one when he saw it. He appreciated good things, not like those idiots, he thought angrily.

All they had to do was abide by the law and silence the exhaust, but did they care about others? No, they didn't, and what were the police doing? Nothing, that's what. Everyone had had enough, and someone had to do something, so why not him? It wasn't right that young lads could terrorise decent, law-abiding citizens.

The law was too soft these days. Riffraff, that's what they were, living in social housing, lazing around, and claiming benefits on everyone else's hard-earned taxes. It was a bloody disgrace, and it had to stop. They had to be stopped. People who don't abide by the law should be taught a lesson. The police need to be firm like they are in America. They wouldn't put up with this crap there.

The bike was so beautiful, too. It seemed such a shame. All it needed was some care and a silencer, but no, they had to ride it through the village, risking lives and annoying nice, decent people. There were places for trail bike riding.

Well, it was too late, and it was their fault. He lifted the hammer he'd brought and began smashing it down onto the trail bike with as much force as possible.

Then, with each lift of the hammer, his rage grew stronger. Pain shot through his hand with each blow, but it was pleasurable. He was doing good. Bits of metal flew around the garage like silver confetti.

He ignored the pain when slivers of metal cut through his glove. He didn't care. He felt exhilarated and powerful. He was putting everything to rights, and it felt good. The hiss from the punctured tyres was music to his ears.

Jim Carter, who the garage belonged to, had dozed off while watching a drama series on television and woke to a banging noise. He turned down the volume on the TV and strained his ears. It was coming from outside.

Fear gripped him, and he started to shake. They were trying to break in. Someone, probably the Nazis, was trying to get into his house.

He should phone someone, but who? He scrambled through the old sideboard drawer until he found his old address book. Written in bold letters on the front page, was, 'In times of trouble, phone the station,' followed by a phone number.

The station, he thought. *Yes, the station should be called and warned. The station would know what to do.*

'Jim Carter here,' he said when DC Luke Carpenter answered the phone.

'Everything all right, Jim?'

'They're smashing things up. I can hear them.'

'Who are?'

'It must be the Nazis.'

'Smashing things up where, Jim?'

'I don't know. Outside, I think.'

Luke was about to appease him when his ears picked up the sound of crashing in the background. 'All right, Jim. I'll be there in a few minutes.'

Needles was about to pull his bedroom curtains when he saw the strange figure outside Jim's house. It was well past twelve. Who'd be knocking at Jim's at this hour? He grabbed the cricket bat he kept under the bed and pulled on his hoodie before walking over to Jim's house, where he saw the man knocking on the door.

'Jim, it's DC Luke Carpenter. You called the station. Can you open the door for me?'

The detective peered through the window into the living room. The television was on, so Jim had to be in there. 'Jim, can you open the door?'

'What are you doing?'

Carpenter swung around and came face to face with Needles and his cricket bat.

'Police! What are you planning on doing with that cricket bat?'

'He ain't done nothing wrong,' said Needles. 'Why are you bothering 'im? He's got Alzheimer's. He'll be scared.'

'Go home, son, and back to bed where you should be,' said Carpenter.

'I ain't going nowhere. Jim's not well.'

'Would you put the bat down, please?'

Needles dropped the bat.

'Who are you?' asked Luke.

'I live a few doors down.'

'That tells me nothing. What's your name, son?'

'Colin Lees,' Needles said reluctantly.

'Mr Carter called us. He said he heard something. He sounded frightened.'

Needles narrowed his eyes. 'Show me your ID.'

The detective nodded and held it up.

Needles stretched his arm to the porch's roof and took down a key. 'I'll go in first,' he said. 'He knows me.' He opened the door and called softly, 'Jim? It's me. Everything's okay, mate.'

They both peered into the living room, where a silent TV was playing. Needles left the room and went to the cupboard under the stairs. There, he found Jim, crouched in the corner.

'They'd told me to go here whenever the Nazis came. I haven't heard any more bombing or crashing. Have they gone? They were knocking on the door,' the elderly man said, wrapping his arms around his quivering body

'They've gone now, Jim. I got rid of the bastards. You can come out. I'll make us a nice cuppa, shall I?'

Luke looked on in amazement as Jim Carter crawled from the cupboard, his face dripping with sweat and his eyes red from crying.

'Needles?' Jim asked, clutching at the skinhead.

'Yeah, it's me, mate. Did you call the old bill?'

'Have they gone?' Jim asked.

'Yeah, let me help you up. There's no need to crawl. There ain't any bombs, not now.'

Jim saw Luke and went to make for the cupboard again.

'It's all right,' said Needles, holding on to him. 'He helped get rid of them. Let's have a nice cuppa.'

Jim nodded, allowing Needles to lead him to the living room. Luke was struck by the older man's extraordinary relationship with this shaven-headed man.

'Did you hear some noises tonight?' Needles asked Jim, whose eyes were now on the TV.

'You called the police about noises you heard,' prompted Luke.

Jim's forehead creased in concentration. 'Oh, the Nazis were crashing around outside like they were breaking something.'

'Can I check your garden and garage, Mr Carter?'

Jim looked confused. 'I don't have a garage.'

'He doesn't remember he has a garage,' said Needles. 'He keeps nothing in there.'

'The banging was close. I could hear it over the phone.'

Needles jumped up. 'He's got nothing in the garage anyone would want.'

'I'll check all the same. Do you know where he keeps the garage key?'

'No idea,' lied Needles, following the police officer to the garage.

'Does he have help come in?' Luke asked as they walked.

'No. No one gives a fuck about 'im, not his sister nor his wanker of a son.'

'Social services should be informed.'

'They're rubbish,' said Needles, his lips tightening in anger. 'He never uses the garage. It's a waste of your time.'

Luke shone his torch on the garage door. 'Is this the one?' It was numbered 38, like Jim's house.

Before Needles could lie and say it wasn't, Luke had shone his torch on the lock, and Needles gasped when he saw it had been forced.

'Looks like someone has been in here,' said Luke.

Needles dived in front of him and lifted the door. He clicked on the light switch and blinked several times, unable to believe his eyes. Chunks of twisted metal lay everywhere, and the sickening smell of spilt petrol and sweat hung over the air like a toxic cloud. Needles slowly became aware of what he was looking at, and it felt like his breathing was suspended for a second. He leant down to pick up a piece of metal.

'Leave it, son,' said Luke. 'Do you have any idea who this bike belonged to?'

Needles was staring at the slashed tyres. 'No,' he said. 'But they're sure going to be upset.'

He spotted something by the side of the tyre. He couldn't think what it was. Did he drop it? Or did it belong to whoever had smashed his bike? Needles told himself he'd return for it later, but then Luke spotted it too. He knelt and studied it before carefully picking it up with a plastic bag. Needles then saw it was a postcard. Luke read aloud the words on it.

'When the law fails to serve us, we must serve as the law. The Vigilante.'

Needles thought he would explode. That fucking vigilante must have followed him. That's how he knew where the bike was. He must have watched him take it out. He fantasised about the violent retaliation he'd take when he found the bastard.

'Are you sure you don't know who this bike belongs to?' asked Luke.

Needles shook his head. 'Nah.'

They went back into the house, where Luke tried again to

question Jim, but he had no idea about a bike or a garage. It seemed he now couldn't remember anything about that evening.

Luke turned back to the young lad who had now ensconced himself on the couch next to Jim. They were both staring at the drama on the TV screen.

'If you hear anything again, Colin, call the station,' he said.

'Sure,' replied Needles.

'I'll forget I saw that bat, but should I ever see you with it again, I'll arrest you. Do you understand?'

Needles shrugged. 'Whatever.'

Luke hesitated.

'You won't get a statement out of him,' said Needles. 'If that's what you're waiting for.'

Luke nodded and quietly let himself out. Needles heard the door close, and his mind drifted from the television to The Vigilante. Who the fuck was he?

CHAPTER SIXTEEN

The coach driver from Saturday night was reluctant to go to the police. He'd never been in trouble with the law. He'd never been inside a police station before, until today. He had spent his life staying on the right side of the law and even feared being called for jury duty. *Keep your nose down* was his motto, but he'd had to report the broken radio to his boss.

'We need to report it,' his boss had said. 'For the insurance claim, you understand. It'll come up at the next meeting. There'll be safety discussions for our drivers, and if we say we didn't report it because we were afraid of a few thugs... well, you can imagine. It's also likely that some passengers have reported it, so we can't waste time.'

'Why can't *you* report it?' he'd asked his boss.

'I wasn't there, was I, Alan?'

It was the right thing to do. Alan knew that. So here he was, Tuesday morning, sitting on a hard chair in the police station waiting room. Then, glancing again at the clock on the wall, he realised he'd been there for fifteen minutes already, and his nerves were leaving him. If someone didn't come soon, he'd leg it. At that moment, unfortunately for Alan, a female police officer walked in. *God, they get younger by the day*, he thought.

'Hello, sir, I'm DC Rawlins. How can I help?'

'Well, it's nothing really,' said Alan, trying to play it down. 'My boss wanted me to come as a matter of routine.'

'Can I get you tea or coffee?'

'Oh no, I doubt I'll be here that long.'

'Come through,' she said, smiling, and he followed her into an interview room. 'Can I take your name?'

Alan hesitated for a second. 'Alan Mitchell.'

'So, why has your boss asked you to come along?'

'There was a bit of an incident on my bus Saturday night, nothing much.'

'So, you're a bus driver. You must see some things on your journeys?'

'The Oxford Tube, actually. The coach from Oxford to London.'

'Oh,' she said, surprised. 'I'm not familiar with that. Is there any reason you came here instead of Oxford police station?'

Alan hesitated.

'So, what happened,' she said encouragingly, opening her notebook.

Alan sighed. 'Some lads, you know, excited after a football match. They most likely had been drinking. They got a bit rowdy, as they do, and picked on some Pakistani lad.' He laughed nervously. 'It happens, you know.'

Ana's eyes registered interest, which dismayed Alan. 'Were they racist towards him?'

'Well, you know, just a little bit, but the odd thing was this masked guy suddenly popped up with a machete, sorted the lads out, and threw them off the coach,' Alan said matter-of-factly, thinking she might not take it too seriously if he made light of it.

'What?' said Ana, looking up from her notebook. 'He had a machete?'

'He didn't hurt anyone,' explained Alan. 'He just threatened them, and then a bit later, he got off too. He did everyone a favour, to be honest.'

Ana looked perplexed. 'I still don't understand why you didn't go to Oxford police station.'

Alan chewed his lip nervously. 'Well, they're a big station, aren't they? It's not like it's a murder or anything, and seeing as I live in Stonesend, I thought...'

'The man with the machete, can you describe him for me?'

Alan shook his head. 'That's the thing. He was wearing a balaclava and called himself The Vigilante. He also wore combat trousers and a khaki top.'

'Did he get on your bus like that?' she asked.

Alan laughed. 'I think I'd have noticed if he'd been wearing the balaclava. I remember him vaguely, but I couldn't describe him.'

'Do you have CCTV cameras on the coaches?'

Alan sighed. 'Yes, but they sprayed them with black paint.'

'Canny little buggers then,' she said. 'Were these the lads causing the trouble that did that?'

Alan nodded.

'So, let me get this straight. Some lads got on your coach, sprayed the CCTV cameras with paint and harassed this Pakistani lad; and then this guy pops up wearing a balaclava and threatens them with a machete?'

'That's it, and he gave me this card,' said Alan, taking out his wallet.

Ana pulled the card towards her using a pen. 'When the law fails to serve us, we must serve as the law. The Vigilante,' she read aloud.

'Shouldn't I have touched it?' he asked nervously.

'It's okay.' She smiled.

'He only threatened the ringleader,' said Alan.

'Right, can you describe any of these lads?'

'No, I was too busy keeping my eyes on the road.'

Ana nodded. 'How about when they got on the coach?'

'I don't rightly recall seeing them. We get a lot of people catching the coach.'

'Can I ask why you didn't use your radio for help?'

Alan sighed. This was getting too intense for his liking. 'One of them smashed the radio with a hammer. That's how I got these cuts on my face and hand. Look, I don't want trouble. I've got a family.'

'There shouldn't be any trouble. It's good you came here,' she said reassuringly. 'I'll need to take a formal statement from you.'

'Is that necessary?' he asked nervously.

'You've just reported a crime, Mr Mitchell.'

Alan's shoulders slumped. He knew he should have kept his head down.

CHAPTER SEVENTEEN

SEVEN YEARS EARLIER

Laurie crossed and uncrossed her legs. The desire to flee was too much. The clock on the waiting room wall said 6.15. Her appointment had been for six. Several times she had eyed the exit. All she had to do was tell the woman at the desk that she felt unwell and needed to go home. The jacket could be left at reception, and that would be that.

Closing her eyes, she tried to take a calming breath. It didn't help. Looking at the shut door opposite, she suddenly jumped up and was about to head for the exit when a voice said, 'Laurie, sorry to keep you waiting.'

Her heart beat a little faster. 'That's okay.' She turned around and came face to face with him. Today, she wore a winter skirt covering her knees and a loose jumper.

He opened the door for her, and she walked in. Her legs felt like jelly, and she walked quickly to the brown leather couch in case they gave way. In the future, whenever she smelled leather, she would think of this room and how her skin, even through her skirt, had stuck to this couch and how the wetness must have dripped onto it.

'I brought your jacket.' She handed it to him.

'How are you today?' His soft, cultured voice washed over her, a sound she could listen to all day.

'I'm okay. I'm sorry about Friday,' she stuttered. Laurie had the feeling he was looking at her differently.

'I'm pleased I was able to come to the rescue.'

'Yes,' she said, blushing at the memory of her low-cut top and short skirt. She hoped he wouldn't mention that.

'It's a bit warm in here. I'll get us some water, and we can begin.'

While he was gone, Laurie forced herself to take several deep breaths before he returned with the water. The glass was cold where he'd added ice, and Laurie held it against her flushed cheek before drinking.

'So, would you like to talk about Friday night?' he asked gently.

God no, thought Laurie. *That's the last thing I want to talk about.* 'Not really.'

'It wasn't a hen night, was it?'

'No, it was, honest.'

He laughed. Laurie thought how handsome he was when he laughed. 'I think you're lying, Laurie.'

She lowered her head. It was like he could see right inside her mind. 'It was just a night out.'

'Do you often have *nights out* like that?'

Laurie swallowed and reached for the water. When she lifted her head again to look into his handsome, caring face, the room spun, and a sudden wave of nausea attacked her. She lifted the glass to her lips and drank, hoping it would help the sick feeling in her stomach.

'No,' she lied.

He smiled at her indulgently. 'You need to be honest with me, Laurie, if we're going to make progress.'

Laurie sighed. 'It's just a few drinks with friends now and

then. Honest.'

He looked deep into her eyes as though he were reading her mind. 'How often do you have drinks out with friends?'

Laurie hesitated. For a moment, she couldn't think clearly.

'Have you been missing school, Laurie?'

She shook her head. It felt funny.

'You did look lovely Friday night,' he said.

Laurie knew he shouldn't be saying things like that and didn't know how to answer. 'We only go out on special occasions,' she said, although it felt like someone else was speaking and not her.

'Are you all right, Laurie?'

His voice seemed far away, and then she realised he was no longer sitting opposite her. He was at the door. Was he leaving? Then she heard a click and wondered why he was locking it. Suddenly, her head felt fuzzy, like it was full of cotton wool. *I need the loo*, she thought and went to stand, but her legs were too heavy and wouldn't hold her up. Instead, she ended up reeling back and falling onto the couch. Then he was there beside her, holding her hand.

She tried to say that she felt funny.

'It's the heat,' he said.

'Why did you lock the door?' she asked, a stab of fear flaring in her stomach.

'You looked very sexy on Friday,' he whispered.

She pushed her hands down onto the couch and tried to get up. 'I have to go,' she said. 'I don't feel well.'

'Here.' He was handing her the glass of water.

It was then Laurie realised. It had been the water. He'd put something in it. That's why she didn't feel well. 'What have you done?' she asked fearfully, but she was now struggling to keep her eyes open.

'You need some rest. You'll feel better soon.' He was too

close, and his unfamiliar hands pulled at her skirt.

'No, no!' She didn't know if the screamed words came out of her mouth or if she just thought them, but then his hand was over her mouth, silencing her. She couldn't understand why this was happening and didn't want to focus on the pain, thrusting and horrific violation. This couldn't be happening. He tore into her as if she were a piece of meat, simply a thing to bear the brunt of his uncontrollable lust.

Laurie told herself she must be dreaming. If only she could think straight and get her body to move, but it didn't feel like her body anymore. It was heavy, and she was weak and so very tired. So she closed her eyes and gave in to the overwhelming sleepiness.

Later, when she came round and saw him sitting at his desk, all she could focus on was the throbbing in her head. Then she felt the soreness between her legs and the ache in her thighs.

'You're awake,' he said pleasantly. 'Feeling better?' he asked.

Laurie's body shook. 'What did you do?' she asked, struggling to stand up.

He raised his eyebrows in surprise. 'What do you mean? We had our session, and you kept saying you were tired, so as you were my last session, I let you sleep. This drinking has to stop, Laurie. The hangovers–'

'I'm not hungover. You drugged me,' she cried, tears rolling down her cheeks.

'Laurie,' he pleaded. 'Don't be ridiculous. Have some water.'

Laurie slapped the glass out of his hand and it landed with a crash on the floor. 'Unlock the door,' she hissed. 'You raped me, and I'm going to the police.'

His eyes met hers, and the hard determination in them unsettled her. 'The door is unlocked, Laurie and always has been. You should be careful what you say, Laurie. Slander is no small thing.'

'I'm underage,' she said, shaking so much that it felt like the floor beneath her was vibrating. 'I was a virgin.'

'I don't like your accusation, Laurie. I never touched you, and you know it. I don't know what your game is.'

'This isn't a game. I'm going to the police,' she said, walking to the door.

'Don't forget, Laurie, that you have a reputation as a drunk, bordering on alcoholism. You come from the trashy side of town and see me to aid you in your recovery. You're known as a bad student at school. I'm a professional with a good reputation and no hint of scandal. Who do you think they'll believe? No one has raped you. It would be best if you didn't make accusations like that. It's girls like you that ruin decent men's careers.'

Laurie's eyes smarted. He was right. People would think she was lying or that she encouraged it. How could her judgement have been so wrong? Standing up, she felt the wetness of his semen run down her thighs. The door opened easily, and she hurried from the room without looking back.

'Excuse me,' called the receptionist. 'You haven't booked your next appointment.'

Laurie ran from the building until she reached a public toilet. She locked herself in the seedy cubicle that stank of piss, wiped her thighs clean of blood and semen, and then stuffed a large wad of toilet paper between her legs. The police station was across the road, but she knew there was no point going there. They wouldn't believe her, a troublesome schoolgirl with a reputation for liking a good time. It would be his word against hers. She felt numb, and she didn't want to cry, not yet.

Ignoring the soreness in her breasts, she left the loo and went home.

'Laurie, why aren't you at school?' called her mum.

'I started my period, so they sent me home. I'm going to bed.'

She crawled under the duvet and sobbed.

CHAPTER EIGHTEEN

Laurie couldn't focus on what the teacher was saying, something about revision and their GCSEs.

'What do ya fancy for dinner then?' Kerry whispered. 'Shall we sneak out for pizza?'

Laurie didn't lift her head from her exercise book. 'I've got to see someone,' she said.

Kerry stopped writing. 'You going for a job interview?'

'No, I've got a doctor's appointment,' Laurie lied.

'What's up with yer?'

Laurie turned. 'Mind your own,' she said, tapping her nose.

Kerry gasped. 'Oh my God, you're not pregnant, are yer?'

'No, I'm not, you silly cow.'

Kerry looked curiously at her. 'You're acting weird. Are you going to tell me or not?'

The teacher hovered over them. 'Less chat, you two.'

The hands of the clock struck one, and the sound of slamming books echoed around the room, followed by the click-clack of shoes as everyone made for the door. Laurie didn't stop to talk to anyone but left the building and walked the ten minutes it took to get to town. The STD clinic was down a side road, and Laurie walked briskly past it, stopping to check no one she knew was behind her before retracing her footsteps and entering.

It was easier than she'd imagined. No one judged her as she'd dreaded, and the examination and swabs were easy. Chances were, he hadn't given her anything, but she didn't want to take that chance. How many other vulnerable girls like her had he drugged and raped? Girls exactly like her, no doubt, with reputations that would go against them in court.

'It looks a bit sore in there,' said the nurse.

Laurie didn't speak.

'Do you want to talk about anything, Laurie?' the nurse asked gently.

Laurie shook her head. Tears were threatening to flow; that was the last thing she wanted. *Keep it together*, she told herself.

'I'll prescribe something for the soreness. You can get down now.'

Laurie got off the couch and sat in a chair opposite the nurse. Sitting down hurt, and she grimaced.

'I'm also giving you a prescription for the morning-after pill. It's your choice whether to take it. If you want to come back anytime, Laurie, feel free to do so, even if it's just for a chat. We should have the results in a few days.'

'Thanks,' said Laurie, taking the prescription, but she knew she would never return. It was humiliating and shameful, and for that, she hated him.

CHAPTER NINETEEN

PRESENT DAY

'Can I have everyone's attention,' Beth said, facing her team.

The clattering of keyboards stopped, and everyone turned to face her.

'You all know by now about our local vigilante, who seems to have taken it upon himself to hand out justice. He thinks we're not doing our job properly.' She turned to Ana. 'You took a statement from the coach driver?'

Ana opened her notebook, and Matt smiled at her keenness. 'On Saturday 12th July, Alan Mitchell, a local man who drives the Oxford Tube coach, said there was an altercation between some skinheads and a Pakistani lad. It got nasty, and one of the lads smashed the coach's radio with a hammer when Alan tried to get help. At this point, a stranger appeared, wearing a balaclava, combat trousers, and a khaki top and held a machete to the throat of who the driver thought might be the head of the gang. Mr Mitchell said The Vigilante threatened to slit the gang leader's throat if his mate didn't drop the hammer. Unfortunately, they blacked out the coach's CCTV cameras, so we have no ID.'

'Any CCTV of them boarding the coach?' asked Beth.

'Seems they deliberately kept their hoods up when boarding.'

'Did the driver describe them?' asked Luke.

'Mr Mitchell claims he didn't see the faces of the skinheads because he had his eyes on the road. I think he's too scared to say. The lads were forced off at Lewknor, and The Vigilante got off about five minutes later after instructing Mr Mitchell to stop the coach.'

'This so-called stranger, our vigilante, likes to leave a calling card, it seems.' Beth held up the business card. 'All it says is "When the law fails to serve us, we must serve as the law." He signs off The Vigilante. His name is the only word he writes. The rest is typed. Luke, you took a call from Ludbook Grove?'

Luke walked to the front. 'Everyone in Longbridge will be pleased to know the trail bike that has been causing problems has been smashed to pieces by none other than our vigilante. He left his calling card,' said Luke, holding it up. 'The bike and card were found in old Jim Carter's garage in Ludbrook Grove.'

'Thanks, Luke,' said Beth. 'Now, we can't be sure that it's the same trail bike, but it seems likely considering no one has reported their bike missing. So we can probably assume the owner is our trail bike rider, who doesn't want to get involved with the police. So, we need to find this vigilante before he acts again.'

'I think we should chat to Will Moulson,' suggested Matt. 'He was keen to take the law into his own hands, as were his neighbours.'

Beth nodded, but her eyes were on the door where she could see Tom Miller speaking to the chief. The sight of him after all this time caused her hands to tremble. 'You'd think someone on that coach would have come forward.'

'People like to steer clear of trouble,' said Ana.

'Ana's right,' Beth agreed. People are afraid to report thugs because they fear they will be pursued. Right, before you all go, the chief would like a word.'

Lewis entered with Tom, who gave her a nervous smile.

'Thank you, DS Harper,' said Lewis. 'You have probably noticed DI Stephens hasn't been in for a few days. Unfortunately, I must inform you that he has been suspended following accusations of sexual harassment.'

There were several gasps, and Beth noticed a few blushes from some of the younger females.

'If anyone here feels DI Stephens was out of line with them, please come and see me. Meanwhile, many of you will remember DI Miller from a few months ago. He's the new DI from today, so make him welcome. That's it. Thank you, everybody.'

Quickly moving on, Beth said, 'Right, DI Miller and I will visit Will Moulson. Ana, chase up forensics about those cards. Matt, see if any neighbours saw or heard anything at Jim Carter's. We must follow up on any social care Carter is getting too. I'll leave that with you, Luke.'

'The young neighbour seemed to be caring for him.'

'We still need to make social services aware. Okay, that's it, everybody. DC Wilkins, my office, please.'

Matt Wilkins closed the door behind him and asked Beth, 'Did you know about Tom Miller? That all seems a bit out of the blue.'

'Did you?' she asked, failing to keep the accusatory tone from her voice.

'What do you mean?'

'Did you tell the chief I'd been drinking?'

Matt's eyes widened in surprise, which quickly turned to anger. 'Is that what you think of me? That I'd go behind your back? I never realised you had such a low opinion of me. Thanks a lot. Frankly, I'd have told you straight to your face.'

Beth instantly felt remorseful and touched his arm. 'Matt, I'm sorry. I just...'

'Yeah, well, let's forget it, shall we?' He turned, closing the door quietly behind him.

Beth exhaled. 'Shit,' she muttered.

Ana saw Matt leave and took her chance to knock on Beth's door.

Beth took a deep breath. 'Come in,' she called.

'Ma'am,' said Ana. 'It's about Vanessa Smith.'

Beth looked perplexed. 'What about her?'

'Would it be okay if I looked into the hit-and-run case?'

Beth raised her eyebrows. 'Why would you want to do that? That case is closed, Ana.'

'I won't step on anyone's toes,' said Ana quickly.

'Do you think we missed something?'

Ana blushed. 'No, of course not. I'm out of line, sorry.'

Ana turned to leave when Beth said, 'Why the interest?'

Ana licked her lips. 'I met her today, and it seemed so wrong that whoever did that is walking free.'

Beth nodded thoughtfully. 'Just don't waste too much time on it.'

'No, ma'am, thank you, ma'am.'

Beth busied herself with some paperwork, but she couldn't concentrate on it. From the corner of her eye, she could see the chief approaching her office with Tom. Then the door opened, and Tom was standing in front of her. A tingling swept up the back of her neck and into her face.

'I parked in a visitor space,' he said, smiling. 'Before you have a go at me.'

Beth felt herself relax. 'Pleased to hear it.'

He'd gained some weight, and his hair was slightly shorter, but aside from that, he hadn't changed much at all.

'You look well,' he said.

Beth smiled. 'Bloody liar. Everyone's been telling me how crap I look.'

'Maybe they can get away with it.' He grinned.

The chief said, 'I've assigned DI Miller to Stephen's office. I'll leave it to you to update him.'

'Fine,' said Tom.

God, Beth thought, *he's better looking than I remember.*

'So, how are you really?' he asked.

'I'm fine,' she lied. 'A few grey hairs, but...'

He nodded, and she could tell he didn't believe her.

'Where are you staying, Tom?'

'Same place.'

'Lots of memories,' she said, reflecting. 'Still enjoying the cemetery?'

'I like the view and the church bells.'

Beth lowered her head.

'You saved my life,' he said quietly.

'You were bloody ungrateful,' she said.

He laughed. 'Good, back on form, I see. Right, fill me in.'

'It's good to have you back,' she said quietly.

'It's good to be back. I've missed your insults.'

Beth grinned. 'I've missed throwing them at you.'

CHAPTER TWENTY

Ana approached Ruth, the administrator, who was tapping madly at her keyboard. 'Hi, I'm DC Rawlins. The new girl,' she added, smiling and holding out her hand.

Ruth didn't look up.

Don't go overboard with the welcome, thought Ana.

'Hi,' Ruth finally replied, tapping away at the keyboard as though her life depended on it. Ana was surprised sparks weren't flying off it.

'I need the file on Vanessa Smith, hit and run about three months ago. I understand you're the person to ask.'

Ruth stopped typing and looked up. Ana stared in amazement at the pink painted fake cupid's bow above Ruth's upper lip and the bright blue eyeshadow smudged across her eyelids.

'That file is closed,' said Ruth, fluttering her heavily mascaraed lashes. Her tone was final, and she returned to her mad typing.

Ana said, 'Yes, I know that, but I still need it.'

'On whose authorisation?' asked Ruth in a pompous voice.

Ana sighed. Miss bloody Gestapo, or what?

'That case is closed,' said Luke Carpenter from behind her.

Ana took a deep breath and turned to face him. 'DS Harper said I could look into it.'

'You're reopening the case?' he asked. 'No one mentioned anything to me. I was in charge of Vanessa Smith's case. Why didn't you come to me?'

Ana looked closely at him. He was in his early forties, she guessed. The gold band on his left finger told her he was married. There was an arrogance about him that she didn't like. Some instinct told her he was most likely a male chauvinist pig. 'I didn't know you were in charge of the case,' she said. 'Otherwise, I would have.'

'Well, I was, and I can't see anything to look into unless you've got a new lead.'

Bloody male ego, thought Ana tiredly. 'I'm not questioning anyone's ability,' she said. 'Obviously, if you're unhappy, you can take it up with the boss.'

'I might well do that.'

'Not a problem.' Ana turned away from him and asked Ruth, 'If you could leave it on my desk.'

Without glancing at Luke, she walked to her desk. Ruth swept past her, leaving a strong, musky scent in her wake. Ana sneezed. A few minutes later, Ruth slapped a file onto her desk. Ana mouthed *thanks*, but Ruth seemed to ignore her.

Ana became aware that Luke was watching her and pretended not to notice. A few moments later, he walked from the station.

'Wanker,' she said under her breath.

The file didn't tell her much at all. A hit and run on a small side road in Summertown. Ana looked up Summertown, a town close to Oxford. CCTV cameras hadn't revealed anything, and there had been no witnesses to give details of the car. An investigation was carried out, but as there were no clear leads, the officers on the case had nothing to follow. Ana sighed. The only witness was Vanessa's friend, who said she'd rushed to Vanessa's aid and couldn't give much information on the car.

Ana grabbed her cardigan and made for the door.

Tim Smith's home was on a housing estate in Longbridge. The front garden was immaculate, overflowing with a variety of shrubs. A woman opened the door. Ana soon learnt this was Vanessa's friend, Penny, who had been with Vanessa at the time of the accident. Ana couldn't believe her luck. Vanessa and Penny couldn't have been more helpful when she explained who she was and why she'd come.

Hot air blasted her as soon as she entered the immaculate hallway. A polished sideboard held a sparkling crystal vase with red roses. Like the hallway, the living room was scrupulously clean and hot, and Ana began sweating. 'It's warm in here,' she said, removing her cardigan.

'Vanessa feels the cold,' said Penny.

What cold? thought Ana. *It's bloody summer. I'll be down to my underwear at this rate.*

'I'll make some tea,' offered Penny.

Ana requested a cold drink, which Penny supplied along with a plate of bourbon biscuits.

'My favourite,' said Ana, taking two.

Ana broached the subject of the accident carefully, explaining she didn't have any new evidence but felt it wouldn't hurt to check they hadn't missed something. Unfortunately, Vanessa couldn't remember anything after leaving the bingo hall. Penny related the incident, and her memory of it wasn't clear either.

'We always got the bus at the stop on the side road. If you

get it in Summertown, you see, the queue is endless where everyone is leaving the bingo hall, so Nessa and I always walked that bit further to get the bus at the first stop. That way, we always got a seat. We were crossing the road to the bus stop when I heard loud booming music and saw this car roaring towards us. Before I knew it, it was on top of us. So I jumped onto the kerb, but Nessa never quite made it.'

Penny stopped and shuddered. She explained that the driver had stopped as though they were coming to help them.

'Then someone else rushed towards us, and the driver closed the door and drove off.'

'What time do you estimate this was?' asked Ana.

'Bingo finished at 9.30, so I guess it would have been about 9.45 by the time we'd walked to the bus stop. I told the other officers this.'

'You say the driver stopped?' said Ana. 'Could you tell what make of car it was? Or the colour?'

Penny shook her head. 'It was dark, and honestly, I don't know much about cars and their types.' Penny's best description was that it was a small car and dark in colour, although she couldn't be sure. Then she remembered something, and Ana sat forward excitedly.

'Something I do remember, though, was a strange squeak when the car door opened like it needed oiling or something. It may not have been the car, though.'

Ana nodded. 'Did you mention this to the police?'

'I don't remember. I may have done.'

'That's really helpful, thank you.'

Ana finished her drink, popped a bourbon into her pocket and stood up. Vanessa and Penny exchanged glances, a policewoman nicking a bourbon. Now, that was one to remember.

'Thank you for your time,' she said. 'If you should remember anything else, please phone me,' she said, handing Vanessa her card.

'I'll give it to Tim,' said Vanessa, looking at the card. 'It doesn't have your address.'

'No, it's not sensible for us coppers to advertise where we live.'

'Oh,' said Vanessa. 'I'd like to send you some bourbons to thank you for looking into this again.'

Ana laughed. 'Oh well, I can't resist bourbons.'

She jotted her address on the back of the card.

Penny grinned. 'Expect more than one packet.'

Outside, the fresh air was a blessed relief. Ana popped the bourbon into her mouth and then checked Google Maps for the road where Vanessa's accident occurred. At that moment, her phone rang.

It was Matt. 'The card samples from the crime scenes show no body fluids when analysed, so we're not going to get a DNA profile from those.'

'Okay, thanks.' Ana clicked off her phone.

Summertown was far busier than Stonesend but Ana soon found the Methodist church hall where the bingo had been held.

Standing at the bus stop where Vanessa and Penny had waited, Ana understood how they had not seen the car approaching the bend at the top of the road. Several houses looked out onto the street, but according to the file, no one heard anything until the sirens. Ana walked up and down the road several times before she saw the security camera outside a house directly opposite the bus stop.

A young man with dishevelled hair and a slightly bemused look answered the door. *God*, thought Ana, taking a step back, *he's bloody handsome, even with the dishevelled hair.* 'Hello, I'm DC Rawlins. Could I have a word?'

'What's the problem?' he asked, running his hands through his hair.

'How long have you had that security camera?' Ana pointed.

He wrinkled his brow. 'I can't remember. Maybe three years. Why? It's not illegal, is it?'

'Could I come in for a moment?'

'Yeah, sure,' he said helpfully. 'I'm in the middle of work. What's this about?'

'A hit and run three months ago. Your security camera might have picked something up. How far is the range?' She was finding it hard not to stare at his gorgeous face.

'I remember that hit and run,' he said. 'It was terrible. The camera does pick up the road outside. Someone tried to nick my car once, so I got the camera.'

'Does the memory go back three months?'

'Yeah, I think actually eight months, but I'm not sure.' He opened the door for her to enter. Ana somehow doubted she would get tea and bourbons here. He took her to the security camera, and she watched while he fiddled with it. Ana had no idea about security cameras, but it looked pretty expensive.

'Yep,' he said. 'Eight months. I'll leave you with it.'

Ana looked alarmed. 'You're kidding. I haven't got a clue how to work these things. Can you do it?'

'Are you serious?'

'No, I'm joking. Us coppers joke a lot about hit and runs.'

'A sense of humour, I see.' He grinned. 'Right.' He sat beside her. 'What date and time am I looking for?'

He smells gorgeous, too, thought Ana. She checked her notes. 'It would be the 14th of April, sometime between 2145 and 2215.' Ana watched the small screen closely.

He fiddled with some buttons, and the camera came to life. 'Okay, here it is, the 14th of April. The lamp outside makes it a bit brighter, but it's still quite dark. There were no cars at 9.45pm.'

Ana leaned in closer to the monitor. She could just make out the bus stop. At 10pm, two figures appeared.

'That must be them,' she said and held her breath.

At precisely 10.02pm, a car flew past and slammed into Vanessa. Ana watched in horror as she landed on the bonnet and fell to the ground.

'Oh my God,' she muttered.

'Shit,' exclaimed the guy at her side. 'He just mowed her down.'

The place where the vehicle must have stopped, was out of range of the camera.

'Damn it,' muttered Ana. 'Apparently, he stopped. Can we go back?' she said, trying to hide her excitement. 'I need to see the car.'

With shaking hands, he rewound the video until the car came into view again.

'Freeze it there,' Ana said, straining to see the car. But it was impossible to make out the number plate or colour. 'Can we go forward a second?' she asked.

'That looks like a Golf or Polo to me,' he said. 'I can't be sure, of course.'

Ana sighed. 'If only I could see the reg.'

'Too dark, and he was driving too fast.'

'Bugger it,' she said, standing up.

'I'd still say that's a Polo or Golf.'

'Why do you say that?' asked Ana.

'I had a Golf. It looks like one of the older makes.'

'Great, thanks for your help Mr...'

'Jonny,' he smiled. 'Jonny Manners.'

'Jonny, thanks. I'll let you get back to work.'

'I was just about to make a coffee if you'd like one.'

She checked the time. What she wouldn't do to say yes, but she had to get back. 'That would have been great, but I need to be somewhere else.'

'Well, if you need more help, this is my number.' He handed her a card: Jonny Manners, Software Developer.

Ana looked up. 'Can you freeze and print photos of the car, make them bigger?'

He grinned. 'Yeah, no problem.'

'Great, call me at Stonesend station.' Ana debated giving him her mobile number, decided against it and said, 'Thanks for your time.'

'My pleasure,' he said with a smile. 'Have that coffee next time.'

'I will.'

Ana wished she could have captured that smile on video.

CHAPTER TWENTY-ONE

L eigh Moulson peered around the net curtain and her heart sank.

Why couldn't they have come this evening when Will was at home? Knowing her, she was bound to say the wrong thing.

'Hello, Mrs Moulson, this is DI Miller,' said Beth pleasantly. 'Sorry to bother you. It's about the trail bike your husband reported the other day.'

'He's at work,' said Leigh, clearing her throat, which had suddenly become very dry.

'Where would that be?' asked DI Miller.

He had a soft, calming voice, and Leigh relaxed. They weren't going to ask *her* any questions after all.

'In Cowley, Rutland's Garage. He's the manager.'

'Great.' Tom smiled, writing in his notepad.

'Could we come in for a moment?' asked Beth.

'Oh,' said Leigh, surprised. 'I didn't see anything that night. I can't really help you. It's Will you need to talk to.'

'It won't take long,' said Tom reassuringly.

'Well,' said Leigh reluctantly, opening the door. She was

embarrassed that the vacuum cleaner was out, and a duster and tin of polish sat on the hall table. Leigh felt a sudden urge to explain. 'Cleaning day. Come into the kitchen.'

'We believe the trail bike has been badly damaged,' said Beth. 'I don't think you'll have any more problems.'

'Oh, did he have an accident?' Leigh asked, careful to keep her tone neutral. 'I'm not surprised if he did. He drove it like a madman.'

'No, someone deliberately smashed it to pieces,' said Tom.

Leigh's mouth opened as though she were about to speak, and then she closed it quickly. *God, Will wouldn't do something like that, would he?* She needed to be careful what she said. 'Oh, when did it happen?'

'We think late Monday night.'

'Your husband did threaten to take things into his own hands,' said Beth.

Leigh forced a laugh. 'Oh no, he's all talk. He wouldn't really do that.'

'Was he home Monday night?' asked Tom.

Beth noticed Leigh hesitate.

'Yes, he was. We watched TV,' she said, averting her eyes, aware that Beth was watching her closely.

'So Will didn't go out at all Monday night?'

Leigh's lips closed tightly together as though someone had glued them.

'It's just to eliminate suspects,' Tom assured her.

'Will has done nothing wrong.'

'We're not saying he has. It's just routine questioning,' said Tom casually.

'No, he didn't go out at all.'

'Well, thanks for your time. Hopefully, you won't hear any more trail bikes.'

Tom reached the front door, saw the Chelsea cap hanging on a hook and said with a smile, 'Who's the Chelsea fan then?'

'That's Will,' she said. 'Won't miss a match.'

'Me neither,' lied Tom with a smile. 'Thanks for your help.'

CHAPTER TWENTY-TWO

Tom drove the car in silence until they reached Stonesend, where he stopped at The Bell pub. 'Share a plate of nachos?' he asked.

Beth looked pleasantly surprised. 'Since when did you share anything?' she asked.

'When weren't you hungry?' he retorted, opening the door.

'This is true.' She grinned.

The pub was pretty quiet – it was way past lunchtime. Jack, the landlord, took one look at Tom and sighed. 'Well, well, look who's back. Like a bad penny, you are. Last time you were here, we had a murder.'

'Well, as you know, I didn't commit it.' Tom smiled.

'What's happened now?' asked Jack, looking at Beth.

'DI Stephens has left, so we have a new DI.'

Jack scoffed. 'Sacked him, did they? It took long enough before someone realised. That bloke would have given one to a tree if it had a hole in it. I'll bring menus over, and don't worry,' he said, looking at Tom, 'nothing is on the house. I wouldn't want to be accused of bribing a police officer like last time.'

Beth held back her smile. 'Jack's got a memory like an

elephant,' she said, adding, 'We're sharing a plate of nachos, and I'll have a Diet Coke.'

'Mineral water for me,' said Tom.

'Don't overdo it,' said Jack.

'Nice to get a warm welcome.' Tom smiled.

Looking at Beth closely, Tom could see the change in her. She'd lost weight, her eyes didn't have the brightness he remembered, and her hair was longer. Today, she wore it tied back in a bun. Strands had stuck to her neck due to the heat. But, for all that, he was still deeply attracted to her.

'Not as hot as last year,' he said without thinking.

'No,' Beth said, remembering.

Jack brought over their drinks and said, 'What's this vigilante stuff about then? Someone said he smashed up that kid's trail bike. Good for him, I say. The bloody thing was a pain in the arse.'

'What else have you heard?' asked Tom.

'That's it, and it doesn't look like I will hear any more from you. So I'll get those nachos.'

'Never been so popular.' Tom smiled.

'This is true.' Beth laughed.

Tom leant his arms on the table and looked into her eyes, and Beth had to fight the desire not to lower hers. 'So, how are things between you and Ben?'

Beth's heart flipped at Ben's name. Bloody Lewis. How dare he share her business.

'How's the drinking?' she asked.

'How's yours?' he shot back.

'I don't go to AA meetings,' she said cruelly.

'Sharp as ever,' Tom noted.

Jack returned with the cutlery and nachos. Beth sipped at her Coke.

'Sorry,' she said, finally. 'That was unnecessary.'

Tom shrugged. 'You've said worse things to me.'

Beth slid some nachos onto her fork and tried not to look at him. Tom was being kind, that's all. Beth realised she'd been stupid to think they had had a mutual attraction. That was a year ago. Tom had been grieving, and her marriage had just broken up. For all she knew, he may already have met someone else.

'Ben and Mark are having a child. They've got a surrogate mother. Ben thought I ought to know. He didn't want me to be shocked if I saw them,' she said, laying down her fork. The cola eased the dryness in her throat but didn't ease the pain in her heart in the way that a large glass of wine would have done.

'I'm sorry, Beth.'

She nodded and quickly changed the subject by pointing at the nachos. 'Let's get some more. I'm starving.'

'What's new?' He smiled.

'So, why would you want to return here?' she asked curiously. 'The worst we get here is dopeheads and trail bikes.'

'And vigilantes,' he reminded her.

'Oh yes, that's this year's big excitement.'

He looked around the pub. 'I missed the abuse.'

'I'll remember that.' She sipped her Coke and asked quietly, 'What was it like, rehab?'

'Let's say I needed it.' He pointed to the nachos. 'Tuck in.'

Beth ate hungrily. 'But why come back here? Why not a different part of London?'

'Why not here? It's peaceful, and there's much to appreciate.' His eyes locked onto hers, and she felt herself blush. 'Besides, the gossip in London isn't half as good, neither are the nachos.'

Beth smiled. 'You should try the beef and ale pie one day.'

'As long as I never have to suffer your homemade soup again, I think I'll survive.' He laughed.

'Ungrateful sod,' she said.

'Back to normal, I see,' said Jack.

'Still eavesdropping, I see,' said Tom.

Beth laughed and realised she hadn't laughed like that for some time.

CHAPTER TWENTY-THREE

Laine crouched in the corner of her bedroom, her arms cradling her legs, trying to stop the throbbing of her thighs.

She was desperate to shower and take a wee, but she felt too shaken to pull her abused body from the floor, and she knew peeing would sting.

She felt guilty. She thought she should have fought back, but she couldn't. It was as though her body hadn't belonged to her. She had tried; she felt sure of that. He must have put something in the water he'd given her. She'd felt fine before that.

She should never have gone. How she wished she'd gone into town with Jassy.

It did occur to her to go to the police, but who would believe her word against his? She couldn't bear to tell her parents or Needles. She felt too ashamed.

The memory of his body on hers made her feel physically sick, and she had to rush to the bathroom to throw up.

'You okay?' her mum's voice called from downstairs.

'Just a tummy upset.' She wiped her mouth of the sick and sat on the toilet to pee, wincing as the urine stung. Finally, she forced herself into the shower and scrubbed herself so fiercely that her body was red and sore when she finished. Lying on her bed, she thought of ways she could make him pay. Laine was quite inventive, and blackmail shot through her brain like a bullet.

He's had my body, and now I'll have something of his. It's amazing what you can learn about a person online. It didn't take long to find him and learn he was married.

'I'm sure you wouldn't want her to know,' Laine said, looking at his photo on a health site.

Oh yes, she could do well out of this.

CHAPTER TWENTY-FOUR

Sajid walked cautiously through the woods. The sun felt hot on the back of his neck. The wind rustling through the leaves made him nervous, and he looked behind him.

Saturday night's incident with the coach had affected him more than he'd thought. He should have gone to the police. Supposing some of the other passengers had and the police had visited those lads? They were bound to believe it was him that grassed them up.

He consoled himself that they didn't know his name or where he lived... But what if they saw him again at another match? A sudden grassy rustle made him jump, and then he saw it was just a squirrel racing to the top of a tree. He sat on the rotten fallen log they'd claimed as their own and waited patiently. The hum of insects calmed him, and he began to relax. The clock on his phone told him it was 12.15. Where was she? He'd have to get back to college soon.

He jumped at the sound of a branch cracking in the distance. He saw a flash of long brown curly hair and sighed with pleasure.

Laine was wearing her school uniform, and even in that, he

thought she was the most beautiful thing he'd ever seen. 'I thought you weren't coming,' he said.

'Don't be daft. I just didn't feel too good earlier. I'm okay.' She wrapped her arms around his waist, and he smelt vinegar.

'You look pale,' he said.

'I'm fine, honest. I had to go to that counselling session this morning – it was a waste of time. I got us some chips,' she said, holding up a bag.

Sajid licked his lips as Laine lifted out the bag of chips.

'I asked for a curry sauce, too,' she said, smiling.

Sajid heard a noise and jumped. 'What was that?' he asked nervously.

Laine looked at him oddly. 'Someone walking their dog, probably. Why are you acting all funny?'

'I'm not,' he said defensively, knowing he clearly was.

'Yes, you are.' She tucked her arm in his and laid the chip bag on her lap. 'Are you finishing with me?'

'Don't be a dumb head,' he said, putting his hand in hers. 'I just worry, you know, what with me being Indian and you being white and all that, and you're underage.'

'I'm nearly sixteen,' she said adamantly.

'Nearly,' he repeated. 'I'm eighteen, don't forget.'

Laine tossed back her curly hair, revealing large silver hooped earrings. 'What do you think?' she asked, fingering them proudly.

'I think you nicked 'em, is what I think.'

She tapped her nose cheekily.

They ate the chips in silence for a while. Finally, Laine said, 'Something's up. I ain't daft, you know.'

Sajid sighed. 'Some racist lads turned on me Saturday night on the coach coming home from the football.'

Laine began to choke on a chip. Sajid pulled a can of Coke from the bag and handed it to her. 'You okay?'

'Is that why you didn't want to meet me on Sunday?' she asked.

Sajid looked upset. 'I felt ashamed. I should have had more balls, but there were four of them. I thought you'd think me a coward. I was shaken.'

Laine put down her chips. 'Was there some other guy with a machete?'

Sajid reeled back. 'You what?'

'Was there?' she persisted.

'How do you know about him?' he asked suspiciously.

Laine sighed. 'What did he look like?' she said in a croaky voice. 'The one that went for you.'

Sajid stared at her. 'You think you know him?'

Laine nodded sadly.

'He had lots of tattoos and said his name was Needles.'

'Shit,' cursed Laine. Her bloody brother ruined everything.

'How do you know him?'

Laine bowed her head in shame. 'He's my brother.'

Sajid closed his eyes, despair washing over him. 'Oh shit,' he moaned. 'If he ever found out about us...' Sajid trailed off.

She grabbed his arm desperately. 'He won't, and besides, he's all mouth. He wouldn't hurt anyone.'

Sajid remembered the venom in Needles' voice and the dark hatred in his eyes. 'He has an irrational hatred of Pakistanis. He's like all racists. He thinks all people of colour are from Pakistan.'

'Honestly, he wouldn't hurt anyone,' she repeated. The truth, though, was that Laine wasn't sure about that.

Sajid looked at her with watery eyes. 'I can't carry on, Laine. I'm sorry. I could put my whole family at risk.'

'No,' she cried, standing up, the chips falling from her lap. 'You can't finish with me.'

He took her hand. 'He knows what I look like, Laine. If he ever sees me with you, well...'

Tears were running down Laine's cheeks. 'You said. You said you would come to the summer village party with me. That we'd show everyone we were together.'

'Laine, it's dangerous and...'

'I hate my stupid brother, Ludbrook Grove, that stupid bloody school, and their stupid bloody social worker. I hate everything. I can't even have the boyfriend I want because he's a fucking coward.' She knew the words would hurt him, but couldn't he see how much he was hurting her?

'Laine,' Sajid reached out to her, but she slapped his arm away.

'Fuck off,' she yelled and ran back through the woods.

Sajid sat with the curry sauce in his hand for a few minutes and suddenly jumped up and threw it at the tree, watching it slide down the bark like yellow pus. He hated being who he was and hated his parents for being who they were. More than anything, he hated Needles for his ignorant prejudice.

CHAPTER TWENTY-FIVE

Ana closed the door of her flat and opened the bedroom windows before shoving a frozen cottage pie into the microwave and pouring herself a large glass of sparkling water. She downed it in one go, poured another, and stood by the window. It was bloody hot on the fourth floor. The flat directly opposite was in darkness. Ana pulled a chair to the window and slumped into it.

Meanwhile, thoughts ran through her mind like a runaway train. There were so many unanswered questions about Vanessa's car accident.

Why hadn't Carpenter checked the security camera at Jonny Manners' house? It hadn't been difficult to spot.

The report hadn't mentioned the car's squeaky door. Maybe Penny hadn't mentioned it at the time. She was most likely in shock.

There must have been a dent in the car from the impact, but Carpenter had only checked local garages. Surely, if the driver had been canny, he would have taken it to a garage further away.

Ana sighed. Bloody lazy cops that couldn't be bothered when there was legwork to do. The microwave pinged, and Ana took the steaming cottage pie and more water back to the chair by the window.

The lights were now on in the flat opposite. Ana picked up the binoculars she'd left on the windowsill and looked into the living room. The woman was alone. Ana ate the cottage pie and watched the woman go out of sight into what Ana presumed was the bedroom.

Was he already there, waiting for her?

The cottage pie finished, Ana opened the file on Vanessa. The report said that all CCTV cameras were checked along routes that led to the bus stop. Although the car showed up, none of the footage was clear enough to show the reg or make.

The woman across the street was back in the living room, and Ana grabbed the binoculars. She was now wearing a pink dressing gown and had a towel wrapped like a turban on her head. Ana watched as she dropped onto the sofa and picked up a book.

'Bugger,' Ana muttered. He wasn't coming.

Realising it was pointless to sit at the window, she made herself comfortable on the couch and studied the file. Maybe she was being too thorough, as usual.

Still, it wouldn't help to check out a few garages further afield. Without the registration, it wouldn't be easy to trace, though.

She exhaled heavily and threw the file onto the coffee table. Tomorrow, she should read through her interview with Alan Mitchell and see if there is anything to pick up on. If only the bloke weren't so scared. Ana felt sure he had seen some of the lads' faces, but he wasn't budging from the 'I had my eyes on the road' story.

She rechecked the window, but the woman was still curled up with her book. Ana switched on the TV in time to catch her favourite crime drama.

CHAPTER TWENTY-SIX

'The police were here this morning.'

Leigh had debated all day whether to tell Will that DS Beth Harper had visited. Some part of her had decided not to, but then she'd realised the police might mention it, and then he'd know she'd kept it back from him.

Will's head lifted, and he turned from the fridge where he'd been getting a beer. Leigh saw his body tense.

'What did they want?' he asked bluntly.

Leigh raked her fingers nervously through her hair. 'Someone smashed that lad's trail bike.'

Will laughed. 'Is that right? If I knew who it was, I'd buy him a pint.'

Leigh felt as if someone had removed a huge boulder from her shoulders. The tension she'd felt all day now flowed from her body like a cool stream, washing away all her worries. It hadn't been Will. Of course it hadn't. It had been disloyal of her to consider it might have been.

'They asked where you were. It happened Monday night.' Leigh knew she had said the wrong thing from the change in Will's expression.

His eyes darkened. 'What did you tell them?'

'I said we watched television all evening.' Leigh was now regretting ever telling him the police had visited. It was always hard to know how he would react. 'I think they may question you. You did say you would take the law into your own hands if they didn't do something. That's why they wanted to speak to you,' said Leigh.

Will slammed the bottle of beer down onto the kitchen table. 'You should have phoned me at work, you daft cow.'

'I did think about it.'

'Think about it? Are you stupid?' Next time, call me. I don't want them turning up at the garage unannounced.'

'Yes,' she said, her voice trembling.

'I'll go and see them tomorrow at the station.'

'You didn't do anything to that boy's bike, did you, Will?'

'Don't be stupid,' he snapped.

Leigh nodded. 'I'm sorry. I don't know why I asked.'

'I need to put some washing on. I spilt oil over my work clothes this afternoon.'

Leigh waited while he fetched his overalls. 'I'll do them,' she said when he returned with a bundle under his arms.

'I don't want them ruined,' he said, walking past her to the utility room.

Leigh bit back her tears. If he saw her crying, he'd get even angrier. She drew in a slow, steady breath and swallowed down her tears. If only she didn't aggravate Will so much. She had tried to be a good wife but was somehow useless. Every woman she knew had got pregnant at the drop of a hat. Why not her? Will was adamant that he wouldn't have any tests.

'There's nothing wrong with me,' he'd said hotly. 'All the men in my family have fathered kids.'

Every month, Leigh prayed that her period wouldn't start, but it arrived like clockwork. The cramps were so bad some months that Will said she kept him awake at night with her fidgeting. Now, whenever it was that time of the month, he would go to the spare room.

If only she could have told Beth Harper that this week had been that time of the month and that she and Will had been in separate bedrooms. The truth was she had no idea if Will had gone out that evening as she'd gone to bed early and taken some painkillers.

CHAPTER TWENTY-SEVEN

Ana waited patiently at the corner of the street, holding her Starbucks paper cup tightly. The time on her phone told her she'd be late if she didn't leave soon. She'd studied the woman's movements and knew she had the time right, so where was she? A few more minutes and she would have to go.

She chewed her lip anxiously, rechecked her phone and was about to walk to her car when the woman turned the corner. Ana took a deep breath, pretended to be studying her phone and then deliberately walked straight into the other woman, splashing cold coffee down the front of her pink flowery dress.

'Oh,' cried the woman, stepping back.

'Oh my God, I'm so sorry,' said Ana, rummaging in her bag for a tissue. 'It was my fault.'

The woman looked up, her features creased in anger. 'It's new,' she said. 'God knows if the stain will come out.' She dabbed frantically at the dress.

She was well-spoken, Ana noted. *Just his type*, she thought.

'I'll have to go back and change,' she said miserably.

Ana dug into her bag. 'I'm really sorry. Here's my number. I'll pay for the dry cleaning.'

Just as Ana hoped, the woman looked at the card. 'You're a police officer.'

Ana nodded. 'Look, give me your number, so I'll know it's you when you call,' she said, smiling.

The woman hesitated for a second. 'Okay,' she said, finally. 'I'm Olivia Wilson. I'll WhatsApp my number when I get home. I'd better rush, or I'll be late for work.'

'Don't forget,' called Ana as Olivia rushed off.

Ana cursed. She'd hoped to get the number immediately. Then, checking the time, she saw she was also late and hurried to her car.

'Beth Harper,' said Will to the copper behind the desk.

'Can I help, sir?'

'I wouldn't be asking for Harper if I thought you could help,' snapped Will. 'Some of us have jobs to do. Can you let her know I'm here?'

The desk sergeant gave Will Moulson a hard stare. He'd become a copper to get respect from people, not this kind of shit. The bugger could wait. 'Take a seat, sir,' he said, pointing to the waiting area.

Will sighed. 'I'll stand.'

'Your choice, sir.'

The desk sergeant tidied the counter and answered a call. Finally, just as Will was getting red in the face, with anger, he buzzed through to Beth.

Will, agitated now, sat down and swung his foot back and forth. 'Is she coming or what?'

'On her way, sir.'

A few seconds later, Beth entered. 'Mr Moulson. Thank you for coming. We didn't request it.'

'Leigh said you came to the house and asked some questions.'

'Just routine. Come through. Would you like tea or coffee?'

'I haven't got long,' he said, his agitation evident. 'I just don't want the police turning up at the garage. Doesn't look good, you know.'

Beth led him to an interview room where Tom was waiting.

'DI Miller,' introduced Beth.

'Thank you for coming in, Mr Moulson.'

'Yeah, yeah,' interrupted Will.

'Is everything all right, Mr Moulson?' Beth asked. 'You seem rather tense.'

'I'm late for work.'

'It was your choice to come in, Mr Moulson. If you'd prefer to do this another time.'

'No, I just want to get things over with. It doesn't look good when the police come to your house. Leigh should have phoned me.'

Tom looked down at the paperwork before him while Beth kept her eyes on Will Moulson.

'You hinted to DS Harper on Sunday morning that if the police didn't do something about the trail bike rider, you would have to take things into your own hands. Is that correct?'

Will laughed. 'I was angry, okay?'

Tom nodded. 'So you weren't serious? Only someone did take it into their own hands and they smashed the bike to bits.'

'Like I said to my wife. I'd like to buy that person a pint. That kid was torturing everyone with that bloody bike.'

Beth noticed Will's finger was bandaged. 'Well, he won't be now. You're the manager of a garage in Cowley, I understand?'

'That's right, and I'm running late.'

Beth fought back a sigh and tried not to let her irritation

show. 'Mr Moulson, may I remind you that you chose to come today.'

'Yeah, I know.'

'You've hurt your finger,' Beth said lightly.

Will looked down at the bandage.

'Yeah, that's working in a garage for you.'

Or from smashing up bikes, thought Beth. 'Another witness told us you chased the lad in your car.'

'Yeah, but he sped down a narrow back lane and was aiming for the Ludbrook estate.'

Tom stood up. 'Well, I don't think we need to ask you any more questions.'

Beth raised her eyebrows. As far as she was concerned, there were plenty more questions.

Will also stood up, clearly relieved the interview was over. 'Great, I'll get off.'

'Your wife said you're a Chelsea supporter?'

'Yeah, I am,' said Will proudly.

'Me too. Did you go to the game on Saturday?'

'Sure did.' Will smiled. 'Great win.'

Beth opened the door for him and he hurried off to work.

Once Will Moulson was out of earshot, she turned to Tom. 'There was plenty more we could have asked him. Like, was he on that coach returning from the match.'

'Let's just watch him,' said Tom thoughtfully. 'He's anxious about something. I don't want him to know we're suspicious.'

CHAPTER TWENTY-EIGHT

Jack, the landlord of The Bell, had three words for the likes of Rory Landon, and they were *rich spoilt brats*.

It was a Sunday afternoon, the day of the Wimbledon final. Jack had plenty of punters in to watch, and the beer was flowing.

In the village hall gardens, the yearly cream teas were happening. Only one thing spoiled the peace of the quintessential English village of Stonesend: the car rally a few miles away. Every fifteen minutes, a joyrider in his fancy sporty car would scream through the thirty-mile-per-hour village, screeching tyres as it took the bends.

'Rich spoilt brats,' spat Jack.

'More money than sense,' said another.

'Wouldn't surprise me if it weren't one of them knocked down poor Vanessa.'

'Nah, that was in Summertown,' said Jack.

The car roared past again, and Jack popped his head outside the door to see a sporty Mercedes, smoke billowing from an open window, whizzing around the corner on its way to Longbridge.

'Expensive car that,' said Jack, who considered himself an expert on cars. 'That's what I mean, rich, spoiled brats.'

A roar went up as the British player scored a vital point.

'I'd better go and have a cream tea with my wife,' said Dan, one of the locals, standing up just as the joyrider skidded to a stop outside the pub.

Rory didn't see the guy hiding behind the bushes of the house opposite. He and his friend Maurice lazily climbed from the car. They stubbed their cigarettes out on the path and then strolled cockily into the pub, smelling of tobacco and expensive aftershave.

'Two large Chardonnays, my man.' Rory laughed.

'You realise this is a quiet village you're racing your car through?'

'We'll call the police,' said Dan.

Maurice laughed. 'Oh, what a hoot. I'll tell my dad, Judge Waters. I'm sure he can afford the fines.'

Jack wanted to throw the wine in their faces. Dan felt that if he didn't leave soon, he'd end up in a fight, which wouldn't go down well with his wife. He opened the pub door and gasped. A man in a balaclava and combats was slashing the tyres of the Mercedes. With each slash of the machete, there was an almighty bang.

'What the hell was that?' said Jack.

Dan watched nervously, too scared to move. From the account he'd heard, this looked like that vigilante. The man glanced up, and Dan moved nervously to one side as The Vigilante approached the pub doors. He walked in, and the place fell silent.

'Who does the Mercedes belong to?' he asked.

Rory turned, stared unperturbed at The Vigilante and said, 'Who the fuck are you? A cheap copy of The Joker?'

Maurice laughed.

The Vigilante pulled the machete from his rucksack.

Jack let out a long breath.

'Whoa, hold on, old chap, no need for that,' said Rory, stepping back.

'Just call me The Vigilante. I'm about to give you a little lesson about the law. Drinking and driving, not to mention speeding, is illegal. That's quite a few laws you're breaking there.'

'Yeah? And what are you going to do about it?' asked Rory with a sneer.

The Vigilante laughed. 'Oh, don't worry. I've already sorted it. I've slashed all your tyres. You must have heard it. You won't be going anywhere soon.'

Jack clapped his hands in glee. 'So, that's what I heard,' he said.

'I'm sure our friendly landlord can get you a lift. How about you phone the police, Mr Landlord?'

'Happy to,' said Jack.

The Vigilante returned the machete to his rucksack and walked from the pub.

'Nice meeting you guys,' he said, passing Dan on his way out. Dan then watched him run along the road, turn the corner and disappear.

Rory raced outside and stared in disbelief at his car. 'Fuck, he did,' he said shocked.

By the time Beth arrived, Rory and Maurice had calmed down and were demanding that she catch the guy who had mutilated their car.

'Did anyone see this person?' she asked, looking around at everyone. The large TV screen had now been turned off.

'It was that vigilante guy,' piped up Jack. He had the balaclava and all the gear we've been hearing about. He decided to take the law into his own hands. If you ask me–'

'Yes, right, thanks, Jack.' She turned to Rory. 'Your car, is it?'

'Racing through here like a lunatic,' added Jack.

Beth ignored him.

'Yes, my car. Bloody expensive it is, too.'

'Were you driving it?'

'Yeah, I was.'

'Okay, so just breathe into this for me,' she held out the breathalyser.

'Look, there's no need...'

'I can smell it on your breath. Are you refusing to take a breathalyser test?'

'Look, I'm not at fault here. It's my car that's been damaged.'

'My father is a judge, so you might want to think about what you're doing,' said Maurice arrogantly.

Beth scoffed. 'I don't care if your dad is the King of England.'

Jack sniggered.

'Now, are you going to take this test? If you don't, I'll have to take your keys and ask you to accompany me to the station.'

'Oh, for fuck's sake,' Rory said, blowing into the tube.

Beth waited a few seconds. 'Right, you're over the limit. I'm afraid you'll need to come to the station with me. Meanwhile, you might want to phone someone to pick up your car.'

She turned to the punters. 'Anyone see this vigilante?'

Several hands went up, including Dan's and Jack's.

'Did you recognise his voice? Did he seem familiar in any way?'

'Nah,' said Jack.

'I thought he was disguising his voice,' said Dan.

'If you could all stay here, I'll have someone come and take statements from you.' *Bloody vigilante*, she thought. *What is he up to? He's becoming the local bloody hero and making us look stupid.*

'If you find that vigilante guy, tell him there's a pint here on the house for him,' said Jack.

Great, thought Beth. *Hero he already is.*

Rory arranged for someone to collect his car and called his lawyer. 'It's pointless you cautioning me. I'll get off,' he said, lighting a cigarette, which Beth whisked off him.

'Not in here. You're not that bloody special. Matt, escort him to the station.'

'I'm coming, bro,' said Maurice.

'Spoilt little buggers,' said Beth.

'He'll get a fine, anyway. Hopefully, he's already gotten points and may well lose his licence,' said Jack.

Life seemed so unfair to Beth. *Still*, she thought, *at least Jack is happy.*

CHAPTER TWENTY-NINE

SEVEN YEARS EARLIER

The first missed period, Laurie put down to stress. Since the rape, she hadn't slept properly, and her mind was foggy, so she couldn't think clearly.

When the second period didn't arrive, Laurie panicked. The constant daily headaches were getting her down. Some days, they made her feel so sick that she had to rush from class to throw up.

Now, she sat in the doctor's waiting room with butterflies fluttering in her stomach. At least she knew it wasn't an infection he'd given her. All those tests had checked out fine.

Laurie tried to avoid looking at the heavily pregnant woman who sat opposite her, accompanied by someone she presumed was her proud husband. Then, another pregnant woman walked in, followed by another. It seemed they were everywhere, like ants crawling out from a nest.

Then Laurie noticed the *Antenatal Clinic* sign and smiled at the irony. She snatched a magazine from the table and tried to concentrate on it, but the chatter in the waiting room and the ringing of phones at the reception desk made it impossible.

Suffocation overcame her, and she felt a desperate need to run. Then, her name flashed up on the screen.

'Laurie McDuff to Room 4.'

The female doctor was kind. Still, Laurie blushed, crossed and uncrossed her legs several times as she described the missed periods.

'Can you pop to the loo and do a urine sample for me?'

Laurie took the container obediently. She was so nervous that she could only pee a small amount.

'That's fine.' The doctor smiled. 'We'll do a pregnancy test.'

Laurie waited nervously, wringing her hands.

The doctor checked the test and looked up at Laurie. 'Well, Laurie, I can confirm you're pregnant. If you've missed two periods already, and taking the date that intercourse occurred. I would put you at about ten weeks.'

The words were like a punch to her solar plexus, and she struggled to breathe. 'What?' she gasped. She remembered the morning-after pill prescription the nurse from the STI clinic had given her. She'd tried to get it after school, but the pharmacy had closed early. She'd managed to get hold of it the next day, but it must have been too late.

The doctor filled a plastic cup of water from the dispenser and handed it to Laurie. 'Here, take deep breaths. It's clearly a shock.'

Laurie took sips of the water.

'I see from your records that you're not on the pill.'

Laurie shook her head. She couldn't think straight, not while her head was all fuzzy.

'Do you know the father?'

Laurie nodded and then started to cry.

'Will he support you?'

Laurie shook her head. 'Do you have to tell my parents?' she asked.

'Only if you want me to.'

'I don't know what to do,' Laurie sobbed.

The doctor pushed a box of tissues across the table and laid a reassuring hand on Laurie's arm. 'Go home and take time to think about it. Come back in a week, and we can discuss your options.'

Laurie wanted to laugh. Options? What bloody options? How could she support a child? Would she even be able to love it, knowing how it was conceived? There were no options.

'I was raped,' she said. The words seem to spew from her mouth of their own volition.

Hearing the words aloud for the first time tightened her gut. She had been violated by a man who should have known better. The anger consumed her like a fire, burning through every part of her he'd touched.

The relaxed face of the doctor now hardened. 'Did you report the rape, Laurie?'

'No, how could I? Who would believe me? He's a professional man with a good reputation. The police would make mincemeat out of me, and so would the courts. I'm the kind of girl they say asked for it.'

The doctor took a deep breath. 'No one ever asks to be raped, Laurie. He exploited you. It was an abuse of power. He took advantage of your age and your background. You must report him.'

Laurie shook her head vigorously. 'You don't understand. If it happened to you, everyone would listen. I'm from a council estate. My mother is an alcoholic. My dad left us when I was a kid. I'm fifteen, but you grow up quickly on a council estate. I know the score.'

'Laurie, it doesn't matter where you come from–'

'Of course, it does. It matters a lot. No, I need to get rid of it.' *Like a bit of unwanted rubbish*, she thought sadly.

'Do you want to tell me who raped you, Laurie?' the doctor asked. 'I'll report it on your behalf.'

'No, I can't.'

The doctor sighed helplessly. 'Think things through, Laurie, and then come back in a week.'

Laurie took the tissue handed to her and wiped away her tears. It wouldn't take a week to decide, but she nodded anyway.

CHAPTER THIRTY

PRESENT DAY

M att approached Ana with two paper bags. 'Custard tarts or jam doughnuts, which is your favourite?'

'Custard tarts.' She smiled, dipping her hand into the bags and pulling out one of each. 'By the way, how do I get into the evidence room?'

'You'll need clearance.'

'Who from?'

'DI Miller or DS Harper.'

'Thanks, mate,' she said. 'I'll make a brew in a sec.'

Matt smiled. Only Ana would have the nerve to take two cakes. 'I thought you didn't like doughnuts,' he said.

'Custard tarts first, then doughnuts.' She smiled.

'By the way,' he said cautiously. 'The village summer fair is on Saturday. I was wondering if you'd like to go. There's live music, a funfair, and a cèilidh in the evening.'

'What's a cèilidh?'

'It's like a barn dance,' said Luke, taking a doughnut. 'You know, do-si-do and all that.'

'Sounds like fun.' She smiled. 'Is there food?'

'Sure is.' Matt grinned.

'The only problem is Matt's got two left feet, so you'd be best off finding another partner. I'm happy to offer.'

'Aren't you bringing your wife?' said Matt sharply.

'I've got tough toes,' Ana said, smiling at Matt. 'I think I can handle your two left feet.'

She waited until Luke returned to his desk before knocking on Beth's door. 'Ma'am, permission to look at the CCTV tapes from the hit and run.'

Beth looked up. 'Any updates on forensics?'

Ana realised she was being put in her place. 'No, ma'am. Analysis showed nothing we could work with.'

Beth sat back in her chair. 'The hit and run had a full investigation, Ana.'

'I beg to differ, ma'am.'

Beth raised her eyebrows. 'Excuse me?'

'A private security camera was overlooked, which showed the accident. The friend said the car stopped, and she heard a squeaky door. I believe the driver would have taken the car further afield to get the damage repaired, but only local garages were the ones checked.'

'We didn't have a registration, Ana.'

'No, ma'am, but with all due respect, I think there are other things to look into.'

'Such as?'

'The private security camera. We might get some leads from that.'

'This isn't going down well with the officer in charge of that case.'

'That's his problem, ma'am, not mine.' Ana knew she sounded gutsy and ambitious but wanted justice for Vanessa.

'I don't want to waste human resources on this. I'll give you forty-eight hours. If you don't come up with something concrete, you drop it. Understood?'

'Yes, ma'am, thank you.'

'I'll authorise Ruth to let you in.'

'Thank you, ma'am. I'm just making a brew. Would you like one? There are some doughnuts on the go.'

'Thanks, Ana.' Beth watched Ana leave. There was confidence about her but also a vulnerability.

Ana made tea while the authorisation went through. Then, taking a mug to Ruth, she said, 'DS Harper put in a request for me.'

Ruth nodded. 'I'll take you through. Thanks for the tea, but I only drink coffee.'

Of course you do, thought Ana, following her to the evidence room.

'There's doughnuts?'

'I'm on a diet,' said Ruth.

Of course you are, thought Ana.

'Drawer 36,' said Ruth, unlocking it. 'Let me know when you've finished.'

Ana rifled through the drawer for the CCTV tapes. At that moment, her phone vibrated, and Olivia's name popped onto the screen.

'DC Ana Rawlins.'

'Hi, it's Olivia. You spilt coffee on my dress?'

Ana's breathing quickened. 'Hi, how are you?'

'I took it to be dry-cleaned and I'm picking it up later.'

'Great, let me have your address and–'

'A bank transfer will be fine,' broke in Olivia.

Fuck, thought Ana.

'Oh please, let me give you the cash. I feel so bad. I bought some chocolates as an apology.'

There was silence at the other end.

'I'm quite safe.' Ana laughed.

'Oh, I know. It's 24 Queens Court.'

'That's right opposite my block,' said Ana, feigning surprise. 'I'll pop by this evening. Is seven okay?' *Or are you seeing him?*

'Yeah, that's fine.'

'Great, see you later.' Ana clicked off her phone and stared at it for a few seconds, at last, some headway.

The CCTV footage showed nothing. If Ana was expecting something to jump out at her, she was disappointed. Still, she had forty-eight hours. It gave her enough time.

CHAPTER THIRTY-ONE

SEVEN YEARS EARLIER

It had been a week, and Laurie still hadn't decided what to do. So many things ran through her mind. If she had the baby, her life would be over. Fifteen years old, and she had no real future ahead of her.

What if she hated it when it was born? Supposing it looked like *him*? The memory of that day would be relived in her mind every time she looked at her child.

There was only one thing to do, and that was to speak with her mum. Trying to carry the burden alone was too much. Surely, she would know what to do. With her mind on the baby, she turned into her street and stopped abruptly. It felt like an invisible hand had suddenly pushed against her chest, preventing her from going forward.

An ambulance was parked outside their house. A man was sitting on the front step, his head in his hands. Several neighbours were outside watching. Then, as she drew closer, forcing herself through the invisible barrier, she saw that the man on the step was Arthur and sitting beside him was Anika.

'Oh, no,' she groaned. 'Arthur?'

He looked up, his face white and drawn. Laurie took one look at his red eyes and tear-stained cheeks and knew.

'Mum?' she said, her voice barely audible.

'Oh, my lovely,' said Anika, wrapping her in her warm arms. The smell of curry wafted from her clothes, and Laurie breathed it in deeply. If she could stay here, then maybe nothing would change.

'She won't go to the hospital. Maybe you can get her to change her mind,' said Arthur, breaking into Laurie's security blanket.

Laurie pulled herself out of Anika's embrace and rushed into the house, where the paramedics were coming down the stairs.

'I'm her daughter,' Laurie said breathlessly. 'You need to take her to the hospital.'

The paramedic looked at her sympathetically. 'We've tried our best. I'm sorry, but she won't go.'

Laurie rushed past them and up the stairs where her mother lay in her darkened bedroom. The room stank of stale alcohol and unwashed bed sheets. The air was muggy and putrid. Laurie pulled her eyes away from the bin that was full of blood-stained tissues and went to draw back the curtains.

'Laurie,' Brenda said weakly.

'Let me open the curtains,' Laurie said.

'No, it's too bright,' said Brenda, her voice hoarse.

'What the fuck?' Laurie said, weeping. 'I thought Arthur was looking after you.' There was a painful ache in Laurie's chest. *I've let her down*, she thought. *I've not been here when she's needed me.*

'He's a man, don't blame him or yourself. I never wanted either of you to know the truth.'

Laurie tried to straighten the bedclothes but couldn't see

what she was doing through her tears. 'I would have looked after you.'

Brenda shook her head. 'You're too young.'

Laurie stroked Brenda's thin hair and wiped her watery eyes with a tissue.

'Two pills,' whispered Brenda. 'The pain–'

Laurie strained to see the bedside cabinet. Several bottles of pills were lying amongst an assortment of tissues and half mugs of cold tea.

'Which ones?'

Brenda pointed to a bottle and Laurie shook out two capsules. Carefully, she lifted her mother's head from the pillow and slipped the drugs into her mouth, using the cold tea to help wash them down.

'You must go to the hospital,' she said, her voice breaking.

'It's too late, darling.' Brenda clasped Laurie's hand with her cold and clammy fingers.

'Mum...'

'My liver is failing. It's time for me to check out.'

Laurie broke out in a cold sweat. What was she talking about, checking out? 'You'll get better if you go to the hospital. They'll have everything you need there. You must go!'

Brenda took a long, labouring breath.

'Don't talk, Mum. I'll get the paramedics to come back.'

'No,' said Brenda firmly, using every ounce of breath she could force from her lungs. 'Promise me–' Brenda coughed forcefully, blood spilling from her open lips.

Laurie lifted her body slightly. God, she was so light. Why hadn't she noticed? Gently, she wiped away the blood from her lips. The wetness of her tears fell onto her mother's nightie. 'Please don't try and talk,' Laurie begged.

'You'll stop drinking. Promise me, Laurie.'

'I promise. Now, will you please go to the hospital?'

Brenda fell back onto the pillows and sighed. 'I've got stage 4 liver cancer. There's nought they can do.'

Laurie dug her nails into her hand until they bled. *Why now, why fucking now?* Why the fuck hadn't she told them? Anger swept like a hurricane through her body. That bastard that raped her, his mother wouldn't die in squalor like this, would she? Oh no, she'd be in a lovely private clinic.

'I've been waiting,' Brenda panted. 'To say I'm sorry.' She squeezed Laurie's hand.

'There's nothing to be sorry for. It's me who should be saying sorry. I've been a disappointment,' Laurie sobbed.

'Oh darling, you've been the best daughter a mother could ever have. I let you down terribly. Forgive me.'

Laurie struggled to breathe. 'No, you didn't. You've never let me down.'

'Forgive me,' pleaded Brenda.

'I forgive you, but you haven't done anything bad. I love you.'

'A bad hand of cards, that's all it was,' whispered Brenda.

'Yes.' Laurie wept. 'A bad hand of cards.' She felt the cold hand in hers loosen its grip.

'Love you forever,' Brenda whispered, closing her eyes. Her hand slid from Laurie's, and at that moment, Laurie felt part of her soul leave her body.

'Love you forever, too. Safe journey, Mum,' she whispered, kissing her. 'I promise with all my heart that I won't disappoint you.'

Gently, she climbed onto the bed and laid her head softly on Brenda's chest, clasping her hand.

Anika peered tearfully around the door, slid down the landing wall, and cried silently for fifteen minutes before entering the bedroom. Then, with the gentleness of an angel, she led Laurie away from her mother's body.

'God has her now,' she said softly. 'She's free from pain.'

Laurie nodded tearfully. She couldn't tell Anika she didn't believe in God and angels, only in good and evil. Her mother had been good, and he was evil. He should be the one suffering.

CHAPTER THIRTY-TWO

Ana had an hour before she visited Olivia. An hour was enough for a road trip to Summertown. She wanted to check the place against the map she had made of the CCTV cameras she'd seen in the evidence room. Also, what better way to get to know the area than a road trip?

She ticked off some of the CCTV cameras on her map, including the one near the bingo hall.

Realising she was low on petrol, she stopped at a garage on the way back, and it was then she saw the camera. Supposing the driver had stopped for petrol? It was a long shot, but still worth checking out. The manager was accommodating and showed her the video from that evening, but there was no sign of a Golf or anything like it.

On the journey back, she passed the rest of the CCTV cameras on her map, but coming through the village of Bladon, she saw another that wasn't. Had she missed it when going through the evidence? It was too obvious not to be seen. Perhaps it was new. Ana made a mental note to check it out. Time was getting on, and she didn't want to be late getting to Olivia's.

The entrance to Olivia's block was identical to Ana's, even

down to the tiled flooring. It felt uncanny as she got into the lift, to find that it was also identical. *I'll be walking into my own flat at this rate*, thought Ana. Olivia answered the door wearing the dress that Ana had spilt coffee over. The faint sounds of jazz music came from inside the flat.

'Just so you know, I really did get it dry-cleaned.' Olivia smiled.

Ana handed over the chocolates, and Olivia opened the door wider. Ana stepped inside and gasped. The flat wasn't identical to hers at all. There was a state-of-the-art sound system, an opulent fireplace, and a mantlepiece decorated with solid silver candle holders. A bouquet of flowers sat in a vase on the dining table and plush corner-to-corner couches covered in colourful tapestry cushions filled the living area. It was like something in a home magazine.

'Thanks for the chocolates,' said Olivia, walking to the kitchen. Here, Ana noted there were more fresh flowers. *Were they from him?*

'I've got red wine or white if you prefer?' Olivia opened the fridge.

'Just a coffee for me. I don't drink the night before work. I'm useless the next day if I do.'

'I'll make a fresh pot.'

'Your flat is beautiful. Is that what you do for a living, interior design?'

Olivia laughed. 'I wish. No, I'm a legal eagle. Mostly high-profile divorces.'

'Wow, I bet that's interesting. Seeing how the other half live.'

'Are you at Oxford police station?' Olivia asked, taking the coffee into the lounge.

'No, Stonesend.'

'It's quaint there,' said Olivia, opening the chocolates. 'I hope you're not on a diet and will share them with me.'

'I don't do diets.' Ana grinned. She looked around for evidence that would prove she had the right woman. 'What do I owe you?'

'Eighteen fifty. Is that okay?'

Ana pulled her purse from her bag and handed the money to Olivia, noting the blue sparkler on Olivia's finger as she did so. 'That's beautiful,' she said, pointing to the ring.

Olivia blushed. 'Thanks, a gift from my boyfriend.'

Ana blew out her cheeks. 'I should have such a boyfriend.'

Olivia poured the coffee and didn't answer.

Ana said, 'I've not been here long enough to meet anyone apart from colleagues, and I'm not sure about dating another copper. However, there is a cute one at the station. He asked if I wanted to go to the summer fair at Stonesend. Are you going?' She helped herself to a chocolate. *Are you going with* him? she wondered.

Olivia looked doubtful. 'I'm not sure.'

'Maybe I'll meet your boyfriend,' said Ana. 'Does he have a friend?' She laughed.

'He works unsociable hours.'

Ana wondered if she was pushing too hard and too fast. 'Well, if you're ever at a loose end and want to go for a drink one night, I'm free.'

'Thanks, that's kind. I heard about that vigilante guy. Are you working on that case?'

'Who told you?' asked Ana curiously.

'A friend was in the pub in Stonesend on Sunday, and everyone was talking about it. They said he called himself The Vigilante.'

'I'm sorry, but I can't discuss ongoing cases.'

'No, sorry, of course not. Should we be afraid?' she asked, leaning back into the cushions.

'Only if you've broken the law and he's unhappy about it,' said Ana, trying to reassure her.

She excused herself to use the loo, closing the living-room door behind her. On her way to the bathroom, she peeked into the bedroom, hoping to see a photo of them together, but there was nothing. Ana cursed. Surely she hadn't got it wrong. There must be something.

The loo was an interior designer's delight. Soft white towels, all lined up neatly on a towel rail, a fluffy, clean white mat to step on when getting out of the shower, and fragrant candles around the bath.

Ana looked at her reflection in the bathroom cabinet, tidied her hair, and opened the cabinet door. Shampoo bottles and face creams sat alongside perfume bottles, and then she saw it. For several seconds she stared at the aftershave bottle before lifting it out. Then, taking off the gold-capped lid, she sniffed the fragrance. It set her head spinning, and she grasped the sink for support as her legs gave way. She put the bottle back with trembling hands and sat on the loo, composing herself.

It was *him*. She had been right all along. Ana didn't know whether to laugh or cry.

CHAPTER THIRTY-THREE

The pub was quiet, and Ana sat at the bar with her drink. Her mind was racing. It had been one thing finding out where he was but another to have it confirmed. In truth, she had expected it to be a lot more difficult. Without realising it, she tightened her hands into fists. The fragrance was still in her nostrils, and her heart raced. Grabbing a tissue from her handbag, she blew her nose. Had she secretly hoped it wouldn't be him? Now the time had come, did she have the courage to do what she'd planned?

'Hello there, drinking alone? Never a good sign.' Ana turned with a start to see Luke. He looked different in casual clothes.

'I was just about to leave,' she said, sliding off her stool.

'Have another on me,' he urged. 'I'll take it personally if you leave just as I've arrived.'

Ana hesitated. Wasn't he married? 'Just the one. I'll get them in. I've got to buy a round sometime.' She smiled.

Luke conceded. 'Equal rights, fair enough. London Pride for me. I'll get us a table. That Jack over there has got big ears.'

'I bloody heard that,' said Jack.

Luke chuckled. 'See what I mean?' Addressing the landlord he said, 'We might talk police business.'

'Yeah, sure,' said Jack, taking Ana's order. 'How you liking it here?'

'Too soon to say,' said Ana.

'Straight to the point, aren't you?'

'Sure am. Thanks, Jack.'

'He's married, you know,' he said softly, nodding at Luke.

Ana smiled. 'I know, but I appreciate the warning. I assure you, he's not my type.'

'So why is a pretty girl like you drinking alone?' asked Luke when she'd sat down.

'What's a married man like you doing in a pub alone?'

'My wife doesn't understand me,' he said with a grin.

Ana smiled and sipped at her drink. The fragrance still lingered in her nostrils, sending a shiver down her spine. 'That's an old one. What's hard to understand?' she asked.

'Let's just say it's complicated,' added Luke. 'How about you? There must be someone in your life.'

Ana shook her head. 'Let's just say it's complicated.'

Luke grinned. 'If you ever need a drinking companion, just let me know.'

'Actually, I only just dropped in on my way back. I've been checking out the neighbourhood.'

Luke laughed. 'I bet that didn't take long.'

'I checked out the journey from Stonesend to Summertown.'

Luke put down his pint. 'You're not still on about that hit and run, are you?'

Ana noticed that Luke's cheeky grin had now disappeared.

'I was wondering, did you check the CCTV camera at Bladon on the A44? Only it's not mentioned in the files.'

Luke frowned. 'To be honest, I can't remember. I imagine

we must have. It will be in the evidence somewhere.' He took another swig from his beer.

'I checked all the CCTV recordings. I didn't see it.'

'Most likely a new one, then. They're throwing the things up all the time.'

'There was also a garage CCTV–'

'What are you after exactly?' Luke glared at her. 'A promotion or something? I notice that you're always crawling into the boss's office.'

Ana took a sip of her drink. 'I'm doing my job, that's all.'

'No, you're looking into someone else's investigation, and that's a bit of an insult,' he said. 'I did a good job. If there had been someone to be found for knocking over Vanessa, I would have found them. This is a close-knit community. Everybody knows Vanessa. We didn't make any mistakes.'

'I'm not saying anyone did a bad job. I like her and–'

'We all like her, so we worked hard to find the bugger who knocked her over, but...' He sighed. 'Look,' he said wearily, his voice softening, 'I think you and I have got off on the wrong foot. I have some personal issues and may have been over-defensive.'

I don't give a fuck about your issues, Ana thought. She opened her mouth to speak, but he held his hand up to stop her.

'Not your problem, I know, but maybe I was dismissive. If you think I missed something, then fair enough. Let's at least work together on it.'

You worked so hard on it that you missed one security camera and one CCTV camera, thought Ana. If there was one thing Ana hated, it was lazy cops, but the least she could do was to be gracious. 'I'm sorry if I've upset you,' she lied.

'No hard feelings.' Luke seemed to have calmed down.

'Good. See you tomorrow,' she said, finishing her drink and standing up.

'Sure. I'll go through all the evidence.'

Ana nodded in response. 'Thanks.'

'Mates?' asked Luke.

'Mates.' She smiled while thinking, *Only mates*.

'Bye, Jack,' she called.

Jack waved. 'See yer,' he said.

Ana knew Luke thought she was a pain in the arse, which was why she had bought the drinks. He most likely saw her as a threat. *Maybe I am*, she thought with a smile.

———

Laine passed people carrying branded shopping bags and sipping on-the-go coffees. *That's what I want*, she thought. *Not just now but always.*

'I could do with one of those,' said Jassy, eyeing up the coffee. 'I'm parched.'

'Let me try on the shoes first,' said Laine, pointing to a pair of red heels in the shop window.

The shoe shop was lovely and cool. 'I love air conditioning,' sighed Jassy.

Boots and shoes lay on the floor where people were trying them on. Ladies with posh voices were strolling back and forth in new shoes. 'I'm really not comfortable,' whispered Jassy. 'All these posh people and stuff.'

'Enjoy it.' Laine smiled. 'Can I try on the red shoes in the window?' Laine asked an assistant.

Laine and Jassy waited while the assistant got Laine's size.

Jassy stared at the shoes in wonder. 'Aw, look at those,' she said, watching with envy as Laine tried them on.

'I love them,' said Laine. 'I want to wear them to the village fair. How much?'

'A hundred and seventy-five pounds,' said the assistant without batting an eyelid.

Jassy gasped. 'You what?'

'I'll take them,' said Laine.

Jassy stared at her in shock. 'What?' she said, grabbing Laine's arm. 'Are you out of your mind? Where have you got a hundred and seventy-five quid to spend on a pair of sodding shoes?'

'In here,' said Laine, pulling out her purse and showing Jassy the wad of notes inside.

'Jesus,' breathed Jassy.

Laine took the branded bag from the assistant and walked proudly from the shop.

'What? How? I mean, blimey,' stuttered Jassy. 'Did you rob a bank?'

'I'm getting a really nice dress too and some jewellery. I want Sajid to see what he's lost.'

Laine pulled a stunned Jassy into Costa Coffee.

'I'll get them,' said Laine, opening her purse.

She saw Jassy looking at the wad of notes.

'Where did you get all that?' Jassy asked, shocked.

'What you don't know can't get you into trouble.' Laine smiled.

Jassy was too dazed to reply.

Laine returned with coffee and muffins. 'Look at your face,' she laughed. 'Don't worry. I can buy us both a nice dress.'

'But–'

'Look, don't ask, and I won't tell. There's more where this came from.'

Jassy looked worried. 'You'll get into trouble, Laine.'

Laine tucked into her muffin. 'I won't, honest. We'll get dresses after this and go to that Thai place for lunch.'

Jassy was finding it hard to swallow her muffin, not knowing where the money came from to pay for it. How could she possibly eat a Thai meal? Then again, she reasoned, it wasn't her problem. After all, she didn't nick the dosh, and it probably came from some posh nob who could afford it.

'Okay,' said Jassy, biting into her chocolate muffin. 'Why not?' Why shouldn't we tuck into a slap-up meal for once in our lives?

Laine smiled. 'Let's enjoy ourselves.'

Deep down, though, all Laine could think of was Sajid. Part of her hated him for being so weak, while the other half understood and wanted to tell the world that Sajid was just like them. He was caring, kind, thoughtful, loving, and the perfect son. The colour of his skin didn't make him a bad person.

At night, she'd lie in bed and listen to her dad snoring in the room next door, and she knew he would never accept Sajid. Sometimes, she imagined them as a modern-day Romeo and Juliet. Both their parents would hate the thought of them together. Needles would go apeshit and cause fights and no doubt get his mates to intimidate Sajid's family. Why did she have to be born into this family? It wasn't fair. It's not her fault she fell in love with Sajid. You can't choose the person you fall in love with.

'Come on.' Jassy was nudging her. 'I'm bloody starving.'

Laine knocked her bruised thigh on the table leg and winced. The memory of what happened instantly shot through her mind. She pushed it away before any tears came.

CHAPTER THIRTY-FOUR

'I can't think of anyone who'd have the guts to take on thugs,' said Ray, turning the roast potatoes. The heat from the oven blasted his face, and he grimaced.

'Like we're all cowards,' said Sandy.

Ray shut the oven door and wiped his hands on a tea towel. 'No, I'm not saying that. I meant it's surely either a criminal, ex-copper, or ex-soldier. Someone confident enough to handle themselves.'

'He has a point,' said Beth.

'Yes. I don't imagine Dan or Jack at the pub would be brave enough,' admitted Sandy. 'You certainly wouldn't be.' She laughed, poking Ray in the ribs.

'Do you mind? I've got muscles.'

'You must be hiding them.' Sandy laughed.

'Doesn't he give anything away on those cards?' asked Ray, refilling their wine glasses.

Beth covered hers with her hand. 'I'll wait until dinner,' she said. 'The cards are printed with the exact words, "When the law fails to serve us, we must serve as the law." He signs himself off as The Vigilante. He might write some other comment on the back. That's it.'

'No fancy pattern on them so that you can trace them?'

'Plain white cards. Thousands of people buy them every day.'

Zoe, Beth's three-year-old niece, flew into the kitchen. 'Snowy's woken up. Can I show Aunty Beth?'

'Snowy?' questioned Beth.

'Snowy the rabbit,' smiled Ray. 'He came yesterday.'

At that moment, the doorbell rang, and Beth glanced at Sandy in disbelief.

'It was Ray's idea,' squirmed Sandy.

Beth shook her head. 'I don't believe you two.'

'Not me, honestly,' persisted Sandy.

'Liar.' Beth smiled.

'Right, let's see this rabbit then,' she said, taking Zoe's hand.

The sound of Tom's voice reached her from the open back door. Beth had known something was up. Sandy had been edgy from the moment Beth had arrived. Why did they have to do this stupid matchmaking?

'I hear we're rabbit visiting,' said a voice behind her. He looked gorgeous as usual – more gorgeous now than when she'd first met him. He'd been thinner and gaunt then, grief for his wife etched across his face. Now, he looked relaxed. The tight lines of anger around his mouth had gone.

'His name is Snowy.' She handed him the rabbit. His hand was warm as it stroked hers. *I so need a drink*, thought Beth.

'He's still a baby,' said Zoe.

Beth raised her eyebrows. 'I can't escape babies, it seems,' she said.

'Me neither,' he said.

Beth closed her eyes and sighed. 'Oh God, I'm sorry. I should have thought.'

He shook his head. 'No, don't be. I don't want people to tiptoe around me. I lost my wife and unborn child, but time does heal, and life goes on, and it will for you too, Beth.'

Tom handed the rabbit to Zoe.

'By the way,' he said to Beth apologetically. 'I honestly didn't know you were going to be here.'

Beth laughed. 'You mean you're still unaware that my sister and her husband are matchmaking?'

'Oh,' he said, surprised.

'Dinner is almost ready,' called Ray.

'Do I call you sir this evening?'

'I'd prefer you didn't.' Tom smiled.

But you'll be counting my drinks, she thought resentfully.

Dinner was roast lamb, Ray's speciality. Beth noticed Sandy didn't top up their wine glasses like she used to. *Or maybe I'm just imagining it.* Perhaps they had been this considerate the last time Tom came to dinner.

'If you ask me,' said Ray, 'this vigilante guy is doing us all a favour.'

'Ray!' said Sandy, surprised.

'Well, obviously, as one of the "so-called public", he probably has inside knowledge.'

'Of what?' asked Beth.

Ray shrugged. 'The locals.'

'My husband, the psychiatrist, turned police officer,' said Sandy.

'Out of curiosity, how would someone like that think?' asked Tom. 'Would there be some baggage they're carrying that's driving them to revenge?'

Ray nodded. 'It could be that he hates injustice and has decided to put things right. Or maybe he hates the police for some reason and wants to show them up. Or maybe he craves power.'

'And if you had this person come to you, you would be able to tell us?'

'If they were a threat, of course.'

'Try telling that to some priests,' said Tom, keeping his voice controlled, but his body was tense.

'Patient confidentiality, I'm afraid.'

Tom scoffed. 'Tell that to the families of murder victims.'

'Right,' said Sandy, 'dessert. Ray, come on.' Ray lifted his eyebrows but followed her into the kitchen.

'They are giving us dinner,' Beth said quietly, topping up her glass. 'Besides, Ray did have a good point earlier. He said that surely only someone who could be sure of taking care of themselves would put themselves out as a vigilante, ex-cop maybe, or ex-soldier.'

Tom nodded. 'Worth looking into.' His foot touched hers under the table, and their eyes met. 'Got a date for the summer fair?' he asked. 'I hear it's good.'

'It is,' she said, taken aback. 'It got cancelled last year, so you didn't see it. It's fun. I'm on call, but I don't have a date. I think everyone is a bit pissed off with me these days.'

'Yeah, I'm a bit pissed off with you too,' he said, grinning at her. 'But I'm free if you can stand it.'

'As long as you buy me a hot dog,' she said, attempting to cover her embarrassment.

'You're on,' he said.

The door flew open, and Sandy waltzed in with a trifle. 'Dessert,' she announced.

'Dishes,' declared Ray.

'Excitement,' said Tom, and everyone relaxed.

CHAPTER THIRTY-FIVE

SEVEN YEARS EARLIER

L aurie had no more tears left.

The funeral had been a quiet affair. Arthur was a pallbearer along with Dil and two other neighbours. Brenda had no family, and her parents were dead, but several people from the estate came to say goodbye and those that didn't, sent flowers. It warmed Laurie's heart that so many people loved her mother. Anika held her hand as they walked behind the coffin.

Today, she knew she had to be strong for Brenda. The vicar was kind and had said nice words about her mum, even though he'd never met her, but it wasn't the same as hearing someone talk about her mum who'd actually known her. Brenda hadn't been a churchgoer. In fact, this was the first time Laurie had ever set foot inside a church. At least her stomach had settled. She'd been terrified that she would throw up during the service.

'Laurie McDuff is now going to say a few words,' said the vicar.

Anika squeezed her hand reassuringly. Laurie took a deep breath and walked to the podium. With trembling hands Laurie opened the sheet of paper that had her speech written on it. It had been well over a week since she'd had a drink. That, coupled with the pregnancy hormone changes, had left her feeling pretty rough.

Laurie swallowed and then leaned in towards the mic. 'My mum wasn't perfect, and she'd be the first to say that. *Don't sugarcoat it* was one of her sayings. My mum didn't have it easy, but she made the best of everything and tried her best to give me a happy childhood. I loved my mum, and she loved me. There are many hateful people in the world...' Her voice broke when she thought of the life in her womb. 'But my mum wasn't one of them. Brenda McDuff was kind and caring and accepted everyone for who they were. *Yes*, she drank too much, but as she would tell everyone, life had dealt her a bad hand of cards. I wish she'd been dealt a far better one because she deserved that. I will miss her every day and love her forever.'

The walk back to her seat seemed endless, but Anika and Arthur's warm embraces finally allowed her the freedom to cry. Anika had arranged for Laurie to move in with her family, and Arthur was set to move on.

'You know I love you, girl,' he'd said. 'But there's nothing here for me now. I'd make a lousy dad, and I know Anika will take good care of you.'

'You've been a great dad,' she'd reassured him.

It had been her mother's wish that Laurie lived with Anika, and Laurie knew that at some point, she would have to tell Anika about the baby and her decision to have an abortion. There was no way she could give birth to that monster's child.

As she watched the curtains drape around her mother's coffin, like warm, comforting arms, she whispered one last goodbye.

When they returned to the estate for the wake at Anika's house, Laurie saw men from the council painting the inside of what was once her home.

'Jesus,' she said, 'look at them.'

Before Anika could hold her back, she was storming towards them. 'What the fuck,' she shouted. 'We've just cremated my mum. This was her home. Couldn't you have waited a few days? Didn't we move out fast enough for you?'

'Sorry about your mum, love, but we're just doing our job,' one of the workmen said, clearly uncomfortable.

Anika pulled her by the arm. 'Come on, Laurie. They don't understand. They're just doing what the council tells them.'

'It's like she never existed,' Laurie cried.

Anika led her away gently. At that moment, Laurie wished she were dead, just like her mum.

So many people hugged her. 'So sorry,' they said. 'If there's anything we can do,' they said. 'Such a terrible loss for you,' they said, and all Laurie wanted to shout was, 'He raped me. I'm pregnant, and I didn't even get to tell my mum. What am I supposed to do now?'

Sometimes, she felt guilty for not telling the police and would think about all the other girls he would do the same thing to. If she did go to the police and it went to court, and she lost, which she surely would because he'd get the best solicitor, wouldn't that be even worse? After all, people like him had friends in high places.

What would she get? Legal aid, that's what. Girls would watch and see how humiliating it was, and it would put them off even more. No, there had to be another way. That's what her mother would have said. It might take her time to think of it, but she would. First, though, she would need to tell Anika about the baby and the abortion, which would be hard to do without a few drinks inside her.

CHAPTER THIRTY-SIX

PRESENT DAY

Luke worked through the paperwork while Ana studied the CCTV footage. It was her third time looking at them, and her eyes were becoming sore.

Taking a sip of cold coffee, she turned to Luke. 'Anything?'

He handed her a folder. 'The friend's statement. The squeaky door was mentioned, and I remember that now, but at the time, I knew that unless we found a car, there wasn't much we could do with the information.'

'Right,' agreed Ana.

Luke continued rustling papers, and Ana rubbed her eyes before returning to the CCTV footage.

'Bingo,' exclaimed Luke. 'Here's the report on the CCTV camera in Bladon. It wasn't working the night of the hit and run, so that explains it.'

He handed it to Ana, who glanced through it. How did she miss it? *I'm too focused on him*, she thought. *I need to concentrate on work properly.*

'I must have missed it,' she said. 'Thanks.'

Luke rose from his chair. 'I think you've reached the end of the road, if you'll pardon the pun, just as we did. Unless you can get a reg on the car, you're buggered.'

Ana sighed, realising he was right.

'Coffee?' asked Luke.

Ana was about to answer when Matt popped his head around the door. 'Someone on the phone for you,' he said. 'Jonny Manners.'

'Who?' she asked.

'He said something about some photos.'

Ana then remembered the security camera outside Jonny's house.

'Hi,' she said, picking up the receiver.

'I have the photos for you, and I was right. It's a Golf. I looked it up, and I reckon it's a Volkswagen Golf estate 1999, so I printed out the details.'

'Great, thanks. Can you drop them into the station?'

Jonny seemed to hesitate and finally said, 'Or I can give them to you over a drink tonight if you're free.'

Ana chewed her lip. It wouldn't hurt. After all, most of her nights were spent reviewing evidence or watching Olivia's flat from her window. 'That would be great.'

'Shall I meet you at the pub in Stonesend at about seven? If that's easier for you.'

Ana felt Matt's eyes on her.

'Sure, see you then.'

Matt raised his eyebrows in interest.

'It's not a date,' she said.

Matt smiled. 'Pleased to hear it. I've booked you for the fair, don't forget.'

'Careful.' She smiled. 'Or I might charge a booking fee.'

CHAPTER THIRTY-SEVEN

SEVEN YEARS EARLIER

The news that Laurie was pregnant had come as no surprise to Anika. Having delivered four children herself, she recognised the signs. There was a slight swelling in Laurie's tummy, and the long time she spent in the bathroom in the mornings was a clear giveaway.

'Who's the boy?' was her first question, and Laurie had been dreading it. She'd already decided to tell Anika the truth. It was the least she owed her.

'I was raped,' she said bluntly.

Bile rose in Anika's throat. Laurie was speaking, but Anika couldn't take the words in. It felt as if she was drowning in them.

Locked the door... Drugged my water.

Her temples began to throb, and she massaged them gently.

Laurie handed her a glass of water. 'I'm so sorry, Anika,' she said tearfully.

Why was Laurie apologising? She'd done nothing wrong.

'Who?' Anika asked, feeling like a sharp icicle was stabbing through her heart. Who would rape her lovely Laurie? Brenda's Laurie? She wanted to kill him.

'The social worker I had to see from school.'

Anika thought she would collapse with the shock. It hadn't even been some drunken slob but a man Laurie had trusted.

'We have to go to the school and the police,' she said, standing up and grabbing her handbag.

'They won't believe us,' said Laurie miserably. 'He's a well-respected professional man–'

'Not in my eyes,' fumed Anika.

'In everyone else's. I'm known at school for always getting in trouble.'

'That doesn't mean he can rape you. No, I'm going to the school and then the police.'

Laurie jumped up and grabbed Anika's arm. 'No, don't you see, I'll be the slag in everyone's eyes? I'll be the one who drank too much, whose parents were never strict enough, and whose mother had alcoholism. The girl who was always asking for it. He'll win. He'll get the best solicitor, and why would they listen to an Indian woman? You know what they're like, Anika. I could be responsible for other girls not reporting when they've been raped.'

Anika's shoulders sagged. Everything Laurie said was true. Anika knew it wasn't who you were but what you represented, and in most people's eyes, they represented the worst of everything. 'Oh God,' she groaned.

'I'll have an abortion. Then I will try hard and get my GCSEs as Mum wanted.'

'Oh, darling.' Anika hugged her tightly. 'We'll get through this together. It'll be our secret.'

Laurie thought *My life is full of secrets.* But one day, the secrets would be unveiled, and the truth would be revealed. He may have broken her physically, but he hadn't broken her spirit.

CHAPTER THIRTY-EIGHT

PRESENT DAY

Ana quickly realised that the local was not the best place to meet anyone. The villagers greedily drank in the stranger sitting with her, their eyes as round and big as saucers. Ana avoided eye contact. She could have sworn her ears were burning. 'Sorry about all the attention,' she apologised.

Jonny seemed amused. 'I hadn't realised I was with a celebrity.'

'Far from it.'

Ana saw Jack approaching and fought back a sigh. 'What can I get you?' he asked.

'I didn't know you did table service.' Ana smiled.

'Depends how busy we are,' he said, looking at Jonny.

Or *how nosy you are*, thought Ana. 'A bitter lemon, please, and a packet of crisps.' Ana wasn't sure if the landlord had heard her because he was still looking at Jonny.

'Pint of your best.' Jonny smiled.

'Haven't seen you in here before. Friend of Ana's, are you?'

'No, he's a criminal. We're just having a quick drink before I handcuff him and take him to the station.'

Jack took a step back. 'You're sharp, you are. You'll cut yourself one day.'

'A bitter lemon, a packet of crisps and a bit of peace.' She smiled.

Jack laughed. 'She's feisty this one. Don't say I didn't warn you,' he told Jonny.

Ana shook her head despairingly. 'Sorry about that.'

'No problem,' Jonny said, pulling an envelope from his rucksack.

The photos were larger than Ana had expected, and she could barely contain her excitement.

'In this one,' said Jonny, pointing. 'You can clearly see the car. I looked it up in this.' He pushed a book across to her. 'It looks very much like a 1999 Golf. Every car from about 1940 is featured in that book. But the most interesting photo is this one.' He pushed another photo across the table. 'If you look with a magnifying glass, you can just make out something on the passenger seat. It's sketchy. Here.' He handed her a magnifying glass.

'I'll get your drink,' he said, standing up. 'Looks like table service has been cancelled.'

Ana studied the photo but couldn't see anything. Then she looked at it through the magnifying glass. Jonny returned with their drinks. 'I can't see anything,' she said, disappointed.

'On the passenger seat, look closely.'

Ana studied it again and then gasped. 'Oh my God, It's a handbag.'

Jonny nodded, looking chuffed. 'Your driver was a woman.' He pushed another photo across to her. 'This one isn't so good. It's the point of impact, but it's under the street light, and you can see the first letter of the reg at the back, which looks like an S to me, which matches my year of 1999.'

Ana tore open the crisp bag. She'd missed lunch and was

starving. 'This is great,' she said. 'We know we're looking for a Golf 1999, S as the first initial on the reg and a woman driver.'

'Doesn't sound like much,' said Jonny, taking a crisp. 'Not when you say it like that.'

'It's a lot.' Ana smiled. This was what she loved most about police work, the putting together of the jigsaw pieces.

'It might be my imagination, but it seems like you haven't eaten all day.' Jonny smiled.

Ana found him very attractive when he smiled. His face was the kind you wanted to keep looking at. *I guess he must be used to that*, she thought. *Women must give him admiring glances all the time.* 'I skipped lunch,' she said.

'Right,' he said, taking charge and scooping up the photos. 'I'm presuming you don't want to eat here, so let's go to the pub in Longbridge.'

'Bossy, aren't you, but seeing as I'm famished, I'll agree.'

CHAPTER THIRTY-NINE

Skinner was scared, and he didn't mind admitting it. It wasn't what they were going to do that scared him. After all, Needles was right. These people raped their women and took their jobs and houses. It wasn't like they didn't have their own country. They should return there instead of expecting the English to fit in with them and allow them to build mosques everywhere. As Needles had pointed out, that ground could have been used for a church or homes for the homeless.

'We need to take care of our own,' Needles had said. 'They'll never go back if we keep making their lives comfortable. England is for the English.'

Skinner was afraid that The Vigilante geezer would turn up with his machete. He'd heard what had happened in the pub. It seemed this vigilante knew everything.

Skinner was surprised to see Digger waiting at the playing fields with Twitch.

'Thought you weren't coming,' said Skinner.

'Well, I figured if we're going to wear balaclavas, then me dad won't know it were me, will he?'

'What if that vigilante bloke rocks up?' said Skinner, looking around nervously. 'Did you hear about those blokes in the pub?'

Digger shook his head. 'What blokes?'

'Got their fancy cars smashed up. I think it was that vigilante bloke. He was wearing the same combats.'

Digger shrugged. 'He won't come here,' he said confidently.

'I hope not,' said Twitch nervously.

Needles was swaggering towards them, and his face lit up when he saw Digger. 'Hey, mate,' he said, giving him a high five. 'Well done.'

Skinner saw, with horror, that in his other hand was a hatchet. 'You never said anything about getting tooled up,' he said anxiously.

'Don't worry. It's not for them. It's just to smash a few things. Let 'em know we mean business.'

Skinner heard the excitement in Needles' voice and began to doubt whether this was a good idea after all, but didn't know how to get out of it.

Needles pulled balaclavas from his pocket and handed them around.

'Maybe we shouldn't take the hatchet,' stuttered Digger.

Needles' face clouded over. 'Are you in the Vipers or not, or are you just fucking cowards?'

'Aw, come on, Needles, it's just me mum goes in there a lot, and they're always helpful and–'

'Bloody 'ell, what are you now? A fucking Paki lover?' Needles sneered, his eyes flashing.

'Let's go,' he said to Skinner without waiting for Digger to reply. Digger hurried after them.

Imran had never liked the skinhead kid with the tattoos, and his wife, Huma, had wanted him banned from the shop.

'For what?' he'd asked her. 'He's not done anything for us to ban him.'

'You know why. He hates us.'

Imran had shrugged. Many people hated them, but an awful lot of people liked them and were their friends. One lad with a few tattoos and something of an attitude Imran felt he could handle. He didn't want to start banning people because they were racist. That kind of thing just fuelled further racism. They'd run the village shop now for five years, and everyone had always been friendly.

He was refilling the coffee machine when he heard the jingle of the door opening. Imran turned with a smile, expecting one of his Longbridge regulars. Instead, he came face to face with three men in balaclavas. At the sight of the hatchet, a spike of adrenalin shot through him.

'What's going on? What do you want?' he asked, trying to hide his fear but failing miserably. Huma was upstairs with the boys. If he called her, she'd hear the fear in his voice and come down.

'I don't want trouble,' he said. 'Take what you like.'

Needles stepped forward, menacingly brandishing the hatchet. 'Don't worry, mate, we will because this shop should be ours and not stinking of your fucking curries. Get some cans of lager, boys,' he said, turning to Skinner. 'We'll have some crisps as well.'

Needles turned back to Imran, his eyes black with hate. 'That fucking coffee you make is shit.'

He brought the hatchet down with a frightening smash onto the coffee machine, sending glass and paper cups flying through the air. The second smash brought Huma rushing down the stairs from their upstairs flat. At the sight of the balaclavas, she screamed in terror.

'Please, just take what you want and go,' begged Imran.

Huma, in her fear, was struggling to breathe. Seeing her, Digger panicked and edged his way to the door, followed by Twitch. 'Let's go,' he yelled.

Needles turned to Digger and said firmly, 'When I'm ready.'

Tim was heading home after a quick pint at the local. He didn't often stop after work, but it had been hot that day, and as his aunt was with his mum, he thought he'd have a quick one before going home.

As he approached the corner shop, he decided to pop in for his mum's magazine and the local paper. Then, as he drew closer, he heard a crashing sound followed by a woman's scream. He ran to the shop, presuming someone had had an accident, but he stopped abruptly when faced with three masked men. On the floor, in the corner of the shop, he could see Huma was hyperventilating, and Imran was rigid with fear.

'Help us,' cried Huma.

'What the hell are you doing?' Tim yelled.

One of the masked men pushed past him at the door. He called over his shoulder to the man armed with a hatchet, 'We should call an ambulance!'

Tim blocked their way. He saw the eyes of the man with the hatchet looking at him scornfully through the balaclava.

'We'll be back,' he said, lifting the hatchet to smash the fridge door.

Tim grabbed his arm to stop him.

'No,' yelled Imram, attempting to pull Tim back. 'He's not worth it.'

Huma's screams tore through the air.

'Oh God,' groaned the third masked man. 'It wasn't supposed to be like this.'

Tim grabbed the hatchet's blade before it hit the fridge and groaned as it cut into the palm of his hand.

'Let's get out of here,' shouted someone.

'You're all fucking cowards, the lot of you,' said the man with the hatchet. 'I should have done the place over myself. I'd have done a better job. You clowns are just a noose around my neck. You'll be telling them your names next.'

He tugged hard on the hatchet, scraping Tim's hand with the blade, causing Tim to yelp and pull his hand back, giving him time to run from the shop.

Ana heard the shouts first, a fusion of panic and fear that pierced the quiet street.

'Did you hear that?' she asked Jonny, her instincts as a police officer already kicking in.

The screams propelled her towards the shop. As she approached, the sight of Tim's bloodied hand and Huma's slumped form on the floor brought her to a halt. Imran, still reeling from the shock, managed to utter, 'One of them has a hatchet.'

Jonny's distant yet distinct voice reached Ana's ears, urging her to call for back-up. 'Call the station,' she instructed Jonny, her voice steady despite the adrenalin surging through her veins.

She didn't have time to wait for Jonny's response, as the fleeing lads nearly knocked her over in their haste to escape.

'Police, stop!' she shouted, giving chase.

One of the men clutched a plastic bag of cans. The other, menacing and defiant, held the hatchet aloft.

Shit, thought Ana, she didn't even have a taser.

'Get back,' screamed the man with the hatchet.

The standoff between them was tense. Ana took a cautious step forward.

'Don't come any nearer,' warned the man. 'I mean it, I'll do yer, I will.'

'And what good would that do you?' she asked, determined not to show him her fear. 'Doing a police officer carries a long jail term. Is it worth it?'

'Don't be a moron,' cried the other lad. 'Just leg it.'

'He's right,' said Ana. 'Attempted assault on a police officer is no minor crime, sunshine, so why don't you drop that hatchet and do us both a favour? You're in enough trouble already for possessing it and using threatening behaviour.'

'You always take their side,' sneered the masked man.

'Whose side?' asked Ana, taking another step forward.

'Stay back,' he warned. 'I ain't scared of bashing one of you lot.'

'If you're so brave, why are you hiding your face?'

'Because you'll arrest me. But you never arrest them, do yer?'

'Who?' asked Ana, while thinking, *Where's the sodding police? Didn't Jonny call them?*

'The Pakis. It makes me sick.'

'So, you thought you'd smash up their shop with your hatchet and teach them a lesson. Not very bright, are you, sunshine?'

'Stop calling me fucking sunshine.'

'Okay,' said Ana, 'tell us your real name, and I'll use that.'

'That should be our shop,' he said viciously.

'I bet you use it a lot, though, don't you?' said Jonny from behind her. Ana didn't turn around. She wasn't going to take her eyes off the hatchet.

The man with the hatchet stared long and hard at Jonny. 'I won't forget your face,' he said threateningly before turning on his heels and running away.

Ana threw herself at the other man, pulling him down by the legs. He scrambled to free himself, scratching like a mole at the grass of the playing field.

'Keep still, you little sod.' Ana cursed, 'You've already twisted my finger.' Jonny knelt across his legs and pulled his arms behind his back.

'You're under arrest for robbery,' Ana said breathlessly. You do not have to say anything, but it may harm your defence if you do not mention something when questioned that you may later rely on in court. Anything you do say may be given in evidence. Do you understand?'

'I ain't done nothing.'

'Do you understand what I've just said?'

'Yeah, but I ain't done nothing.'

Ana pulled off his balaclava. 'Well, if it isn't "Mr I'm good at everything". Stand up and don't even think of running. I've seen your face, and it won't take long to find you.'

Skinner heard the police siren and sighed heavily. He was in deep shit now with just about everyone. Why couldn't they have nicked Needles?

Beth wasn't happy, and it showed on her face.

'You could have been injured, Seargent Rawlins. I don't know how they do things in Liverpool, but here we wait for back-up.'

'With all due respect, ma'am, I'd have lost them by then.'

A crowd of locals was milling around the shop while a

paramedic checked over Tim and Huma. Imran, sitting beside her, suddenly recognised Skinner and lunged at him.

'I know you. Your parents come in all the time. I've been nothing but kind to you all. Look what you've done to my wife. You're a racist coward.'

Matt gently pulled him away. 'It's okay, sir. We've got him now.'

'It wasn't me,' said Skinner, almost in tears.

Ana watched as he was taken to a police car, aware that Beth's eyes were on her.

'Good work,' she said softly. 'What happened to the one with the hatchet?'

'He got away.'

'Next time, think of your pretty face and wait for back-up.'

Ana nodded. 'Ma'am.'

They both knew she wouldn't.

Beth liked her, and something about Ana reminded her of when she was a young copper, all eager and ready to take on the world. 'Well done,' she said.

'Thank you, ma'am.' Ana smiled.

'Sorry your evening has been spoilt, but we'll need your statements.'

'Of course,' said Ana.

'It will just be a later dinner.' Jonny smiled. 'God, you're bloody stubborn,' he said, relieved to see her safe.

'And you're bloody mad. You're not even trained, you madman.'

He grabbed her hand. 'I'm mad for you,' he said.

CHAPTER FORTY

Skinner cried throughout most of his interview to the point where Matt thought they would run out of tissues. The lad even offered to pay for the beer and crisps. Finally, he was released with a caution. His dad gave him a bashing around the head to knock some sense into him, and then Skinner went to Benson's garage to assure Needles he hadn't mentioned any names.

'Good lad,' said Needles, slapping him on the back, much to Skinner's relief. He'd already decided to tell Needles that he wanted out of the Vipers. He'd get tanked up first and then tell him. Needles was getting out of control, and it frightened Skinner.

He'd just turned the corner into his street when the panda car passed him, and for one awful moment, he thought he might vomit in the road, but the car didn't stop, and he could breathe again.

Matt pulled up outside the garage, and he and Ana got out. 'I don't think the guy you're after would have brought his car here,' said Matt.

'Not for the damage, maybe, but it might have been convenient before the accident to bring it here.'

Needles recognised her immediately and tried not to show it on his face. They weren't here about yesterday. Skinner assured him he hadn't told them his name.

'Your boss in?' asked Matt.

Needles pulled his eyes away from Ana, who was looking around the garage.

'He's out testing a car for its MOT.'

Ana nodded. 'I'm sure you can help. Didn't you have a Golf, reg beginning with an S, come in for repair around April 15th or sometime after that?'

Needles relaxed and pulled a book from a drawer.

'Old school?' said Matt.

'Yeah,' said Needles, flipping through the pages. 'No, nothing around that time,' he said.

'Any other time?' asked Ana.

Needles sighed, licked his thumb and flicked through more pages. 'Only an MOT on a Golf, reg SD51 OMR in December last year.'

Ana felt a tingle of excitement run down her spine and noted down the registration. 'Do you have the invoice for that work?'

'You'd have to ask Margaret for that. She handles the invoices and keeps them on her laptop. She's in on Wednesdays.'

'Thanks,' said Ana.

'They letting you off early for the village do later?' asked Matt.

'Yep, early finish.' Needles smiled.

'Sure is a big thing around here, this fair,' commented Ana.

Needles watched with relief as they walked to the door when Ana suddenly turned and said bluntly, 'Your voice is familiar. Have we met before?'

Needles shook his head.

'Maybe around the village?' Ana smiled.

'Yeah, maybe.'

The door opened, and a man in grubby overalls strolled in. 'Afternoon,' he said, taking in their uniforms. 'Something wrong?'

He glanced over at Needles.

'Richie Benson?' asked Ana.

'Yeah, that's me,' he said gruffly. 'What's the problem?'

'We're enquiring about a Golf, reg beginning with an S,' said Matt. 'Possibly involved in an accident on the 14th of April.'

'Driver most likely a woman,' added Ana, but already she had seen his face blanch. He knew something.

'Would be in the ledger,' he said.

'Okay,' said Ana, smiling. 'So you didn't repair a Golf in April?'

His brown, beady eyes met hers. 'Like I said, it would be in the ledger.'

'Nothing in there,' piped up Needles.

'What about a change of ownership?' persisted Ana. 'You wouldn't keep those in a ledger, would you?'

Benson gave her a dirty look. 'We keep those in the filing cabinet, but everything in there would be logged in the ledger.'

Ana was getting irritated. 'Maybe you wouldn't mind checking the filing cabinet for us?'

Benson looked put out. 'Right,' he said, walking towards the back office. Ana and Matt followed. 'It's all alphabetical. You're welcome to check.'

Ana did precisely that while Benson patiently waited.

'No, nothing.'

'Thanks for your help,' said Matt.'

They returned to the panda and Ana said, 'He knows something, but the question is what?'

Back at the station, she pulled the note she'd made of the registration and phoned DVLA.

'Doughnuts or custard tarts?' Matt asked. 'I'm off to get some.'

'Custard tarts. Lots. I'm on hold, and this crackly repetitive music is driving me to slash my wrists.'

'Hello,' said the DVLA woman. 'I have those details for you. That car was scrapped in June of this year.'

'Who was the owner?' asked Ana.

'Hold on,' said the woman.

Ana was about to turn to Matt when the woman said, 'Miss Beth Harper, address–' Ana didn't hear the rest. Instead, she vaguely heard herself saying yes to a Costa Coffee to Matt and then felt her head swim.

'Bet you'll still steal a doughnut,' Matt was saying.

It didn't mean it was the same car that had hit Vanessa. *Loads of people drive a Golf*, Ana argued with herself. All the same, it was the same year, the same area, and there was this rumour that Beth had been drinking a lot the past few months, supposing, just supposing...

She forced herself not to lift her head and look across at Beth's office. It would explain a lot. The sudden piece of evidence she was sure she hadn't missed that said the Bladon CCTV camera wasn't working that night. What if Beth had removed incriminating evidence and added the evidence that said the Bladon CCTV wasn't working? *Christ*, thought Ana, *am I working for a bent cop?*

She dropped her head into her hands. *Jesus, who could she talk to about this?*

No one.

'You all right, Ana?'

She snapped her head up to see Luke staring at her. 'Yeah, thanks. I had a bit of a dizzy spell. Just popping to the loo.'

Alone in the loo, Ana convinced herself she was barking up the wrong tree. A strong coffee, a doughnut and custard tart, and she'd drop this investigation. She sighed. The thing was, she knew she wouldn't.

CHAPTER FORTY-ONE

The country fair was the highlight of the year. The committee decided to use the playing fields at Stonesend and erected several marquees for beer tasting, selling homegrown vegetables from the local allotment and a much larger marquee for the cèilidh.

Jack hired a burger van and hung bunting outside the pub. It was the best day of the year for him, and the money he made on the fair day was more than he made all year. The smell of candy floss and popcorn filled the air, and folk music from the Morris dancers and loud rock music from the bumper cars pounded through Tom's head.

'Not your thing?' laughed Beth.

Tom's face was horror-stricken. He'd expected it to be a small fete, not a huge fair. A colourful looping roller coaster made him nauseous just looking at it. Balloons of all colours were being carried around by over-tired toddlers. Music seemed to come at him from every corner of the field. Friends were yelling and screaming at each other. It was a tsunami of noise that he felt might overwhelm him. 'Not quite, but maybe it's time for me to let my hair down.' He smiled.

Beth had never really enjoyed the fair herself. It was an open sesame to the local burglars. Most of the village attended, which meant many empty houses. Some she knew never locked their doors, never imagining a burglary might happen to them, even though she warned them every year. Then, of course, there were the drunks who got out of hand as the evening wore on.

The smell of candy floss and fried doughnuts made Tom's mouth water. 'Right, where do we start?' he asked.

'How about a drink? They do a nice lemonade.'

Under the warm embrace of the summer sun, the funfair came alive.

The scent of freshly popped popcorn wafted through the air. 'Fancy some?' asked Matt.

Ana grinned. 'Absolutely! A large bag, please.'

Matt bought the popcorn and they wandered deeper into the fair, the popcorn crunching between their fingers.

'What do you think?' asked Matt.

'Well, I wasn't expecting sheep shearing for a start.' Ana grinned. They passed the bumper cars, and laughed as the cars bounced in to each other. 'Or dodgems.'

Matt reached into the popcorn bag and encouraged Ana to do likewise. She lifted her face up to feel the warmth of the sun, the taste of butter lingering on her lips.

They sat on a hay bale and watched as some kids tried to catch floating ducks in an attempt to win a soft toy.

It was a relief to get her mind onto something else. The loud music and raucous laughter drowned out her thoughts. People were having fun. That's what she should be doing. Maybe Jonny Manners was here. She scanned the crowd but couldn't see him. Their dinner after the shop incident had been really enjoyable. He'd told her about his previous marriage.

'Too young. We drifted apart as often happens.'

She hadn't shared much. He'd tried, but she'd managed to be elusive as usual. He'd said he like to see her again, so she gave him her number.

'Enjoying it?'

Ana looked up to see Beth and DI Miller.

'We're off to the drinks tent.' Beth smiled.

'I thought you were on duty,' Ana said, belatedly realising her tone had been sharp.

Beth looked at her oddly. 'I am. They do soft drinks, too.'

Ana spotted Skinner walking with his mates, holding plastic pint cups of beer in their hands. 'Trouble with a capital T.' She nodded in their direction.

'We'll keep an eye on them,' said Beth. 'See you later.'

Ana decided she'd keep an eye on them, too.

———

Laine studied her reflection in the mirror. The pink chiffon dress hugged her slim waist perfectly, but the hair wasn't right. Maybe she should wear it up in a bun. She'd read somewhere that boys liked to see a girl's neck. It was sexier, the magazine said. After clipping it with a slide, she admired her reflection again. Another dab of blusher, and she was ready.

She removed a brown envelope from the bedside cabinet, took several five-pound notes from it, and slid it back into its hiding place. There would be more to replace that soon enough. One last look in the mirror convinced her that Sajid would change his mind.

———

Sajid had decided not to go to the fair until his mates persuaded him otherwise.

'Sajid, you're letting these racist bastards spoil your life. If it has to be us against them, so be it. There are five of us and four of them,' said Kasem.

'I don't want a race war,' argued Sajid.

'Nor do we, bro,' agreed Khalid, 'but we ain't gonna let them stop us from living. Anyway, they may not even be there.'

Sajid thought that wishful thinking, but he did want to go just to see Laine if nothing else. Everyone in the village was talking about how the local shop had been smashed up, and at first, when Sajid had heard they were wearing balaclavas, he'd wondered if it had been The Vigilante. Then he remembered how kind he'd been to him on the coach.

Now, he felt sure it had been Laine's brother and his cronies. Huma had been severely shaken, Sajid's dad had said.

Maybe the lads were right. They shouldn't give in. Instead, they should show these bullies that they weren't afraid of them.

CHAPTER FORTY-TWO

SEVEN YEARS EARLIER

L aurie entered the clinically white building with Anika's hand clutched tightly in hers. This was their secret. It's not like she would be punished. Some girls at school had said that God punished women if they had abortions, but Laurie didn't believe in God. If there were a god, he wouldn't have taken her mum away, not when she'd needed her the most.

Some days she felt numb with shock; others, she was so emotional she couldn't stop crying. How could he have done this to her? She often wondered if her grief was for her mum, her unborn child, or maybe both.

How could she kill a child, but how could she keep it? While she was killing her baby, other mothers were shopping, buying cots and baby clothes. If only she could ask her mum what to do. Mum would have known, wouldn't she?

Anika guided her to a chair in the warm waiting room. It was quiet and peaceful. It was hard for Laurie to imagine babies being killed here every day. She shuddered.

Anika gripped her hand tightly. 'You okay, Laurie?'

Laurie nodded.

A nurse came out of one of the treatment rooms. *She doesn't look like a murderer*, thought Laurie. The woman's face was gentle, her eyes soft and caring. 'Laurie McDuff,' she said gently.

Laurie stood up and her legs turned rubbery. Anika supported her, and they followed the nurse into the treatment room.

'Everything is going to be fine,' the nurse said reassuringly.

Why did Laurie not believe her?

CHAPTER FORTY-THREE

'Ray in the beer tent?' asked Beth.

'Where else?' Sandy said, her cheeks flushed. 'He's been looking forward to the beer tasting for months.' She drained her plastic cup of wine. 'I'm off to get another. You want one?'

'I'm on duty, remember?'

Sandy grimaced. 'Oh yeah, I forgot, bad luck. I'm going to make the most of not having a toddler to race after. God bless babysitters.'

Beth made a tutting noise.

'Bad mother, not letting your child enjoy the fair,' she teased.

'She'd be whining within thirty minutes, and you know it.'

Beth was only half listening to her and had her eyes on a group of lads at the firing range.

'Trouble?' asked Sandy.

'Ludbrook Grove lot,' said Beth. 'I bet there'll be trouble before the night's out, especially now they've arrived.'

She nodded to the gang of Asian lads that were hovering around the fish and chip van.

'It wouldn't surprise me. After what happened at Imran's shop, there's bound to be a bit of aggro,' Sandy said, eyeing up the lads. 'Don't envy you tonight. That was a bloody disgrace. Poor Imran and his family.'

Jassy and Laine wobbled past them on their high heels, their potent perfume floating on the air.

'To be young again,' said Sandy wistfully. 'I couldn't get into a dress like that now if I tried,' she said, admiring Laine's clothes.

Beth smiled. 'Oh, yes, you could.'

Sandy wobbled towards the drinks tent, swinging her handbag. 'See you later.'

'Yeah. See you later.' *And most likely, you'll be pissed by then*, thought Beth.

Tom returned with two hot dogs. 'Not bad, these,' he said, handing her one, stroking her hand as he did so. Beth shivered. Was that deliberate?

'Need to watch that lot,' she said, nodding at the lads.

Beth looked around, taking everything in. Will Moulson, she noticed, was unsteady on his feet. A plastic cup of beer wobbled in his hand. Leigh looked uncomfortable when she met Beth's eyes, so Beth turned away and looked over to the dodgems, where she saw Ana and Matt. The person she was really looking for was Ben. When they'd been together, they'd gone to the fair every year, but he was nowhere to be seen.

Hale was eyeing up some girl on the carousel. She couldn't have been more than fifteen. *Jesus*, thought Beth, *what's wrong with these men?*

'You're dripping.'

Her head snapped up, and she felt the wetness of the ketchup on her hand.

'Not like you to forget to eat.' Tom grinned.

'Cheeky sod,' she said, taking a large bite.

She was some way off, but Ana knew it was her. Olivia's face and body were etched on her brain like indelible ink. She would know her anywhere.

A man was with her, and they were watching the sheep shearing competition. Ana's heart quickened and her hands shook. She swallowed several times to relieve the dryness of her throat and heard herself say hoarsely, 'Shall we watch the sheep shearing?'

'Sure,' said Matt, but Ana didn't move.

She'd imagined this moment so many times. She had practised what she'd say over and over again, but she hadn't prepared herself for the fear that now gripped her insides and paralysed her legs.

Olivia turned, saw Ana, and waved. At that moment, Ana felt the bile rush up into her oesophagus and she struggled to keep it down. She waved back and then grabbed Matt's hand, aware that her own was rather sweaty. She kept her face averted from the man, who was still intently watching the shearing.

'Hi,' said Olivia. 'It's good fun, isn't it?' She waved a hand to take in the fair.

Ana turned her attention to the back of the man standing next to Olivia.

'This is Matt, my work colleague,' said Ana. Ana realised her mistake immediately by the hurt look on Matt's face. Shit, she should have said friend, not work colleague.

'Oh, I'm sorry,' said Olivia. 'This is Ana,' she said to the man beside her. 'She lives opposite me. I told you about her. Ana, this is my boyfriend...'

Olivia's voice became fainter, and it seemed to Ana that she was falling into an abyss. She felt her legs give way and she grabbed Matt's arm.

He looked at her oddly. 'You okay?' he said softly.

The man turned around and held out his hand to Ana.

———

Laine flirted with almost every boy she bumped into at the fair, knowing Sajid was watching her the whole time. She laughed loudly at a dirty joke one of the boys told her.

'It's not even funny,' said Jassy, unimpressed. 'Why are you winding Sajid up like this? It's not nice.'

'He could at least say hello,' moaned Laine.

'So could you,' argued Jassy.

'I'm not going to be the first to speak.'

Laine's expression suddenly changed as though an invisible cloth had wiped it away, turning her rose-pink cheeks to porcelain white. Jassy followed her gaze to the beer tent where several men were swaggering about laughing.

'Laine?' said Jassy, but Laine seemed not to hear her. 'Laine, what is it?'

Laine seemed to snap out of her reverie and smiled. 'Nothing. Come on. I'm going to see Sajid.'

Jassy followed with a sinking feeling in her stomach. Laine had already had two drinks. God knows how she got them. It seemed to Jassy that Laine could get anything she wanted. It still worried her where Laine got all that money. From the corner of her eye, she could see Needles and his mates watching them.

'Shit, Laine, wait.'

But Laine wasn't listening, and Jassy reached her too late. Laine already had her arm around Sajid's waist.

'Shit,' Jassy muttered again. 'This is going to be bad.'

CHAPTER FORTY-FOUR

Amidst the whirl of merry-go-rounds and the tantalising aroma of cotton candy, there lies a corner that beckons both the seasoned marksmen and the curious novices – the rifle range. Here, the air crackles with anticipation, and the rhythmic pop of air rifles punctuates the air. It was the one stall Needles loved, but he was sidetracked by Skinner.

Skinner was getting too drunk for Needles' liking. Drunk people inevitably ended up saying things they shouldn't, and the last thing Needles wanted was Skinner mouthing off to everyone about the shop they'd done over. So far, he'd kept his mouth shut. Needles figured if Skinner were going to grass him up to the cops, he would have done it by now, but after a few drinks, people's tongues loosened, and there were enough coppers on and off duty to hear him.

So he shoved a bag of chips into Skinner's hand. 'Eat something,' he ordered.

Skinner looked down at the greasy chips and grimaced. 'Needles, listen, could we have a quiet chat?' he said uneasily.

'A quiet chat?' Needles laughed. 'Where the fuck do you expect to have a quiet chat here?'

Skinner shrugged. 'I don't know, maybe near the woods.'

Needles barely heard him for he realised that DI Miller was right at his side at the rifle range. Needles stared at him with a mixture of curiosity and admiration. So, this was the guy who'd mixed with real East End gangsters. He'd looked him up after that murder case in Stonesend. He'd put an actual brutal gangster away. He had some guts, and Needles had to credit him for that.

'I think you have an unfair advantage,' said the guy, handing him the rifle.

'Beth wants a teddy bear.' Miller laughed.

Needles watched in awe as Miller took a steady stance, rested the rifle easily on his shoulder, gently placed his finger on the trigger, and, with a sharp aim, managed to hit every target. Needles whistled in admiration and felt an overwhelming urge to congratulate Miller when Digger nudged him in the ribs and said, 'Look! What the hell is Laine up to?'

Needles turned to see his sister laughing with the group of Asians he'd seen earlier. What was the little bitch playing at, mixing with Pakis and Asians? Embarrassing him in front of his mates, too.

'Right, I think it's time they moved back to their own patch. Come on, lads.'

'I don't know,' said Skinner. 'Best if we leave them. It will only mean more trouble.'

'Don't be a fucking gutless wonder,' snapped Needles.

Digger, fuelled by drink, followed eagerly with Twitch at his side, while Skinner followed reluctantly. Skinner heard Needles say in a menacing voice, 'Get your filthy Paki hands off my sister or...'

'Or what?' said Khalid, stepping in front of him. 'You gonna beat us up?'

'Yeah,' said Digger.

'I remember you,' said Needles to Sajid. 'You were the Paki on the coach the other day. I just told you to take your filthy Paki hands off my sister.' He shoved Sajid hard in the chest.

'Laine,' said Jassy, her voice trembling. 'Let's go.'

Sajid's body tensed. His warm eyes were suddenly hard and cold. He was angry with Laine for being provocative, furious because he had to struggle all the time because of his colour, angry that he couldn't have the girlfriend he wanted and angry with Needles for his ignorance. His nails bit into his palms.

He was furious with the whole fucking world, and at that moment, all his hatred was directed at Needles, and before anyone could stop him, he was pounding his fists and kicking his feet at any part of Needles he could reach.

Needles, taken by surprise, yelped in pain and fell to the ground, covering his head with his arms. Digger let out a primal scream and jumped on Sajid's back, knocking the breath out of him.

Then all hell broke loose. Skinner was winded when Laine punched him in the stomach. Sajid could hear her screaming obscenities. Khalid had dragged Digger off Sajid and brutally punched him in the jaw. Before Digger could retaliate, Kalid hit him again.

'Here we go,' said Beth in a resigned tone. 'Sooner than I thought.'

Through blurry eyes, Sajid saw Needles being dragged away by DS Harper.

'You all right, mate?' said a voice. 'You look a bit winded.'

Sajid nodded. Through the haze, he could see a crowd had gathered, and the police were moving people on.

'What's going on?' said Ray.

'The usual fair punch-up,' said Sandy, her voice slurred.

'You're a twisted racist bastard, Colin,' screamed Laine.

The paramedic had somehow got Skinner up, and he

realised he was sitting on a hay bale. The Asians, bleeding and bruised, were on the other side, also being seen by paramedics.

Needles gave Laine the finger. Laine returned it and walked off with Jassy, who was shaking so much she couldn't walk straight.

Sajid was dizzy; all he could see were black spots in front of his eyes, but he knew he'd beaten the shit out of Needles, and it was the best feeling in the world.

After the police searched them, Tom stood before them and said firmly, 'Right, you lot. We're giving you two choices. One, you leave the fair right now, or two, you stay away from each other. I'm putting this down to too much drink and excitement, but I'll arrest all of you next time. Make your choice.'

Sajid got up. 'Come on,' he said to his mates. 'Let's enjoy the fair.'

They nodded in agreement and followed him, dabbing at their wounds.

'Wanker,' Needles said.

'We'll be watching you,' said Beth.

'Good luck with that,' said Ray.

Sajid was shaking but feeling more confident. His sides hurt, but he imagined Needles hurt even more, and that made the pain easier to bear. Laine had been right. They shouldn't be ashamed of their relationship or let anyone bully them into splitting up. He looked around the crowded field, but spotting her amongst the crowd was impossible.

He fumbled in his pocket for his phone to call her, but it wasn't there. He must have dropped it during the scuffle. He searched everywhere he thought it might have fallen, but it was nowhere.

'It's gone, mate,' said Khalid. 'Anyone could have it by now.'

Sajid punched the air in anger. There was so much he needed to tell Laine.

The man next to Olivia turned. Ana had been holding her breath, and there was an uncomfortable tightening in her chest. Now that the moment she had been waiting for had arrived, she didn't want him to turn around. Instead, she wanted to run and keep on running. But there was no time for her to run. Ana's eyes focused on his hand. The smell of his aftershave made her want to vomit.

'Hi, Ana, nice to meet you,' he said, his hand closing over hers.

She held her breath in anticipation, then forced her eyes from his hand to his face and gasped.

It wasn't him.

But that couldn't be right. It didn't make sense. He'd gone to Oxford, they'd said. A new job. A promotion. A private detective said he was married with two kids and lived in Banbury.

'He's got a fancy piece. Lives in a nice apartment. Olivia Whitman.'

It didn't make sense. He had the correct name, so why wasn't it him?

'You okay, Ana?' asked Matt.

Ana struggled to control her emotions. 'Nice to meet you,' she said, but it didn't sound like her voice. It was fake and empty of feeling. *Why the fuck aren't you him?* her head was yelling. *You're supposed to be him. You've got his fucking name, and you even fucking smell like him.* But, of course, if she'd used a bit of common sense, it would have been obvious that loads of men probably wore the same scent.

'You're a police officer,' he said. 'You must have your hands full tonight.'

I should fucking arrest you for nearly giving me a heart attack, thought Ana.

'We're not on duty,' said Matt, looking at Ana, who was staring at the other guy like he was an alien.

'Olivia said you work odd hours too,' said Ana.

He smiled. He didn't look at all like him, not in the fucking least. Ana's anger was overwhelming her. If this wasn't him, then where the fuck was he? How much fucking time had she wasted?

'I'm a surgeon at the JR hospital.'

'Have you always lived in Oxford?'

'Twenty questions or what?' Matt laughed. 'Once a police officer, always...'

Ana glared at him.

'Yes,' he said, looking confused.

Ana forced a smile. So, she'd been chasing a dead end all along. She'd got the right person, except it wasn't the man she wanted. So how the hell was she supposed to find the fucker now?

'Hello.'

Ana turned to see Tim with Vanessa and forced a smile. 'Oh, hi. Are you enjoying the fair?' she asked.

'We'll only be staying a little longer.' Tim smiled. 'It's a bit noisy for Mum. Thanks, by the way, for looking into the accident.'

Ana felt embarrassed. What if she didn't find anything? 'Well, don't raise your hopes too much,' she said.

'At least you're trying,' he said.

'How's the hand?' Ana asked, noticing the bandage.

'It's getting better. Right, Mum wants some chips to take home. Enjoy yourselves.'

Tim wheeled Vanessa across the field towards the chip van.

The place was swarming with people now, and Ana found herself jostled into the highly fragranced body of a woman.

'Oops, sorry,' said the woman, trying not to slur her words.

'You okay, Lisa?' asked Matt.

Ana cringed at how provocative the woman suddenly became, fluttering her eyelashes and stepping closer to Matt, asking, 'You haven't seen my useless other half, darling?'

'Luke? No. Have you checked the beer tent?'

So, this is Luke Carpenter's wife, thought Ana. *Not quite what I'd expected.*

Lisa wagged her finger in Matt's face. 'No, but I will.' She glanced at Ana and then, sliding her arm into Matt's, said, 'Fancy buying me a drink, darling?'

Matt smiled politely. 'I'm sure Luke will buy you one when you find him.'

'Huh, that tight old tosser,' she said caustically, throwing her handbag over her shoulder. They watched as she strolled off in her short dress, swinging her hips provocatively.

'She looks a right tart,' said Ana, without thinking.

'Don't let Luke hear you say that.' Matt laughed.

CHAPTER FORTY-FIVE

The sun was slowly setting, casting long shadows through the trees in the wood beyond.

The cèilidh was in full swing now, and those who weren't dancing were laughing at those who were.

Beth looked around the tent and then wandered outside where Tom was. 'Not dancing?' she asked, with a smile.

'God, no. Anyway, I'm on duty.'

'Any excuse.' Beth laughed.

It was that time of evening when everyone had consumed too much alcohol. So Tom kept his eye on the rival gangs that seemed to be behaving well so far, but he knew never to be complacent.

An arm suddenly draped itself around Beth's shoulders, startling her.

'All right, my lovely,' said Lisa Carpenter. 'Have you seen my "pain in the arse" other half by any chance?' She asked drunkenly, wine slopping from the glass in her hand onto Beth's shoe. 'Is he on duty?'

'No, I haven't, Lisa. Is he in the cèilidh tent?'

Lisa roared with laughter. 'Have you seen him dance? Trust

me, it's no treat, I'll tell you that.' Lisa's hair was a tangled mess, where strands had escaped her bun. Then, through lipstick-smudged lips, she muttered something about finding 'The Loser' and wandered off. Beth watched her bump into Will Moulson, who stumbled, spilling beer over Ray's white shirt.

'Hey, watch it, you stupid fool,' snarled Will, tumbling to the ground.

'That'll teach me to wear a white shirt,' said Ray, trying to laugh it off.

'You all right, sir?' said Tom, helping Will up from the ground.

Will groaned and clutched at his groin. 'I need a pee. Have you seen the queue for those portable things? Quicker to go home.'

'Mind how you go,' said Beth insincerely.

He spat on the ground near her feet.

'Mind the road,' she said.

'Well, I was going to check on the babysitter,' said Sandy. 'But I think you'd better go now, Ray, and you can get changed out of that shirt while you're there.'

'Ray, keep an eye on Moulson, will you? I don't want him falling over,' said Beth.

Ray smiled. 'Sure. I'll walk with him.'

'Anyway, why don't you just phone the sitter?' asked Beth.

'Because I want to be sure she's not snogging her fella rather than looking after my child,' said Sandy.

'That's unlikely,' said Ray.

'All the same, I don't want them in my bed...'

'Right,' said Beth, not wanting to hear anymore.

'I don't think that's happening,' said Ray.

'Don't you remember being young,' said Sandy.

'No comment.' Ray grinned.

Sandy smiled and went back into the cèilidh tent.

'See you later,' said Ray, hurrying to catch up with Will.

'Just think, we could have been somewhere nice and quiet, having a lovely hot mug of chocolate,' sighed Beth.

'Well, how about later at my place?' suggested Tom.

Beth inhaled. She hadn't been expecting that. She shrugged. After all, she didn't want to seem too keen. 'All right,' she said, just before Lisa turned up again and vomited at Tom's feet.

'Can't find the bugger,' she said.

'Maybe he's gone home for a pee,' said Beth. All this talk of peeing was making her feel pretty desperate herself. 'Just...' she said, pointing to the Portaloo.

'If you see Luke, remind him he's got a wife,' called Lisa.

Will wasn't wrong about the queue.

'Might be quicker to go home,' said the young woman in front of her. 'I've been here for what seems like half my life.'

'Yeah, except I'm on duty.'

'Great do, isn't it? I'm Caroline. My husband Hale and I moved to Longbridge last year.'

'Is he here tonight?' Beth asked as they moved forward.

'I'm not sure where he is,' she said, looking around. 'He had to find somewhere quiet to take a work call. It never stops. Gets me down a bit. Still...'

'I know the feeling.' Beth checked the time on her phone. It was only 7.30pm, three and a half hours before she could get off.

CHAPTER FORTY-SIX

The sky had turned a beautiful scarlet red, and Frankie admired it appreciatively before throwing up onto the dry earth behind a tree.

The music from the fair faintly reached her ears. She wiped her lips with a tissue and, confident that no one else was in the woods, she pulled down her knickers and peed on the dry grass.

Frankie liked the fair. It allowed her to pick up new clients and have fun at the same time. Pulling her dress back down, she turned to go back when she heard raised voices. Peering around the tree, she saw a girl gesticulating angrily.

In front of her was a man, but Frankie couldn't see him properly. He had on a baseball cap and what looked like combats. The girl held her hand out like she was expecting the man to give her something.

Frankie knew she should creep away, but supposing they heard her? The man turned, and Frankie stepped quickly behind the tree. Had he seen her?

Laine was halfway into the woods when Jassy gave up.

'I just want to be alone,' Laine had shouted.

Laine had hoped Sajid would at least talk to her after the fight, but he hadn't. He'd just ignored her as if she didn't exist.

'Maybe he's waiting for things to calm down,' Jassy reassured her. But as the evening wore on, Laine drank more and became tipsy and unreasonable.

When the text came through, Laine ignored it at first. She didn't want to bother with her phone. Instead, she wanted to be somewhere quiet where she could think, and the woods were always the best place. They backed onto the playing fields so she could still hear the raucous laughter from the fair, but at the same time, she could sit and watch the sunset while she decided what to do. *Perhaps me and Sajid could run away together. If I got enough money...* But Sajid wouldn't do that. She knew how crucial his studies were to him.

She clicked on the message. It was from Sajid.

Meet me by The Oak in 15 minutes. I love you.

Her heart leapt. The oak tree wasn't far from where she was, and she hurried to it. Everyone knew it as 'The Oak' because it was one of the largest trees in the centre of the woods. Was Sajid going to make up with her? *Oh please, God, let him make it up.*

She arrived at the tree and looked around for Sajid, but there was no sign of him. 'Sajid,' she called softly.

A crackle of a branch caused her to turn. 'Oh,' she said. 'What are you doing here?'

Frankie didn't know what to do. She didn't want any trouble. If only she could return to the fair and have fun, but she was too scared to move. If only she'd stayed in that fucking Portaloo queue. The man was yelling angrily now and waving his fists at the girl, who stepped backwards. Frankie could see the fear on her face and hear her shouting, but she couldn't make out what she was saying.

He was grabbing at her handbag. Then the girl started running towards where Frankie was hiding. She could hear footsteps thudding hard on the ground as the man chased her. Frankie's heart was banging in unison. If only her stupid legs would move.

Then she saw the man's face. He was wearing a balaclava, which meant only one thing. It was The Vigilante, and he would have a machete. Everyone knew the stories about him.

To her horror, the girl slipped and fell. The man was on her immediately. Frankie bit back a scream.

———

Jassy felt like breaking down in tears. Already, she could feel them welling up behind her eyelids. Why did Laine have to be so stubborn? Where the hell was she? It was not the time to run off into the woods alone. If only it weren't so dark. Then she saw Sajid and let out a massive sigh of relief.

'Sajid,' she called. 'Have you seen Laine?'

He shook his head. Jassy gasped at his swollen eye and cut forehead.

'She ran into the woods. She said she wanted to be alone. But that was ages ago, and I'm too scared to go into the woods now it's getting dark,' she said tearfully. 'I've texted her, but she's not answering.'

'I'll find her,' he said.

Jassy nodded, reassured. 'She's probably gone to The Old Oak. That's where she usually goes when she's upset.'

Sajid nodded and made for the woods.

She took a deep breath and then saw Needles approaching her, and her body froze. 'Where's Laine? Ain't see her in ages?' he asked.

'I haven't either,' she said, but her eyes betrayed her and he followed her gaze to where Sajid was entering the woods.

'Fucking Paki,' he growled.

'No, wait,' said Jassy, panicking. 'You don't understand.'

But he was already running into the woods.

Frankie couldn't move. She tried, but her body wouldn't let her. It was paralysed with fear. Her mind pleaded with her to scream, but no matter how hard she tried, her paralysed vocal cords prevented her. She ought to run and get someone, but she wouldn't stand a chance if he heard her.

Then he was up, looking around. *Please don't come this way.*

As if answering her plea, he turned and ran into the woods.

Frankie stayed in the same position for nearly three minutes before she felt safe enough to move, and then she ran faster than she'd ever run in her life, tripping over stray twigs and stones. Twice she stumbled and fell and had to drag her trembling body upright. Finally, she heard the sound of voices close by and began to weep.

Sajid had almost reached the Old Oak when he saw something lying on the ground. The shadows cast by the moon created a sharp, stark contrast against the surrounding area on the blood that flowed from Laine's head. Dazed, he stared at the body, afraid to move nearer. He stiffened with shock, and his skin tingled with fear as he moved closer. It couldn't be Laine. Then he recognised Laine's dress.

He shook his head.

'No, no,' he said, shuffling back in shock.

Finally, he moved forward towards her and fell to his knees. 'Laine,' he sobbed, shaking her. 'Laine, wake up.'

It was as though someone had just plunged a knife through his heart. He clutched his chest, struggled to take a deep breath, and then howled like a wild animal.

'Help me!'

Needles, who'd charged after him, recognised Laine's dress and screamed. 'Laine? Oh Jesus, what have you done to her?'

'I–' began Sajid, but he never got to finish.

Sajid could never recall how long the beating lasted, but it seemed an eternity. He felt the heavy punches to his face, but they didn't matter. Part of him was numb from finding Laine's body. The heavy boots pounded into his ribs, followed by a hammer of abuse. Needles had become a lightning bolt of anger.

Only the final kick Sajid remembered because someone arrived then and pulled Needles, still spewing vitriol, off him.

CHAPTER FORTY-SEVEN

Frankie screamed as she approached the edge of the woods, her legs bleeding from where she'd tripped.

Jack, the landlord, who was enjoying a quick fag, quickly dropped it and ran to Frankie. 'Are you all right?' he asked, knowing it was a stupid question as anyone could see she was far from all right.

'The vigilante,' she said, vomiting and just missing his shoes. 'He's done something to a girl in the woods.'

'What?' he asked, stunned. 'What girl?'

'Are you fucking deaf,' she screamed, dragging a hand across her face to wipe away her tears. 'Help her,' she said, grabbing his hand and pulling him to where Laine was. 'It was The Vigilante. I saw him.'

Much to the man's relief, he saw Matt and the new DC running towards them.

'Help her,' Frankie begged hysterically, tears running down her face.

'What's happened?' asked Matt, pulling out his mobile.

'The Vigilante, he's attacked a girl in the woods.'

'Show me,' said Ana calmly.

'No, wait,' said Matt.

But Frankie had grabbed her arm and pulled her into the woods to the Old Oak tree where Sajid was lying beside Laine, and several men were holding back Needles.

Ana stopped abruptly.

'We heard the shouts,' said one of the men holding Needles. 'He was beating the other lad like a madman.'

'You've got to help her,' Needles cried. 'She's bleeding from her head. It's my sister. It was him,' he said, pointing at Sajid. 'He tried to kill her. You need to get her an ambulance.'

'Let him go,' said Ana. 'I think he's got it out of his system.'

'It wasn't him,' said Frankie, pointing to Sajid while trying to avoid looking at Laine's still body. 'It was The Vigilante. I saw him arguing with her.'

Ana knelt by Laine's body and felt the warmth of her blood seep through her dress and onto her skin. Even in the darkness, the gushing blood from her head glinted under the moonlight. Watching Laine ebb away, her eyes growing steadily dull, Ana felt like her guts were being torn out.

'Jesus,' she groaned, feeling the prickle of tears behind her lashes. She bit hard on her lip until she tasted blood. *Keep it together*, she reprimanded herself.

Matt arrived, panting at her side.

'She's still breathing,' she said, feeling Laine's weak pulse.

Needles fell to his knees beside his sister. 'Please save her, please.'

'Stay with me, darling,' Ana pleaded. 'We need an air ambulance,' said Ana, nodding towards Sajid. 'He's also in a bad way.'

'Air ambulance needed at Longbridge playing fields, Oxfordshire. Two seriously injured,' Matt said into his mobile.

Ana turned to Sajid, who was breathing heavily. 'What's her name?'

'Laine. Elaine Lees.'

Ana leaned close to Laine's ear. 'Laine, can you hear me? My name is Ana Rawlins. I'm a police officer.'

Laine moaned softly. 'We're getting you to the hospital, okay?' She grasped Laine's cold hand. 'I'm going to stay with you. You're going to be okay. Try and stay awake.'

'Is she alive?' asked Frankie.

'Yes,' said Anna. 'Get DC Harper and DI Miller,' she said, turning to Matt. 'We need to cordon off the whole area. We need to preserve evidence. Don't let anyone near.'

She turned to the crowd that had now gathered. 'Unless you witnessed the incident, then, with all due respect, I need you all to bugger off. This is a crime scene now.'

Matt was staring down at Laine's battered head. He could feel nausea rising within him. Sajid beside him was crying uncontrollably.

'What happened?' asked Ana.

'I don't know. I found her like this.'

'What's your name, lad?'

'Sajid. She's my girlfriend, and that's her brother. He just beat me up. I think my ribs are cracked.'

'You've killed her,' screamed Needles.

'Matt, get Beth and Tom Miller,' she said again, this time more sternly.

Matt shook himself as though coming out of a nightmare, but Beth and Tom were already hurrying towards them.

'What the hell's happened?' asked Tom.

'Sajid here found the body. Her name is Elaine Lees, and that's her brother,' Ana said, nodding towards Needles. 'There's a phone and handbag here, but I haven't got gloves. There's also a card.'

Tom pulled on rubber gloves and carefully placed everything into bags.

'He did it,' Needles screamed, tears running down his face. 'That Paki killed my sister.'

'Air ambulance on the way,' said Matt.

Beth radioed control to send forensics, and then she and Tom sealed off the area.

'I wonder if Jack is right about you,' she murmured to Tom. 'Every time you come here, someone gets hurt.'

CHAPTER FORTY-EIGHT

The village fair ended abruptly, with police telling everyone to leave. Some left peacefully, while others demanded to know what was going on.

Jassy begged a policeman to tell her what was happening. 'Only my friend has gone off,' she said. 'She hasn't returned yet, and I'm really worried.'

Then she saw Needles being escorted to a police car and hurried over to him. 'Where's Laine?' she asked.

Needles turned his red, tear-stained face towards her. 'I think the Paki bastard killed her.'

Jassy gasped. 'What? What do you mean?' Hysteria was building up inside her.

The sudden roar of the air ambulance deafened them. Its bright lights lit up the field, reminding her of a concert she and Laine had gone to, where the whole arena had lit up in the same way. But this wasn't a concert. It was an ambulance for Laine. Jassy shielded her eyes.

The police were hurrying everyone out of the area. Jassy slid to the ground crying hysterically, and Beth rushed to help her.

'It's okay. No need to be frightened. We're just getting everyone out so the ambulance can land.'

'No, you don't understand,' sobbed Jassy, shaking her head. 'Laine is my best friend. Is she dead?'

'She's being flown to the hospital now. As far as I know, she was still breathing. Let me have your number and I can phone you later when I know more.'

Jassy wiped her eyes with the tissue Beth handed her and wrote her name and number on Beth's pad.

'Needles said Sajid did it, but he wouldn't hurt Laine,' she sobbed.

'Needles?' questioned Beth.

'Laine's brother, Colin,' Jassy explained. 'That's what everyone calls him.'

The helicopter's lights illuminated the field, and Beth saw what a mess the place was: empty crisp bags, crushed beer cans, empty plastic mugs, and cigarette butts littered the area. It seemed like forever before the ambulance took off, and all Jassy could think was, would it take longer if Laine were dead and then she sobbed more. Beth and Jassy covered their ears as the helicopter took off. People were hurrying from the field, their faces white with shock and disbelief. Beth called over a constable to take Jassy home.

'Who is it?' she heard someone ask. 'What's happened?'

Beth turned to see Sandy.

'A young girl. Elaine Lees. Does the name ring any bells?'

Sandy shook her head. 'What's happened to her?'

'She's been attacked. Someone said it was The Vigilante.'

'Oh my God,' she whispered. 'Is she badly hurt?'

Beth nodded. Sandy then saw Ray and ran into his arms.

'Hey,' he said, alarmed. 'What the hell is going on? I almost couldn't get back in. Has someone had a heart attack?'

'A girl was attacked in the woods, apparently.'

Lisa stumbled towards them and collided with Sandy. Ray just managed to stop Sandy from falling. 'Hey, careful,' he said.

'You seen my waste of space husband?' she slurred.

'He's probably left,' said Beth. 'You should too.'

'Waste of space,' she muttered and wandered to the exit.

'We should get home,' Sandy said and then burst into tears. 'This is all so horrible,' she cried. 'People being hurt and shops vandalised. I don't...'

'I think you've drunk too much and are a bit over emotional,' Beth said, hugging her.

'You'll be pleased to know the babysitter wasn't having sex in our bed,' Ray said, trying to make her smile.

'Oh Ray,' she said and cried even more.

'Where was she attacked?' asked Ray. 'It wasn't one of those lads causing trouble earlier, was it?'

'I don't know,' said Beth.

Sandy sniffed and let Ray take her hand.

'Let us know when you hear more?' he asked.

'Of course,' Beth said.

Who is this fucking vigilante? thought Beth. *And why would he want to kill a young kid like Laine?* The card had read, 'The police should deal with blackmailers. When the law fails to serve us, we must serve as the law. Vigilante.'

Had Laine been blackmailing someone? And if so, who and why?

The doctors were waiting at the helipad, and Ana watched as they lifted Laine carefully from the air ambulance before rushing her into the operating theatre.

'I'll need her clothing for evidence,' said Ana.

'Of course. We'll remove them as carefully as we can, but

we may have to cut some of the garments. My job is to save her life.'

'My job is to catch the person who has done this to her. You wouldn't be trying to save her life if he hadn't tried to take it. Her clothes will help find her attacker,' Ana said.

He nodded. 'You've made your point, and we'll be as careful as we can not to contaminate. We've handled cases like this before, but please remember our objective is to save lives, and whatever we have to do to do that, we will.'

You'd think I was the enemy, Ana thought, taking a seat in the waiting area. Sajid waited silently with her until a nurse called him in.

Ana found the loo and locked herself in a cubicle. She sat on the toilet seat for a few seconds with her head in her hands until, finally, the tears came. Tears because it hadn't been him and she didn't know the first thing to do to find him, then tears for Laine, a young girl she didn't even know, but who was only a few years younger than her, now lying on an operating table with half her brains hanging out.

'Jesus,' she muttered, looking down at the blood on her dress. Using cold water from the tap she did her best to remove some of it.

Almost an hour passed before a man dressed in scrubs came to the waiting room. 'DC Rawlins?' he asked.

'Yes,' she stood up.

'Dr Marcus,' he said, shaking her hand.

'Is she going to be all right?' Ana asked hesitantly. *Please don't say she's dead. Please don't.*

He glanced at the blood on her dress but didn't say anything. 'We're operating on her now. The head injury isn't as serious as we initially thought, but she's having trouble breathing. We have her on a ventilator, and we've taken some blood to see if she took anything at the fair that could be causing the breathing problem. The good thing is that she's alive, but it's not looking great.'

The doctor continued, 'The lad Sajid took quite a beating. He's suffered several broken ribs and we'll need to keep him in for a CAT scan to ensure there are no internal injuries. So are you contacting the next of kin?'

Before Ana could answer, a couple walked into the room. The woman stared at Ana's dress, and sobs tore from her body. *Shit*, thought Ana, *I should have phoned for a change of clothes.*

'They said a copper who came with our Elaine was in here,' said the man. His face was mostly obscured by a scraggly red beard that clung to his skin like winter-ravaged ivy tendrils. His nose was unusually crooked, and Ana wondered if a fight had damaged it. He seemed the type that wouldn't take any nonsense. His eyes were a sparkling brown speckled with green, and he was looking directly into hers. His strong arms seemed to hold up the woman by his side, and Ana imagined she would crumple to the floor if he released her.

'That's me,' said Ana. 'DC Ana Rawlins.'

'Where's my daughter?' he asked bluntly.

Not one to mince words, thought Ana. She beckoned for them to sit down. 'The doctor can tell you more about her injuries.'

Her mind drifted as the doctor began to talk. Why would someone want to kill a young girl? Vigilantes don't go around killing people. A vigilante was supposed to keep crime off the street, not be the cause of it. Something didn't add up. Her attention was sharply drawn back to Mr Lees.

'What actually happened?' he asked.

'We're not sure. Her body–'

Mrs Lees sobbed at the word body, and Ana bit her lip before continuing.

'...was found in the woods by her boyfriend–'

'She doesn't have a boyfriend,' interrupted her mother.

'He said he was her boyfriend. Your son beat him up quite badly. The doctors are treating him as we speak. Your son is in custody.'

'I know,' said Mr Lees. 'The little bastard beat up a Paki, didn't he? We never brought him up to be racist. I want to make that very clear.'

Except you just called the lad Paki yourself, thought Ana. 'No one is calling your family racist,' she said. 'We believe that someone who calls himself The Vigilante attacked your daughter.'

'But why?' sobbed Mrs Lees.

Ana knew her blood-stained dress was a problem for Mrs Lees and didn't want to prolong her agony. 'Was your daughter involved with anyone else besides the lad who claims to be her boyfriend?'

Mr Lees stepped closer to Ana. Ana determined not to be intimidated, didn't move. 'She was no slag,' he retorted. 'And she didn't have a Pakistani boyfriend.'

Ana turned to the door. 'Thanks for answering my questions.'

'You'll find him, right? This bastard,' said Mr Lees sternly.

'If it's the last thing we do,' she reassured him.

Sajid was arguing with the nurse when Ana entered the ward. The surgical smell of hospitals had always had a bad effect on her, and today was no different. The sooner she was out of there, the better. The nurse took in Ana's blood-stained dress and hurried over.

'I'm okay,' Ana quickly assured her. 'I'm the police officer that came in with the air ambulance. I need to ask your patient a few questions.' She fumbled for her ID and remembered she didn't have it on her.

'Not too long,' said the nurse. 'We've given him a mild sedative.'

Sajid looked at Ana pleadingly. 'I need to see Laine,' he said, his voice breaking. 'They won't let me. Is she going to be all right?'

Ana pulled a chair next to the bed. She felt emotionally drained. 'I don't know,' she said honestly. 'She's in theatre, so you can't see her.'

He looked crestfallen, and Ana gently reached out a hand and laid it on his arm. 'Anything you can tell us, Sajid, will help us catch who did this.'

He wiped his nose with a tatty tissue. 'We'd argued.' He sniffed. 'A few days ago. It was about her brother. He's a racist. He intimidated me and others on a coach back from a football match–'

'Hang on. Did The Vigilante stop him?' she interrupted.

Sajid nodded. 'Anyway, they started on us at the fair, and we had this fight. I was going to text Laine, but I must have dropped my phone during the fight and I couldn't find it. Jassy said Laine was upset and had gone into the woods, and as she liked it by the Old Oak, I went there to look for her and...'

He burst into tears and Ana looked around the bedside cabinet for tissues. 'Here,' she said, handing him one.

'She was just lying there. I thought she'd fallen, and then I heard that girl say The Vigilante did it.'

Ana chose her words carefully. 'Had she been spending more money recently?'

He shook his head. 'I don't think so. Why, what's that got to do with it?'

The nurse approached and said softly, 'His parents are here.'

'Okay,' said Ana, standing up. 'Someone will be back tomorrow to take your official statement.'

Sajid's parents were younger than Ana had anticipated.

'Thank you for coming here with him,' said the woman, holding out her hand.

Ana took it. It was warm in hers, and a strong memory assailed her and she wobbled slightly on her feet. 'Just doing my job,' she said.

'The police have filled us in,' said the father, walking towards his son. Ana only had eyes for the mother and realised her hand was still in hers. She pulled it away, said goodbye.

Then she walked briskly from the ward until she came to reception. 'Can I order a cab?' she asked. The sooner she was home, the better.

CHAPTER FORTY-NINE

Frankie refused to speak to anyone other than Ana.

'I trust her,' she said. 'She's more like us, she is. I know your lot, you'll twist everything so it looks like I'm involved, and I'm fucking scared. What if he saw me?'

Needles had gone wild in the interview room, demanding to see his sister. He'd had to be restrained, and the tables and chairs he'd thrown over put back before Beth and Tom could question him. Once told that his sister was alive, he calmed down.

'Your parents are with her,' Beth reassured him. 'The head injury isn't as severe as we thought, but she's having trouble breathing for some reason. Did your sister take drugs?'

'Fuck,' he cursed, dropping his head into his hands. 'No. I don't think she did. I don't really know.'

'Colin, can you tell us all you know about what happened tonight.'

He heard the whirring of a tape recorder and lifted his head. 'You recording this?'

'It's the procedure,' said Tom.

'Don't I need a lawyer?'

Beth sighed. She'd hoped to get the questioning over with.

'We can get you one,' said Tom.

'Well, I aint saying nothing until I have one,' Needles said firmly.

Beth scraped back her chair. 'Right, we'll arrange it.'

Ana felt weary. She couldn't get rid of the ache in her heart. She stripped off the blood-stained dress and took a shower. As the hot water washed over her, she found herself unwillingly thinking about him again.

The bastard could be fucking anywhere. It was hard for her to hold back the tears. It seemed she would never find him.

She massaged her aching temples. Thoughts swirled through her mind, memories pinging back and forth as the rage built within her. She dug her nails into her scalp to stop the thoughts and try to calm the rage, but it built up like a volcano about to explode.

She'd returned to the clinic after passing her exams to confront him, but he'd gone.

'Transferred to Oxford,' they told her. 'A few years ago.'

She used some of her savings to pay a private detective to find him. So how could it not be him?

'Where the fuck are you? You fucking deviant bastard,' she screamed, slamming the bathroom cabinet so hard that the glass shattered. She stared at her distorted image in the mirror. *I vowed he'd never break me*, she thought, but there was her broken image staring back at her. The fucking prick had won.

Blood was dripping into the sink, and she realised her right cheek was bleeding. Glass must have flown into it. She was cleaning it with some antiseptic when her mobile rang. Her temples were throbbing so much she thought her head would explode.

'Hi, it's Matt. DS Harper is asking if you're still at the hospital?'

'No. There was no point staying. There won't be any news on Laine Lees for a few hours.'

'Beth wants you to visit Frankie. She refuses to speak to anyone except you.'

'Frankie?' she questioned.

'The sex worker who saw the attack.'

Ana sighed. 'I'm officially off duty.'

'Don't shoot the messenger,' he said, and she heard the smile in his voice.

She looked longingly at her bed and then pulled a blouse and pair of jeans from the back of the bedroom door. She'd be buggered if she'd put her uniform on. The glass would have to wait until later.

CHAPTER FIFTY

Frankie's flat reminded Ana of her home back in Kirby. Frankie shared the flat in Ludbrook Grove with a girl she introduced as Sharon. The flat had water-stained ceilings, grimy windows and ripped wallpaper. Ana figured the rent was probably cheap, or they paid the landlord in kind. She knew that went on all the time in parts of Liverpool.

The noise of next door's TV could be heard clearly through the thin walls, making Ana's nerves jangle and her head ache even more. Frankie lit another cigarette with shaky hands and told Sharon to move some magazines from a chair so Ana could sit down.

'Fag?' said Frankie, offering her the packet.

Ana shook her head. 'I don't smoke.'

Frankie exhaled and the flat was quickly immersed in a haze of blue smoke. 'What 'appened to your face?'

Ana touched the cut and winced. 'I had a fight with a mirror, and the mirror won.'

'You look nicer out of your uniform,' said Frankie. 'You could have been a model.'

'That's not for me.' Ana smiled. 'Are you okay, Frankie? It must have been pretty frightening to see that girl attacked.'

'She was in a right state earlier,' said Sharon. 'Do ya want a cup of tea or something?'

'Yeah, tea and a couple of paracetamol would be great if you've got some.'

Frankie stared at her, took a deep drag on her cigarette and said through mouthfuls of smoke, 'How come you're a copper? I mean, you're more like us than the rest of them.'

Ana took the tea from Sharon and downed the paracetamol with the scalding liquid. 'Maybe I don't like bad people,' said Ana. 'Maybe I thought by being a copper, I could stop them.'

'And have you?' asked Sharon, who'd never spoken to any cops as casually as this.

Ana massaged her temples. 'Not all of them.' She smiled.

Frankie fumbled in her tatty handbag and brought out a bottle of pills. 'Here, take one of these. Codeine, I get them from the doctor for my period cramps.'

Ana swallowed one of the pills, and Frankie and Sharon looked at each other.

'Fucking hell,' said Sharon. 'That could be anything we just gave you.'

Ana smiled. 'I think I know who I can trust. Do you want to tell me about earlier?'

Tears slipped from the corners of Frankie's eyes. 'It was horrible the way he chased her. She looked so scared. Is she all right? She's not dead, is she?'

Ana shook her head. 'Her name is Laine Lees and–'

Sharon gasped. 'Oh my God.'

'You know her?'

'Only from seeing her around. She's just a kid.'

Frankie rubbed at her eyes.

'Can you tell me what happened, Frankie?'

Frankie stubbed out her cigarette, lit another then poured Southern Comfort from the bottle on the coffee table into a glass. 'You want some?' she asked.

Ana shook her head and waited for Frankie to take a sip.

'I was having a pee,' she said. She explained how she'd seen this couple arguing and that the man suddenly turned aggressive and tried to grab the girl's handbag. She shivered at the memory. 'She tried to run from him. She looked so scared.'

'Did she fall, Frankie or–'

'She fell, but then he was on top of her.' Frankie started crying again. 'She was trying to crawl away, but she must have been injured because she was barely moving. I thought he was trying to help her. It looked like he was giving her a drink or something.'

Ana could feel her headache easing. She sipped more of her tea and tried to figure out why The Vigilante would have given Laine something to drink. 'Was he big, tall, muscular-looking?'

'Not big, I don't think. He was taller than her. What if he saw me?' she said nervously. 'He might come looking for me.'

Ana stood up. 'If you couldn't identify him, then I doubt he could identify you either, or that he even saw you. But I'll get someone to patrol around here at night. So keep the doors locked, and any punter who seems odd, don't bother with him.'

Sharon stood up and hugged her. 'Thanks for not judging,' she whispered.

'I'm in no position to judge,' Ana said.

After notifying all the parents, Beth found herself more emotional than usual. Maybe it was memories of what had happened a year ago. So when Tom had offered the hot chocolate, it seemed the safest thing to do. She knew that otherwise, she would go home and finish the half bottle of Chardonnay that sat invitingly in her fridge.

'It's a good one. Belgian chocolate,' he said as though talking about an expensive bottle of champagne.

She took the hot mug, inhaling its sweet aroma. The cottage hadn't changed at all. The only thing missing was the photo of Tom's wife.

He sat beside her on the couch, and she moved slightly as his hip touched hers.

'Cheers,' he said, touching her mug with his. 'Lewis tells me you're a trained firearms officer now.'

She sipped at the sweet liquid. 'I don't want to make any mistakes should there ever be a second time.'

He gently removed the mug from her hand. 'You saved my life. That wasn't a mistake, was it?'

She opened her mouth to reply, but his warm lips were on hers. The kiss was unexpected, and for a second, she didn't respond, and then her arms were around his neck, and their bodies slipped easily into a passionate embrace. It was like the last two pieces of a jigsaw finding each other, and everything was finally perfect.

'Stay,' he whispered, the passion thick in his voice. 'I haven't stopped thinking about you since the day I left.'

She pulled back gently. 'I don't want you to feel rushed,' she said, taking his hand.

'When have I ever done anything I didn't want to do?' He smiled.

She nodded. 'It's been a long time since I've...' She hesitated.

'I know,' he said, pulling her into the warmth of his body. 'Me too. It'll be okay.'

The truth was Beth was terrified of being a disappointment. Lovemaking with Ben, she realised now, had been very different. 'I don't want to let you down,' she said, not looking at him.

'No chance of that.' He smiled, and she relaxed.

That night, Beth realised what it was to be loved.

CHAPTER FIFTY-ONE

A na was late for the briefing, but at least she didn't look as hungover as some.

'Sorry,' she apologised.

'Considering you did some off-duty work yesterday, Sergeant Rawlins, I think we can let you off,' said Tom.

Ana took the empty seat next to Luke. He leaned across to her and whispered, 'Mixing with tarts isn't doing your reputation any good, you know.'

The anger and tension coursing through her body and lack of sleep made her lose it. 'Fuck you,' she said.

'Christ, someone fell out of the wrong side of someone's bed. It looks like you've been in the wars. Had to break up a bitch fight over a client, did you?'

Ana gritted her teeth and focused on DI Miller. She listened as he explained that no DNA was found on the card.

'We've managed to get DNA from Laine's clothes, but there was a lot of contact at the fair. We're still checking the database for any matches.'

'So, he wore gloves as usual,' said Matt.

'Sajid Singh,' said Tom, pointing to his photo on the crime

scene board, 'lost his phone during the altercation with the skinhead lads and claims he didn't send the message to Laine asking her to meet him at the Old Oak. His friend Khalid has also confirmed that Sajid had lost his phone. So, it seems likely the attacker had stolen the phone and left it by Laine's body to implicate Sajid. Elaine Lees's phone still hasn't been recovered.'

'Maybe she didn't have it with her,' suggested Luke.

Ana glared at him. 'All youngsters have their phones on them,' she snapped. 'Why else would she have gone to the exact place mentioned in the text?' *Wanker*, she thought and wished she had the guts to say it.

'Right,' said Tom, sensing the tension. 'DS Harper, can you bring everyone up to date?'

Beth passed the card around.

She's blooming, thought Ana, and then she glanced at Tom. His eyes were on Beth. *God, I hope I'm wrong about her and it wasn't her that knocked down Vanessa.*

'From the words on the card, it seems Laine was blackmailing someone. So the question is who, and is that person also The Vigilante?'

'I know this is tough, but we need to question everyone we knew was at the fair,' said Tom.

'Bloody hell,' groaned Luke.

'Any news on Laine?' asked Ana.

'She's in a coma. I want you and Matt to talk to the social worker and her friend, Jassy. See what she knows,' said Beth.

'It seems Colin Lees, or Needles, was part of the gang that harassed the Pakistani lad on the coach. That lad was Sajid,' said Ana.

'Ah, the fight at the fete,' said Beth.

'What happened with Frankie?' asked Tom, and Luke grinned at her.

'She's scared. She said he didn't attack Laine, but they were arguing. Apparently, Laine ran off after he tried to take her bag. He ran after her. Frankie said Laine slipped. He seemed frantic to get at her handbag. I'm presuming it was her phone he was after. Frankie is scared he may have seen her. I said we could patrol that area for a bit.'

Luke sat forward, the veins in his neck standing out. 'Are you serious? It'll cost a fortune. We should be arresting them, not bloody safeguarding them.'

'Afraid you'll be seen?' Ana smirked, taking the card being passed around.

There was a moment of silence.

'Can you get her to come in and make a statement?' asked Tom.

Ana nodded. She was staring at the card. Something wasn't right about it, but she couldn't work out what. 'I don't feel this was The Vigilante,' she said. 'Smashing up bikes and cars that are speeding is one thing. Murder is the opposite of what he does, surely?'

'Good point,' said Beth. 'We need to keep all options open, one last thing. Sajid Singh is not pressing charges against Colin Lees. He thinks it will aggravate an already tense situation.'

Ana felt an overwhelming urge to laugh. Here was Luke Carpenter making sexist comments about her visiting prostitutes and more sexist comments about how they should be arresting them and not protecting them, and no one said a word. 'What about the sex workers at Ludbrook Grove estate, ma'am?' she asked, trying to keep the anger from her voice.

'Sex workers,' scoffed Luke. 'Is that what we're calling them now?'

Ana turned on him, her face tight with anger. 'Incidentally, where were you last night? Your wife was staggering around drunk, looking for "her waste of space" husband. It seems she couldn't seem to find you. Do you have an alibi?'

Matt gasped.

Luke's face turned red with anger.

'DC Rawlins, my office,' said Beth.

'Doesn't he have to account for his whereabouts just because he's a cop?' asked Ana.

'Not in a roomful of people he doesn't.'

Ana thought Luke would slap her, and she almost wished he would. Maybe this terrible anger would leave her then.

Beth closed the door of her office. 'Remain standing, constable,' she said firmly.

Ana held her chin high. 'He was making sexist comments,' she said. 'He said mixing with tarts wasn't doing much for my reputation. Or words to that effect.'

'You need to show some self-control, constable. I'm sure you're tired, so I will overlook this.'

'Thank you, ma'am.'

'I'll have a word with DC Carpenter. You may leave, and we will patrol the area where Frankie lives.'

Ana nodded. 'Sorry, ma'am, just lack of sleep.'

Beth smiled. 'I've been there many times. Take this evening off. In fact, if you've got nothing planned, maybe we could have a quick snack at the pub later?'

Ana tried not to show her surprise. 'Yes,' she said. 'Sure, what time?'

'Seven?'

'See you then,' said Ana, closing the door behind her.

Beth watched her. There was something intriguing about Ana, but she couldn't fathom what it was. Beth had looked into her background but could find nothing unusual. All she heard was how brilliant and dedicated a copper she'd been from day one.

Someone well worth having on the team, the Kirby chief had said.

'Why did she want to leave?' Beth had asked.

'Said she was sick of breaking up fights at the footie.'

Beth somehow thought there was more to it than that.

CHAPTER FIFTY-TWO

SEVEN YEARS EARLIER

The nurse had a kind face with rosy-red cheeks like the Pink Lady apples that Laurie had sometimes stolen from the boxes outside the greengrocer's shop. They could never afford to buy them, and she remembered thinking what a lovely name they had and how exquisite they must taste. So one day, she stole two, and they tasted just as she expected: deliciously sweet, just like syrup.

'You've had the counselling, Laurie. Are there any questions you'd like to ask me?'

The taste of the Pink Lady apples left Laurie's lips as she pulled herself back to the present. She shook her head.

'You're happy to go ahead?'

'Yes,' she said so quietly that the nurse barely heard her.

Anika squeezed her hand tightly. 'I'll be here the whole time,' she assured her.

Laurie's legs had begun to tremble, and she was sick with nerves. Somehow, she couldn't stop thinking of the life inside her. Surely, this was no different to murder, but the counsellor had assured her repeatedly that it wasn't like that and had explained everything to her, showing her diagrams to help.

'It isn't a fully formed life yet,' she'd told her.

'This way,' said the nurse, leading her to a cubicle and handing her a green gown. 'If you'd like to change into this, leave your clothes on the chair. I'll be back in a moment.'

Laurie stepped out of her clothes, forcing herself not to think. The sterile gown slipped on easily, and she then sat on the chair holding her clothes and waited. If only Anika could be with her the whole time. Then there wouldn't be any chance to think. Laurie jumped when the door opened.

'Okay?' asked the nurse.

'A bit nervous,' said Laurie.

'That's normal, but there's no need to be.'

Laurie followed the nurse along the corridor and then felt it. It was so fleeting, just a tiny flutter, like a butterfly's wings. She stopped abruptly and laid a hand on her stomach. Could she do this? *You'll be a useless mum*, a voice in her head whispered. *You've failed at everything else. What makes you think you'll be a success at this? It will live in a shit hole and turn out just like him.* There it was again, the flutter. Was it nerves? They said it was too early to feel the baby.

CHAPTER FIFTY-THREE

PRESENT DAY

Ana was just about to sit at her desk when DI Miller came out of his office. 'Round everyone up, please, Matt. Briefing room, five minutes.'

Ana's phone lit up. It was a message from Jonny. She replied:

Urgent briefing. I'll call you back.

Luke deliberately pushed past her. 'Perhaps this vigilante has murdered one of your mates,' he whispered.

'What's your problem?' she asked.

'You're my problem,' he hissed. 'Trying to make me look incompetent at my job.'

'I don't know what you're talking about.'

'I thought you were dropping the hit and run, but no, you're still pushing it and making me look like a dick.'

'Yeah, well, that's not hard to do, is it?' she sneered. She walked past him and into the briefing room, stared at the photo of a smiling Laine on the crime scene board, and felt stupidly weepy.

When everyone was settled, DI Miller pointed to the image. 'I'm sorry to have to tell you that the hospital just informed us that Elaine Lees had a cardiac arrest in the night. She didn't make it. There will be a post-mortem later today. We need to find the person she was arguing with at the fair. We're now looking at manslaughter.'

Ana couldn't speak. She couldn't believe Laine hadn't made it. Yesterday, they'd said her brain injury wasn't as serious as they'd first thought.

'Fuck,' muttered Matt.

There was a chattering of voices, but she wasn't listening to what was being said. It was like she was falling into a dark abyss. 'Would you like to attend the post-mortem with me?' Beth asked.

Ana's head jerked up.

'Don't eat first,' Luke said with a smirk.

'Yes,' she replied to Beth.

Jonny said he had more information on the car for her and asked if she fancied trying the new French restaurant that had just opened in town. Ana felt a heaviness in her body. She found herself doing what she vowed she would never do. She was obsessing over *him* again. He was stealing her life. It was time to let him go. She wasn't going to find him. It was impossible to trace the nameless. So she told Jonny yes, but not this evening as she was meeting her boss for a drink.

Ana had never attended a post-mortem. Beth checked with her several times before they entered the mortuary.

'I'm not good at this myself,' Beth admitted.

It was the smell that hit her first. The smell of death. A faint, sickly sweet odour, disguised by litres of antiseptic. She donned the mask and scrubs handed to her and shivered uncontrollably as the cold air from the mortuary hit her in the face.

Laine's body was covered with a white sheet. Ana thought she looked peaceful, and she felt grateful. The blood had been washed from her hair, which now framed her pretty face, and so she appeared angelic. The open wound in her head had turned purple. Ana tried not to look at it.

'Hello, I'm Gina, one of the pathologists. As you can see here, there is a head wound corresponding with the evidence of her falling onto a piece of stone. The debris removed from her injury during her operation shows she hit her head quite hard when she fell. There is no evidence of her being hit with anything. There are several bruises on the body, which correspond with the fall.'

'Cause of death?' asked Beth.

Ana could see that Beth wanted to escape the post mortem as soon as possible.

'This is where it gets interesting,' said Gina, her eyes brightening.

Ana saw Beth turn white and thought any moment she would throw up.

'The head injury wasn't good, but it wasn't fatal. However, we found a high level of Rohypnol in her blood.'

Ana felt a cold finger stroke her back, and she shivered. 'Rohypnol?' she repeated.

'It's often used to spike people's drinks and—'

'Yes, I know,' interrupted Ana. 'But it's not enough to kill someone, is it?'

Gina shook her head. 'No, I agree with you. The amount to spike a drink is sufficient to incapacitate a person but not to kill them. This kind of dose was fatal.'

'Thank you,' said Beth, making her way to the door. 'If you

could send over your report as soon as possible.'

'The person who witnessed the encounter saw the man kneel beside Laine and give her a drink. It could have been the Rohypnol he'd given her,' suggested Ana.

'That's supposition,' said Beth.

But most likely, thought Ana.

'Was she a virgin?' she asked.

Gina raised her eyebrows. 'No, she wasn't, but it's interesting that you ask. There was no evidence of recent sexual activity, but there was some bruising on the breasts and a fair amount of soreness in the vagina which would suggest previous sexual activity may have taken place without the victim being aroused or perhaps she had indulged in rough sex.'

'Or while under the effects of Rohypnol,' suggested Ana.

'That's not something I can comment on. I can only tell you that there were no signs of sexual activity that evening.'

'DNA?' asked Beth.

'Loads. She would have had contact with many people at the fair.'

'Great, thanks.'

The sound of a door closing told Ana that Beth had left. Ana glanced around at the other bodies lying on gurneys, some with tags on their feet, others covered with sheets. She found herself wondering how they died. Were they good people? Or had they done evil things like him? Something deep within her told her she was close and that he wasn't that far away after all.

'So, she was murdered?' asked Ana.

'That's my conclusion, or someone gave her too much without thinking, in which case you're looking at manslaughter.'

Ana found Beth waiting outside.

'She was murdered,' said Ana.

Beth nodded. 'Possibly. It seems we're not just looking for a vigilante anymore.'

CHAPTER FIFTY-FOUR

'Harper,' said Tom, walking from his office.

Beth looked up, a half smile playing on her lips. The memory of the fair night was so fresh in her mind that she could still smell his body's musky scent. Now, here he was, calling her Harper as if nothing had changed between them.

'We're visiting Elaine Lees' school. See if we can find anything more about her and who she'd been mixing with. Luke, organise a police presence outside the flats where Frankie Reece and the other sex workers live.'

Luke gaped at him. 'I didn't think we were taking that seriously.'

Tom stared into Luke's eyes until Luke found it so uncomfortable that he dropped his gaze.

'We are. We don't want another attack on our hands when we could have prevented it.'

'Right, sir,' said Luke.

Tom saw Luke glance over at Ana, anger shining in his eyes. Ana Rawlins was clearly pissing Luke off.

'Harper?' questioned Beth once they were in the car.

Tom smiled. 'I knew you'd complain.' He briefly rested his

hand on her knee before returning it to the gear stick. 'I quite like calling you Harper.'

Beth laughed. 'It always was Harper this, Harper that.' She pulled a chocolate bar from her pocket.

'It never stops,' he said, pulling into the car park.

'That's because you never give me time to eat.'

They arrived just as the students were leaving. Beth recognised Skinner, who looked downcast. He saw them approaching, and his shoulders tensed.

'We're here to talk to the headmistress,' she assured him.

'I hope you get that fucking vigilante. He's mad. God knows who he'll go after next. He attacked Needles on the coach coming home from football. Scraped his neck with a machete.'

Tom stopped. 'Needles?' he asked.

'Colin Lees,' said Skinner. 'Laine's brother. Everyone calls him Needles on account of his tattoos.'

Skinner couldn't care less anymore. Needles was in a right state. He wouldn't leave Jim's house. He said he couldn't stand the sound of his mother's crying. Skinner was devastated about Laine. The more he told them, the better chance they had of getting that mad bastard.

'So you were also on the coach that Saturday with Lees, who smashed the radio and blacked out the security cameras,' said Beth.

Skinner looked like he was going to burst into tears. 'We were wasted, you know. It was just a bit of fun. But he had this machete. We shouldn't have done it, but he didn't have to kill Laine. Why would he do that?' Tears spurted from his eyes and Beth rummaged in her bag for a tissue.

'Come to the station later and make a statement,' said Tom, walking ahead of her into the school.

'Thanks,' said Skinner, taking the tissue.

'All heart,' she said, catching up with Tom.

'Too soft,' he replied.

Before she could answer, the headmistress was greeting them. It turned out that Laine had barely attended her lessons. Her behaviour had been so antisocial that they had referred her to a social worker. The social worker, Rufus Jones, said he found her difficult during their sessions. The headmistress had planned to follow up after the fair.

'But...' She stopped, trying to control her emotions. 'I never got to do that.'

When they arrived at his office, Rufus Jones was in the middle of a session, so Beth and Tom accepted the administrator's offer of a coffee.

'We have some doughnuts if you'd like one. You know what offices are like. You can never stay on a diet here.'

'Sounds lovely,' said Beth.

Tom rolled his eyes. 'I'm surprised you're not the size of Buckingham Palace,' he commented.

Twenty minutes later, a tall young man came out of one of the therapy rooms and invited them in. Throughout the interview, he seemed edgy to Beth and stroked his chin nervously between his thumb and finger until the skin became angry and red.

'She was referred to me because of her continual absences from school and for abusing the teachers,' he explained. 'There was no parental support, although I did invite them to the sessions.'

'How did you find her?' asked Beth. 'Was she responsive?'

'She didn't communicate with me. She was resentful at being here,' he said. 'She'd fidget or look out of the window.'

'Did you form any kind of relationship with her?' asked Tom, observing him closely.

'What do you mean relationship?' Rufus asked anxiously.

'We're not accusing you of anything,' said Beth reassuringly.

'We need to know if she shared anything with you that might help us find her killer.'

'Did you have a rapport with her?' asked Tom.

Rufus sighed heavily. 'Look, I'm a social worker. I saw her for three visits. One time, she didn't even turn up.' He lowered his eyes. 'She could be quite provocative, and I wasn't comfortable with that.'

'In what way?' asked Tom, still watching him closely.

'She would lie and then admit she was lying.' He licked his lips nervously.

'Lie about what?'

Rufus rolled his neck to release the tension in it. 'She'd talk about all the boys she'd slept with and what they'd done, and then laugh and say "Got you." She said she could easily make accusations against me because we were alone in the room.'

'I see,' said Tom.

Rufus looked up, his face flushed. 'That's always a worry, you know. We don't have cameras in here because of patient confidentiality. Look, I did nothing to that girl. I did the professional thing and asked for her to be referred to someone more qualified.'

Beth pulled out her notepad. 'Who was that?'

'Dr Raymond Grace.'

Beth stopped writing. So Ray *had* known the social worker for the Ludbrook Grove school. Why hadn't he said that? She glanced at Tom and saw him roll his eyes. He'd asked Ray at dinner about the patient confidentially. She inwardly groaned. Beth had known Ray wouldn't divulge much. He was very hot on confidentiality.

'Thanks for your help,' said Tom, standing up. 'We might need to question you again.'

Rufus looked panic-stricken. 'Why?'

'Nothing to worry about.' Beth smiled, following Tom.

'You intimidated the poor guy,' she said once they were outside.

'Why the hell hasn't your brother-in-law come forward to say he treated her?' Tom asked, starting the car and angrily struggling with the gears.

Beth winced as he crunched into first gear. She struggled to find an answer, at least an answer that would make sense. 'Maybe he never got to see her,' she suggested. 'We don't know. Perhaps she skipped those appointments too.'

'Bloody patient confidentiality,' he said between gritted teeth. 'Well, we'll soon find out.'

Beth sighed. 'I can't interview him. You know that. I don't think you should either. Let Rawlins and Matt do it.'

'Bloody vicars and...' He took a deep breath before agreeing with her. This whole thing of being able to withhold evidence had been simmering within him for years. The number of murders he'd known that could have been prevented if one of these so-called professionals had opened their mouth in time.

CHAPTER FIFTY-FIVE

The brass plaque on the door read *Dr Raymond Grace MRCPsych and Dr Michael Rust MRCPsych.* The building was impressive.

As they entered, Ana held her stomach as if in pain. Anxiety moved through her body like a current. The walls were blindingly white and two modern paintings hung on each.

Fear gnawed at her stomach, and she kept swallowing to ease the anxiety rising within her. Her hands trembled and her head ached. Then, for the first time in months, she dug out the Valium from her bag and swallowed two while Matt talked to the receptionist.

'Jesus,' she muttered, as memories flooded her brain until she thought she would drown in them. *They're just memories,* she told herself. *They're just the same as nightmares. They'll go soon.*

'It's okay,' she whispered. 'It's okay.'

'First floor,' said Matt, startling her.

They stepped into the lift and Ana could feel herself hyperventilating.

'Jesus, Ana,' said Matt, concerned. 'Are you okay?'

Ana struggled to take deep breaths. 'I hate these sort of places.'

Matt frowned. 'Right,' he said, thinking it odd, considering she had been in the mortuary earlier. Nowhere could be worse than that.

The lift opened, and Ana went straight to the water dispenser and took another Valium.

Matt flicked through a magazine in the waiting area while Ana paced the room. *Jesus, how much longer would he be?* 'Have you ever met him?' she asked.

'Vaguely, in a pub once when it was DS Harper's sister's birthday.'

Ana didn't think she could take much more. Her stomach was cramping unbearably, and she was about to excuse herself to the loo when a tall, handsome man opened the consulting room door. A young woman followed. They exchanged a few words, and then he turned to Ana and Matt. 'Come in,' he said.

Adrenalin rushed through Ana as she entered the room. The cramps in her stomach got worse. Her head swam, and she suddenly became unsteady on her feet.

'Ana?' questioned Matt, concerned.

There was a tingling in her chest, and she just wanted to escape. Her eyes fell on the sofa on the other side of the room, and she had to swallow constantly to stop vomiting.

Matt helped her into a chair, and slowly, the Valium began to calm her. 'Maybe a delayed reaction to your morgue visit,' suggested Matt.

Shit, she could feel tears pricking her eyelids. Was it relief or ghostly memories?

'I know I wouldn't cope with a visit to the morgue.' Ray smiled.

Ana swiped at her eyes. Before she knew it, Ray was standing in front of her with a plastic cup of water.

'This might help,' he said,'

Ana's whole body shook. 'No,' she shouted, slapping the cup from his hand.

Ray, taken aback, just looked at Ana before Matt broke the silence.

'Shit,' he said, grabbing several tissues from a box on the coffee table and attempting to soak up the water. 'Sorry about that.'

'It's fine,' said Ray. 'I'll fetch a towel.'

Ana forced herself to take several deep breaths. *Hold it together*, she told herself firmly.

'What the hell is the matter, Ana? You look terrible?' whispered Matt.

'I'm fine,' she said tersely.

Ray had mopped the floor and now sat in a chair opposite them. 'Are you feeling a bit better?' he asked her.

'I'll be fine,' she said, although her heart was hammering so fast that she held her hands tightly together to stop Matt and Ray from seeing them tremble.

'I try to avoid the morgue.' Matt smiled, trying to lighten the atmosphere.

'We're here to discuss your sessions with Elaine Lees?' Ana said bluntly.

Ray frowned. 'The girl that was attacked at the fair?' he asked. 'That was awful.'

Matt nodded and looked down at his notes. 'Her social worker, Rufus Jones, referred her to you. He found her hard to handle and a bit provocative.'

Ana watched as Ray tapped into his laptop. She noticed he had a bald patch at the top of his scalp.

'Ah, yes, he did. He thought she had attention-seeking issues and that she was trying to harass him in some way. He's quite young, if I remember. So I booked her in and arranged for my receptionist to be present. I thought it safer, although the receptionist would have left if the client had refused to have her present in the room.'

'When was this?' asked Matt.

'The 3rd of June at seven. She never attended the appointment. I booked another one for a week later. She arrived for that one. I didn't expect her to, so I didn't arrange to have anyone in attendance.'

He scrolled down the screen. 'I can read my notes, as there is nothing confidential in them. The client arrived, seemingly irritated to be here. She refused to answer questions and was silent most of the session. She spent much of the time biting her nails and checking the time on the clock.'

Ana glanced over at the clock on the clinical white wall.

'It's the client's right to spend their hour here as they wish. The client then made it clear she wouldn't be returning,' Ray explained.

'How did she make it clear?' asked Ana.

Ray closed his laptop. 'I'm sorry. I can't share that. It was personal reasons.'

Ana clenched her fists. 'But she's dead. We're investigating that death.'

'Nothing she said in our session would be connected to her death. She gave her reasons for not attending again, and I respected them. I asked her if she would prefer another psychiatrist and referred her to Dr Rust.'

Ana felt her body slightly relax as the Valium travelled through her bloodstream, and she looked cautiously around the consulting room as though expecting a monster to jump out of a corner of the room. Her eyes took in the bare white walls, the couch, the cabinet full of...

'Do you ever need to sedate any of your patients before you begin therapy?' she asked.

Ray cocked his head. 'Excuse me?'

'Sedate them?' she repeated.

'Sedate them?' he asked, surprised. 'What for? They're not having an operation. If they're a bit anxious, I'll do deep breathing with them.' He looked at Matt and then back to Ana. 'I'm sorry, but I don't understand your question.'

'There was a high level of Rohypnol in Elaine Lees' blood,' said Ana.

He didn't look surprised. 'Was she perhaps using it recreationally? After all she was at a fair with lots of young people,' he said.

Matt met his eyes. 'It was a fatal dose.'

'A therapist wouldn't give that to a patient,' he insisted. Ray checked his watch and then stood up.

Ana could see from the glint in his eyes and the sudden tightness of his mouth that he was angry but trying not to show it.

'I've told you everything I know about Leanne Lees and–'

'Elaine Lees,' corrected Ana.

'I apologise. I have a patient in a few minutes, and I can assure you we do not use sedating drugs such as Rohypnol during our sessions. It would leave the patient powerless to talk; therapy is about sharing feelings, not preventing the patient from doing so.'

Ana glanced over at the couch, and her stomach turned over. *Not here*, she pleaded, *not here*. 'Thanks for your time,' she said.

She didn't bother waiting for Matt but hurried straight to the loo directly opposite reception. The paintings on the wall now looked fuzzy and distorted. Her stomach lurched and gurgled. The cubicle door locked safely behind her; she fell to her knees and threw up into the toilet bowl. It seemed like the retching would never end. Her phone pinged several times.

Probably Matt, she thought. Her head thumped with every beat of her heart.

'Ana?' It was Matt.

Ana grabbed some toilet roll and wiped the sweat from her forehead. 'I'll be out in a sec. Sorry, must have been something I ate.' She rinsed her mouth with cold water and then splashed her face. Finally, she took several deep breaths before walking out of the toilets.

'Christ, Ana, you had me worried.'

She walked quickly to the doors. 'I need some air, that's all.'

The door was pushed open, and Ana stepped back to prevent it from colliding with her. The air she so needed was still out of her reach.

'I'm so sorry.'

Ana found herself forced back into the clinically white reception area, and a man was stepping on her toe. Ana shivered, pulled her foot away and started shaking again.

'Are you okay?' the man asked, concerned. He touched her arm reassuringly, but she recoiled like she'd received an electric shock.

'Dr Rust, I have a call for you,' said the receptionist.

'One moment.' He turned to Ana, who was struggling with the door. *Why the fuck didn't Matt open it?*

'Let me get you some water,' Dr Rust said kindly.

She ignored him, yanked open the door, and took a lungful of air while grasping the railings surrounding the building to keep herself upright.

Matt seemed concerned and said, 'Let's get you home. I'll explain that you came over unwell. I'll come back and question Dr Rust.'

No, I'll come with you,' she said, but deep down, she knew she couldn't do it. She couldn't face Dr Michael Rust's consulting room, see his couch, or look at the whiteness of the walls. She took a deep breath before saying, 'I think I should go home after all.'

Matt nodded. Ana hoped Matt would connect her feeling unwell after visiting the morgue. Hopefully, he wouldn't realise it was a panic attack. She could tell from his expression he was confused. She knew she was acting oddly, but how could she explain why to Matt?

'Is there something wrong?' he asked.

Ana steered the conversation back to Elaine Lees, and eventually, he gave up, and they drove home in silence.

Jassy's mum had made a chicken casserole and told Jassy to take it to Jim and Needles. Jassy wasn't keen. Needles had always frightened her, and Jim said things that didn't make sense, and she never knew how to answer him.

'Make sure they eat it,' her mum had ordered.

The smell of the food made Jassy sick to her stomach. How could anyone eat knowing Laine was dead? It seemed to Jassy that time had come to a standstill. The shock and disbelief were palpable throughout the village. She kept expecting Laine to WhatsApp and tell her it was another of her silly jokes. But Laine didn't WhatsApp or text. Jassy had told the police that Laine had started to throw a lot of money around, but Jassy didn't know where it came from. The night of the fair, Laine wanted to impress Sajid.

'She wanted to win him back,' she said. 'He would never hurt her. He just didn't want trouble with her brother.'

They asked her about the social worker, and she said she didn't think Laine ever went. 'Said it was a waste of time.'

Jassy couldn't face the fact that she'd never see Laine again.

Laine had been so happy in her lovely dress and new shoes that night. So why had Sajid ruined everything?

'Oh, Laine,' she whispered, tears watering her eyes. 'I miss you so much.'

Needles opened the door and Jassy gasped in shock. He was unshaven, his eyes red and sore, and he wore a shabby top with food stains on it.

'Mum made a casserole,' she said.

He looked at the stoneware pot and opened the door wider.

'Who is it?' called Jim.

'Just a friend. It's okay.'

Jassy followed him into the kitchen, where he placed the pot on the counter that had toast crumbs peppered all over it. She wrinkled her nose at the smell of the overflowing bin and offered to empty it, but Needles said he would do it later. Jassy didn't know what else to do, so she walked to the kettle, ignored the rust-stains on the sink and dirty dishes, and filled it from the juddering tap.

'The tap isn't working properly,' she told Needles.

'It's good enough.'

'Shall I make Jim one?'

'Nah, he'll just forget it's there. He's probably dozed off again.'

Placing the tea on the kitchen table, she sat opposite Needles. 'It wasn't Sajid. He wouldn't hurt Laine for the world.'

'I know,' He nodded. 'It was The Vigilante. He disrespected me on the coach. He smashed my bike. And now he's killed my sister because he hates me.' Jassy thought the same, but why did this hooded fucker hate Needles so much that he'd kill his sister? First, the incident with the coach, then the bike, and now Laine. There had to be a connection.

'You're coming to the candle-lit vigil tomorrow night, aren't you?' asked Jassy. 'Loads of people are going to be there. We need to show Laine how much we love her.' She burst into uncontrollable tears. 'I should have followed her into the woods instead of being such a coward,' she sobbed. 'I could have saved her.'

Needles stood and walked around the table, and then they were hugging and crying together. 'He might have attacked you, too. I'll get the bastard,' he said. 'I'll make him wish he'd never been born.'

CHAPTER FIFTY-SIX

Ana's headache was worsening, and she knew she needed to go somewhere quiet to ride out the storm within her brain.

Matt dropped her off outside her apartment block. He whistled in admiration. 'Bloody hell. I need to ask for a pay rise,' he joked.

'It belongs to a friend,' she lied. 'She's travelling, so I'm using it.'

Before he could ask any more questions, she climbed from the car and waved as she entered the building. The headache was almost blinding her, and all she could do was swallow more pills and then lie on the bed with the curtains closed.

Ana was scared. She was out of her depth. The flat was costing her too much. She closed her eyes, but the memories were persistent and harsh. *What are you going to do now?* her inner voice asked.

'I want to go home.' She wept, turning over and burying her head in the pillow. If what she'd discovered was true, who could she trust now? Her eyelids closed as the Valium and painkillers started to work. In that quiet, peaceful moment between waking and sleep, she idly wondered if she should have mixed the pills.

———

ONE YEAR EARLIER

They'd raced to the red-light district, sirens blaring and blue lights flashing. Ana led the way, the ambulance behind her. She'd been dreading this happening. How many times had she warned them?

'The pimps are supposed to take care of you.'

'A punter's a punter,' Cherry would say.

'You're selling sex, Cherry,' Ana warned. 'They're not paying to rough you up. No matter how much they pay, you don't deserve that.'

Ana knew who the pimps were and had warned them several times, but if Cherry and the girls kept working for them, what the fuck else could she do? She sighed at the sight of the crowd that had formed outside Southfield Park flats. She abruptly stopped the police car, and she and Arif hurried into the dilapidated building, followed by the paramedics.

'Clear the fucking vultures,' Arif yelled to the policemen behind them.

Ana was running up the stairs with the paramedics behind her.

'Oh God, Ana,' sobbed a young girl, falling into her arms.

'Where is she?'

The girl took Ana's hand and led her into flat 13. The smell of cigarette smoke, booze and sweat assaulted Ana's nostrils. But the overriding smell was the coppery stench of blood. It seemed the whole flat was covered in it. The walls looked like blood-stained graffiti. The other girls sat in shock staring at Cherry, who lay groaning on the floor.

'He went at her with a billiard cue,' said one.

'We tried to stop him.' Another wept. 'But he was fucking mad.' She held up her arm, and her hand was hanging strangely.

'You must go in the ambulance, Sonya,' Ana said. 'That wrist looks broken.' Ana knelt beside Cherry and held her hand gently as the paramedics lifted her onto a stretcher. 'Which one?' Ana asked.

No one answered.

'I know it was one of your pimps,' said Ana.

'The Glaswegian,' whispered a young girl in the corner. 'It was my fault. This guy wanted… He wanted to do–' She broke off and began to cry. 'Cherry said no, that I was too young and…'

'So it was McQuire,' said Ana. She felt a pain in her jaw and realised she was grinding her teeth.

They all stared at her. Fear was evident in their eyes.

'Fucking tell me,' she demanded.

'It was him,' whispered Sonya.

Ana nodded. 'You go with the girls in the ambulance,' she said to Arif.

Arif shook his head. 'No way.' He clicked into his radio. 'Woman has been badly beaten at Southfield Park. Her name is Cherry Miles. Back-up needed to arrest the assailant.'

Ana smiled gratefully at him. He could have called her a prostitute, but he didn't.

'Message me how she is,' she told Sonya, who nodded tearfully.

They knew Alistair would be in one of two places: either the The Fox pub just along the road or his fancy house on the outskirts of Kirby. Ana hoped it would be the pub. At least his wife and kids wouldn't have to witness the arrest.

It was a Saturday night, and The Fox was heaving. They passed the placard announcing a live band was playing that night and entered to the sound of pulsating music and shouting punters struggling to be heard above the din. As soon as Ana and Arif were spotted, the noise slowly diminished until only a lone musician played. Ana nodded toward them, and the music stopped.

Shane, the landlord, walked towards them. 'What the hell?'

'Sorry to break up the fun,' said Ana.

'Yeah, you look it,' said Shane.

Ana ignored him and walked towards Alistair McQuire, standing by the dartboard.

'Turn around,' she said, her voice sharp.

'What for? I ain't done nothing wrong,' he sneered.

'I said, turn around. Don't make me ask a third time.' Ana pulled handcuffs from her pocket. 'You're under arrest for grievous bodily harm.'

He laughed, looking around the pub for others to laugh with him. 'Oh, come on. Sometimes you have to give those whores a slap or two. How am I supposed to run a business?'

Several of the men laughed. Ana stared at them for a second and before McQuire had time to react, she'd whipped out her baton and brought it down hard on the back of his knees. The next thing he knew, he was on the floor. Arif knew that McQuire was in big trouble now.

'Fucking bitch,' yelled Alistair. 'I only gave her a slap.'

'I'd shut up if you know what's good for you,' warned Arif, pulling him up and handcuffing him.

'You shit-faced bastard. The whole fucking room is decorated with her blood,' spat Ana.

'The place needed a clean-up,' he sneered.

It was the smirk that did it. Arif wasn't prepared, and when her baton came smashing down on McQuire's head, he leapt back in shock.

'You fucking no good piece of scum,' she yelled, the baton coming down repeatedly.

'Christ, Ana, stop,' said Arif, as McQuire's blood splattered onto his face. He pulled the baton out of her hand just as she was about to strike again.

'Get this piece of shit out my sight,' she said, the emotion thick in her voice.

He dragged McQuire from the club. The Glaswegian pimp was already screaming his revenge.

'Okay, the party's over,' said Ana, a slight tremble in her voice.

'You were out of order,' said Shane.

She ignored him and left the pub, her heart banging in her chest. She got into the police car and turned to McQuire, who was now quiet, blood flowing from a cut on his head.

'He's going to need a doctor,' said Arif. There was no criticism in his tone.

Ana nodded.

'I have to report it, Ana. You used unnecessary force.'

She shrugged. 'I know. I'm going to the hospital. Can you arrange some protection for the girls for a few nights?'

He nodded. 'Sure, I'll see what I can do.'

Cherry was lucky, they said. She had a broken collarbone and a few fractured ribs. 'One of her kidneys looks damaged,' said the doctor. 'I'll need to open her up to see how bad it is. But from the CAT scan, I'm not hopeful I can save it. I'm sorry.'

Ana swallowed, trying to take everything in. 'I understand,' she said.

'When she comes out, she'll need somewhere safe and quiet to stay. We keep patching them up, Ana, but...'

'I know. I have somewhere she can stay.'

Cherry tried to smile when she saw her, but her face was so bruised and bloated that it was almost impossible.

'I hit him too many times,' Ana said softly.

Tears rolled down Cherry's cheek. 'Oh, Ana.'

They held hands silently for a time.

'You need to do it.' Cherry finally whispered. 'You need to get rid of the anger. You know where he is.' Her voice was hoarse, and Ana had to lean close to hear her.

'I know.'

Of course she knew. She'd known when she got the address in Oxford six months ago, but the thought of facing him again was too much for her to deal with.

'When you leave here, you'll be looked after, okay?'

Cherry nodded and closed her eyes. 'They think I might lose my kidney.'

'You're going to be fine. Besides, some of the best people only have one kidney.'

A loud ringing tore through Ana's eardrums and she woke with a start. She'd set the alarm so she wouldn't oversleep.

'Cherry,' she said, looking around. Then she remembered she was in her fancy flat in Oxford. She called Cherry's number and was relieved to hear her voice.

'Hey, girl, how's it going?'

Ana closed her eyes and pictured Cherry in her mind. That deep richness of her black skin, the brightness of her eyes, the colour of acorns. That broad smile and contagious giggle that was uniquely hers.

'Good, how about you?'

'You sounding posh, babe.' Cherry laughed and then said, more seriously, 'Found him?'

'I will.' Her eyes landed on the bedside clock, and she remembered the drink with Beth. 'Shit. I have to go. Drink with the boss.'

'Okay, girl. All is well here. No worries.'

Ana hung up.

Had beating McQuire helped get her the transfer? She'll never know, but she's here. McQuire had been done for attempted murder, and still, Ana hadn't got her man. *But I'm close*, she thought. *I'm so close.*

CHAPTER FIFTY-SEVEN

PRESENT DAY

Ana glanced around the pub before spotting Beth. 'Quiet tonight,' commented Ana.

'I think the locals are a bit unnerved. They don't like knowing someone is walking around capable of attacking a young girl.' Beth had a glass of wine in front of her.

Ana apologised for being late, explained she'd had a bad headache. Then she wondered if Matt had said anything about how oddly she'd behaved at the psychiatrists.

'What do you prefer, red or white?' asked Beth.

'Just a tonic water, thanks. I don't think my head could take a wine right now.'

Jack waved and Ana waved back. Beth leaned down to retrieve her bag and Ana looked at it appreciatively. 'New handbag?'

Beth laughed. 'Hand me down. My sister is the designer queen. I don't even know if this is a good make. It's a Radley. I've had it a few years now.'

'It's a good make,' Ana assured her. 'Must have cost well over a hundred.'

Beth gasped. 'Blimey, I'd better treat it with more respect.'

While Beth went to the bar, Ana checked her phone. There was a text from Jonny.

> Not sure when I'm seeing you, but here's a brilliant blow-up photo of the bag. I have a mate who is a genius at this stuff. It's got initials on it. Looks like SG or SO. It could be a designer logo. When are you free?

Ana replied.

> How about tomorrow.

She zoomed in on the photo and there was the bag. It was pink, but she couldn't make out the letters very well. However, there was something vaguely familiar about it.

'Tonic water,' said Beth, making her jump.

Ana took more painkillers and tried to relax but couldn't bring herself back to the present since her dream. Her thoughts were chaotic. The pub was vaguely similar to The Fox. The woman sitting across the way, laughing with her male companion, could easily have been Cherry. The bright red lipstick was certainly Cherry's.

'So how did you find Ray? Discover any more about Elaine Lees?'

'Ray?' Ana asked, confused.

'My brother-in-law, the psychiatrist.'

An invisible hand punched Ana in the solar plexus. 'Ah, yes. Not much helpful information.'

Beth sighed and leaned back in her chair. 'Don't tell me. The whole confidentiality thing?'

Ana nodded. Brain fog was making everything seem unreal. She shouldn't have taken so much Valium with the painkillers.

'It makes Tom pretty angry. Matt said the other doctor was

the same. They always claim they would tell us if anything could be connected to a murder. Tom's argument is, how would they know.'

'I agree. Awkward for you, though, with him being your brother-in-law.'

'I guess he believes he's doing the right thing. So what made you come to Oxford?' asked Beth, changing the subject.

ONE YEAR EARLIER

The chief had ordered Ana into his office when she'd returned from the hospital.

'What the hell did you think you were doing? A whole pub full of people saw you.'

'He was resisting arrest,' she said quietly.

'He was handcuffed, Sergeant Rawlins.'

Ana lowered her head. 'He was making abusive comments.'

'Which you should have ignored.'

'Yes, sir.'

'Lucky for you, he's not pressing charges. It's taken a lot for you to get here, Ana; don't ruin it now.'

She chewed her lip thoughtfully and then hesitantly asked. 'Could I be transferred? There's a vacancy at Stonesend station in Oxfordshire. I'd like to learn more. I don't want to spend my life arresting pimps and hooligans at football matches.'

The chief lifted his eyebrows. 'Oxfordshire? Why not London? If it's the action you want.'

'That's a big jump, sir.'

He nodded in agreement. 'Let me look into it.'

'I got tired of breaking up riots at football matches,' she told Beth.

Beth looked at Ana over the rim of her glass. 'Was that the only reason?'

Ana's eyes met Beth's. 'Yes,' she said, perceiving from the look in Beth's eyes that she didn't believe her.

'Oh, I meant to ask you.' Beth took a handful of peanuts from the dish on the table. 'Any luck with the car investigation?'

It was said so casually that Ana was annoyed that she blushed. She considered her words carefully. 'Not really. I've reached a dead end,' she lied. 'Talking of cars. I really need a new one. Mine's had it. You've got a Clio, haven't you? How do you find them?'

The sudden change of subject took Beth by surprise. 'Erm, it's okay. I miss my old Golf. That was an excellent little car, but the last MOT cost me so much that it seemed sensible to get a new one.'

Ana studied Beth, looking for any signs of discomfort or wariness, but there was nothing. Either that or she was hiding it well.

'I'd like a Golf,' said Ana, wishing her head would stop aching. 'How did you sell yours? I don't want to get fiddled.'

Beth was looking a bit bemused now. 'It was scrapped.'

Ana nodded. Beth's eyes on her were making her uncomfortable, and she sipped on her tonic water. 'So you've learnt the car that hit Vanessa was a Golf, have you?'

Ana almost choked on her drink.

Beth smiled. 'You're very bright, Ana, but I'm far from stupid. If I had hit Vanessa, I would have owned up to it. If you'd done your homework, you would have discovered I was on a firearms course in Leeds that day, so I took the train.'

Ana could have kicked herself. The pub door opened, and

several people strolled in laughing. Ana was grateful for the short reprieve. But unfortunately, it didn't last long.

'I think it's time you dropped the case,' said Beth.

Ana nodded, feeling stupid. Why hadn't she checked out Beth's movements? It should have been the first thing she'd done.

'I'm sorry. You're right,' Ana said, pushing back her chair. 'I hope you don't mind, but I have a terrible headache. I think I ought to go home.'

Beth stood up. 'Of course, let me see you to your car. You don't look good at all.'

Ana acquiesced and apologised again.

'Don't worry,' Beth assured her. 'At least you were thorough,' she hugged Ana reassuringly. 'By the way, my sister, Sandy, and her husband have invited you for dinner. They regularly do this when new staff members arrive. I think they're just bloody nosy, to be honest. I'll send you the date, see if it suits you.'

Ana forced a smile. 'Thank you, that would be nice.'

Ana was about to get into her car when Lisa Carpenter called out to them. She was strolling along the street in a thin summer dress, and Ana could see her nipples standing out through it. With her were two other women, whom Ana surmised were her friends, all dressed similarly. The potent smell of their perfumes made Ana's head throb more.

'We're having a girlie night. Why don't you join us,' enthused Lisa, trying to slip her hand through Beth's arm. Ana noticed the other two girls didn't seem keen on having two coppers on their 'girlie' night out.

'Work tomorrow,' Beth said, with a fake smile. 'Ana's not feeling too well, but thanks, maybe another time.'

Lisa shrugged.

By this time, Ana was already in her car, where the perfume

still seemed to permeate. She opened the window, allowing a further wave of perfumed air into the car.

'I'll give you a lift,' she said to Beth.

With humour in her voice, Beth climbed in and said, 'This car seems okay to me.'

'I've got the message,' said Ana, looking into the rear-view mirror before pulling away.

Lisa and her friends were swaggering along and laughing loudly. Then, as they turned into the pub, Ana remembered.

'Ana!' Beth yelled.

Ana looked up to see she had swayed onto the wrong side of the road. 'Shit,' she said, swerving. 'Sorry, it's the headache.' But she knew it wasn't the headache. It was everything happening at once and happening too fast.

'I'm not sure you're safe to drive, Ana. Look, here's my place. Let me call you a cab, and you can collect your car tomorrow.'

Ana had no choice but to agree.

'Anything you don't eat by the way?' asked Beth.

Ana shook her head and felt like a knife just sliced through it. 'I eat anything,' she said, struggling not to think of food.

'Great,' said Beth. 'Here's your cab. Rest that head.'

Beth's phone rang just as she pushed the key into the lock of the cottage. 'DS Harper,' she said answering it.

'I lied.'

Beth stopped with the key halfway in the lock. 'Who is this?'

There was silence, and Beth waited for the inevitable hang-up.

'It's Leigh Moulson. I lied about that night the trail bike got smashed up. Will wasn't home. He didn't get home until late after the fair either.'

Beth made a note to check with Ray. Hadn't she asked him to see that Will got home okay? 'Why are you telling me this now?'

Leigh started weeping. 'I don't know. He gets so angry sometimes and...'

Beth pulled the key out of the lock. 'Does he hit you?'

Leigh sounded shocked. 'Oh no. He's a rough diamond. I know that, but he's not a wife-beater. It's just, well, I know he doesn't do everything by the book, but I know he wouldn't kill someone, but he was angry about the bike. We had put up with it for a long time, you know.'

'Well, thank you for telling me.'

'You won't tell him it was me, will you?'

Beth assured her she wouldn't and hung up.

CHAPTER FIFTY-EIGHT

She should have told Beth, but it would have sounded so unlikely that Ana felt sure she wouldn't have believed her.

Ana sent the text. She knew the reply would be instant, and she knew he wouldn't resist. He was weak. Ana had picked up on that immediately. Part of her empathised with him, but only a tiny part. He should have been stronger. But everyone had a right to explain themselves, even him. The least she could do was give him time to do that before she reported it. She downed a glass of water and waited patiently.

It was funny how things come to you, thought Vanessa. After all this time, it took a television programme to bring it all back. Tim had brought home a curry. He did that sometimes if he worked late. So they'd finished it with half a bottle of wine from a few nights before.

'Any news on who attacked that poor girl?' she asked Tim.

Tim broke a poppadum in half and shook his head. 'Not yet.'

'I wish they'd find that vigilante. It frightens me.'

'They will,' he assured her.

Tim washed up, and Vanessa took the leftover poppadums and wheeled her chair to face the TV. Tonight was the last episode of a detective drama she'd been watching. She finished the poppadums while she waited for Tim.

'I'm making tea,' he called. 'Then I'll be in. You start watching.'

Tim wasn't interested in the drama. He'd pretended to be to please his mother. But he wasn't into detective programmes.

'If you're sure,' said Vanessa, who had been looking forward to the final episode all day.

'I'll watch it later on catch-up,' he called.

While Tim washed up and made tea, Vanessa wrapped a blanket around her knees and turned on the TV. The drama, as anticipated, had an exciting final episode. Vanessa became so entranced that she barely noticed the tea and bourbons Tim placed in front of her.

'Good is it?' He smiled.

'You're missing a great episode.'

'I'm just going to print out a few invoices. You enjoy.'

She vaguely heard Tim tapping on the computer and talking on the phone, but his words didn't register.

Vanessa became so enthralled that her tea grew cold and she forgot the bourbons. As the show's final minutes ended, Vanessa gasped and yelled, 'Tim, Tim.'

Tim hurried into the living room, almost tripping over the hall rug.

'What's wrong?' he asked worriedly.

'It was a woman,' she said excitedly.

He glanced at the TV screen, bemused. 'A good ending then?' he remarked.

'No. You don't understand. The person who hit me. I

remember now. It was a woman. Something in the programme reminded me. Penny said she heard a squeak when the driver opened the door, but it wasn't the door. I remember it was a woman wailing. The driver was a woman, Tim.'

Tim's face lit up. 'You're sure about that?'

Vanessa nodded. 'Oh yes. Something in the programme brought it flooding back.'

Tim grabbed his mobile. 'We should let Constable Rawlins know.'

He arrived on time. It didn't surprise Ana. She opened the door and immediately smelt his aftershave. She wanted to laugh but fought back the urge. It was typical of him to think there was something on offer. Such a fucking huge ego. As if she'd ever consider sex with him. The thought of it made her nauseous again.

'You've got a fancy gaff,' he said, looking around. 'Too fancy for a copper's wages.' She heard the suspicion in his voice.

'It's not mine. I'm house-sitting for a friend,' she said, turning on the music player. 'Until I find something I can afford.'

'Rich friend,' he said, impressed. 'Open-plan, nice. What does this friend do then?'

'He's a property developer. A friend of my dad's,' she lied. It was almost laughable, considering she hadn't seen her dad in years and didn't for one moment think he'd have a property developer friend.

If only they all knew how she'd blown all her savings on this place for one reason and one reason alone.

'I'd offer you a beer, but I'm all out,' she said, filling two glasses with fruit juice. It had only been a short time since she took the last lot of painkillers. It felt like a Zulu dance was going on inside her head. The more stressed she became, the worse it got.

'I'm supposed to be on duty anyway. Quiet night, luckily,' he said, and she felt his breath on her neck.

He was close, too close.

She turned quickly, pretending she was unaware of his presence. He stumbled backwards, and she walked past him to a chair. There was no way she was going to risk sitting on the sofa with him.

'Bit late for a chat,' he said, a half smile on his face.

'I'm sure the station can cope.' She smiled.

From the satisfied look on his face, she knew he thought he was on to a good thing.

'I had a drink with the boss tonight,' she said.

She saw his face cloud over slightly. *He's wondering where this is going.*

'Harper or Miller?' he asked.

'Harper, we went to the local. You'll never guess who we saw?'

He looked uneasy and began fidgeting in his seat. 'No idea,' he said, trying to sound disinterested.

'Your wife, with her friends. They're having a girlie night.'

He sighed with relief. Ana, horror-stricken, then realised Luke thought she had invited him over because his wife was out.

'Yeah, she does that.' He smiled. 'They like their little girlie night drinks.'

'Beth asked me to drop the Vanessa hit and run,' she said, getting up to refill her glass. God, her head hurt.

'Probably a good move.'

She stood in the archway that led from the living room to the kitchen. 'The thing is, I can't,' she said.

He frowned. Ana could tell he fancied her but was wary of her at the same time. He placed his glass on the coffee table.

'If Beth Harper said to drop it, then you should.'

She sighed and shook her head. 'You see, I can't. The problem is I know who did it, and so do you.'

His expression changed in an instant. His face turned white as if an invisible paintbrush had stroked across it. His eyes narrowed, and Ana heard the crack of his knuckles. He stood up abruptly. 'I don't know what on earth you're talking about.'

'I have photos of the car.' Ana knew this was a huge bluff, and she couldn't be sure he would fall for it. 'You missed a private security camera in Somerville Road with footage of the accident. Your wife was driving the car, wasn't she? Her fluffy pink handbag with her initials on it was on the passenger seat. I remember seeing her with it at the fair. You've been covering for her. The longer the cover went on, the harder it became to tell the truth because your job would have been on the line, wouldn't it?'

Luke slammed his glass onto the coffee table and started for the door. 'I don't know what the fuck you're talking about.'

'The CCTV camera in Bladon photographed your car. That's why you destroyed the evidence.'

He turned to face her. 'This is bollocks, and you know it.'

Ana sighed. She needed to get to bed and take something for the blinding headache. 'It's not bollocks, and you *know* it, Luke. I can understand why you'd want to cover for her. She's your wife. I didn't want to be the one to tell Miller. I thought it *would* be better coming from you. They'll understand you must have been under a lot of stress and–'

She stopped. He was glaring at her, and the anger in his eyes unnerved her.

'If you'd kept your bloody nose out of it, everything would have been fine. You don't know what Lisa's been through since it happened or what I've been through. I had to protect my wife.'

At last, she'd got him to admit it. Ana put a hand to her head. She felt light-headed.

'I'm begging you, don't tell anyone?' he pleaded.

Ana sat down before she fell. 'You scrapped the car, Luke. You took it to Robbie Benson's, didn't you? I could tell from his face he was hiding something when we questioned him. Your wife left a crime scene, and you destroyed evidence,' she said wearily. 'I'll let you tell your side of the story. It will look better for you.'

Ana was taken by surprise when he pulled her from the chair and shook her roughly. 'Don't you understand, you stupid bitch?' he yelled. 'I'll lose my job, my pension. We'll have to leave the village. All her friends are here and—'

It felt like pebbles were crashing around in her head. 'Luke, please. I think you should leave.' She tried to pull away from him, but his grip was tight. His fingers dug into her arm muscles.

'I can't let you tell them about Vanessa. Our lives will be ruined.'

The trilling of her phone silenced them both. Ana grabbed it before Luke could stop her, but he snatched it from her and threw it to the ground. Ana only hoped she'd managed to push the answer button and hadn't hit *end call* instead.

'Hello, is that Constable Rawlins?' Tim asked.

There were sounds in the background, but he couldn't determine what they were.

'Constable Rawlins, it's Tim, Vanessa's son. Mum has just remembered something that I think might be important.'

Still no reply, and then he heard a man's voice in the background.

'What is she saying?' asked Vanessa.

He put a finger to his lips to silence her. The man had used his mother's name, and Ana wasn't answering the phone. Something was wrong.

———

'Luke, I'd like you to leave, please.' The shake in Ana's voice was unmistakable, and she hated herself for it. She leaned down to pick up her phone, but Luke kicked it away.

'The minute I leave, you'll tell Miller, won't you? In a split second, you'll ruin our lives.'

Ana realised that she'd made a terrible mistake. She hadn't thought things through. She had wanted to make things easier for Luke by letting him tell Harper or Miller. Now she could see that all she'd done was make him more desperate, and a desperate, bent copper was unpredictable.

'In a split second, Lisa ruined Vanessa's life. She was over the limit, wasn't she?'

He sighed and rubbed his eyes. 'We've had problems. You don't understand. It's not like Vanessa died. I mean, she still has a life and does things.'

Ana stared at him, stunned. 'She's disabled for life, Luke. Her life will never be the same again, nor will her son's.'

He pushed her back onto the couch and clawed his fingers through his hair. 'Just be quiet. I need to think.'

———

Had he heard right? He clenched and unclenched his hands. Adrenalin shot through his body. Now, it all became clear. The bastard had been covering for his wife. The whole time Tim had believed him to be looking for the hit-and-run driver, he had instead been covering up for them. Now Ana Rawlins had discovered the truth. The pounding in his ears was so loud that he barely heard his mother when she said, 'What's wrong, Tim?'

'Damn,' he cursed. 'I don't even know where she lives.'

'Who?' Vanessa asked, puzzled.

'Ana Rawlins. I think she is in trouble.'

'What kind of trouble?' she asked anxiously.

'I'm not sure,' he lied. It was best not to tell her the truth – at least not yet.

'Yes, we do,' Vanessa said, remembering. 'It's on the back of her card.' Vanessa felt guilty then. She'd asked for the address to send biscuits and then, as usual, had forgotten all about it.

'Ring the police, tell them I phoned Constable Rawlins at home and I think she is in danger.'

He grabbed the card and his rucksack and hurried to the door.

'Tim, I don't think you should go,' Vanessa said anxiously.

Tim turned and said, 'There's every reason I should go. Do you want me to call Penny?'

The landline phone sat on a small table beside her. 'I'll phone her. Please be careful, Tim.'

'Don't worry about me,' he said confidently. 'Don't forget to call the police.'

Ana realised how foolish she'd been. Not only foolish but soft, which was unlike her. If she'd been sensible, she would have gone straight to Beth, but she'd felt she owed Luke some forewarning. Of course, now she could see how idiotic that had been. All she'd done, in his eyes, was put him in an even worse position.

'Look, I'm pleading with you. I've got a son starting university soon,' he said, wringing his hands. 'Lisa has depression. I've tried to get her to stop drinking...'

'Luke, I think you should leave,' said Ana, standing up and making for the door, but he shoved her roughly before she could reach it.

'No,' he said.

Ana wobbled; the effects of the painkillers mixed with the Valium had made her unsteady. She lost her balance and fell, hitting her head on the corner of the coffee table. For a few seconds, her head spun and then exploded into a frenzy of pain. Something wet ran down her cheek. She wiped it away then gasped at the bright red blood on her fingers. She frantically looked around for her phone.

Panicking, Luke hurried to help her up. 'Ana, I'm sorry, I didn't mean to...'

'Get away from me,' she cried, scrambling away from him, her hands grasping at the rug and feeling the stickiness of her blood.

'Oh, why did you have to go poking your nose into things that don't concern you? Can't you see you've left me with this awful dilemma?'

Luke reeked of desperation, and too late, Ana realised she was in grave danger. She crawled backwards and using the arm of the couch as leverage, lifted herself to her feet, ready to try for the door again. But before she'd had time to steady herself, his fist crashed into her jaw. Ana found herself back on the floor, helpless, with her head throbbing unbearably and her ears ringing.

In that terrifying moment, it occurred to her that Luke Carpenter might be capable of killing her.

CHAPTER FIFTY-NINE

Tim had assumed that Constable Rawlins lived locally, so he was surprised to find her address was in a plush area of Oxford. He was driving too fast. He was angry, but most of all, he was fearful for Ana. She was alone with a man who had a lot to lose. Ahead of him, the lights had turned red.

'Shit,' he groaned.

For a moment he considered calling 101 himself, in case his mother forgot, but a honking behind him jolted him back to the present moment, and he saw that the lights had turned green. He pushed his foot down on the accelerator. He was minutes away from Rawlins's apartment block. At first, he wasn't sure he had the correct address. He checked the card. It had to be right; Ana had signed it herself.

After a few seconds of thought, he decided to buzz the flat below, hoping someone would be in.

'Hello,' said a man's voice.

'Hello, sorry to trouble you. I can't get a reply from number 8. I wonder, would...'

'I'm not surprised,' said the man. 'She's got the music on so loud, I doubt she can hear anything else. Can you ask her to consider the neighbours? It's past ten.'

'Yes, of course.'

The door clicked and Tim rushed into the foyer. He could hear the pulsating music. Ignoring the lift, he raced up the stairs.

Ana screamed, the punch taking her by surprise. Fearing someone might hear, Luke turned up her music player.

'What would you do in my position?' he shouted, standing over her, his voice shaking. 'Would you allow some jobsworth to ruin your life? Because that's what you're doing.'

Ana's jaw was throbbing, and the metallic taste of blood filled her mouth. She knew her eye was swollen because she had trouble opening it. 'You know this is making things worse,' she said. It was difficult to open her mouth, and there was a strange clicking sound when she did. *Shit*, she thought, her hands trembling. *He's broken my jaw. How is he going to explain this? There's no way he's going to let me go.*

Her mind tried to organise itself into coherent thoughts, but there was too much pain to focus on. Somehow she had to sidetrack him and get to the kitchen, where she could grab some sort of weapon, but even then, she would most likely be too weak to tackle him.

A loud banging on the door startled them both. 'Turn that bloody music down, or I'm calling the police.'

Luke turned to her. 'Don't make a sound,' he warned. Then he called, 'Sorry, mate, turning it down now.'

The banging on the door continued. 'Open up, you arse 'ole.'

'Shit,' mumbled Luke. He lifted Ana from the floor and into an armchair before going to the door. He slid the safety chain across and then opened the door, his mouth partly open with the apology he was about to make, but he'd barely got the first word out when a machete sliced through the chain.

The man kicked the door open, and Ana saw he was wearing a balaclava. The Vigilante. Ana wasn't sure whether to be relieved or afraid.

She gasped when The Vigilante punched Luke hard in the stomach. Luke heaved as he struggled to breathe but was punched again several times, first in the face and then the groin. He battled to fight back, but the rage in The Vigilante burnt wildly, enhancing his strength.

Luke fell to the floor only to have The Vigilante kick him violently in the ribs several times.

Ana sat frozen in shock. Her eyes locked on the machete that The Vigilante had dropped to the floor. Luke was struggling to protect himself and had curled his body into a trembling ball of fear, but The Vigilante was not stopping, and Ana felt Luke's warm blood as it showered onto her dress.

'You no good piece of scum. Covering for someone who'd knocked down an old lady. What kind of a policeman are you?' yelled The Vigilante.

'Stop,' screamed Ana. 'Please stop.' She forced her shaking legs to work, pulled herself from the chair, and dived for the machete. 'I said stop!' she screamed. The machete wavered dangerously in her hand and Ana stood, shaking, her eyes not leaving The Vigilante.

'I should slit his throat,' he said menacingly, looking down at Luke, who was now groaning and grovelling to escape. 'You covered up that accident. You don't deserve to live.'

'I'm sorry,' quivered Luke.

Blood seeped from his cheek onto the snowy white carpet and Ana oddly wondered how much it would cost to clean.

Luke attempted to stand, but his legs collapsed under him.

'He needs an ambulance,' said Ana.

The distant sound of sirens eased the rush of adrenalin pulsating through her veins, and her body relaxed.

The Vigilante turned to the door. 'Thank you,' he said when they were outside.

Ana gripped the machete. Why the hell was he thanking her? She swiped the back of her hand across her mouth, where it was wet with blood.

'I don't know who you are, but I know you saved me, and I'm truly grateful for that. I'm in no fit state to arrest you, but I beg you, please hand yourself in.'

He closed the door behind them and lifted the balaclava.

Ana gasped. Of all the people they'd imagined The Vigilante to be, it had never occurred to anyone that it could be Tim. Quiet, unassuming Tim. But, of course, why wouldn't it have been him? After all, he'd been let down by the police. The accident had changed his life, and his mother's, forever. Thinking about it now, she realised how that anger must have crushed him. The police had seemed to do nothing, and he had been right. They hadn't done anything to find the culprit because Luke had known who it was all along.

Tim held his hand out, and she obediently passed him the machete.

'I heard your conversation over the phone,' he said. He looked at her closely. 'You need an ambulance. I think your jaw is broken.'

She knew he was right. The pain was becoming excruciating now.

Tim sighed wearily and clicked into his phone. 'Just me, Mum,' he said. 'Is Penny with you? ... Oh, good. ... Yes, she's fine. She had an accident. ... All okay. I'll be home as soon as I can.' He hung up.

Ana continued to stare at him in silent shock.

He pulled the balaclava over his head. 'It's not the time, not yet,' he said. 'But I will hand myself in. I didn't kill that girl, you know that?' He dropped the machete into his rucksack.

'I know,' she said.

He didn't even ask how she knew. 'They'll be here soon,' he said. 'I need a huge favour from you.'

'I won't tell anyone until we find Laine's killer,' she said.

He smiled and handed her a card. She didn't have to read it to know what it said.

She watched him quickly walk down the corridor to the lift, then she sat on the hall floor and waited for the ambulance to arrive. In all the panic, she knew no one would notice Tim. It seemed several occupants of the flats had called the police, too, and within minutes, Ana's apartment was cordoned off.

CHAPTER SIXTY

After all he'd done for her, Beth noticed that Lisa Carpenter didn't ask about her husband's condition until the very end of her interview, and even then, it was as though she'd only just remembered his existence. When confronted with the accident, she immediately broke down.

'I didn't know what to do. I was going to help,' she said, sobbing. 'But others came, and I panicked. I know I shouldn't have driven off, but I'd been drinking, and Luke said that Robbie Benson would take care of the car and after I found out she hadn't died...'

She stopped when she saw the expression on DI Miller's face and then started sobbing again. 'I've been depressed,' she said as though that explained everything. 'We've had some money difficulties.'

'Lisa Carpenter, I'm arresting you for driving without due care and attention and causing a near-fatal accident while intoxicated. You do not have to say anything, but it may harm your defence if you do not mention when questioned something that you may later rely on in court. Anything you do say may be given in evidence. Do you understand what I've just said?'

Lisa nodded and lifted her tear-stained, blotchy face. 'You know me, Beth, I wouldn't hurt anybody. There's no need to arrest me.'

'You can't just knock people down with your car, Lisa, and get away with it, and Luke should never have covered up a crime or destroyed evidence.'

'I would have handed myself in, but Luke said it would affect his pension and everything.'

Christ, thought Beth. *She is trying to squirm her way out of it by blaming Luke.*

Lisa's eyes widened. 'Is he okay? You said The Vigilante beat him up.'

Beth shook her head in amazement. *Now she's concerned for him. For all she knows, he could be dead.* Beth explained Luke had been badly beaten but would be okay and Lisa could visit him if she wished after making her statement at the station.

Tom was still trying to figure out how The Vigilante knew to go to Ana's flat. Had he been following Luke, and if so, why?

'It's badly bruised but not broken,' the doctor assured Ana. 'I'll give you some painkillers and muscle relaxants for when the pain is severe.'

She'd messaged Jonny to say she couldn't meet with him as she'd had a minor accident. He was at the hospital within half an hour, his face creased in concern. 'My God, what happened?'

She briefly explained, ending with, 'I was stupid. I shouldn't have invited him to my flat.'

'Well, I'm taking you home to your flat, whether you like it or not,' he said forcefully.

At that moment, Ana liked someone deciding for her, but

her fierce independence kicked in quickly. 'It's fine. I can get a taxi,' she said.

Jonny was not even listening. 'I'm bringing the car round.'

Ana, realising she was too tired to argue, simply nodded.

CHAPTER SIXTY-ONE

The vigil for Laine Lees was held on the playing field. Ana was stunned at the number of people who turned out. It saddened her when they spoke of their hate for The Vigilante, and she had to force herself not to look over at Tim.

She'd gone over all the scenarios as to why someone would want to kill Laine, and each time, she came to the same conclusion, which terrified her.

The playing field was a flood of grief. Most people were wearing black and holding red roses. It was a unique and moving sight. A bleak atmosphere hung over the village like a dark shroud had draped itself over everyone. The unnatural stillness was unnerving. The gloomy mood affected everyone, and the air of suspicion touched them all. In their mind was one thought. Was The Vigilante standing next to them?

Candles and torches lit the dull night. The rain had been predicted, and people had brought umbrellas. The fragrance of the numerous bouquets placed at the entrance to the woods could be smelt as far back as the village green.

Matt and Ana watched everyone, trying to catch an

expression that might indicate guilt. But all they saw was grief etched on people's faces.

Sajid looked down at the red string bracelet Laine had given him. He stroked it several times before taking a deep breath and strolling across the field to where Needles stood beside Jim in his wheelchair. Before Needles could speak, Jim said, 'Hello, lad. How are you? Javid, isn't it?'

'Sajid. I'm okay, Jim, a bit sad.'

Jim shook his head in disbelief. 'It's the end of the war. Why is everyone sad? It should be a party. Be glad. Those Nazis have lost.'

'Yeah.' Sajid smiled, aware of Needles' eyes on him.

'I didn't know you knew Jim,' Needles said suddenly, his tone stern.

Sajid nodded. 'My mum makes him curry sometimes.'

'Sajid doesn't like it when the Nazis come, do you, lad?' said Jim. 'Well, it's over now.'

Sajid took a deep breath, felt the pain in his ribs, and let out a small groan before reaching into the pocket of his jeans. Before Needles had a second to react, Sajid had pulled out a pen knife.

Needles stepped back. 'I'm not fighting with you today.'

'No, no more fights,' replied Sajid.

Needles watched, fascinated, as Sajid tore the blade through his own flesh. He held his cut arm out for Needles to see. 'Look, my blood is the same colour as yours.'

Needles couldn't speak. It was all too much: the vigil, the memory of Laine in her lovely dress and now this.

'My heart beats just like yours,' continued Sajid. 'It's broken like yours too. My family are mourning Laine just like your family are. I love football just like you do. I like music. Laine once told me you liked the same music as me. We're the same, except my skin is darker than yours. Otherwise, we could be brothers. What Laine wanted most of all was for us to be friends. Can we not give her that? If only tonight?'

Needles struggled to stop the tears, but he couldn't. It was as if a dam had burst inside him. He swiped at his eyes, but more tears followed. They wouldn't stop; it was like an overflowing river, and he could not stop it.

'Here,' said Sajid, handing him the knife.

Without hesitation, Needles cut his left arm above the tattooed words 'Laine'. Sajid then held his bloody arm against Needles'.

'Blood brothers,' he said.

People held their candles and torches high as Jassy walked to a makeshift platform. The silence was eerie. Jassy tried to smile, but Ana could see it was a considerable effort. She hesitated for a moment as if weighing up her words.

'Thank you for coming tonight. Seeing so many people coming together to remember Laine is wonderful. As you can imagine, her parents and brother are devasted, so I will talk about Laine on their behalf.'

She took a deep breath.

'Laine was my best friend. She wasn't perfect, but none of us are. Laine was too young to die. She had so many dreams and plans.'

Jassy broke down then, and Ana wanted to hug her but knew she couldn't.

'She used to love dancing and having fun, and we're all still trying to understand why anyone would want to kill our lovely Laine.'

Jassy took a deep, trembling breath. 'Laine's parents ask that if you know anything – anything at all, or noticed a stranger that night, or anything odd – that you please get in touch with the police. Help us find this vigilante and stop him from doing this again.'

Ana and Matt looked around the crowd. Matt was looking for The Vigilante, and Ana was looking for the murderer. Matt nudged her in the ribs and nodded over at Will Moulson and Hale. It looked as though Hale was passing a brown envelope to Will. Will looked around as if to check that no one was watching.

Their attention was turned back to Jassy, who had started speaking again. 'One of Laine's favourite songs was "Before You Go" by Lewis Capaldi, and I think it's fitting, so we're going to play that now.'

There was applause as she stepped down tearfully from the platform, and Ana felt herself tear up.

'You okay?' asked Matt, putting his arm around her shoulder.

'Just my jaw hurts,' she said, covering her emotions.

The music began playing, and Ana saw Beth Harper and Tom Miller approach Will and Hale.

'I'm just going to speak to Jassy,' said Ana.

There was no need for words. Ana hugged her briefly and then handed her a card with her number. 'If you ever need to talk.'

Ana looked around at the vast gathering, remembering the night of the fair. Jonny said he couldn't make the vigil as he had a deadline. It then occurred to her he hadn't been at the fair either. Ana realised then that Jonny had been absent on the two nights that involved Laine.

An arm hooked itself into hers. 'You okay, Ana?'

Ana turned to see Frankie, who immediately pulled her into her arms. 'You're special, you know,' whispered Frankie.

It felt like being home, and Ana knew at that moment that

soon it would be over, and she could go home.

CHAPTER SIXTY-TWO

'How are you feeling?' asked Tom.

Ana thought how strange it was that she should be the one being questioned and not the other way around. 'I'm okay. The pain meds help.'

'Good.' He smiled.

Ana thought how handsome he was. Everyone at the station knew he and Beth had a thing going on. They weren't good at hiding it.

'Obviously, we have some questions about that night with Luke. He's owned up to everything, but there are some loose ends I'd like to clear up. I'm curious, DC Rawlins, why did you invite Luke Carpenter to your flat and not question him at the station? That would have been the correct procedure.'

Ana sighed. 'I know. I was stupid, basically,' she said honestly. 'I wanted to give him a chance to own up. I thought it would look better for him. I guess I didn't want to be a snitch. I honestly wasn't expecting him to lose it like that.'

'I don't want you to make that mistake again, Ana,' Tom said firmly.

She lowered her head. 'No, sir.'

Tom leaned his arms on the table and looked closely at Ana. She was a good cop, he knew that, but he also sensed she was holding something back. 'It was very fortunate The Vigilante came when he did, wasn't it?'

Ana lifted her eyes and kept them focused on his. 'I've been thinking the same thing. The only thing I can come up with is that he came to the same conclusion about Luke as I did. Or Lisa revealed something one night when pissed. It could have just so happened that the night Luke came to me was the night The Vigilante planned to get him.'

'Convenient,' Tom murmured. 'And there was nothing familiar about him.'

'Nothing,' Ana lied.

'You didn't recognise his voice?'

'No,' she lied again. *Don't lose eye contact*, she told herself. 'In all honesty, I'm grateful to him. I think Luke was quite capable of killing me.'

'I'm not excusing him, but he's changed over the years. His financial situation is a mess,' explained Tom. 'I think he got desperate.'

'No one is above the law,' Ana said sharply, taking Tom by surprise.

Tom realised then that Ana Rawlins was razor-sharp, which came from a place in her past. He recognised the hardness and the couldn't give a damn attitude. It came from an injustice. She was a copper to watch. One for her own safety and two for whatever was driving her.

'I agree. Can you give us some idea of The Vigilante's age? Clearly, he was fit.'

Ana chewed her lip thoughtfully. 'He had a youngish sounding voice, so maybe late thirties.' *At least that's not a lie*, thought Ana.

'Thanks, Ana. Take some time off. Give that jaw time to

heal.'

'Thank you, sir,' she said and left his office.

———————

Beth phoned Will and asked if he would mind coming in to help clear up some of their enquiries. 'Just an informal discussion.' Beth sensed his hesitation. 'Just a few loose ends to tie up. Sorry if it's inconvenient.'

'Well, I suppose I could,' he'd said finally.

He arrived looking nervous.

'It's just a friendly chat,' said Beth Harper. 'You know DC Wilkins?'

Will didn't even look at Matt. 'I don't know what this is all about. I told you everything I knew about that trail bike and–'

'Did you go straight home after the fair?' asked Matt.

Will shot him a dirty look. 'Why don't you ask my wife?'

'We did,' said Beth. 'But I don't believe she told us the truth.'

Beth saw the confusion cross Will's face. He knew that if his wife had covered for him, then he wouldn't be at the station being questioned. So, what else was going on? Beth gave him a few minutes to answer, and she continued when it became clear he wasn't going to.

'Were you on the coach returning from the Chelsea match when some skinhead lads attacked a Pakistani boy?'

Will looked puzzled. 'I don't use the coach. I get the train.'

He could be lying, thought Beth. 'I know you didn't go straight home when you left the fair. I had someone follow you just to be sure you'd be okay, and he claimed that after ten minutes of walking home, you didn't seem drunk and didn't aim for Longfields but went into a house in Stonesend.'

Will gave her a dirty look. *He'd like to smack me in the face*, thought Beth.

'I only did that so he'd stop following me.'

'If you didn't go home, then where *did* you go?'

Will sighed. 'I did go home,' he insisted. 'I don't know what the fuck you're insinuating,' he scoffed, standing up. 'Unless you tell me what I'm supposed to have done. Then I'm leaving.'

'Why don't you sit down and tell us where you were, who you were with, and what was in the envelope Hale gave you? If you don't tell us, I'm sure he will.'

Will fell heavily into the chair. 'You guys are killing me. Okay. The night the trail bike was smashed, I was writing out fake MOT certificates in my office. Two clients came to collect them. You can check it out with them. They'll be pretty fucked off with me when you turn up.' He sighed. 'I left the fair early because I was meeting this woman I've been seeing. I suppose you'll want her name too?'

Beth nodded.

'The envelope was money for fixing Hale's car where that little sod with the trial bike had damaged it and arranging a fake MOT. Okay? Fucking happy?'

'I'd be delighted if you'd give us those names,' she said, pushing a pad and pen towards him.

Will shot her a murderous look and then wrote the names. 'Look, she's married too. Her bloke's a rough bugger. So, can you be discreet?'

Look who's talking, thought Beth. *Talk about the kettle calling the pot black.*

'Can you please question her when he's not around?'

'It shouldn't be a problem,' said Matt. 'We're not here to judge your private life.'

'I might supply the odd fake MOT, but I ain't no murderer, and whoever killed that girl, it sure wasn't me,' Will said, scraping back the chair and storming out.

'Nice fella,' remarked Matt.

CHAPTER SIXTY-THREE

The death of Anika's husband Dil was the catalyst for Laurie. At his funeral, she was reminded how short life was. She'd tried to forget the past, but it would come back to haunt her at unexpected moments.

Going to her grave without taking her revenge was unthinkable. It would take some planning, but she figured she could do it. She'd tried hard to follow Anika's advice and put it behind her, but she knew that she could never lead a normal life while *he* went unpunished.

'Are you sure this is the right thing? Isn't it best to let it go? It's been nearly five years,' Anika asked cautiously. She'd learnt to be careful with Laurie when broaching the subject of *him*.

'Do you know how many nights I've lain awake wondering who else he's done it to since or even before me? I should have stopped him, but who would have believed me then? No one. But, don't you see, now I can? Now, I'll be respected. I can't let him continue doing it.'

Anika had reached her wrinkled hand across the table and taken Laurie's. 'Your mum would be proud. Her daughter now a police officer.'

It hadn't been easy, any of it. She'd lost friends. Who wanted to be with a loser who wouldn't have a drink on a night out and studied most of the time to get her A-levels? Of course, to them, the biggest betrayal had been becoming a police officer.

'We'll have to watch ourselves now.' Her mates had laughed, but Laurie knew their laughter had been forced. But they had no idea. No idea at all what she'd been through.

'Don't you see,' said Laurie tearfully. 'Now I can find him. I'll have the resources; wherever he is, I'll go.'

Anika nodded, resigned. Once Laurie's mind was made up, Anika knew there was no point trying to change it.

'Another thing. I changed my name before joining the force.'

'Ana Rawlins,' Anika said.

'You knew?' asked Laurie.

'I thought you did it because you felt ashamed.'

Laurie smiled. 'I don't want him pre-warned. I did it properly. Deed poll and that.'

All Laurie had to do was get transferred, which turned out to be easier than expected. Then Ana Rawlins was in Oxford, determined to get her man, which, without Anika's support, she could never have done.

CHAPTER SIXTY-FOUR

It was good to be back working in the office, although it felt odd with Luke not there, and she sensed a change of attitude towards her from some of the other officers.

'They think betraying one of your own is, well, you know, not the done thing,' Matt said quietly across their desks.

'Intelligent, adult thinking,' she said, her anger rising. 'What was I supposed to do? Just let him get away with it?'

Matt shifted uncomfortably in his seat. 'Maybe you should have gone to professional standards.'

'Jesus, Matt, do I have to hear this from you? Tim is one of your good friends.'

'I'm on your side, Ana.'

'Well, that's good to hear.' She returned to her computer screen and checked Jonny's alibi for the night Laine was killed.

'A great hotel in Gloucester,' he'd told her. 'Beautiful gardens. I wish you could have seen them. It was a good conference.' Six top hotels held conferences, and she phoned them all. Jonny hadn't checked into any of them that night, and her heart sank as she messaged him.

> My friend wants to stay in a fancy hotel while they're in Gloucester. What was the name of the one where your conference was held?'

He answered immediately.

> The Belmont. I recommend it. Are you free for dinner tonight? It's great that you caught the driver of the car. Let's celebrate.

She'd checked The Belmont. He'd lied.

> Dinner would be great.

And so would some answers, thought Ana.

They went to a curry place in Cowley. 'The food is supposed to be excellent here,' he said.

The restaurant was packed. The spicy smell of dhal and chillies swept up Ana's nostrils and memories of Anika's home-made curries took Ana's breath away. 'Smells good.' She smiled.

The waiter took them to their table, commenting on Ana's face as he did. 'Looks like you've been in the wars. I hope the other person looks worse.'

Ana automatically stroked her jaw. 'He does.' She smiled.

'At least you got the bastard,' Jonny said once they'd sat down.

'It seems not all my team members are happy about it. They feel I should have gone to the professional standards. I think some of them are glad he bashed me about.'

'Wankers,' he muttered.

The waiter came over, and Jonny asked, 'What wine would you like?'

'Just tap water for me, thanks.'

They ordered, and then Jonny looked at her oddly before

asking, 'Why don't you drink? I've noticed you always have an excuse for not drinking alcohol.'

'Why did you lie about the conference in Gloucester?' she said, taking him by surprise.

He seemed to open his mouth to answer her and then closed it again. Ana watched him swallow nervously. Finally, he lifted his eyes and met hers. Then the realisation hit him.

'You think I killed that girl?' he said, shocked.

'You lied about where you were.'

He sighed heavily. 'I was with my daughters. Chloe and Sophie. It was my weekend to have them. You'd seemed so impressed with my job and so-called single life that I thought if you knew about my kids, it would put you off before you even got to know me.'

He pulled his phone from his pocket and scrolled into the photo app. He pushed it across the table to her.

'Chloe and Sophie taken on the day of the fair. You can see the date on the metadata. Those were taken at Pizza Hut at about eight, and then we went bowling. There are a few photos of that. I didn't kill that girl.'

Ana could see the resemblance to Jonny in both girls. She closed her eyes. Deep down, she knew he hadn't killed Laine. She just needed to be sure. She couldn't afford to make any more mistakes. She handed him his phone. 'They're beautiful,' she said. Then, after a second's silence, she added. 'I'm sorry.'

He shrugged. 'I guess it looked suspicious.'

'I don't drink because my mother was an alcoholic, and I was getting close to becoming one too. I made a promise to her on her deathbed that I'd stop drinking. My real name is Laurie. A man drugged and raped me when I was fifteen. I'm from Kirby and I belonged to a working-class family with a bad reputation. The police would never have believed me. So, I became the law, and I'm here in Oxford because this is where *he* is, and I'm going to bring him to justice if it kills me.'

Her heart felt like it would burst. Her breathing slowed and the huge weight that had hung over her for years lifted, as if someone had removed a massive rock from her back.

Jonny blinked several times and then took a large gulp of his wine. 'Jesus, Ana– I mean Laurie,' he said, clearly stunned.

'Call me Ana.' She smiled. 'I've got nothing against kids, by the way.'

He leaned across the table and took her hand. 'I know they'll like you.'

It was a relief for them both and made the evening one of Ana's most relaxed since coming to Oxford. For once, she could be herself. When they reached her flat, it seemed natural to invite Jonny in, where he stayed until the following morning. During breakfast, he took her hand in his and said, 'You're very impulsive, you know. I worry about you.'

'Don't be silly.' She laughed.

'I'd be happy if we shared our location on Google Maps. I promise I won't stalk you – just for safety.'

She mulled it over. 'Okay. Seeing as you're not a pervert.'

He kissed her hand.

CHAPTER SIXTY-FIVE

S andy parked her car and was about to get out when the sound of a shotgun being fired made her jump. 'Oh my God,' she muttered.

Then her client, Miriam, had calmly walked around the cottage, shotgun in her hand. 'Bloody rabbits,' she grumbled. 'Good for a pie tonight, though.'

Sandy sighed with relief. Inside the cottage, it smelled of damp, smelly carpets and the musty odour of antiquated furniture.

'My sister wants me to stay with her next week. She's not well. How can I say no? But I can't go unless I can get someone to feed the chickens and cat.'

'I'll feed them,' said Sandy, without thinking. One week of not having to sit in Miriam's house for an hour suddenly seemed idyllic. A quick in and out to feed the animals, and she'd be done.

Anyway, she assured herself, it was a good idea for Miriam to get away. It was too isolating living alone on a farm. Miriam had strange ideas about spirit gods. Sandy had always ignored Miriam's mumbo-jumbo, but she knew many people went to see

Miriam for tarot card readings. Sandy had always thought it was a load of nonsense.

That day, as she was heading for the door, Miriam asked, 'How's your husband, dear?'

Sandy turned and gawped at her. 'What?'

'Your husband, dear,' repeated Miriam, frowning deeply. 'Something's troubling him.'

Sandy was flummoxed and didn't know what to say. Miriam looked absent-minded and said, 'Don't forget the chickens and cat.'

Sandy could feel anticipation building within her. She wanted to know more about Ray. She took a deep breath and asked, 'Is it another woman?' It had always worried her. Ray went to many conferences. There were always going to be pretty women there.

Miriam smiled. 'Isn't it always? Chicken feed is in the shed, and cat food is under the sink.'

The door closed on Sandy.

CHAPTER SIXTY-SIX

O ver a week had passed since Laine's death. Needles was becoming increasingly frustrated with each day because the police still hadn't caught The Vigilante who'd murdered his sister. So, he arranged a meeting. It was set for eight that Wednesday at Jim's garage. He didn't want any cops seeing them in a pub.

Sajid and his friends stood some way back from Jim's garage and waited. Each glanced at the other to gauge what the other was thinking. Sajid shuffled his feet and Khalid cracked his knuckles. Dilip said, 'Well?'

Sajid hesitated. What if they were tooled up? The agreement had been that no one would be, but could he trust Needles?

'Okay, let's go,' he said finally.

The others followed, and Sajid knocked on the garage door three times as Needles' text had instructed. The door swung up.

'We're taking your word that you haven't come tooled up,' Needles said.

Sajid stared at the small scar that wrinkled Needles' arm in almost the same place as his own.

'We don't break our word,' said Khalid.

'Nor us,' responded Needles.

They stepped into the garage, which smelt stale and unused. A few old forks and spades were hanging on hooks, their rustiness showing their lack of use. The air was cool and slightly damp and the smell of petrol still lurked in the air from where the bike had been smashed. Fluorescent lights buzzed quietly overhead, casting a stark white glow over everything. A ladder was clamped to the wall, but Sajid could tell nothing in that garage had been used in years.

The two gangs stared suspiciously at each other.

'A beer?' said Needles, trying to break the ice.

Sajid nodded, and Needles handed round cans of London Pride. After they'd cracked open the cans and taken a few gulps, Sajid sensed everyone relax.

'We're all here for the same reason,' said Needles. 'To find that fucking vigilante that killed Laine. The police are getting sodding nowhere.'

'Where do we start?' asked Digger.

The million dollar question, thought Sajid. *Where* do *we start?* There wasn't a single clue to lead them to The Vigilante. There had been no other attacks since Laine. The more they discussed it, the more depressed Needles became. It seemed an impossible task.

'The machete,' blurted Sajid. 'The clothes, the rucksack. What if they were recently bought.'

Needles scoffed. 'Probably bought online.'

Sajid shook his head. 'But what if they weren't?'

'I think he's got a point,' said Digger. 'After all, what else have we got? It's a start.'

Needles didn't have any other ideas, so he agreed. Laying out a large piece of paper on the floor, Needles outlined a plan. 1) Make a note of everyone locally who carried a rucksack. 2) Check local garages for machetes and similar clothes to what The Vigilante wore. 3) Make a list of potential suspects. 4) See if they could find shops that sold similar clothing.

Sajid didn't want to ask Needles what they would do if they found The Vigilante. He thought they should go to the police, but somehow, he doubted that was Needles' plan; and Sajid knew that's when the trouble would start.

CHAPTER SIXTY-SEVEN

Tom was getting frustrated. There had been nothing at all that would lead them to The Vigilante and now the chief had called a meeting.

'I'm under real pressure here. Have we got nothing at all?' he asked the team.

'We're presuming he's local,' said Matt. 'Perhaps we should be looking further afield.'

'Where exactly?' asked Tom, and Beth recognised the irritation in his voice. They were feeling the pressure, especially after what had happened with Luke. The villagers had lost faith in the officers of Stonesend and Beth couldn't blame them. It was worse for Tom. It seemed to them that trouble had been running amok in their village since he returned.

Laine's parents were talking to the newspapers, expressing their disappointment at the police's lack of progress, and Chief Lewis was constantly on their backs. The vigilante had been on the run for too long in everyone's opinion. He needed to be caught.

'The news of a bent copper has not helped,' he growled at Beth and Tom. 'How the hell did that happen? It took a constable to figure it out, Jesus! What the hell were the rest of you doing?'

Beth had lowered her head, knowing she'd been so focused on Ben and his baby and Tom returning to the division that she'd overlooked things that had been clearly under her nose.

'I don't think the person who killed Laine was The Vigilante,' said Ana.

The room turned silent, and all eyes turned on her.

'What makes you think that?' asked Tom, surprised. 'I thought the girl, Frankie, told you it was him.'

Ana shook her head. 'She said it was a man wearing a balaclava. That doesn't have to mean it was The Vigilante. Anyone can wear a balaclava. If it was The Vigilante, why didn't he kill Laine with his machete? Secondly, all The Vigilante cards have been signed *The* Vigilante. This one was signed *Vigilante*. Why suddenly change his signature sign-off?'

Matt leaned across to her. 'Good thinking, Sherlock.'

'He could have panicked,' said Tom.

'I don't think he's the type to panic,' disagreed Ana.

'So you're saying we're looking for two people. The Vigilante and the person who killed Laine Lees?'

'Yes,' said Ana with certainty.

'But it began as an accident,' said Beth. 'Maybe his original intention wasn't to kill her, but when she fell–'

'He gave her a large dose of Rohypnol,' said Ana.

'We don't know how that got into her body,' argued Tom. 'Anyone at the fair could have spiked her drinks several times.'

'No one else has complained of their drinks being spiked,' said Matt. 'So, it would be odd if she were the only one.'

Ana smiled at him gratefully. 'It was an exceptionally high dose,' she said.

Tom sighed and looked at the board with Laine's photo and all the information they had gathered.

'Right, question the social worker again and her friend Jassy. Laine was blackmailing someone. The question is who? That's our main focus, and remember that The Vigilante and the murderer may not be the same person. Have you had any luck with the DNA?'

'There were loads. She would have had contact with lots of people. One match that came up on the data was her brother. He was done for nicking a car once. But he was in a fight and being watched by us, so it wasn't him,' said Beth.

As chairs began to scrape back, Tom quickly added, 'There will be a lot of speculation in the village about Luke Carpenter. Everyone knew him. The correct answer is "No comment". It's bad enough that the local rag is making the most of the case coming to court next month.'

Everyone nodded.

'He was a good copper,' someone said, looking directly at Ana.

Ana met his eyes and said, 'No one is above the law,' before leaving the station with Matt.

That night, Ana sat on her couch, the bottle of wine she'd bought earlier staring at her from the coffee table like the devil himself, tempting her to commit what to her would be the worst sin.

Tomorrow was the dinner at Sandy's, or was it Sarah's? She could never remember her name. Except now it would be a barbeque, and a few other people had been invited. She couldn't imagine getting through it without a few drinks first.

'DI Miller is coming,' Beth had said. 'And my brother-in-law has invited his colleague. It should be an interesting and fun evening. Sandy suggested you should bring your bloke Jonny.'

Jonny had agreed, but she'd made him vow not to tell anyone her secret. The problem was, could she trust him?

The prospect of tomorrow evening was the first time she had felt the need for a drink. She'd even considered packing a bag and going home. Right this minute, she could do it. God, how desperate she was to go home, to see all those familiar faces and smell those familiar smells that represented where she truly belonged. She scooped up the wine bottle and emptied its contents down the sink. She'd waited too long for this to blow it all now by falling off the wagon. She was that close, and best of all, he had no idea.

———

The dress was perfect. It was light, ideal for the humid evening. Ana had chosen it carefully. It took her ages to pin her hair into a French knot because her hands trembled so much. She tipped out the contents of her make-up bag, decided against mascara and applied a small amount of blusher and a touch of lip gloss. Then, finally happy with her appearance, she walked into the living room and re-read the letter confirming the early end of her tenancy. At that moment, the buzzer went.

'Your carriage awaits,' Jonny said into the intercom.

'Coming,' she said. She slipped on her shoes, picked up her handbag from the sofa, took a deep breath and opened the door.

———

'I can't remember if her name is Sandy or Sarah,' said Ana.

'It'll work itself out,' Jonny reassured her.

The house was huge. However, Ana considered it probably not that large for Oxford. Back home in Kirby, a place like this would belong to someone very influential or well-known. The driveway was wide enough for four cars. A black Mercedes and a Land Rover sat alongside another vehicle, which Ana recognised as Beth's.

'I'll park outside,' said Jonny. 'Leave space for the important people.'

'What do you mean?' She smiled. 'I am the important person.' She hoped it would relieve her nerves, but it didn't. To Ana's relief, Beth opened the front door.

'Love the dress,' said Beth, hugging her warmly.

The desire to flee was so overwhelming that she wasn't aware of Jonny pulling her forward.

'Thanks for the invitation,' Jonny was saying.

The smell of the barbeque reached Ana's nostrils, and the sound of laughter and clinking of glasses was all too much. God, she was fucking hyperventilating.

'Hi,' said a bright voice. 'I'm Sandy. How's your jaw feeling?'

A woman now stood beside Beth. Ana thought she looked like a celebrity with perfectly coiffured hair and bright red fingernails. Her perfume wafted over Ana, and she could tell it was expensive. She was as unlike Beth as anyone could be.

Ana was struggling to breathe. 'It's better, thank you.'

'Great. Come through and meet everyone.'

'Can I use your loo first,' she asked breathlessly.

Sandy directed her to the downstairs toilet, which was as fragrant as her. Ana rummaged shakily through her bag for the Valium she'd brought with her and swallowed two. God, what she wouldn't do for a drink. After taking several deep breaths, she left the loo. The hallway was empty. Boisterous laughter could be heard from the garden. Ana looked at the doors that led off the hallway. Then her eyes locked on the front door. She could run now. Grab her stuff from the flat and be on her way home.

'Are you lost?' said a voice behind her. Ana felt a tingling in her chest as she turned around. He appeared to be one who had learned how to look confident as a survival skill. One couldn't deny his handsomeness.

Her lips trembled when she smiled. 'Looking for the garden,' she said.

'Follow me,' he said in an almost playful tone. 'I'm Michael, by the way, Michael Rust. Ray's partner at the practice.'

'Ana,' she said.

He nodded knowingly. 'Ah, yes, we met briefly. How are you? You looked rather unwell when I last saw you.'

'Something I'd eaten,' she lied.

'Well, nothing here should make you ill. No rabbit stew or pigeon pie.' He laughed.

Sandy appeared then. 'Did I overhear you talking about my cooking?'

'Only that awful rabbit stew. One of Sandy's clients spends much of her time shooting rabbits, pigeons, and pheasants, of which we get the pleasure of eating.'

Just the thought of a rabbit stew made Ana nauseous.

'Is she licensed to have a shotgun?' she asked.

Sandy pulled Ana to one side. 'Honestly, he should know better than to discuss my clients. I visit her at home. I'm a counsellor, by the way. She has a lot of land and needs to keep it under control. So I'm always getting dead rabbits and pigeons. She's quite safe. I have been seeing her for years,' Sandy assured her. 'She's eccentric but not unstable.'

The noise was getting closer. Where was Jonny? They walked through the living area, which seemed cluttered with toys, out through some French windows and onto a patio where tables and chairs had been laid out.

'You're from up north,' Michael said. It wasn't a question.

'Kirby, Liverpool. Do you know it?'

He shook his head. 'Never had the pleasure.'

Ana shivered, even though it was extremely humid.

At the barbeque were Tom and Raymond Grace. The smell of frying burgers and sausages permeated the air. The garden beyond was immaculate with bursts of colour, from red roses to marigolds and bright orange sunflowers. Ana could hear the hiss of a running sprinkler. To her, it was a dream home.

'There you are,' said Jonny, taking her by the arm. 'I thought you'd left me.'

The Valium was kicking in, and at last, she felt she could do this.

CHAPTER SIXTY-EIGHT

'I don't understand why you don't get it?' Tom was saying.

Ana looked down at her half-eaten burger. No matter how hard she tried, her throat struggled to swallow it as if it was made of stone. Jonny kindly covered for her when the wine was being poured.

'Give Ana a soft drink, Ray. Alcohol affects her stomach.'

Michael Rust rolled his eyes. 'Get that stomach sorted. You don't know what you're missing.'

'I do. I'm missing a rotten hangover tomorrow,' she replied acidly.

'You don't seem to get the importance of patient confidentiality,' said Ray, continuing his argument with Tom. 'Michael, help me out here,' he called.

'If it were your daughter, you'd feel differently,' snapped Tom. 'You'd want everyone to tell us as much as they could and fuck any confidentiality.'

'Well, we do,' said Michael. 'Obviously, we wouldn't hide a crime.'

'Tell that to Catholic priests.'

'Okay, you two,' broke in Beth. 'That's enough. Let's change the subject.'

The evening dragged on relentlessly, and Ana kept glancing at her phone to check the time. At least her heart had stopped racing, and she was able to eat some of the fruit salad, but she was still shivering even though it was humid, and she ached all over from tensing her muscles.

The discussion turned to books and films. Recommendations were made, and everyone seemed keen on Ana's book suggestion.

'You must WhatsApp us the link, or we'll have all forgotten by the morning.'

Ana took all their phone numbers. She couldn't have planned it better if she'd tried.

'We should make a move,' she said. 'If I could just use your loo,' she added.

'Use the upstairs loo. I think someone is in the downstairs cloakroom,' said Sandy.

The fruit salad was now threatening revenge. Inside, she tried to appreciate the prettiness of the decoration, but knowing what she was about to do made her appreciate only the toilet bowl as she threw up the fruit salad.

There was a cry of 'Mummy', followed by the sound of running footsteps.

Ana scrolled through her phone. It didn't take long to find the photo she wanted. It brought back so many memories that she forgot where she was for a moment.

'At least smile,' she could hear Arthur saying.

She'd hated having her photo taken when she was younger. Still did. Constantly having to force a smile when you didn't feel like it.

She clicked on WhatsApp, attached the photo with the

words 'Remember me, Laurie?' to one of the numbers, and attached the book link to the others.

Now, her heart was ready to burst. Her throat was dry, but there was no time for a drink. She pulled the chain, washed her shaking hands, opened the door, and hit the send button on all the messages. She turned off her phone and went out to the garden. It was getting dark now and chilly. No one was looking at their phones.

'Sandy's doing mother stuff upstairs,' explained Beth. 'Do you mind waiting until she comes down?'

Fortunately, they didn't have to wait long before Sandy bounded down the stairs. 'So sorry to disappear just as you're leaving,' Sandy apologised. 'Zoe sometimes has bad dreams.'

Ana thanked her for the evening, and before anyone could hug her goodbye, she was out of the front door, with Jonny still saying his goodbyes.

'Blimey, that was a quick exit,' remarked Jonny once they were in the car.

'It's complicated,' said Ana. She knew that from this point on, it would only get more complicated.

CHAPTER SIXTY-NINE

When they arrived home, she asked Jonny if he wouldn't mind just dropping her off. 'I've got a terrible headache. I'm sorry.'

He pulled her to him and kissed her passionately on the lips. 'Of course not. You've had a stressful few days. Sleep well. I'll message you in the morning.'

Ana clicked on her phone the second she closed the flat door. No message. She stared at it uncomprehendingly. What was he doing? She locked the door and slid the top and bottom bolts that she'd recently installed.

She cleaned her teeth and waited for her phone to ping, but nothing happened. The suspense was driving her mad. She hadn't gotten it wrong this time – she knew it – so why wasn't he responding to her?

She climbed into bed and lay there, tense and anxious, clutching her phone tightly. It got to one in the morning, and still nothing. He hadn't even come back online since reading it. Her eyes began to grow heavy. She needed to sleep off the Valium, but what if he messaged? She turned the volume up full and closed her eyes.

While Sandy and Ray had their barbeque, The Vipers, with Sajid and his mates, searched some local garages. It wasn't as easy as they'd hoped. Many had padlocks and Sajid was against breaking them.

'It could be any of those padlocked garages,' argued Needles.

'Most likely is,' agreed Skinner. 'The Vigilante isn't going to have an unlocked garage.'

Sajid still argued they should search the unlocked ones before breaking into any. 'Need to keep a low profile,' he said.

Needles agreed on one condition: they started on the unlocked garages, and if they found nothing, they'd move on to the locked ones.

Sajid agreed. He wanted to find The Vigilante as much as Needles did, but there were so many garages that it could take them forever. Unless they had a stroke of luck, it could be months before they found anything. He felt so useless. He was already in therapy because of his guilt for letting Laine die. He shouldn't have ignored her. She wouldn't have gone into the woods if he'd spoken to her and not been so dismissive. He wondered if Needles carried the same guilt. Maybe she wouldn't have gotten upset and run into the woods if Needles hadn't started the fight.

For both Sajid and Needles, finding The Vigilante and taking their revenge was the only thing keeping them going. Only then would they have closure.

They never considered the murderer could have been someone other than The Vigilante.

Ana awoke with a start to the sound of a phone alarm. Memories of the previous night hit her like a sledgehammer, and she grabbed her phone, dropping it in her haste. Clicking into it, she saw three messages and her heart raced. But one was from Beth:

> How are you feeling this morning?

Another was from Jonny:

> Feeling okay this morning. Free later?
> Jonny x

The third was from Matt asking if she was coming in to work today.

Damn it, the fucker still wasn't online. What the fuck was he playing at? This wasn't the response she had been expecting. It unnerved her. Surely, he'd make contact soon.

'Seems The Vigilante is back at work,' said Tom.

Ana sat beside Matt and resisted the temptation to check her phone.

'You okay?' he asked.

'Fine,' she said.

Tom was relating how several garages in Ludbrook Grove and Longbridge had seemingly been searched the night before. There were no actual break-ins, as the doors had no padlocks, but the garages had been ransacked.

'Doesn't sound like The Vigilante,' said Matt. 'He's usually taking the law into his own hands, not breaking it.'

Ana nodded in agreement.

'We're looking for someone with a garage obsession, then,' said Beth.

Meanwhile, the pressure was mounting to find The Vigilante. The Lees family wanted to have a funeral for their daughter. Ana surreptitiously glanced at her phone and cursed.

'DC Wilkins and DC Rawlins check out these garages. See if anything connects them, similar items taken, that kind of thing. DS Harper and I are going back to the murder scene with forensics. We may have overlooked something.'

Everyone scraped back their chairs, and Ana winced. God, she was more stressed than she thought.

'Ready,' said Matt, looking over at Ana. 'What about you?'

'Just need the loo.' She had noticed that Matt had been watching her closely ever since her odd behaviour at the clinic. He seemed puzzled by her friendship with the sex workers, and Ana was aware that he'd noticed her frequent phone-checking. Although he obviously sensed that something was amiss, he refrained from asking her.

'Ready,' she said, breaking into his thoughts.

Most of the garages had become dumping grounds for storage or workshops for home projects. Some had been converted into workout rooms or man caves. It seemed that only a few were used for storing a vehicle. Not one garage owner had found anything missing.

'It makes no sense,' said Matt when they returned to the car, but Ana wasn't listening. She was checking her phone and getting more agitated by the minute

'What's wrong, Ana? I know there is something up. Why don't you share it with me?' asked Matt.

Impatiently, she threw the phone into her handbag. 'It's just that time of the month,' she said.

Matt sighed. 'Have it your way,' he said dismissively.

'What does that mean?'

'You've become very secretive these days. You're different to when you first arrived on this patch.'

'Sorry, it's all a bit complicated.'

Matt laughed, but there was no humour in it. 'It always is,' he said.

CHAPTER SEVENTY

Ana parked her car at the edge of the Ludbrook Grove estate. She didn't want to come out and find her car minus wheels. It was almost ten and getting dark. Although she could see where she was going, she still pulled a torch from her bag and walked slowly, occasionally looking behind her. The anorak hid her face, but she felt it was unlikely she would see anyone she knew.

She pushed the buzzer to Frankie's flat, and immediately the door clicked open. 'Why didn't you check it was me?' said Ana. 'I told you to be extra careful.'

'I keep telling her,' said Sharon.

'I knew you were coming,' said Frankie. 'That's why.'

Sharon rolled her eyes.

Ana glanced at her watch. He was already a minute late.

'He'll be here,' said Frankie. 'Chill.'

The buzzer sounded, and Ana wiped the sweat from her face. He looked like the smart boy from next door. *He's only a few years younger than me*, thought Ana. *God, I hope he knows what he's doing.*

'This is Vicky,' said Frankie, pushing Ana forward. 'This is Spike. Have you got her stuff?'

He grinned and pulled his rucksack off his back. 'Would I be here otherwise.'

He pulled out a small bag. Ana swallowed, checked it, and saw a syringe in the bag. 'Just a useful little gift.' He smiled. 'It's clean.'

'Thanks.' She smiled. God, why was she sweating so much?

She handed him an envelope of money, which he carefully checked, and then, with a cute smile, said, 'Nice doing business with you, Vicky. I'll see myself out.'

Ana let out a long breath. 'Jesus,' she huffed.

Frankie laughed. 'Who'd have thought it,' she said.

Ana smiled.

'This badass girl is going to get things done,' said Frankie.

CHAPTER SEVENTY-ONE

Sajid was returning from the library when he passed Tim's open garage. The library was the only place he'd found sanctuary since Laine had gone. Sajid knew she'd want him to continue his studies and work hard, and he told himself he would do it for her. He'd get top grades and make her proud.

If they caught The Vigilante, then Laine could rest in peace. Nothing would bring her back, but at least justice would have been served.

Now, he and Needles were no longer enemies. That would have made her very happy. Sajid felt sure of that.

Tim was putting away his gardening tools. Sajid had meant to visit Tim and Vanessa after DC Carpenter had been arrested to express his and his family's satisfaction that the driver had been found.

'Hot day for gardening,' commented Sajid.

Tim turned, and Sajid saw his hair was soaked in sweat. 'Bloody is.' He smiled.

'We were pleased to hear they arrested the person that knocked down your mum.'

Tim picked up a towel from the floor and wiped his face and hair. 'Fancy a beer?' he asked.

But Sajid's eyes were stuck on the combat trousers that had been lying beneath the towel.

'Thanks, but I need to get home. Mum hates it if I'm late for dinner.'

'No worries.'

Sajid felt the sweat run down his back until it itched like crazy. It couldn't be Tim. Sajid couldn't comprehend it, gentle Tim, who took such excellent care of his mother. It was just a pair of combat trousers. It didn't mean anything. Sajid tried to remember if he'd seen Tim wearing combats, but he could only picture him in jeans. Maybe he used them for working on the car.

'Jesus,' he mumbled, thinking he'd go mad trying to work out why Tim would have combat trousers. He needed to forget it. It wasn't Tim. Tim would never have killed Laine. Then he remembered the backpack. Tim always wore a backpack, but Sajid couldn't remember what it looked like and only vaguely remembered The Vigilante's backpack. He pondered whether to tell Needles or break into Tim's garage himself. Yes, that's what he'd do. Safer that way.

CHAPTER SEVENTY-TWO

It amazed Ana the number of things you could buy in B&Q that held sinister undertones and were innocently scanned by the till assistant, who, of course, had no idea how dangerous those items could be in the wrong hands.

Ana packed her bag into the boot of her car like all the other shoppers and then drove to the playing fields at Longbridge. After parking her car, she removed the B&Q shopping bag and walked into the woods. She avoided the area where Laine's body had been discovered. There were too many memories there that she didn't want to revisit.

Slowly continuing through the woods where her colleagues had searched for clues after Laine's death, with just the dry leaves crackling under her feet and the chirping of birds, she finally reached the old ramshackle barn, which she imagined had once been a hunting lodge, now long forgotten. Leaves rustled in the light breeze as she strolled around it. The sloping roof was covered in dead leaves and twigs. There were no footprints leading to the barn. Clearly, the place had been abandoned for years.

Ana had spotted it during the search, but this was the closest she'd been to it. The creaky front door needed a shoulder to push it open. The place smelt of damp wood and soot. Ana wrinkled her nose at the sight of mouse droppings on the floor. A spider web tickled her face, and she leapt backwards. Her hands began to shake when she realised what she was planning to do, but it was coupled with a feeling of excitement and the knowledge that inevitability was in sight.

The text message she sent was threatening. She'd been too soft before.

> Meet me here tonight at 7, or I'll not only go to the police and tell them you killed Elaine Lees. I'll contact the press, too. They'll look into you, and your life won't be the same again. They'll take a copper's word for it.

She'd added a Google Map link to the barn.

> Don't mess with me. I have all the proof I need.

The quick response took her by surprise. He'd taken so long, and now this.

> What is it you want? Money? How much?

Ana knew he'd planned to finish her off, too. What choice did he have? Perhaps that's why he'd taken so long. He'd been trying to work it out like she'd been doing. She tried to imagine his fear every time the doorbell rang. Maybe he'd been waiting for her next move and was relieved it had now come. She typed back:

> £20,000 and bring it in cash.

Now she was mad as hell. Did he think she was totally stupid? He wasn't coming to pay her. He was coming to kill her.

A cluster of dead wasps lay on the soft padding of an old creaky chair – a wasp coffin waiting for its burial. Ana shuddered and dusted them off, pulling the chair into the middle of the room. She took a few things from the B&Q bag and then put the bag in the corner of the room.

Back outside, it took her longer than anticipated to attach the padlock to the door. The wood was so old and damaged it just splintered. Eventually, it was done, and she replaced the tools into the B&Q bag, padlocked the door and walked back through the woods to her car, knowing that no one could enter the barn until she returned.

Back at the station, she pretended to study something on her computer. At six, she stood up, yawned and said, 'Just going to check a lead at the woods.'

'Want me to come?' Matt asked.

'No, I'm due to knock off soon, so I'll probably go home after and rest this jaw.'

Jonny was convinced that he'd done something wrong. Ana still hadn't answered his text. She had acted weird after the dinner at Sandy and Ray's, and he couldn't understand why.

He'd gone over and over in his head the events of that evening and couldn't remember anything that might have upset her. Had she regretted sharing her past with him? He was reluctant to call her. What if this was her way of pulling back? He knew he had fallen in love, but had he made a big mistake? Had he moved too fast? An email pinged into his inbox and he pushed Ana from his mind. He was on a deadline. He'd phone her later.

Sajid cycled to Tim's house to try to get into the garage. Maybe he could tell Tim's mum or her carer that he had a puncture. Hopefully, they'd let him into the garage to pump it up. He couldn't break in. He didn't have it in him to do that. At the house, Tim was loading up his van.

Careful that Tim didn't see him, Sajid bent down to fiddle with his bicycle. He had to push the nail hard into the tyre to puncture it. 'Oh no,' he said, pushing the bike towards Tim.

'You okay?' called Tim.

'I was going to the library and must have gone over a nail. I don't suppose you've got a puncture kit?'

'Sure. I think it's in the garage. Come on in.'

Sajid followed Tim and looked around as Tim searched for the puncture kit. 'It ought to be here somewhere,' he muttered.

Sajid surreptitiously glanced around the well-ordered garage.

'You know what?' said Tim, making Sajid jump. 'I think I left it in the shed. Hold on.'

Tim entered the house from the back of the garage. Sajid held his breath and then cautiously began looking around. He couldn't see anything unusual and then spotted the rucksack on the floor in the far corner. He hurried over to it, listening for footsteps before unzipping it. He'd only moved a few things inside before he reeled back in shock at the sight of the shiny blade of the machete and the balaclava beneath it.

'I've got it,' called Tim.

Sajid pulled the zipper closed and almost fell in his haste to drop the bag.

'Let me fix it for you,' said Tim helpfully. 'It's only a temporary job, but it will get you home.'

Sajid stared at Tim's back as he pumped up the tyre. Was he really looking at Laine's murderer?

CHAPTER SEVENTY-THREE

To say Ana was frightened would have been an understatement. She'd already made one mistake with Luke, but she had to do this alone. There was no one she could tell. Not yet. This was her revenge and hers alone. It was personal. The physical signs of fear were manifesting themselves on her body. She could smell the sweat from under her armpits. Her breath was bursting in and out of her chest like that of an asthmatic. Fuck. It was too warm to wear a police uniform, but she wanted as much equipment on her as possible.

What if he didn't show? What the hell would she do then? She pulled her phone from her pocket. It was 6.45. He should be on the playing field or close to it.

Then, to her horror, she saw she had no phone signal. How could she have overlooked something so important? *Damn it.* She checked and double-checked everything, but it wasn't easy because her hands shook so much. She needed to calm down. One mistake, and it could be the end for her.

A terrible thought entered her head. Should anything go wrong, Tim was bound to get the blame. Eventually, they'd discover he was The Vigilante, and he'd go down for everything.

Oh God, she thought, her breath catching in her throat. *If anything happens to me, he may well hand himself in.* She should have told Jonny the whole truth. At least he could have saved Tim.

A slight crackle reached her ears, and Ana froze. The sound of footsteps trampling on the leaves drew closer.

Oh. My. God. He's come.

Sajid just wanted to escape from Tim, but Tim was chattering about how pleased they were that Luke Carpenter had been arrested and that his mother had finally got justice for what had happened to her.

'If it hadn't been for Constable Rawlins...' Tim said. 'I can't praise her enough. That's the police doing their job properly. Of course, we know now why Carpenter didn't do his properly.'

'Yeah.' Sajid nodded. 'But most coppers are honest, aren't they?' He fidgeted on his feet. How much longer was Tim going to take to fix his puncture?

Tim smiled. 'They sure are. There you go. I've patched it up. You're ready to go.'

'Thanks,' said Sajid, almost snatching the handlebars from Tim. 'See yer,' he called over his shoulder and cycled home as fast as his legs could pedal. The only safe person he thought he could talk to was Jassy. Surely, she'd know what to do. They could go to the police together, but Needles would never forgive him. Weren't they blood brothers now?

If only it had been anyone else but Tim. But why? Why would Tim kill Laine? What reason would he have had? It didn't make sense. Could it have been revenge for what Needles and the Vipers did to Imran's shop? Tim's hand was severely injured, but surely Tim wouldn't kill someone because of that and certainly not Laine. It didn't make sense. But there was no doubt Tim had everything that would make him The Vigilante.

What if they got it wrong and it wasn't Tim? Getting him arrested on suspicion of being the murderer would make the village turn against him, even if it was untrue, and there was Vanessa to think about.

'Oh, Laine,' he pleaded. 'Tell me what to do.'

Jonny tried Ana again. This time, it went straight to her voicemail. He then sent her a WhatsApp.

> Are we okay? Message when you can.

It wasn't like Ana not to respond. He'd give her a bit longer and then try the station.

'She just lies on her bed, looking at the photos on her phone,' said Jassy's mum. 'I'm really worried about her. She misses Laine so much. We need the funeral.'

'Is it all right to go up?'

'Of course.' She smiled. 'I think the company will do her a world of good.'

Jassy barely looked up when her bedroom door opened.

'Hi,' said Sajid, standing on the threshold. He'd never been in Jassy's house, let alone her bedroom.

Jassy lifted her eyes. 'Hi,' she said. 'Come in.'

He stepped into her room. On the dressing table, he saw a photo of her with Laine at a birthday party. They were both carefree and laughing into the camera. He turned his eyes away.

He would cry if he looked at it for too long. Posters of her favourite celebrities adorned the walls.

'What's up?' asked Jassy, seeing his worried expression.

'I think I know who The Vigilante is,' he said quietly.

'What?' Jassy sat upright, her eyes widening in surprise. 'Who?'

Sajid hesitated. 'I think it's Tim.'

Jassy stared at him, disbelief written across her face. 'Shut up,' she said finally. 'Why would Tim want to be The Vigilante? That's mad.'

'Think about it,' said Sajid.

It then clicked in Jassy's brain. 'OMG,' she whispered. 'His mum?'

Sajid nodded. 'They let him down, the cops. It turned out they were covering it up, even.'

'Only one officer,' Jassy corrected him. 'It's not Tim. I don't believe it.'

Sajid took a deep breath. 'I saw the combats, the rucksack and the machete in his garage.'

Jassy's face turned white, and for one awful moment, Sajid thought she would be sick.

'Tim wouldn't kill Laine. I know he wouldn't. Why would he?'

'I don't know. I don't understand it, either. Maybe she learnt the truth about him and was blackmailing him.'

Jassy got up and paced the room, shaking her head. 'No, it's too crazy.' A thought crossed her mind, and she turned fearfully to Sajid. 'You haven't told Needles?'

Sajid shook his head and Jassy sighed with relief.

'Anyway, Tim doesn't have the kind of money that Laine was spending. I think we should phone Sergeant Rawlins. I've got her number. She's all right, she is.'

Sajid shook his head. 'We need to think about it.'

CHAPTER SEVENTY-FOUR

Ana struggled not to hyperventilate. Her pulse was racing, and she could hear it thrashing in her ears. The footsteps grew closer and then stopped.

Ana wiped her sweaty palm on her trousers, took the hypodermic from her pocket, and grasped it tightly. *Please don't let me drop it*, she prayed. She fought back the vomit that threatened to surge violently from her oesophagus.

'Ana,' said a voice that sent a chill through her.

She opened the creaky door.

'Couldn't we have done this somewhere more civilised?' he asked. 'Or is this more what you're used to.'

His scathing words were the final slap in the face, his way of gaining control over her again by making her feel small and insignificant. His hand slid into his pocket. She panicked. Had he not done that, she might have been more gentle. Instead, she stabbed the needle deeply and viciously into his neck. He cried out and staggered in shock.

'Jesus, what the fuck was that?' he said, panicking, his hand flying to where she'd injected him.

'Rohypnol,' she said and was surprised at how calm her

voice sounded. 'Sorry I couldn't offer it to you in a glass of water, but it works quicker this way.'

His eyes filled with fear and he went to lift an arm to hit her, but she backed away.

'I've researched the drug. That was a fairly high dose,' she said, aiming her taser at him. 'I don't think the taser and the drug combined would be pleasant. So, if I were you, I'd do exactly as I ask. Sit in the chair.'

'Bitch,' he slurred, the drug starting to affect his body.

Ana pointed to the old chair in the middle of the room. He just made it before losing control of his muscles.

'Now you know what it feels like,' she said triumphantly, grabbing the B&Q bag. Her hands weren't even trembling. How could that be?

She waited patiently with the taser on him until he almost flopped forward and fell from the chair. Pushing him back, she carefully and methodically removed the cable ties from the bag and used them to tie his hands in front of his chest. Then she tied his legs. Just to be sure, she used another cable tie to loop them together. He was now slumped forward in the chair, unable to move.

'I could do anything I want with you,' she whispered into his ear. 'But I'm going to wait until you come round because I don't want you to miss anything.'

Ana then sat on the floor opposite the chair and stared at Ray Grace.

It was impossible to deny his handsomeness. Wasn't that what had appealed to her all those years ago? He was older now, of course. There were streaks of grey in his hair that she hadn't noticed before, but then she'd been too panicky to look too closely at him. Slowly, she stood up and approached his slumped body. A slight tremor of fear washed over her. Visions of him pulling free and grabbing her around the throat made her hesitate for a second. Realising she was being stupid, she slowly and carefully went through his pockets.

The sharp blade nicked her finger, and she removed the Stanley knife and his mobile phone. She could tell it was an expensive jacket, and the urge to slash it with the knife was hard to suppress. The other pocket held his wallet and a bottle of Rohypnol. Two great minds think alike; she thought and smiled at the irony. If he was really on the level, the wallet should contain £20,000.

Ana opened it to find two credit cards, a driver's licence and a £20 note. He had no intention of paying her anything. He was intending to finish her off like he did Laine. Now, she was really pissed off.

After pushing his thumb onto the phone and seeing it magically open, she sat back on the floor and began going through his messages, emails and photos. If he'd ever exchanged messages with Laine Lees, he had deleted them.

The images were innocent enough: photos of him and Sandy at after-conference parties, pictures of their child, holiday photos and images of them with Beth. He had albums for everything: *Holidays, Family, Friends, Zoe and Work.* She could imagine him being very organised. She fiddled with the phone while waiting for him to wake up. Suddenly, she found herself in a file marked 'hidden'. She eagerly clicked into it only to find it was password protected.

'Fuck,' she muttered.

Then he groaned. She looked up, and his eyes met hers.

He struggled with the cable ties, cursing her the whole time, but they were too tight, and he was too weak.

'You only brought £20,' she said, sounding insulted.

He saw she'd emptied his pockets. 'I haven't done anything wrong,' he said, struggling against the ties. 'Why should I pay you £20,000?'

'Do you remember me?'

His expression told her everything. Beads of sweat had built up on his forehead.

'Of course you do. I was a virgin when you raped me. A fifteen-year-old virgin. That must have been a thrill, or have they all been virgins?'

'You're delusional,' he scoffed. 'Always have been. I never raped anyone.'

'You said no one would believe a low life like me over a professional man like you, that I was nothing. But I'm not a nothing now, am I?'

His expression showed his fear, although she knew he was trying to hide it.

'You can't use evidence you've obtained under duress,' he said triumphantly. 'So, if you're recording this, you're wasting your time.'

She continued talking as if he hadn't spoken. 'How many before me?'

'Like I said, you're delusional.'

Ana laughed. Her revenge had finally come to fruition, and she was enjoying it. Maybe that made her as bad as him.

'I'm not recording this,' she lied. 'There's no point. This is my revenge. I want you to know what you did to me. I was fifteen. I suffered from post-traumatic stress disorder afterwards. You see, I had no one to turn to. You abused your position of trust in an environment that should have been safe for me. My mother died before I had time to tell her what a perverted psycho had done to me. Do you know how alone I felt?'

Something changed in his expression. Was it shame, guilt, sadness? Ana couldn't tell.

'You thought you could change your name and come to Oxford and just forget scum like me, didn't you? Or did you realise I was stronger than the others?'

She stared into his face. 'You were clever, though. I stupidly looked for a Richard Stephens, but you changed your name, didn't you? I nearly gave up and went home, and then Elaine Lees got attacked, and I interviewed you. In a warped way, I've got Elaine to thank for that.'

She laughed then.

'I used a cheap detective. Cheap as chips, as we say back home. I was so fucking angry. He'd found a Doctor Raymond Stephens in Oxford, and he presumed that was the right one. I only recently discovered he found another Dr Stephens who'd changed his name before starting work in Oxford, but he didn't think it worth telling me about him, and apparently, I hadn't paid for two names. So it must have been fate that I found you.'

Ray Grace looked at the attractive woman before him and wanted to say, 'Yes, I remember you. You were the best I ever had.'

CHAPTER SEVENTY-FIVE

Ray's life had become a living hell after receiving Ana's WhatsApp message. Looking back, if he'd noticed her enough, he would have seen that the resemblance to Laurie had been obvious. He'd struggled to think how she'd managed to find him. It had been seven years. He had a different name. Every day, after the barbeque, he'd expected the police to knock at his door. When they didn't, he presumed it was money she wanted. That would be easy enough. No, it had to be more than that.

He'd tried so hard, too. After the last girl in York, he'd promised himself he would control it. He'd been lucky. They'd all been too frightened to tell anybody, but it was risky to stay there. He could start again. All he had to do was find a new position and move. So he went to Liverpool, and life had been perfect. He'd met Sandy, who was studying there, and they had become engaged.

He'd vowed to himself it would never happen again, and it hadn't until Laurie. What did these girls expect when they walked half-undressed through the streets at night?

The sight and smell of her in his consulting room that day had been too much. Visions of her in that skimpy skirt and low-cut top had haunted him for days. He was so overcome with lust for her and the power to control her that he knew he had to do it, no matter how wrong it was. He had to dominate her and make her his. Teach her a lesson for flaunting herself. But she'd been different from the rest. Stronger. There was no fear in her. Her anger had been tangible. He'd felt scared. Worrying she would go to the police.

Finally, he'd told Sandy. 'She's accusing me of rape,' he'd lied to her. 'She's delusional. She threatened to go to the police if I didn't pay her.'

'You must go to the police,' Sandy had insisted.

'I can't. I panicked and stupidly paid her,' he lied. 'That will go against me, won't it?'

Sandy had been distraught. She'd loved their life in Liverpool, but when he told her he had been offered a position in Oxford, she jumped at the thought of being where her family was.

Then his stepfather died, and Ray felt guilty. He'd promised to take his name. After all, he'd always been more of a father than his real dad, but he had a massive heart attack before they could sign the legal adoption papers. Before leaving Liverpool, Ray changed his name by deed poll and explained the delicate situation of his stepfather to the university. They were more than happy to change his name on his qualifications.

Now, he was completely safe. Life had been perfect, too, and he'd controlled himself until that bitch Elaine Lees. She'd deliberately flirted with him. It wasn't fair to do that, so he'd had her. After that, she'd hounded him every day, wanting more and more money. It wasn't like she'd even been worth it, not like Ana.

Needles was on his way home when he saw Sajid ahead of him on his cycle. He was about to call out to him when Sajid stopped and seemed to puncture his tyre deliberately. Needles was puzzled as to why Sajid would do something like that. He was about to hurry forward and offer to help when Sajid wheeled it towards Tim's garage.

Needles kept his distance. He didn't want Tim to recognise his voice. Sajid seemed to be in there forever, but finally, he came out and pedalled so fast down the road that even if Needles had called out to him, he would never have heard. Instead, he hurried to Tim's garage, where the door was still open.

Tim turned. 'Can I help you?' he asked.

'Just passing,' said Needles. 'I am allowed to walk the streets.'

Needles tried to see into the garage, but Tim pulled the door down.

———

'She's not answering,' said Jassy. 'Shall I leave a message?'

Sajid nodded.

'What do we do now?' she asked after clicking off her phone.

Sajid had no idea and could only shrug.

'We could ask Tim,' she suggested.

A shout from her mother downstairs stopped Sajid from answering. 'Colin's here, love.'

'Don't mention anything,' whispered Jassy.

Needles didn't bother to knock. He looked from one to the other and said, 'Having a meeting without me?'

CHAPTER SEVENTY-SIX

A na could see the drug was wearing off. His face turned pale and Ana remembered how sick she felt when she'd come round.

'Can't you loosen these ties?' he asked.

The hate in her eyes told him what a stupid question that was.

'Like that's happening,' she said. She held up his phone like a trophy. 'Nice photos of you and your family, especially of Zoe.'

His eyes showed his fear. 'Don't say my daughter's name,' he barked.

She looked away from him and fiddled with the buttons on his phone. It was getting cooler now, but still the air was heavy, and Ana was sweating buckets. She removed her jacket and resisted the temptation to open the barn door.

'You see, I think your pleasure didn't just come from that moment. I imagine you wanted to relive it over and over because you're a fucking pervert.'

He didn't reply.

'I've heard about people like you. I was obsessed. You like to keep your trophies. Where are yours, Ray? In your hidden folder, am I right?'

Ana imagined his back was aching intolerably now, and his wrists must be raw from rubbing against the cables in his bid to escape.

His eyes flashed with anger. 'You won't get away with this.'

Ana was sick and tired of his ego, which was bigger than his bank balance, and she was weary now. She wanted it over. 'What's the password to the hidden folder?' she asked, her throat croaky and dry.

She took a long gulp from the bottled water she'd brought without offering him any. 'You must be thirsty,' she said. 'Give me the code to the hidden folder.'

He grinned at her. 'Fuck off,' he snarled.

Ana slammed the water bottle to the ground, picked up the Rohypnol bottle and syringe, and walked slowly towards him. After all she had suffered, there was no way that she'd ever let him win. She'd come this far. There was no turning back now. She scowled at him.

'Don't fucking mess with me, you sniffling little prick. If you don't give me the password, I'll inject you again and cut off your dick with your own Stanley knife. If you think you feel sick now, think how sick you'll be after that.'

She leaned in closer. 'Don't underestimate me, arsehole, because nothing would give me more pleasure than stopping you fucking young girls.'

Ray struggled to breathe. She was close, so close, close enough. He lifted his head and head-butted her viciously. Ana, unprepared, slipped backwards under the impact, her head pounding. Ray fought for release like a caged animal, but she'd done too good a job.

Ana scrambled around for the syringe and leapt at him, screaming, 'You fucking asked for it.'

Ana would never know if she would have gone through with it. Another dose so soon after the first would most certainly have caused him serious breathing issues if not death.

'Life2live,' he yelled. 'It's Life2live.'

The look of satisfaction on her face made him want to kill her.

'It had better be,' she said, backing away from him. Her knees were weak from the shock, and her head felt muzzy. She felt his eyes scrutinising hers as she typed in the password. Watched in fascination first as her eyes flinched away, then as the colour drained from her face, and finally, the small whimper that came from her lips before she turned from him and retched onto the dusty floor of the cabin. When she'd finished, she wiped her hand across her mouth and forced herself to look at him.

'You buggered her, you buggered Elaine Lees,' she said, her tone strangled.

He'd videoed it all. There were seven, some even younger than she'd been. He'd even made them perform oral sex on him. Thank God, she couldn't remember everything he'd done to her. Without even being aware of what she was doing, she picked up the Stanley knife and walked towards him.

'You killed Elaine Lees. You injected her with Rohypnol and left her to die.'

'It wasn't like that. You have to listen to me.'

'Why the fuck should I listen to you?' she spat.

'If you kill me, the truth will never come out.'

'What makes you think I'm going to kill you? Maybe I'm just going to chop off your perverted prick, you fucking bastard.'

His head was fuzzy. He was struggling to keep his eyes open. He could feel a throbbing in his forehead where he'd head-butted her. He just needed time, time to think his way out of this.

'So, just what was it like, *Ray?*' she asked, emphasising his name.

'She was blackmailing me dry. I never meant for it to happen. It was an accident.' It was true. He'd never intended to hurt Laine, let alone kill her. If only she hadn't been so difficult. 'I tried to reason with her.'

He could remember it all as if it had happened only yesterday. 'I told her, "Don't you understand, Laine? You can't just keep demanding money. You said it was a one-off".

'"Yeah, well, I lied," she said flippantly. "Give me the money, else I'll tell the police and your wife".' He paused, and then continued. 'I'd looked at her then. At her over-made-up face and slinky dress. She was a narcissistic little bitch who probably never gave anyone else's life another thought.'

He'd forgotten by now how he'd raped and buggered her.

He looked at Ana. 'She wasn't like you,' he said, almost affectionately, making Ana want to puke. 'She was a selfish, uneducated piece of scum who used people for her own means. I told her no one would believe her, but she'd laughed straight in my face. "I'm not a stupid kid, you know," she said, smiling. "I recorded the second time. I have it on my phone. Your groaning and everything".'

His expression turned angry. 'She had no right to record anything. I panicked and demanded her phone, but she wouldn't hand it over. In the end, I tried to grab her bag off her.'

'She shouted, "Get off me! My boyfriend will be here soon." But I had her boyfriend's phone,' he said proudly. 'That shut her up.'

He was getting carried away with the story, almost boasting

now. He was so immersed that he'd forgotten where he was. 'You should have seen her face when I held it up.'

Ana fought the urge to slap him.

'I was in control again, and she knew it. I could tell by the fear on her face. Then the stupid bitch began to run, but in her drunkenness, she lost her footing.'

He suddenly seemed to remember that Ana was there. 'It wasn't my fault she knocked her head on the ground, you know that, don't you?'

He was breathing heavily now as he remembered looking down at Laine, layers of pine needles sticking into her face. He could remember the earthy smell of decomposing leaves and the sight of her sticky, bloody face. He'd watched as she'd scrambled in the dirt, trying to crawl away from him while in a weak voice, begging, 'No, please,' as she felt her bag pulled roughly from her shoulder.

'She should have given me the phone. It was that simple. I felt her pulse. It was too weak. Jesus, why did she have to run? It was her fault she slipped and smashed her head on a rock. It wasn't as though I'd pushed her. If anything, she'd pushed me with her threats. Pushed me to the limit.'

Sweat was pouring off him. The heat and anxiety of what Ana would do next were taking their toll, and he was feeling light-headed.

'It wasn't supposed to be like that,' he said, tears running down his cheeks. 'It was to frighten her. Just slap her around a little. Hand her the card and run off. I just wanted her to back off. She'd become a vampire, draining me of emotion and money. I couldn't concentrate. I'd lie awake at night, worrying that the police would knock on our door.'

'My heart bleeds for you,' said Ana caustically.

He didn't seem to hear her. 'That's all it was meant to be, a frightener. But she'd seen me. So what the fuck was I supposed to do? She'd arrived before I'd had time to put the balaclava on. It was her fault. We could have avoided all of this if she hadn't come early.'

He clenched and unclenched his hands several times. Adrenalin was rushing through his body. He looked around anxiously, remembering the blood gushing from her smashed skull. Even with the wetness of her blood running into her eyes, she'd still pleaded with him.

'Oh Jesus,' he'd moaned. 'Jesus, why did she have to run? The laughter from the fair seemed all wrong. She'd fallen, and it wasn't even my fault, and they were laughing, having fun. I'd laughed like that once before she came into my life. I got scared. What if she confided in someone? Or got brave and went to the police? I couldn't let her do that. Everything we had, as a family, would be gone in a flash.'

'So you murdered her?'

'No,' he denied hotly. 'She was dying. It was her own fault. I put her out of her misery,' he said, his voice bland. 'She would have died anyway. I had one of those cards ready for when they found her slapped about. They'd blame it on The Vigilante.'

'Then, you wiped Sajid's phone and put it back on the ground. What did you do with Laine's phone?'

'I threw it into the lake on my way back through the meadow.'

Ana took a deep breath. 'What were her last words?' she asked through the blurriness of her tears.

'Sajid,' he said, without emotion.

Rage that had slowly been consuming Ana now burst into flames, and she flew at him, the Stanley knife shaking with her anger. Ray desperately tried to free himself, but it was useless. Neither of them heard the creak of the cabin door. Ana's mind was focused on one thing. She wasn't thinking of the consequences, or maybe at that moment, she didn't care.

'Stop,' said a voice from behind her.

Ana turned to see Sandy Grace pointing a shotgun at her.

Jonny checked his phone. His messages hadn't even reached Ana's mobile. He tried to ring her again but got her voicemail like before. It was getting late. Surely, she would have turned her phone on by now.

Something wasn't right. He could sense it. This wasn't like Ana. He rubbed his chin thoughtfully and then phoned the station.

'DC Wilkins.'

'Oh, hi, it's Jonny Manners.'

He heard Matt sigh. 'She's not here,' he said.

'Do you know where she is exactly? Only I can't get hold of her.'

'I can't divulge that information to a member of the public, I'm afraid.'

Jonny felt sure that if Matt stood before him, he'd punch him in the face.

'As far as I know, she's finished for the day,' said Matt.

Jonny cracked his knuckles. 'Thanks.'

He hung up, stared at the unread messages, and then tried her phone again, only to get her voicemail. He hesitated and finally tapped into Google Maps. That showed him where Ana was and had been for the past two and a half hours. Perhaps she was okay and just had no signal. If she really wasn't interested, the last thing he wanted to do was hassle her.

He ran his hands through his hair and finally stood up. No, something wasn't right. He just sensed it. He grabbed his keys and phone and made for the front door.

CHAPTER SEVENTY-SEVEN

Jonny tried Ana's mobile but again got her voicemail. He decided to go with Google Maps, which showed she was somewhere near the playing fields.

He turned the car and headed for the playing field car park. He immediately saw Ana's car. A red Land Rover that he vaguely recognised sat beside it. Where had he seen it before? He was sure it was recently. He looked around for Ana and called her name several times but got no response. The only other place she could be was the woods.

He opened the boot and took out his car jack, feeling stupid as he did so. What the hell he thought he was going to do with that, he couldn't imagine. His scalp crawled as if with lice. What the hell was Ana doing in the woods on her own?

It then occurred to him that she may not be alone. What if he was interrupting something? He shook his head, dismissing the idea. Ana wasn't a quick shag in the woods type. He knew that.

He rechecked his phone and saw he had no signal. His heart was doubling in speed now. He had no idea what lay ahead of him. As he drew nearer to the red mark on his map, he spotted a dilapidated building. As he got closer, he heard voices. One was Ana's, and the other he recognised as Ray Grace's. That's where he'd seen the Land Rover before, on Grace's front drive the night of the barbecue.

Ray had been acting oddly again all day. He'd been like it since their barbecue. When she'd asked what was wrong, he'd blamed work. Now, suddenly, just as Sandy was preparing dinner, he said he had to go out. She had heard his phone ping seconds before, and her heart had sunk. So it was another woman. After all they'd sacrificed to get where they were, he was going to throw it away? For what? A young nurse at the clinic or an intern at the psychiatric ward? Christ, she'd put her dreams on hold so he could study. They finally had it all, and he was just going to throw it away.

'Where do you have to go to this time of night?' she'd asked.

He'd looked irritated. 'It's work. A difficult patient.'

'Surely someone else there can handle it?' she'd said.

'They can't,' he'd snapped.

Sandy couldn't ever remember him snapping at her like that before. She had been tearful ever since Miriam Bradshaw had mentioned the other woman. The thought of Ray leaving her and Zoe was unbearable. That afternoon, not even knowing why, she'd taken the shotgun after feeding the chickens. She had no intention of using it. She was just feeling depressed and hurt. *Tomorrow, I'll put it back*, she'd told herself.

She phoned their babysitter, Bridget, and said they had an emergency. Could she come and sit with Zoe? She'd pay her double. If Ray was having an affair, she wanted to know who it was with. Bridget said yes immediately, but she was at a friend's house and would have to get a taxi.

Not wanting to sound desperate, Sandy had told her that was fine. She could trace Ray's movements on her phone. *He's forgotten that*, she thought.

Then, a horrible thought went through her mind. What if he'd turned the tracking off? She checked. He hadn't.

Bridget arrived thirty minutes later, and after checking her phone, Sandy left. She was surprised to see that Ray had gone to the playing fields. She noticed two other cars were parked there. So he was meeting someone.

She parked her car down a side road. He'd lied to her. How long had it been going on for? Tears rolled down her cheeks as she sobbed. He'd broken her heart and ruined their happy family.

There was no sign of anyone at the playing fields, so she began the walk through the woods and then suddenly slid to the ground, clutching the shotgun, the dry leaves beneath her still warm from the day's hot sun.

Did she really want to know who it was? Hiccupping between sobs, she finally pulled herself up. Why was he meeting her in the woods? It didn't make sense. *He can afford the best hotels*, she thought cynically.

As she neared the cabin, she heard voices and recognised Ana Rawlins. From their conversation, she knew it wasn't a love tryst. She heard Laine Lees's name mentioned and froze. The more she listened, the more the adrenalin charged through her.

A rush of emotions smothered Sandy until she could barely breathe. Her hands wouldn't stop fidgeting, and her jaw hurt where she'd been clenching it. Why would Ray do this to her?

Jonny crept towards the hut. Cautiously, he inched his way around the other side of the building and peered in through one of the dusty windows. He had to fight back his gasp at seeing Ray tied to a chair like a hostage. What the fuck? Was that a knife Ana was holding at his throat? Before he had time to react, Sandy bolted into the room and aimed the shotgun at Ana's head.

'Stop,' she yelled.

Without hesitation, Jonny dived in after her. Hearing the door creak, Sandy swung around, and Jonny quickly raised his hands.

'Drop that,' said Sandy, nodding at the car jack.

Jonny let it slip to the floor. His eyes met Ana's, and she nodded at the ground. He partly followed her gaze, one eye still on the shotgun. He then saw the taser sticking out of Ana's jacket.

'You won't get away with this, Sandy,' said Ana, trying to get her attention away from Jonny. 'Think of Zoe. If you're caught, she'll lose both of you. I understand what you're going through, Sandy.'

'No, you don't,' said Sandy, turning back to Ana, whom she now had difficulty focusing on through her tears. Poor Zoe, what had they done to her?

'Show me the videos.'

'No,' yelled Ray. 'Put the gun down, Sandy, please. Let me explain,' he pleaded.

A sudden surge of adrenalin rushed through Ana as Jonny moved closer to get at the taser.

'Don't look at them,' said Ana.

'You should have left us alone,' said Sandy. Her hand shook as she lifted the shotgun. Shaking hands cause accidents, and there was a good chance Sandy would pull the trigger in error. Ana didn't have much time. She nodded at Jonny, realising it was simply a matter of seconds before her life would be over.

'We had a good life. Why couldn't you have left us alone?'

Sandy snarled. 'You've ruined our life,' she screamed at Ray. 'How could you?'

'She's lying, Sandy,' he said, his voice hoarse.

Sandy kept the shotgun aimed at Ana. 'Show me the videos,' she demanded.

Ray's head fell forward, defeated.

Ana handed her the phone. The album was still open. Sandy's expression didn't change.

'Our whole life ruined,' she said, letting the phone slip to the floor. 'Thanks to you,' she said, turning to Ana. 'Why couldn't you just let it go?'

'Because he raped me,' snapped Ana.

Jonny dived for the taser, feeling his knee crack as he did so. 'Stop,' he yelled.

Sandy turned in surprise.

'Aim the red dot,' screamed Ana.

'No,' said Sandy, determinedly, turning away from him.

Jonny aimed the red dot at Sandy's back just as she cocked the barrel.

Ana squeezed her eyes shut. *Oh God*, she prayed, *please not now. I can't go now.* But it was too late. The reverberation from the firing of the shotgun threw Jonny to the ground. Wood debris rained down on them like curled ribbons. Jonny didn't think he would ever forget in the mesmerising blackness, the silver-blue twirls of smoke from the shotgun or that terrible sound of Ana's horrified screams.

CHAPTER SEVENTY-EIGHT

'It's not exactly a meeting,' said Jassy, avoiding eye contact with Needles.

'Well, it's not a love tryst, is it? At least, I hope not, seeing as Laine hasn't even been buried yet,' Needles said scornfully.

'Don't be stupid,' said Sajid. 'Laine meant the world to me.'

Needles narrowed his eyes suspiciously. 'You're shutting me out from something. Please don't take me for a fool because I'm not one.' He shot a suspicious glare from one to the other. 'I saw you puncture your bike so you could get into Tim's garage.'

Sajid lowered his gaze from Needles', confirming his guilt.

'It's not Tim,' said Jassy. 'He wouldn't lay a finger on Laine.'

Needles rolled his eyes in an exaggerated gesture. 'You two, honestly. You've found someone that looks like he could be The Vigilante, and we know The Vigilante killed Laine.'

'We can't be sure it was The Vigilante,' argued Jassy.

A muscle twitched in Needles' cheek. 'So now you're defending him?'

Sajid didn't know how to appease Needles. Once he had an idea in his head, there was no removing it.

'We should call the police first, tell them of our suspicions and then if they do nothing, we can–'

'Fuck that,' spat Needles. 'That bastard killed my sister, and he will pay for it.'

Sajid grabbed him by the arm and got punched in the face for his efforts.

Jassy gasped. 'Stop it,' she shouted. 'Both of you.'

'Either you're with me or not,' said Needles, making for the door.

Realising he had no choice, Sajid followed him, with Jassy behind.

The Code Zero turned the quiet police station into chaos. Beth checked the destination.

'Code zero,' she yelled. '6553, it's Ana. Matt, we need everyone. Ambulance, MIT, the lot,' she said, pulling on her jacket. 'One person down.'

Matt felt like someone had punched him in the stomach. 'Not Ana?' he said quietly.

Beth inhaled. 'It wasn't her that radioed it in. I don't know, Matt, but we'd better be prepared.'

'Gun requests?' she asked Tom.

'Yes, get on it.'

'Everyone head to the destination, NOW,' yelled Tom.

Jonny's eyes were smarting from the debris. In front of him, he could see Sandy on the floor, staring into space, her dress covered in blood. Anger tore at his every being, and he wanted to taser Sandy until she begged for release. The smell from the gunfire made him feel sick. His eyes were sore from the smoke, so he could barely see. He crawled along the floor, blood sticking to his hands.

'Ana, oh God, Ana.'

Then he saw it and immediately vomited. Ray Grace's head had been blown to pieces. The gunshot that had thundered in their ears was the one that ripped Ray Grace from this existence, silenced his laugh forever and took the light from his eyes.

Sandy Grace had shot her husband through the head close to point blank range. Jonny didn't know whether to laugh or cry. Bits of Ray's brain were sprawled across the floor. Jonny fought back his nausea and moved further along the blood-stained floor. *Please don't let me find her dead*, he prayed.

'Ana,' he howled repeatedly until a small voice said, 'Here.'

Squirrelled in a corner was Ana, her face splattered with Ray's blood. 'I'm okay,' she said shakily and then burst into tears at the sight of Jonny.

'I was convinced she was going to kill me, and then suddenly, she turned the shotgun and deliberately aimed it at him. It wasn't an accident. She said he wasn't fit to be a father and then pulled the trigger.'

She struggled to sit up. 'I can't move my leg. I think I did something when I fell. You must Code o on my radio and get the shotgun off her.'

Jonny nodded and stepped gingerly towards Sandy, who didn't even seem aware of his presence. Carefully, he took the shotgun from her hands. Sandy gave no resistance. He then hurried to Ana's radio, hitting the code o button.

'Hello, can you hear me. My name is Jonny Manners. We need an ambulance ... to the derelict building in the woods, not far from the playing fields. One person is injured and one is dead.'

He hurried back to Ana and cradled her in his arms.

That was how the police found them when they arrived, huddled together amidst a bloody carnage.

Tom turned to Steve and Matt. 'Secure the scene. I don't want any evidence contaminated. Bag up that rifle.'

Beth was leaning down to Sandy. 'Christ, she's got blood on her. Sandy, are you hurt? Speak to me.'

Sandy began to weep.

'I need a paramedic here,' Beth yelled.

Sandy was staring at Ray's lifeless body. She tried to speak, but the shock was too much.

'Who shot Ray?' demanded Beth.

Sandy leant to the side and vomited. Beth held her hand, waited, and then wiped her mouth clean with a tissue before gently taking her into her arms. 'Who shot Ray, Sandy?' she repeated gently.

'I did,' said Sandy hoarsely.

Beth frowned. 'What? What are you talking about?'

Tom forcibly pulled her off Sandy.

'Let go of me, Tom,' she snapped, struggling to escape his grip.

'Step down, Beth,' Tom ordered.

'What? This is my sister.'

'That's why you need to step down.'

She shook her head emphatically. 'No, no,' she shouted. 'She wouldn't have killed him.'

'Stand down, DI Harper, and wait in the car. May I remind you that you'll be disobeying a higher-ranking officer's orders if you don't.'

She glared at him before storming out to the police car.

Tom leaned down to Ana and took her hand. 'The ambulance is here. You're going to be fine. I need you to answer one question, Ana. Can you do that?'

Ana nodded.

'Who shot Ray Grace, and why?'

Ana began to sob uncontrollably for the first time since she'd arrived at the old building.

'Sandy Grace with the shotgun. Everything you need to know is on his phone.' She handed it over with her bloodied hand. 'Including me.'

Beth was in a state of shock. She was having trouble breathing. She saw a paramedic sitting with Sandy in the rear-view mirror. *Oh, please, God, don't let her be badly hurt.* The car door opened and she jumped.

'Sandy's not injured. It's most likely Ray's blood on her top. Beth, I need you to stay calm,' Tom said, climbing beside her. 'Ana has confirmed that Sandy shot Ray using a shotgun–'

Beth went to protest, but he put his hand up to stop her.

'Ray killed Laine Lees...'

'No, no.' She shook her head in denial. 'What the fuck are you talking about? Sandy wouldn't know how to get a shotgun, and Ray had no reason to kill Elaine Lees. Who's telling you all this bollocks?'

'She was blackmailing him. He sexually abused her while she was sedated with Rohypnol. He's abused others, Beth, using Rohypnol while he was supposed to be treating them. He had videos on his phone.'

He hesitated. 'One of them was Ana. He raped her seven years ago.'

'No, no, no,' Beth screamed, covering her ears.

He pulled her into his arms and kissed the top of her head. 'Oh, Beth, I'm so sorry. Know that I love you and will support you through all this.'

Beth clung to him like a life raft.

'I'm arresting Sandy; you must trust me with this.'

Beth dropped her head into her hands and began sobbing. 'No, no, it's not possible. Sandy wouldn't hurt a fly. How could Ray do such terrible things? What about Zoe?' she said tearfully.

'She's with a sitter. Do you want to be with her? Or we can send someone there if you want to stay with Sandy.'

He took both her hands in his. 'You have to trust me with this, Beth. I promise I'll keep you updated.'

Beth swallowed. Her throat felt like parched earth. 'I want to be with Sandy.'

He nodded. 'I'll get someone to drive you to the hospital.'

Beth barely heard him. All she kept thinking was Ray had abused Ana seven years ago. So, that had been Ana's agenda all along. Beth had known there was something.

Jassy was praying hard that Tim wouldn't be home. Her heart sank when she saw the lights on in the living room. 'We really should call the police,' she said.

'I wish you'd shut the fuck up,' Needles snarled. 'It's taken them all this time, and they still haven't found that vigilante bastard. Well, we've got him. Now he'll know what it's like when others take the law into their own hands.'

At that moment, Jassy saw Tim waiting by the wall. Of course, it was fish and chip van night. Beside him was Will. Neither Tim nor Will seemed to have noticed them standing outside Tim's house. Will was too busy moaning about the police.

'You would think they'd be out looking for real criminals rather than someone just wanting to earn a few bob on the side. I ask you. Who can afford to get their cars done after failed MOTs these days?'

Tim hoped the van would come soon. He didn't agree with Will at all. 'Hopefully, they'll catch this vigilante soon,' he said. 'You know what. This van is later than usual. I think I'll give it a miss.'

Tim turned and saw Needles, Sajid and Jassy enter the gate to his house. 'Hey, what do you think you're doing?' he shouted.

'Little bastards,' said Will, hurrying along with him. Everyone froze when they saw the knife in Needles' hand.

'We've come to give you what you deserve, you stinking rat, an eye for eye, isn't that what they say?'

Jassy quickly reached for her phone.

The X-ray showed that Ana had broken her foot. Tom was waiting with Jonny outside the X-ray room. Ana hobbled out, took the painkillers offered by the nurse and turned to Tom after swallowing them.

'Are you feeling up to telling us what happened?' Tom asked.

Ana took her phone from Jonny and idly glanced at the screen. There was a message from Jassy.

'Help us. I daren't phone. Needles might turn on me. He's got a knife. He's going to kill Tim. Hurry.'

There was a missed call from her, too, Shit, when were they sent?

'No time,' she said, hobbling towards the door.

'What are you doing?' asked Jonny, alarmed. 'You're not going anywhere.'

'Colin Lees has found The Vigilante, and he has a knife. Jassy messaged me about fifteen minutes ago. They're going to hurt Tim. We have to hurry.'

Tom looked shocked. 'What are you talking about?'

'Tim is The Vigilante, but as you know, he didn't kill Laine, but Colin Lees doesn't know that. Please get to Tim. They might hurt Vanessa too.'

Tom reached for his radio. Ana struggled to get up.

'Don't you dare move,' Jonny instructed.

Tom hurried from the hospital, and Ana flopped into the chair. The truth was, she couldn't walk without help.

———

'What are you talking about,' said Will, although he was beginning to regret ever getting involved. 'An eye for an eye for what?'

'Him,' said Needles, venom spilling from his angry lips. 'He's The Vigilante. He murdered my sister.'

Tim turned pale. He knew it would be a matter of time, but he'd expected the police, not this.

'What? Are you stoned?' Will laughed. 'If there is one person I know isn't The Vigilante, it's Tim.'

Needles edged closer.

'Okay, I'm calling the police,' said Will. 'This is ridiculous.'

The fish and chip van had pulled up, and people came out to collect their dinner. Sajid could smell the chips and wished he wasn't standing here with Needles and Jassy but with Laine, getting their chip butties as they used to and then sneaking into the woods to eat them. He looked at Tim, whose face was now white and frightened. Sajid couldn't believe it. It couldn't be possible – not gentle Tim.

'Open your garage,' Needles ordered Tim.

Tim reluctantly pulled the key from his pocket and unlocked the garage. Needles raced in.

'Where did you see it?' he asked Sajid.

Sajid could see Needles was really hyped up and watched as he began throwing things everywhere. He was totally unaware that Will had called the police.

At the sight of the combat trousers and balaclava, Needles lost his mind. That was the only way Sajid could describe it when the police questioned him.

'It was like something exploded in his head, and he slashed at Tim with the knife like a madman. All I could see was blood spraying everywhere.'

Sajid couldn't recall how long the attack went on. He remembered he and Will had somehow got the knife off Needles and he'd heard it clatter onto the concrete floor. Will's arm had been slashed in his efforts to help Tim, who was now lying on the floor. Sajid thought he didn't look too bad, just a cut above his eyebrow, the scarlet blood flowing into his eyes.

But Sajid knew the injuries were much worse. It was his body that was damaged. Blood was up the walls, all over the floor, and Sajid saw, to his horror, also over his own shirt and jeans.

Vanessa was screaming from the other side of the garage door, and Sajid was relieved when a paramedic entered. The ambulance arrived before the police.

When the paramedics cut away his clothes, the blooming purple patches told of internal ruptures, likely organ damage. The paramedics had looked at Sajid with encouraging faces. 'He's going to be okay now,' one said.

And all the while, Jassy was crying in the background like her heart had snapped in two.

Ana got a call from Matt, telling her that Tim had suffered horrific injuries, but the doctor said they were not life-threatening.

'Oh, God, if only I'd seen the messages earlier.'

'You can't blame yourself, Ana.'

'Has Sandy said anything?' she asked.

'No, she's waiting for her solicitor. He'll no doubt tell her to say "no comment" to everything. Why didn't you tell me you knew who The Vigilante was?'

'It's a long story.'

'Sounds like a bloody novel, Ana.'

CHAPTER SEVENTY-NINE

Beth's visit wasn't unexpected. She looked pale and weary, and Ana's heart went out to her. Jonny left them alone with the excuse that he had work to do.

'It worked out, then,' Beth said, smiling as Jonny closed the door.

Ana nodded and then lowered her eyes.

'Beth, I'm so sorry. I know you probably think I should have told you. But...' She looked up. 'What was I supposed to say? Someone raped me when I was young; I think he's here. Then, I learn it's your brother-in-law.'

She could see Beth trying to understand. 'Did you ever think of Sandy and Zoe?'

Ana's eyes then blazed with anger. 'No, I didn't. I'll tell you who I thought of. All those girls he abused and those he would have gone on to abuse.'

Beth's eyes filled with tears. 'She's lost everything.'

Ana stood up. 'I'm so sorry, Beth. I didn't pull the trigger, she did.'

Beth swallowed, and Ana could tell the following words

were a struggle for her to say. 'You could say the gun went off by mistake, that she didn't intend to kill him.'

Their eyes met. There was mutual pain in both. Ana didn't want Sandy to suffer any more than Beth did.

'After all, weren't you about to stab him to death yourself with a Stanley knife?' asked Beth quietly.

Ana's eyes didn't leave Beth's. Would she have done it if Sandy hadn't come in at that moment? She was out of her mind with anger and grief. If she was honest with herself, she had probably been capable of stabbing him multiple times.

'I've already made my statement,' she said.

Beth leaned forward and grabbed Ana's hands in hers. 'You could change it – for Zoe and us. You know she isn't a murderer.'

Ana knew that Sandy was denying killing her husband. That the gun went off accidentally. It was her word against Ana's.

A picture of a little girl running through a wood of bluebells, her long flowing curls blowing in the breeze, suddenly ran through Ana's mind. Her pretty face glowed as she looked back and smiled at the camera. Ana smiled at the memory. Her hands were warm in Beth's.

'For Zoe,' she said. 'I'll do it for Zoe.'

Beth went to hug her, but Ana pulled back. 'Children shouldn't have to pay for the sins of their father,' she said, getting up and opening the door. 'I'm sorry again, Beth.'

Beth walked to the door, touched Ana's hand and said, 'Thank you.'

CHAPTER EIGHTY

THREE MONTHS LATER

Jonny taped up the last of the boxes. There weren't many. Ana hadn't collected much in the short time she'd been in Stonesend.

'Are you sure you're making the right decision?' she asked. 'It's a different way of life.'

'If I'm with you. I'll be happy anywhere.' He smiled. 'We'll come back to see my girls every other weekend.'

'Oh, you big romantic,' she said, kissing him. 'By the way, that day in the woods. How did you know where to find me?'

'Ah,' he said, embarrassed. 'I, er, tracked your phone using Google Maps.'

Her eyes widened. 'You little bugger.' She smiled.

'You okay?' he asked, looking deep into her eyes.

'I will be.'

Jassy held out her hand and without even looking at the black ink mark left there, waited along with the other wives and girlfriends until they were allowed into the large hall.

Needles smiled widely at the sight of her. Each time she saw him, she was amazed at how different he looked – happier and more content.

'How are you doing?' she asked, smiling.

'All the better for seeing you.'

Everyone around them was chatting. Some of the women were crying. She'd befriended some of them. After all, it wasn't their fault their husbands had gone off the rails. Sometimes, when she could, Jassy would look after their children so they could visit.

'I'm doing me GCSE in English,' said Needles.

'Oh yeah, that's brill.'

He nodded. 'Yeah, I'm going to do more when I get out. Only three months to go.'

They were silent, the children's screaming piercing through their brains.

'How is Tim?' he asked finally.

'Doing well. Did they tell you that your kidney was a good match?' Tim feels it is right.'

He nodded. 'The operation is set for next week.'

'He's going to be okay, Colin,' she said, touching his hand. He clasped it tightly. 'You'll be saving a life with your kidney. Laine would be proud.'

He nodded, fighting back his tears.

Sajid found a university in Liverpool. He couldn't face staying in the village where he would always see Tim and Needles and be reminded constantly of Laine. He needed to move on. The funeral had been amazing. So many people had turned out that there hadn't been enough room in the church and crowds had gathered outside. The flowers were still there, hundreds of them. You could smell them whenever you were close to the church.

He'd wanted to tell Sandy Grace it hadn't been her fault. She'd wanted to attend the funeral, but Laine's family wouldn't allow it. He thought that had been wrong. She'd suffered as much as anyone.

That morning, he laid a single rose on Laine's grave and told her again how much he loved and missed her. Then slowly, with his suitcase in hand, he walked to the bus station.

Ana felt Sandy had also been the victim of the man who had raped her. No matter how much Tom disagreed with her, she retracted her statement. Ray had been a monster in Ana's eyes but a loving husband in his wife's.

Beth had offered to resign, but Tom and the chief refused to accept it.

'You've done nothing that merits your resignation,' said the chief. Beth agreed to stay but assured them she would always support her sister.

Sandy sat pale-faced in the car park opposite Ana's flat for almost an hour. There was an aching in her chest that had been with her since Ray died. Her eyelids were sore and gritty, and she rubbed at them without realising it. She knew that she'd been withdrawing and turning inwards, punishing herself. She gripped the door handle and forced herself to exit the car.

She hadn't expected Jonny to open the door and found herself unable to breathe. Ana walked from the bedroom and stopped at the sight of Sandy.

'I'll get her some water,' said Jonny.

Ana caught her before she fell. Sandy's head collapsed onto Ana's chest, and she began to weep.

'Sometimes, I can't breathe. I lie awake at night and look at his photo, and then I think of what he did to you and then, and then...'

Jonny handed her the water. Ana was trembling. This was something she hadn't expected.

'My husband raped you. I'm sorry. I never knew, I promise you. I just want this pain to go.' She wept.

Ana wrapped her arms around her. 'You're a good person. Good overcomes evil. I can move on, and so can you. You have Beth, and Zoe needs you.'

Sandy nodded, stood and walked unsteadily to the front door. 'I'm so grateful. I'm sorry for what he did. I hope you find something good in your life.'

An image came into Ana's mind, and she smiled.

CHAPTER EIGHTY-ONE

SEVEN YEARS EARLIER

Laurie wished the butterflies fluttering around in her stomach would disappear. With the gown on, she sat on the bed and swung her legs over so she was lying flat. Placing her hand on her tummy, she couldn't stop wondering if her baby was a boy or a girl. Would it feel any pain? She didn't want there to be any more pain.

The nurse asked, 'How are you feeling?'

'Okay,' said Laurie.

'I'm just going to insert an IV and then give you a mild sedative. Okay?'

Laurie nodded.

'If you could lift your feet into these stirrups. There's a good girl.'

Brenda used to call her a good girl all the time. Would she think she was a good girl now?

'Will it hurt?' asked Laurie.

The nurse assured her that her cervix would be numbed and that she might feel a few stomach cramps.

'No, I mean, will it hurt the baby?'

'No, it won't.'

Laurie felt the butterflies again. Thought of the monster that had done this to her and said, 'Stop.'

The nurse stepped back.

'I've changed my mind,' said Laurie.

'Absolutely, your right,' said the nurse, helping Laurie get off the couch. 'Of course. It's important to remember, however, that if you leave it too late, we won't be able to terminate.'

Laurie nodded her assent. All she wanted to do was get out of there. Anika didn't seem surprised to see her so soon.

'You changed your mind,' she said, smiling.

Laurie began to cry. He was the monster, not her, not the living thing inside her. It was pure, innocent, and had the right to live.

'Let's go home,' she said, taking Anika's hand.

CHAPTER EIGHTY-TWO

LIVERPOOL

Now, just over three months after the shooting of Ray Grace, she was home again – this time to her own house, which she'd bought a year before. The front door opened before she stepped from the taxi.

'Mummy!'

The dark-haired child ran into her arms. Jonny immediately saw the resemblance to Ray Grace and wondered how Ana coped with it.

Anika stood tearfully at the front door.

'Is your work finished?' asked the little girl.

Ana lifted her eyes to meet Anika's. 'Completely finished,' she said.

'You won't be going back?'

'Not ever.'

Ana turned to Jonny. 'This is my adopted mum, Anika,' Ana said. 'Jonny is the man I told you about.'

'You sound like the kind of man I've dreamt of for my Laurie.'

'Well, I don't know about that.' He laughed. 'And what do I call you, Ana or Laurie?'

'Ana.' She grinned.

The child was tugging at Ana's hand.

'Come on, we have so much to show you,' she cried, her dark eyes sparkling excitedly.

'Say hello to my friend Jonny first.'

'Hi, Jonny,' she said.

Ana smiled.

Before they had left Oxford she had slipped a note through Sandy's letter box.

We were both victims of Raymond Grace. Zoe is blameless and gorgeous. Here is a photo of her half sister. Maybe one day they can meet.
Sent with best wishes
Ana.

'Meet my daughter, Grace,' said Ana.

Jonny started. Grace? She'd called her daughter Grace.

Ana saw his expression. 'I had no idea then about his name change,' she said.

'But out of something bad has to come something good.' She took his hand and led him into the house.

THE END

ALSO BY LYNDA RENHAM

Remember Me

Secrets and Lies

Watching You

The Lies She Told

A NOTE FROM THE PUBLISHER

Thank you for reading this book. If you enjoyed it please do consider leaving a review on Amazon to help others find it too.

We hate typos. All of our books have been rigorously edited and proofread, but sometimes mistakes do slip through. If you have spotted a typo, please do let us know and we can get it amended within hours.

info@bloodhoundbooks.com

Printed in Great Britain
by Amazon

46221753R00212